Andy McDermott is th[...]e
Chase adventure thrille[...]s
and 20 languages. His de[...] novel, *The Hunt for Atlantis*, was his first of
several *New York Times* bestsellers. *The Knights of Atlantis* is the seventeenth
book in the series, and he has also written the explosive spy thriller *The
Persona Protocol* and the action-packed Alex Reeve thriller series.

A former journalist and movie critic, Andy is now a full-time novelist.
Born in Halifax, he lives in Bournemouth with his partner and son.

Praise for Andy McDermott:

'Adventure stories don't get much more epic than this'
Daily Mirror

'*Operative 66* is an action-packed thrill ride . . . twists and
turns that will keep you guessing at a blistering pace
that never lets up'
Adam Hamdy

'A writer of rare, almost cinematic talent. Where others'
action scenes limp along unconvincingly, his explode
off the page in Technicolor'
Daily Express

'If Wilbur Smith and Clive Cussler collaborated, they
might have come up with a thundering big adventure
blockbuster like this . . . a widescreen, thrill-a-minute ride'
Peterborough Evening Telegraph

'True Indiana Jones stuff with terrific pace'
Bookseller

By Andy McDermott and available from Headline

Featuring Alex Reeve
Operative 66
Rogue Asset
Ghost Target

Featuring Nina Wilde and Eddie Chase
The Hunt for Atlantis
The Tomb of Hercules
The Secret of Excalibur
The Covenant of Genesis
The Cult of Osiris
The Sacred Vault
Empire of Gold
Temple of the Gods
The Valhalla Prophecy
Kingdom of Darkness
The Last Survivor (A Digital Short Story)
The Revelation Code
The Midas Legacy
King Solomon's Curse
The Spear of Atlantis
The Resurrection Key
The Temple of Skulls
The Knights of Atlantis

Standalone Thriller
The Personal Protocol

ANDY McDERMOTT
THE KNIGHTS OF ATLANTIS

HEADLINE

First published in 2023 by
HEADLINE PUBLISHING GROUP

First published in paperback in 2024

1

Cataloguing in Publication Data is available from the British Library

ISBN 978 1 0354 0085 0

Offset in 10.5/13.57 pt Aldine 401 BT by Jouve (UK), Milton Keynes

Printed and bound in Great Britain by Clays Ltd, Elcograf S.p.A.

Headline's policy is to use papers that are natural, renewable and recyclable
products and made from wood grown in well-managed forests and other
controlled sources. The logging and manufacturing processes are expected
to conform to the environmental regulations of the country of origin.

HEADLINE PUBLISHING GROUP
An Hachette UK Company
Carmelite House
50 Victoria Embankment
London EC4Y 0DZ

www.headline.co.uk
www.hachette.co.uk

For Kat and Sebastian

Prologue

Portugal

The day's oppressive heat endured even after nightfall. Guilerme Braga paused in his patrol to drink some water, then splashed more on his hand to wipe his brow and neck. Damn weather! Each summer was hotter than the last. Fine for the tourists, he supposed. Less good when you had to live in it.

He fanned his face with his peaked cap. He was supposed to wear it at all times while on duty, but to hell with that. He and his fellow security guard Fausto Carvalho were the only people here. The International Heritage Agency facility they were protecting was on the shore near Bobadela, north of the Portuguese capital Lisbon. A motorway ran along one side of the grounds, a railway the other. It did not see many casual visitors. In the year he had worked here, Braga remembered only two unexpected arrivals. One was a group of kids trying to sneak through a fence, the other some archaeologists turning up from Nepal or somewhere equally far-flung.

Whatever the archaeologists worked on was valuable enough to need armed guards. He knew a lot of stuff recovered from the ruins of Atlantis, deep beneath the Gulf of Cádiz, came here. But in all honesty, he wasn't especially interested. The job was simply a steady paycheque for straightforward, if boring, work. Patrol the grounds, make sure the main building's entrances were secure. He reached one. A keypad on the door showed a solid red light. Locked. Everything was as it should be.

Braga checked his watch. Past midnight. Another circuit, then he would return to the security office for a snack. He rounded the building, glancing into the dark sky over the Tagus estuary – and froze.

Something was flying towards him.

He at first took the light to be a firework. But it was coming in from over the water. A distress flare, a boat in trouble out in the bay? He reached for his phone to report it—

The light changed direction.

Not a flare. It had altered course, but was still heading for the facility. He snatched his walkie-talkie from his belt. 'Fausto!' he said. 'There's something over the bay, coming towards us. I think it's a drone.'

'I see it too,' came the reply. 'It's heading for the north wing. I'm on my way.'

'I'll meet you there.' Any boredom was gone, replaced by urgency. The north wing was the highest-security area. Braga had never been inside, but guessed it was where treasures from Atlantis were kept. He broke into a trotting run.

The light dropped behind part of the building. Braga increased his pace. 'I've lost sight of it,' he reported.

'It's coming down,' Carvalho replied. 'It's—' Silence from the radio for a moment, then: 'My *God*!' The exclamation was one of shock – and amazement.

'What is it? Fausto! What is it?'

No reply. Braga kept running. 'Fausto!' Still nothing – but he heard a noise, an echoing crack of impact. And again, as he hurried around a corner. 'Fausto! Where are—'

Carvalho was sprawled unmoving on the ground – but any concerns for his comrade's welfare were overcome by the sight of the figure standing over him.

An angel.

Braga stared in stunned disbelief. Glowing wings extended

from the figure's back. A rippling resembling heat-haze masked its body, obscuring detail. All he could see was that it was apparently wearing armour, golden metal catching reflected glints from the building's spotlights. Its head was hidden by a bright sphere of light. A halo.

Braga did not consider himself especially religious. But he had still been raised in a country where the influence and iconography of the Catholic church was omnipresent. Awe, or fear, or both, froze him. The angel's back was turned. It hadn't seen him yet. Was that what had happened to Carvalho? One look into the eyes of God's messenger had felled him?

The angel shifted, seemingly surveying the building, then raised a hand. It held something: a saucer-sized golden disc. The being drew back its arm – and flung the disc. It shot upwards, somehow changing direction mid-flight—

It hit a CCTV camera, shattering it.

The sight jarred Braga from his paralysis. Other cameras, he saw, had also been destroyed. Why would something sent by God care about being caught on video?

It wouldn't. Whatever he was looking at was no angel. It had attacked Carvalho, and was now trying to break into the building.

Adrenalin overpowered fear. He hurriedly drew his gun. 'Hey! Hey, you! Stop!'

The figure turned, the disc snapping back to its hand like an oversized yo-yo. Braga still couldn't see its face through the halo – but knew it was looking straight at him. A brief shiver, but the gun gave him confidence. 'Get down on the ground! *Now!*'

No movement for a moment – then the angel drew back its arm to hurl the disc—

Braga fired.

He had never done so at a live target before. But the bullet struck the figure centre-mass, as he'd been taught—

A flash from the point of impact. The figure flinched – but didn't fall. Instead, it advanced.

Braga pulled the trigger again. Another flash, an odd ringing sound accompanying it. He aimed higher, fixing his sights upon the halo. 'Get back! I said, get back!'

The figure kept coming. Another shot. This hit its face – or rather, in *front* of its face. For a split-second, the flash revealed a man's features within. The bullets weren't reaching him, stopped short by some invisible force. Braga backed away, fumbling for his phone. With the cameras destroyed, the main security hub in Lisbon wouldn't know what was happening. He had to call the cops, the army – somebody! He turned to flee—

Another angel descended from the sky ahead of him.

This held a spear rather than a disc. It stopped a metre above the ground, hovering silently, impossibly. Braga halted in terror – then shouted an order to his phone. 'Uzz, call the police!' The screen lit up as the Uzz app made the connection—

The floating figure raised the spear. A sharp *tchack*, and what Braga had thought was the spearhead sprang apart, turning the weapon into a trident. The two outer blades were razor-edged spikes. The middle one, though, was blunt, ending in a bulbous cup a few centimetres across. Something glinted within it, a gemstone, sparkling with an inner light . . .

The trident tipped towards Braga. He stared at it in fearful bewilderment—

A flash from the gemstone, the air pulsing as if ripping apart – and Braga exploded.

The hovering figure descended, touching down just short of the bloody mess that a moment before had been a man. Braga's pulverised phone lay amongst the shredded flesh. The 'angel' regarded the carnage in impassive silence.

The other intruder, though, reacted more forcefully. 'What did

4

you *do*?' cried a distorted voice, in Spanish. 'You *killed* him!'

'He was going to raise the alarm,' came the reply, voice also hollow and echoing. 'You know we can't let anyone see us.'

'Yes, but . . . my God!'

The other figure rose back into the air, its wings' glow brightening as if with the effort of defying gravity. 'We still have a job to do. Come on.'

The pair glided silently to a doorway. The trident came up. Another pulse of air-shredding energy – and the barrier blew apart.

The two figures landed and marched through, their wings smoothly shrinking to nothing, absorbed into the glinting armour on their backs. Another door stood at the end of a reception area. It disintegrated as explosively as the first. Beyond was a large, dimly lit room, filled with rank upon rank of storage units. An archive, a vast catalogue of archaeological discoveries.

The intruders were interested only in a select few. They strode through the rectilinear maze, counting off racks before making turns to stop at one particular locker. A flick of the hand and the spinning disc, blades snapping out from its body, sliced it open. A protective case inside was removed. Its contents were rapidly checked, then the pair moved on. More counting, more turns. Another locker was torn open and emptied, then more.

Finally, laden with their prizes, they reached another door. This was larger, more like the entrance to a bank vault. A biometric lock glowed upon it.

The two figures put down the cases, then the second aimed his trident at the wall *beside* the door – and fired another blast. Both intruders were showered with flying debris, the shimmering energy fields surrounding them sparking with the impacts. They recoiled, coughing as dust wafted around them. It cleared . . . revealing a gaping hole.

The pair clambered through the ragged opening into the hangar beyond. Low lights picked out a shape at the chamber's centre: a flattened egg of smooth golden metal fifteen metres long. It was surrounded by workstations and equipment, ranging from delicate probes and sensors to the brute force of powered saws.

Both intruders went to the ovoid object, entering a large open hatch at its rear. More monitoring equipment cluttered the interior. Dim illumination seeped through a broad window at the front.

'Here,' said the first intruder, halting beside a rib arching across the ceiling. A line of crystal set into the metal protrusion glowed faintly as his fingers brushed against it.

His companion went to another rib. 'Let's do it.'

Each took a rectangular object from a chest harness: blocks of C4 plastic explosive. Their hands passed without resistance through the invisible fields surrounding them. They pressed the explosives against the ribs, then pushed buttons on attached timers. Digital displays lit, showing a sixty-second countdown.

'Ready,' said the first man. 'Three, two, one – now.'

They pushed the buttons again. Both timers started to tick down in unison. The pair hurried from the golden craft and exited through the hole.

They did not make their way back through the labyrinthine archive. Instead, the second intruder aimed his trident at the high ceiling. A surge of power from his weapon – then the metal panels above blew apart. The pair collected the cases, then with seemingly nothing more than an effort of willpower extended their wings again. The trident's wielder brought it down behind his shoulders, where it attached to the armour between the wings as if held by a magnet. They took off, rapidly accelerating to whip through the hole in the roof.

Below, the timers continued their countdown. Three, two, one – then nothing as everything inside the strange craft was obliterated.

* * *

The two angelic figures flew eastwards across the Tagus estuary, ascending to a kilometre in the air. At that height, their glow was almost invisible to observers below. Not that there were any. The nearest bridge was several kilometres to the south, and their destination was dark, a nature reserve at the mouth of the river Sorraia. This late, the whole area was deserted.

Moonlight let them pick out their landing site. A car was parked on a track through the wetlands. They touched down behind it. Their wings retracted, folding in upon themselves with a faint chittering until they were gone. Then the shimmer surrounding the first 'angel' vanished, halo blinking away to reveal a black-haired man in his early twenties. The armour he wore appeared to be made of a glinting metallic fabric, flexible yet strong. Then in a blink it was gone, somehow flowing away to reveal ordinary clothing beneath. All that remained of the armour were chunky golden bracelets and anklets, and a torc necklace as thick as a finger.

The man put down his cases. 'Oh, God,' he said, dismayed. 'We killed someone!'

The other figure remained shrouded. 'We had to. If he'd raised the alarm, the cops would have arrived before we could finish.'

'I know, but . . . we *killed* someone,' the first man repeated.

'If we're going to change the world, there'll be casualties.' The glowing figure opened the car's tailgate. 'Let's load these and get out of here.'

The dark-haired man reluctantly nodded. He waited for his companion to deposit his own cargo and retreat, then put his stolen items into the cargo space. 'I . . . I don't know if we've done the right thing. Yes, the world needs to change, and we have the power to do it. But—'

The other figure stepped up behind him, raising its left arm. Another metallic chitter – and a slender blade, shining with an

7

unnatural blue-tinged light, stabbed outwards from above his wrist.

Its tip punched effortlessly through flesh and bone into the organs beneath. The man gasped, convulsing as his heart was transfixed by the paper-thin stiletto. The blade retracted back into the armour's sleeve. The young man crumpled to the parched ground, twitching.

'I'm sorry,' said the hollow voice. 'But there can only be seven of us. And I need to make room . . . for *her*.'

The killer moved quickly, removing the bands that had formed his victim's armour before dragging the body to the track's side. He had prepared for this moment. A shallow trench had been dug behind scrubby bushes. The dead man was hauled into it. A sheet of earth-coloured canvas was concealed beneath the vegetation; it was quickly draped over the shallow grave. Stones and dusty dirt were kicked on to the covering. The track was one of several routes to the nature reserve, not a destination in itself, and even then was far from highly trafficked – it would be days or even weeks before the body was discovered.

The 'angel' stood over the grave, emotions unreadable. Finally, it turned away. The light vanished as it reached the car, armour shrinking to nothing. The figure drove off, leaving only silence behind.

1

New York City

Three Days Later

Nina Wilde entered her apartment's living room – then stopped, standing in silence.

Her husband, on the couch, looked up from his phone. 'What is it?' asked Eddie Chase.

'It'll be like this all the time soon, won't it?' said the redhead, faint regret in her voice.

'Like what?'

'Quiet.'

The bald Englishman grunted in amusement. 'After eighteen years of having a kid, I thought you'd appreciate some peace.'

'So did I. But now it's happened, it's . . . weird.'

'Baby bird's got to leave the nest sometime,' said Eddie. 'Besides, Macy'll be back. She's only gone on holiday.'

'I know.' Nina sat beside him. 'But it's her first vacation without us. I'm . . .' She sighed. 'I'm worried. I know, I shouldn't be. Macy's an adult now, and perfectly capable of taking care of herself. But even so . . . I'm her mom. I can't help it.'

Eddie put a comforting arm around her shoulders. 'She'll be fine, love. She's in the French Riviera, not a war zone. And she's not on her own. Rain's a sensible lass. She'll look out for her.'

'Hmm.'

After a quarter of a century together, Eddie knew the uncertainty behind her noncommittal sound. 'You don't think she will?'

'No, I like Rain. It's this damn trust fund.' Nina's late grandmother had been a woman of considerable family wealth – which Nina considered to have been accrued through unsavoury means. She had made it clear she had no desire to inherit 'dirty money'. So instead, Olivia Garde's entire estate was placed into trust for her only other blood relative: Macy Wilde Chase.

The trust was transferred to Macy on her eighteenth birthday, making her a multi-millionaire overnight. There had been no purchases of Ferraris or castles or gold-plated shoes, and nor had Nina imagined there would be; she knew Macy well enough for that. It was another, more insidious effect of sudden wealth that concerned her. 'Macy was accepted to Harvard, and I didn't expect otherwise. But . . .'

'But you're not sure if she wants to go?'

'She said before she left that if she likes it in Europe, she might not come back.'

'She was joking.'

'Maybe. But . . . she's said other things too. And she doesn't *need* to go to college. She doesn't *need* to earn a degree, or get a job at the end of it. Hell, Rain seems more interested in archaeology than Macy now. It feels like she's changed her mind about going.'

'Maybe it's just about Harvard. She could get in anywhere else with her grades. And her money.'

It was said with humour, but to Nina, it was serious. 'That's the thing. She *has* all this money now – it's taken a few months, but I think it's finally sunk in that she can use it to do whatever she wants. What she wants to do is party! You've seen the pictures she's sent to us from France, and I suspect those have been very carefully curated.'

'She's eighteen!' said Eddie. 'Obviously she'll want to party. I did at that age. I was in the army, but when we had leave we absolutely made the most of it. I bet you did too.'

'When I was eighteen, my parents disappeared in the Himalayas,' she reminded him. 'I wasn't exactly in a party mood.'

'Oh. Right,' was his sheepish response. 'Sorry.'

She squeezed his hand and smiled. 'It's okay. But I'm worried that Macy might decide, "You know what? Life *can* be one big party if you have money!" And then eventually the money runs out, and she's left with nothing – and she doesn't have an education to fall back on.'

'I think you're underestimating her,' said Eddie. 'I mean, she's got a Yorkshireman for a dad, so if there's one thing I've taught her it's how to be tight.'

Nina grinned. 'To be honest, I'm kind of alarmed about some of the things you've taught her.' Her husband was a former Special Air Service soldier, and had passed on some of his training to their daughter in the interests of self-defence.

'Well, better to know this stuff and not need it than the other way round. Anyway, you don't need a fancy degree to succeed in life. Loads of people have made it without one.'

'Like you say, it's better to have it and not need it . . .'

'If you're that worried, we're seeing her in a couple of days. You can talk to her about it then.'

'I suppose. Assuming I don't spend the whole time trying to finish writing everything I promised for the anniversary event.'

'You're still not done?'

She shook her head. 'It turned out to be a lot more work than I expected.'

'How come? I mean, you literally wrote the book on discovering Atlantis. Just cut and paste stuff from it, bang, done.'

'Trust me, I considered it,' Nina told him ruefully. 'But that would have felt like cheating – especially for something this important. It's twenty-five years since I discovered Atlantis! Just recycling my old work for that big a landmark wouldn't feel right. The problem is, there have been so many discoveries since then, about Atlantis and the spread of the Atlanteans across the ancient world, that I *didn't* have anything to do with. I thought I'd kept on top of them, but I guess I spent more time teaching than learning since I became a professor.' She sighed. 'Now I have to keep track of finds made by other people. When was the last time *I* made a big discovery?'

'Three years ago,' Eddie said immediately. 'When you found the Temple of Skulls and Earthbreaker and all that in Guatemala.'

'I meant about Atlantis,' she huffily replied. 'Just in the past year, there have been Atlantean sites found in Egypt, Iran and Uzbekistan. I had nothing to do with discovering them.'

'You had *everything* to do with it,' her husband countered. 'Without you, nobody would even have been looking for 'em. *You* found Atlantis. Nobody else believed you would, but you did. Anything else is all because of you.'

She couldn't deny that. 'Thanks. You always manage to make me feel better.'

'I've been looking out for you for a long time now,' he said. 'Not planning on giving up.'

'At least you don't need to stop people from trying to kill me any more.'

'Tchah!' he exclaimed. 'Now you've jinxed it. Next time someone knocks on the door, don't answer – it'll probably be a hitman.'

'A very polite one, if he knocks,' said Nina, amused. She stood. 'Well, I'd better get on with—'

Her phone rang.

'Don't answer it,' said Eddie. 'Hitman.'

'What, they can kill you through your phone now?' She raised the phone, seeing its screen. 'Huh. It's Oswald. Haven't heard from him in a while.' She answered. 'Hello, Oswald?'

Oswald Seretse was a senior official at the United Nations, who had been Nina's liaison with the organisation when she was the director of the International Heritage Agency. 'Ah, good afternoon, Nina,' said the Gambian. 'I trust you and the family are well?'

'We are, thank you. Eddie's fine, he's here, and Macy's on vacation in Europe.'

'Yes, I had heard.'

She was surprised. 'You had?'

'Curtis mentioned it.' Curtis was Seretse's youngest son, a year older than Macy. Nina knew they knew each other, but she hadn't thought they were especially close. 'They were chatting on that augmented reality app, Uzz. I believe Macy was in Cannes. Curtis was quite jealous.'

'To be honest, so am I,' said Nina. 'But Eddie and I are flying over to the Riviera in a few days.'

'Are you staying with Macy?'

'No – it's her vacation, we're just meeting her for a day. We don't want to impose. Well,' she admitted, 'maybe I want to make sure she's okay, too. It's her first vacation without us.'

'I am sure she will be fine,' said Seretse.

She suspected from his tone that he wanted to conclude the small talk. 'So, Oswald. What can I do for you?'

'I was hoping you might be able to help us.'

'Us? As in . . .'

'As in, the IHA. And the wider United Nations, in truth. There has been, how can I put it? An *incident*, of considerable concern.'

'What kind of incident?' She noticed Eddie react with wary interest to her side of the conversation.

'The IHA has a facility in Lisbon. Its public function is to catalogue and analyse artefacts recovered from Atlantis.'

'I'm guessing it has another function that you're less open about.' Eddie joined her; she switched the phone to speaker. 'I've just put Eddie on as well. Is that okay?'

Seretse's reply was tinged with reluctance. 'It is . . . acceptable. He had security clearance when he worked for the IHA, after all.'

'Ay up, Ozzy,' Eddie chirped. 'Something wrong?'

'One could say that. The Lisbon facility's classified function is as a research centre for other artefacts that fall within the IHA's global security purview. Some of them you are familiar with. The remains of the Crucible, for example.'

'I remember it,' said Nina. *All too well.* The Crucible, an artefact capable of transmuting mercury into gold, had been the source of her grandmother's family wealth. More disturbingly, it could also turn uranium-238, an isotope useless for nuclear power or weapons, into plutonium-239: the core material of hydrogen bombs.

'It and other items of what are now termed an "extraordinary nature" are undergoing analysis there,' Seretse went on. 'Under conditions of great secrecy, naturally. Despite that . . .'

'Somebody broke in and nicked one of them?' Eddie said suspiciously.

'No.'

'Well, that's a relief,' said Nina.

But Seretse hadn't finished. 'Somebody broke in and stole *several* of them.'

Eddie rolled his eyes. 'That's a pretty big balls-up. Who's in charge of security, Paul Blart?'

'This is no laughing matter, Eddie. A guard was killed during the raid.'

'Oh, no,' said Nina, suddenly grim. 'What happened?'

'We are still trying to piece events together,' Seretse told her. 'There is very little definitive evidence. CCTV cameras were destroyed, and the story told by the only eyewitness, a surviving guard, was . . .' A long, unhappy exhalation. 'Difficult to believe, to say the least. Which is why we would like you, Nina, to help investigate.'

'Me?' she said, surprised. 'Why? I haven't worked for the IHA for a long time now.'

'Nineteen years, I believe.'

'Has it been that long? God, yes, it must have – I left before Macy was born.'

'Before she was *conceived*,' Eddie added.

'I don't think Oswald needs that level of detail,' Nina hurriedly said. 'But the point stands; I haven't worked for the IHA for almost two decades. And to be honest,' she continued, disapproval entering her voice, 'I disagree with the direction the IHA's taken in the meantime, especially with John Hoffman as director. The agency's become less about archaeology and protecting any – how did you put it? – artefacts of an "extraordinary nature" from misuse, and more about resource extraction and trying to *duplicate* these things.'

'I cannot argue with you there, regrettably,' said Seretse apologetically. 'But I have not had any direct influence over the IHA for some time. Recent American administrations have pushed for a more extractive, as you say, operational policy, and as the IHA's largest financial backer, they received what they demanded.'

'But that goes against the IHA's whole purpose! Didn't you object?'

'I did. Repeatedly. But as punishment for my outspokenness, I was promoted.'

Eddie frowned. 'Wait, to shut you up they gave you *more* power? How does that work?'

'Some promotions are intended solely to distance one's hands from the actual levers of control. Complaining would be churlish, since it is to the benefit of myself and my family, but the intent was clear.'

'So why are you the one coming to us now?' Nina asked.

'It was felt that in light of our prior friendship, I would have a better chance of securing your agreement than Dr Hoffman. But,' Seretse added, 'I would not have done this if I did not feel it was vital. Powerful, potentially dangerous artefacts have been stolen –

some of them, we are sure, involve earth energy. You are well aware of the threat this represents.'

'I am,' Nina agreed. Over the past quarter of a century, she had discovered numerous items that drew upon the little-understood energy field of the planet itself as a power source – to sometimes incredible effect. What had prevented such artefacts from being used for malevolent purposes was the diligent work of the IHA, at least during her tenure, and a quirk of genetics: only a small percentage of humanity was able to channel and control the earth energy flowing through them. Nina was one of these people, but for anyone without the requisite snippet of Atlantean DNA in their genome, the artefacts were inert, useless. 'Then what do you want me to do?'

'Come to Portugal, and give your insight and deductions regarding the stolen items. Whoever took them was very specific: they gave preference to these over artefacts that would seem more valuable. We are at a loss to understand *why* they took what they did. Your knowledge of Atlantis and its people is unmatched; you may find a connection that others have missed which will lead us to the perpetrators.'

Nina laughed sardonically. 'Funny. I was just saying to Eddie that my knowledge of Atlantis *isn't* unmatched any more.'

'You sell yourself short, Nina. Everything now known about Atlantis has come about because of your work – your tenacity.'

'That's what I told her,' said Eddie. 'So you want us both to go to Portugal?'

Seretse paused before replying. 'I don't recall using the word "both".'

'Either we both go or neither of us goes,' Nina insisted, before giving Eddie a questioning look. 'You actually *want* to go?'

'I'm not bloody letting you go on your own,' he snorted. 'Things have a tendency of *happening* when you do that.'

'Looks like it's both of us, then,' she told Seretse.

Eddie interjected before he could reply. 'Oh, wait! First class flights, open return. And five-star hotels an' all.'

'Eddie, we can afford our own flights,' Nina chided.

'Yeah, but we shouldn't have to. Since we'll be missing the ones we've already booked to France.'

'Damn, so we will,' she realised. 'Eddie's right, Oswald. If we help you, it'll cost us our vacation, so it had better be worth our while.'

'I am sure Dr Hoffman will agree to the expenditure under the circumstances,' was the Gambian's wry reply. 'Very well. I shall pass on your conditional agreement to him, and ensure you receive the necessary details as quickly as possible. My under-standing is that he would like you to fly out tonight. I'll speak to you again soon.' He said his farewells, then rang off.

Nina lowered the phone. 'I'm surprised you agreed to that,' she said to Eddie. 'I thought you were looking forward to this vacation.'

'I still am,' he said with a broad grin, exposing the gap between his front teeth. 'Time it right, we fly to Portugal, you look at this stuff – then we head on to France to meet Macy when we were supposed to. And we get free first-class flights into the bargain.'

She matched his grin. 'Cunning. We might still have to change our plans, though. I don't know long this will take.'

'Better call Macy and let her know.'

Nina glanced at her watch. It was after two in the afternoon in New York; France was six hours ahead. 'That's assuming she's not out tearing up the town already . . .'

2

France

'How do I look?' asked Macy Wilde Chase, twirling and flicking her shoulder-length hair to show off her outfit.

'Very nice,' replied Rain Belcourt approvingly.

Macy smiled. 'And what does everyone else think?'

Macy and Rain were the only people in the rented villa, but several of their friends were also present – albeit virtually. Rain held up her phone, colourful anime-style creatures dancing on its e-ink case, to video the redhead. In the room Macy was surrounded by only empty space, but on screen the Uzz app overlaid the augmented reality avatars of several young men and women around her. The latter offered vocal admiration, while the former mostly limited themselves to approving nods.

'Thanks, guys,' said Macy, smiling again. She had bought the dress of shimmering green metallic fabric in Monaco earlier that day, hoping for a favourable reaction. Raising her own phone, she turned to see her friends. She and Rain had scanned the room with their devices' cameras and lidar sensors, creating a replica on the screens of their friends in New York that they could move around in simply by changing position in real life. 'And doesn't Rain look stunning too?' She pointed her phone at her housemate.

Rain blushed. 'Oh, no no no,' she said, flapping her hands as if to shield her face.

'No, Rain, you look great,' said Lily Rubin over the phone. The spatial audio effect from its speakers placed her to Macy's left; she turned slightly to bring her into frame. 'Did you tint your hair blue? It's cool. And that's such a cute top. Does it have an Uzz code? I'd like to scan it.'

'I think it does,' Rain told her.

Macy watched as the on-screen rendition of Lily stepped closer to Rain. Her body was entirely digital, Uzz's AI simulating its movements, but her face was mapped in real time onto the avatar's head. Lily's own phone – or rather, its CGI clone – was in her hand. She raised it to take a picture of Rain's low-cut top.

'Got it,' said Lily. For a moment, her live expression was replaced by a previously scanned neutral image, her hand obscuring the front-facing camera as she tapped at the screen. Then her real face returned, lips pursed. 'Oof, fourteen hundred kudos? That's pricey.' Uzz had its own virtual currency, earned by engagement with others in the app.

'So was the real thing,' said Rain apologetically.

Lily shrugged. 'Ah, what the hell, it's not real money. I'll just eyeball some ads and earn it back.' Another tap at the screen, and her avatar's clothing changed with a flurry of virtual sparkles to match Rain's. 'Ta-da!'

'You didn't want to scan mine?' Macy asked.

A grin. 'I already did. Four thousand kudos is a bit rich, even for me. I don't even want to guess how much the real thing cost you.'

'It was . . . pretty expensive,' she admitted. It was actually the most she had ever spent on an item of clothing. In her mind, she heard her father's gruff Yorkshire voice complaining: *'Ow much?*

But what she spent her money on was no longer her parents' concern. It was *her* money, after all. Her mother might not approve of where it had come from, but what mattered now was that it was put to good use.

'So you're clubbing in Monte Carlo tonight?' said another voice, seemingly to Macy's right. She turned, bringing Curtis Seretse into view. The handsome young man, his accent a smooth melange of Gambian and mid-Atlantic American from his father's years of diplomatic postings, grinned at her. 'You keep making me jealous, Macy. Are you going to a casino?'

'Afraid I'm not into gambling, Curtis. But maybe I'll put ten euros on a roulette table for you. You pick the number, and—'

The lower quarter of Uzz's display was, as always, a constantly scrolling list of notifications, recommendations and advertisements, the last of which disappeared once the phone's eye-tracking confirmed they had been seen. But now, an alert dropped down from the screen's top, accompanied by a ringtone. She sighed when she saw who was calling. 'Guys, hold on. It's my mom.'

'Just invite her into Uzz,' said Lily.

'She won't use it, she's too old. She's calling on *FaceTime*, for God's sake.' Her friends' reactions ranged from amusement to mock-horror. 'I'll have to drop out of Uzz to answer. Back soon.'

She switched to the video messenger. Her mother appeared. 'Hi, Mom. What's up?'

'Hi, Macy,' Nina replied. 'You look nice. Are you about to go out?'

'Yeah, Rain and I are going clubbing in Monaco.'

A flicker of Nina's expression told Macy she considered the prospect akin to hell on earth, but the thought remained unvoiced. 'I'm sure you'll enjoy it,' she said instead.

'We will,' Macy agreed. 'But our cab's on the way, so I can't talk for long. Is Dad there?'

Nina turned her phone to reveal Eddie on the sofa. 'Ay up, love,' he said, waving. 'Going partying?'

'Yeah.'

'Cool. Don't drink too much. Just remember, "beer before wine, you'll be fine".'

20

'Don't encourage her,' said Nina, disapproval plain. 'She's not twenty-one yet.'

'The legal drinking age in Europe is eighteen, Mom,' Macy reminded her pointedly.

Her mother brought the camera back to herself. 'Remember that when you come back home. I don't want you to get busted for underage drinking because you've gotten into the habit.'

Macy sighed. 'Is this why you called me, Mom?'

'No, no. Sorry. You have a good time. Just . . . not *too* good a time, okay? No, I called to tell you that Dad and I might have to change our plans. Something's come up, to do with the IHA.'

Macy was puzzled. 'You don't even work for them any more. And I thought you didn't like the way the new guy in charge runs it.'

'I know – this is a favour for Oswald Seretse.'

'Huh, that's a coincidence. Curtis was just here.'

'What, he's in France?' Eddie piped up in the background.

'No, we were hanging out on Uzz.'

Another facial twinge from Nina, this one vocalised. 'I don't get the appeal of that app, at all.'

'What's not to like?' Macy protested. 'It lets you be with your friends, wherever you all are in the world.'

'It shoves ads and clickbait down your throat and acts like a Skinner Box by giving you pointless rewards for looking at them,' came the counter. 'And I don't even want to imagine how much personal data it's accumulating on you.'

Macy had heard it all before. '*Anyway*, what are you doing for Curtis's dad?'

'There was a break-in at an IHA facility in Portugal, and some Atlantean artefacts were stolen. Oswald asked me to help with the investigation. So your father and I are flying over there, probably tonight. I don't know how long it will take, so we might not be able to meet you in France. I'm sorry.'

'Oh, you won't be able to come?' said Macy – more brightly than she had intended. She hurriedly tried to cover it. 'That's a shame. I hope you can. Really.'

Nina saw right through it. 'You don't have to sound so thrilled about it, Macy.'

'I wasn't! No, of course I want you to come.'

'You could have fooled me.' She shook her head. 'Do we cramp your style so much that you don't even want to see us for a day?'

'No, a day is fine, obviously!' said Macy.

'That long?' Eddie chipped in sarcastically. 'Glad you could spare so much time.'

Macy tutted in exasperation. 'Dad, you know that's not what I meant. If you're coming here, then yes, I definitely want to see you. If you can't make it because of whatever you're doing in Portugal, that's okay too. It's not as if I won't see you when I get back to New York. I mean, I still live in your apartment!'

She could tell her mother was fighting to contain a comment on her use of 'your' rather than 'our'. 'I just wanted to let you know what was happening,' Nina said instead, rather frostily. 'We'll tell you more once we have the details. In the meantime, you go enjoy yourself.'

'Have fun, love,' added Eddie, leaning into frame.

'Bye,' said Macy, giving them both a small wave before ending the call. She lowered the phone with a huff. 'God! Parents. You're so lucky that yours are always chilled out.'

Rain had ended the Uzz meet-up, their taxi due. 'Not always,' she said, with a smile. 'They're just on their best behaviour for you.' Rain's mother was French-Vietnamese, her father French, the family dividing their time between Europe and New York to oversee the American branch of a charitable organisation.

'Yeah, but I can say the same about my parents – for which I apologise.'

Rain giggled again. 'Don't be silly! I like your mom and dad. Your mom's made all these incredible discoveries, and your dad? He's so . . .'

'Rude?' Macy offered.

'I was going to say funny. Even if, yes, he is a bit rude.'

'Maybe we should swap parents. I'm sure yours wouldn't constantly be on my back about what I'm going to do with my future.'

'But what *are* you going to do with your future?'

'Don't you start.'

Both young women laughed. Then Rain continued: 'Harvard is lucky to have you. Any archaeology department in the world would love to have Nina Wilde's daughter as a student.'

'That's the thing,' said Macy. She went to the wide window and gazed out. Monaco sparkled below at the foot of the rocky hills, the yacht-dotted Mediterranean a shimmering azure plain beyond. 'Do I *want* to spend my entire life as "Nina Wilde's daughter"? What if I want to be myself, and do what *I* want to do?'

'You don't want to study archaeology?'

'I don't know.'

'What do you want to do?'

Macy slumped her shoulders and drooped her head. 'I doooon't knooooow,' she said, flapping her limp arms. 'Hellllp meeeee.'

Rain laughed. 'Come on,' she said, taking her friend's hands, 'our ride is here. Let's have some fun.'

'That,' said Macy, 'sounds like a very good idea.'

3

Macy had hired a car for the vacation, but as she would be drinking, she and Rain took a taxi into Monaco. Their rented villa was in France, yet only a kilometre from the tiny Mediterranean principality's harbour, on the hills above the densely packed tax haven. The cab was electric, as were a good percentage of the cars Macy had seen in Europe, to her approval; sales of internal combustion vehicles were only a few years from being banned in the EU. It was a far cry from the States, where gas-guzzling SUVs and trucks still ruled the roads.

Despite the prospect of a fun evening, Macy was still unhappy about the conversation with her parents. 'Do they think I don't want to see them any more?' she asked.

'No, of course they don't think that,' Rain assured her. 'But you're an adult now. You get to make your own decisions.'

'If I knew what decisions to make. All of a sudden I have so many options open to me, but . . . I've got choice paralysis. And I don't just mean about whether I even want to go to college. I've got this money, and I don't just want to spend it on fancy foreign vacations and sexy dresses.' She indicated her shimmering green outfit. 'It's nice to be *able* to, but I don't fancy spending the rest of my life slacking off by a swimming pool – whatever my mom might think. I want to do some good in the world!'

'You can,' Rain assured her. 'There are all kinds of ways you could use your money to improve things.'

'I know. I can think of like a dozen off the top of my head. And that's the problem.' She sighed. 'There's so much wrong right now. We've got massive income inequality, fascism's on the rise, Russia's breaking apart and rogue nukes are being sold on the black market, new pandemics keep starting . . . And the whole time, the world's getting hotter and hotter.' She looked out at the hills over Monaco. Even in the dusk half-light the landscape was visibly parched, yellow and brown rather than green. 'I want to make things better, but . . .' Another sigh. 'I could give away every penny I have, but it wouldn't even scratch the surface. No matter how many people I helped, there'd be even more who still needed it. And . . . who am I to decide who deserves help and who doesn't? Am I worthy of that responsibility?'

'What do *you* think?' Rain said.

'I don't know – that's why I'm asking you!'

'That's a question only you can answer.' She gently squeezed Macy's hand. 'But I think . . . because you are asking it, you probably are.'

'You think?' Macy asked.

Rain nodded. 'And you don't need to help everybody. If you do it for the right reasons, helping a few might make all the difference. Or even just helping one person.'

Macy smiled. 'That's very philosophical of you.'

'I'm French,' came the reply, with a lackadaisical shrug. 'Philosophy is one of our national pastimes.' They both laughed as the cab entered Monaco proper.

The nightclub was in a part of the tiny state that had not existed when Macy was born in 2015. The district of Le Portier, north of the harbour-mouth, had been reclaimed from the sea during the following decade. Other similar projects were ongoing: Monaco had long ago run out of space for development.

The taxi dropped off the two young women outside the building complex housing the nightclub. Macy felt the heat the moment she left the air-conditioned cab. Night had arrived, but the temperature was still over ninety Fahrenheit. She was glad her dress left a fair amount of skin exposed.

She and Rain went to the entrance. Macy had already booked their admission via Uzz, but the doormen – Monaco was too upmarket for mere bouncers, she thought with amusement – still checked their IDs, even after scanning the confirmation on her phone. There were no problems, though: her passport proved she was eighteen, and that put her on the right side of the local law. 'It's nice to get carded and be told "sure, come in" rather than "you're too young, get lost",' she said to Rain as they entered the club's lobby. 'Europe's very civilised. Although is it true they even let kids drink alcohol in France?'

'Yes, but the stories are exaggerated,' Rain told her. 'I could have wine with a meal when I was sixteen, as long as my parents allowed it. It's not as if kids can go into a bar after school finishes for the day.'

'My dad said he used to. He started going into pubs in England when he was fifteen.' She was caught between disbelief and a reluctant admiration. 'Mind you, that was a long time ago. I suppose things were different back then.'

'How old *is* your dad?' Rain asked.

'Fifty-eight. Born in 1975. My God, that really *was* a long time ago. No wonder he married Mom; he'll need her archaeological skills to remember his childhood!' Rain laughed, then they sauntered on their high heels into the nightclub proper.

Outside, a man in his early sixties watched the two young women disappear from view. He checked his watch, then ran a hand through his sweat-bedraggled sandy hair and started walking back towards the harbour, lighting a cigarette as he went.

The club was expensive and exclusive, drawing a wealthy clientele. Macy had thought she would enjoy the experience of mixing with well-heeled people from all around the world; she was, after all, one of them. But while she found it fun to chat with others in multiple languages, after a while she began to feel . . . *dispirited*, was the only suitable word. The faces eventually blurred together, as did their accessories. *Look at me, look at my hand-made Italian suit and shoes, my Swiss watch, my supercar key fob.* The scents of pricey perfumes and aftershaves blended into a faintly overpowering gallimaufry.

She genially but firmly said goodbye to an Indian man in his thirties who was trying to hit on her and regrouped with Rain. Her friend was receiving similar attention from someone even older. She was smiling, but even after a few drinks Macy could tell it was just a veneer of politeness. 'Sorry, I want to talk to my BFF,' she said, gently guiding Rain away from her wannabe suitor.

'Thanks,' said Rain, with relief. 'I didn't want to be rude to him, but he wasn't my type. Too old, for a start.'

'None of them seem to have heard of the "half your age plus seven years" rule,' Macy agreed. She led Rain to a less busy spot. 'Are you okay?'

'Yes, sure. What about you?'

'I'm fine. Just . . .' She chewed her bottom lip, thinking of how best to verbalise her thoughts. 'Do you think this is where I belong?' she said at last.

The answer was immediate. 'No. This?' Rain gestured at the noisy, gaudy room. 'It's not you, not at all.'

Macy smiled. 'Thanks. I just wanted to be sure. It's weird. I was enjoying it, but . . . only to a point? These people have a lot of money, but all they want to use it for is to buy *things*, that show off to everyone else how rich they are.'

'Welcome to Monaco,' Rain said with a grin.

'Yeah. It's like I'm at a zoo, or a theme park. It's fun to visit, but I'm not sure I'd want to live here, even if it did mean I wouldn't have to pay any taxes. It's not me.' A small shrug. 'My mom'll be pleased about that, at least.'

'I think it proves what we were talking about in the taxi. You want to do something good with what you have, and I don't just mean money – I mean everything you have as a person. You want to make the world better for everyone. Perhaps you'll find a way to do that.'

'I hope so.'

'You will. I'm sure of it. If you get the chance, you should take it.'

'My BFF *and* my life coach. Thanks.' Macy raised her bottle of flavoured schnapps to toast her, only to wobble on her heels. 'Oops, better not have many more of these!'

Rain was also drinking fruity schnapps, but while Macy had tried several different flavours, she had stuck to the same one – surely not *literally* the same one? – all evening. 'A good idea,' she told her friend over the pulsing dance music. 'You don't want another hangover.'

Their first night out together on the Riviera had led to regrets the following morning, at least for Macy. She had told herself she wouldn't do the same again, but . . .

Well, she *was* on vacation. She finished her drink and held up the empty bottle. 'Maybe one more. How many have I had? Three, four?'

'Seven.'

'Shit!' she exclaimed, startled. 'No wonder I can't stand up straight, I'm drunk off my ass! What time is it?'

'Almost midnight.'

'Okay, I'm definitely ready for bed.'

Rain raised her phone. 'Uzz, we need a taxi.' A notification appeared, and she nodded to Macy. 'It'll be here in five minutes.'

'Good. Gives me time to stagger to the exit.' Rain smiled, then tapped in a message as Macy found her footing. 'Who are you texting?'

'Um, my mom. I forgot to tell her something.'

Macy smiled. 'Scatterbrain Rain.'

Her friend stuck out her tongue, then offered her arm to the redhead. 'Shall we?'

'We shall,' Macy replied with a glassy-eyed grin. She waved to everybody and nobody as they headed for the door. 'Ta-ta!'

They made their way outside. Even this late, the night was still hot. Their ride soon arrived. A white electric cab, a European model Macy didn't recognise, whined to a halt nearby, and they boarded.

The shabby man, lurking behind a palm tree as he smoked a cigarette, watched them go.

The cab returned them to their villa. It was owned by a man who lived opposite; his lights were still on, Macy noticed. She paid the driver using Uzz, then she and Rain went indoors. '*Amelie, allume les lumières, s'il te plaît,*' said Rain as they entered. The house's digital assistant obliged, turning on all the lights.

Macy squinted at the sudden brightness. 'Aah! *Amelie, réduire la luminosité.*' The lights dimmed. She fumbled with her shoes' straps before kicking them off. Even with her feet planted firmly on the floor, she put a hand against a wall for support. 'Oh, God. I really *am* drunk.'

'Do you need me to help?' Rain asked.

'Just point me towards my bedroom. Everything's spinning.'

It was meant as a joke, at least partially, but Rain still ushered her upstairs. 'Do you want me to stay with you tonight?' she said as they reached the doorway.

'Better not,' Macy mumbled. 'I might need to get to the bathroom in a hurry, if you know what I mean. But thanks.' She gave her friend a smile. Rain returned it and entered her own room across the landing.

Macy half-walked, half-staggered to the bathroom. This was not the first time she had been drunk – even with America's stricter alcohol laws, finding ways to get buzzed without parents

29

finding out was a senior year rite of passage – but it *was* possibly the most hammered she'd ever been. 'Oh, man,' she muttered as she cleaned her teeth. Her mother definitely wouldn't approve.

But . . . she wasn't here. And no laws had been broken. It might have been ill-advised, and she would regret it in the morning – but it was her decision to make. Wasn't that what being an adult was all about, learning from your own mistakes? Certainly she'd learned never to drink seven bottles of flavoured schnapps again.

She stumbled to the bed, peeling off her dress before flopping onto the mattress and fumbling for the switch beside the bed. The room went dark – but there was still a line of painfully bright light beneath the door. 'Goddammit.' She didn't want to get up again, then remembered she didn't have to. '*Amelie? Éteignez toutes les lumières.*'

The landing light went out. As did all the others in the house – her command had been too general. A startled yelp came from Rain's room.

'Oops! Sorry,' she said. 'G'night.'

She was fairly sure her friend replied, but by then a swirling, turgid sleep had swallowed her.

Macy's suspicion that she would regret her excesses the following morning proved correct. 'Oh, what the hell was I thinking?' she moaned.

'Are you awake, Macy?' called Rain from across the landing.

'By the strict dictionary definition, yeah.'

'How do you feel?'

'Well, I've learned that drinking is a lot more fun during than after, so the experience wasn't a total waste.'

Rain laughed sympathetically. 'Can I come in?'

'Sure.' Macy donned a long T-shirt, then dropped back onto the bed.

Rain, in a similar state of dress, entered. 'Good morning.'

'Oh, if only. What time is it?'

'After nine.'

'Ugh. I need about another eight hours' sleep.'

Rain smiled. 'Just in time to go to another club, yes?'

'No, no, no.' Macy put her arm over her eyes. 'I think tonight'll be a quiet one.'

'I'm fine with that.' Rain sat beside her. 'Do you want anything? Breakfast, coffee?'

'Strong French coffee would be much appreciated.' She raised her arm to look up at her friend. 'You take good care of me, you know. Thank you.'

Rain smiled again. 'What are friends for? I'll bring it to you.'

'Thanks.' Macy covered her eyes again as Rain left the room. She still felt queasy, so stayed still, listening to the sounds of Rain working in the kitchen below . . .

A warbling chime came from the screen mounted on the wall. The whole house was connected to the digital assistant; someone was messaging her. 'Yes, *oui*, what?' she said, assuming it was Rain.

It wasn't. 'Hello, I want to talk to you,' said a male, French voice.

'Shit!' Macy gasped, jerking upright and hurriedly pulling her T-shirt lower. The screen had split into two images; one was Rain in the kitchen, viewed from the screen in that room. The other was a frowning middle-aged man with frizzy hair. She scrambled out of frame to find some leggings. 'Monsieur Pluc, you can't just videocall me when I'm in the bedroom!'

'You were the one who answered it,' her landlord replied. 'But good, you are both there.'

'What do you want to talk to us about?'

'You made too much noise when you came back last night.'

'No, we didn't,' Macy protested. She couldn't remember doing so, at least.

31

Pluc's frown deepened. 'You did. I was asleep, and you woke me up. It is very clear in the rules that there is to be no noise after ten at night – and this was not the first time.'

It was Rain's turn to object. 'All we did was get out of the taxi and go into the house. Then we went straight to bed. We *didn't* make any noise.'

'The taxi did.'

'It was electric!' Macy hooted, stepping back into view. 'And your lights were on when we arrived. We didn't wake you up.'

Pluc drew in a sniffy breath. 'If it happens again, you will have to find somewhere else to stay. I don't care how many more days you have booked. The rules are very clear. No noise after ten. Break the rules again, and you will be gone. I am giving you a friendly warning, so you cannot claim you have not been told. Now, goodbye.' He disappeared, Rain's section of the screen expanding to fill the whole thing.

'But, wait—' Macy said helplessly, before grabbing her phone and stomping downstairs, hangover all but forgotten in her outrage. 'What the hell?' she demanded as she entered the kitchen. 'We weren't making noise!'

'I know,' Rain agreed, filling a cafetière with freshly ground coffee beans. 'But he's one of those people who complains just because they can, so they can pretend they have authority.'

'He has the authority to get a boot up his ass,' Macy griped. Seeing that Rain hadn't yet boiled the water, she took a metal kettle from a cupboard and filled it before lighting the gas hob.

Rain let out a little laugh. 'That is how everyone can tell you're an American. There's an electric kettle, right there.' She gestured at the appliance beside the sink.

'Doing it the American way makes me feel better,' Macy replied, putting the kettle on the hob. 'God, I can't believe that guy! Does he think he can push us around because we're women? Or because we're young?'

32

'Perhaps both.'

'Yeah.' She stared at the blue flames beneath the kettle, feeling a similar heat of her own rising. 'What an *asshole*! We're paying enough to rent this place. Pluc should be bowing and scraping to us, not acting like the lord of the manor!'

'He should,' agreed Rain. 'But it's okay. It's the first time you've ever done anything like this without your parents; they would have dealt with trouble, not you. How would they have handled it?'

Macy snorted. 'Dad would have rolled Pluc up like a basketball and dunked him into a trash can. Mom wouldn't have taken any crap from him either. She's had people point guns in her face. She wouldn't let some creepy little guy with pube-hair talk to her like that.'

Rain laughed. 'You have a special way with words.'

'I get that from my dad. He has a weird insult for every occasion.'

'Have you heard from your parents? You said they were going to Portugal.'

'I haven't checked, actually.' She raised her phone, seeing notifications. 'Text messages! Welcome to the nineteen-nineties.' She read them. 'Huh, they flew out last night. They'll be arriving in Lisbon soon. They really did drop everything to help the IHA. Must be more important than Mom was letting on.'

'You should call them when they land,' Rain suggested.

'Maybe. Although I'd rather get rid of the hangover first. That way, they won't get to wag their fingers at me.' The kettle had started whistling while she spoke; it finally reached its shrill crescendo. 'Oh, good. Caffeine versus hangover, round one. Fight!'

Rain grinned, then poured the water into the cafetière.

4

Portugal

Nina and Eddie cleared customs at Lisbon's Humberto Delgado airport. 'Ozzy got a car for us?' Eddie asked.

Nina checked the people waiting beyond the arrivals gate. 'Yes, there.' A man held a card reading PROF. N. WILDE.

'Just you? So I have to walk, do I?'

'Be glad you didn't have to walk all the way from JFK.' They started towards the chauffeur, Nina taking the opportunity to check her phone. 'Huh.'

'What?'

'Macy didn't reply to my messages.'

'Maybe she's got a massive hangover,' joked Eddie.

Nina responded with a sigh rather than a laugh. 'Maybe. I really thought we'd gotten past our loggerheads phase.'

'You've both seemed okay to me. I mean, you've had arguments, but not like when she was younger.'

'Until she turned eighteen,' said Nina. Another sigh. 'Ever since Macy got all that money, it's changed things between us. It's changed *her*. I'm worried she's going to make a big mistake with her life because she thinks having money makes you invincible. But I know that's not true, first-hand. Remember after I first joined the IHA? I went from splashing out on three-hundred-dollar haircuts to being unemployed in the space of two years.'

'It was *five* hundred dollars,' corrected Eddie, with the air of a Yorkshireman who had been brooding over the sum for decades.

'The point remains,' she insisted. 'But she doesn't want to listen to me because, well, who wants to listen to their mom tell them to be careful?'

'Macy's not stupid,' said Eddie. 'She's just . . . young. Sometimes you've got to learn from your own mistakes rather than have someone tell you. Only way it sinks in.'

'That doesn't stop me from trying to protect her.' They reached the chauffeur. 'Hi. I'm Nina Wilde?'

'Yes, Professor Wilde,' he replied. 'I will take you to Mr Seretse.'

The drive to the IHA facility at Bobadela did not take long. Lisbon's expansion over decades meant the airport had been swallowed by the city's sprawl. Three guards checked the car and its occupants at the main gate, other uniformed men patrolling the perimeter fence. 'Fair bit of security,' Eddie noted as they drove on to the main building.

'From what Oswald said, I suspect it's a case of locking the stable door after the horse has bolted,' Nina replied.

More guards watched at their destination. Waiting under the baking sun were two men. One was Oswald Seretse, urbane and formally dressed as always despite the heat. The other was someone Nina had only previously met briefly but had developed an antipathy towards, purely because of what he had done to 'her' agency. John Hoffman was in his mid thirties, wearing his hair in a short ponytail. 'Professor Wilde – Nina,' he said as the new arrivals exited the car. Like her he was American, but from Oregon rather than New York. 'Good to see you again.'

'And you, John,' Nina replied politely. They shook hands. 'This is my husband, Eddie Chase.'

'Hello,' said Hoffman, giving Eddie a more cursory handshake. 'Thank you for coming all this way.'

'Oswald expressed the seriousness of the theft,' she told him as she greeted Seretse. 'I'll do what I can to help.' She faced both men. 'So exactly what's been stolen?'

'I'll tell you inside,' said Hoffman. He led the group indoors.

To Nina's relief, the facility was air-conditioned. Hoffman led them through a security checkpoint – the doors appeared new, unpainted – into a large room filled with aisle after aisle of storage cabinets. 'This is our main physical archive,' he explained, guiding them through the cavernous maze. 'The bulk of our collection is in here.'

'This is from where the stolen items were taken,' Seretse added.

'So what *are* these items?' Nina asked.

'I'll show you,' said Hoffman. At one side of the chamber was a cabin-like structure; he entered and showed them into a conference room. The rear wall was one large screen. He invited the visitors to sit, then activated the video wall.

The image that filled it was something Nina recognised at once. 'That's not Atlantean,' she said. 'That's a baraka – a Nephilim artefact.' The spear-like weapon was a product of the ancient humanoid race that over a hundred millennia earlier had attempted to build an empire. The Nephilim were products of interbreeding between another ancient race, the Veteres, and primitive humans; the Veteres had ultimately defeated their offspring, only to be driven into extinction themselves by their smaller, less intelligent, but more aggressive and vicious cousins, *Homo sapiens*.

Hoffman nodded. 'It was recovered from the Nephilim craft that landed in Australia. It's damaged; the crystal that gave it its power was broken.'

'So whoever took it didn't want you to have it even though it was knackered,' Eddie suggested.

Nina got straight to the point. 'Were you trying to reverse-engineer it?'

36

'It was one of numerous artefacts undergoing deep systemic analysis, yes,' said Hoffman.

'Oh, is that what you call it now?' She regarded the image with disquiet. Barakas drew upon earth energy to unleash bolts of raw power that caused whatever they hit to explode – whether an inanimate object or a living being. She had both used and been the target of such fearsome weapons. 'What else was stolen?'

Hoffman clicked through more photographs. The first was a gauntlet or vambrace, a piece of armour protecting the wearer's wrist and forearm. The metal was a distinctive reddish-gold: orichalcum, an alloy of gold and other elements, often used by the ancient Atlanteans. A thin line of glinting crystal was set into the metal, running from the back of the hand to a pro-truding slot midway along the armour's length. 'What's that?' she asked.

'We're not sure,' Hoffman admitted. 'The crystal is the same kind found in the baraka and other artefacts, which suggests it channels earth energy. But its function?' He shrugged. 'All we know is that the next stolen item fits into it.' He showed it.

'Looks like a bird,' said Eddie. A ruler alongside revealed the missile-like artefact to be roughly six inches long, a stylised orichalcum bird of prey with a sharp pointed beak of silvery metal. Small crystals represented its eyes. Fine feather-like patterns were inscribed around its body.

'It's missing something,' Nina noted. 'Wings.'

'We'd thought there was another piece we hadn't found,' said Hoffman, 'but there are no holes or pegs anything could mount onto. It's interesting, though. We x-rayed it. See the feather markings? They're not carved into the body, but are individual sheets of metal. Very small and thin, thousands of them. Whoever made it put a hell of a lot of work into it.'

'You said it fits into the vambrace?'

Another picture appeared, showing the golden bird sitting atop the slot in the armour. 'Yes, perfectly. But there's nothing to hold it in place.'

Nina pursed her lips thoughtfully. 'Maybe if the wearer can channel earth energy, it would stay put.'

'It's a possibility. Not one we've been able to test, though.'

'You don't have anybody at the IHA who can do that?'

Hoffman gave her a patronising look. 'It turns out that the percentage of people who are descended from the Atlanteans *and* have the specific genes that let them channel earth energy is very small. If you express that number as a subset of people who are also qualified archaeologists and have the necessary security clearance to work at the IHA . . .' He smirked. 'Perhaps you should come back and work for me.'

'I'm happy where I am, thanks,' said Nina firmly. 'What else was taken?'

The last item Hoffman showed was different from the other artefacts: a stack of orichalcum sheets, the topmost inscribed with what Nina immediately recognised as Atlantean text. Unlike the other pictures, there was nothing present to provide scale. 'These are a very recent discovery,' said Seretse. 'So recent, they have not even been publicly revealed. Do you know Dr Salman Zaidi?'

'I've heard of him,' Nina replied. 'He's been working in Central Asia, hasn't he?'

The diplomat nodded. 'His most recent dig was in Uzbekistan, where these were found. They had only just been delivered to the IHA.'

'Two days before they were stolen,' added Hoffman. 'We hadn't even started working on them. Dr Zaidi took this in Uzbekistan just before they were shipped out. It's the only one we have of them, at least in a semi-clean state. He catalogued their unearthing, of course, but they were covered in dirt. Most of the text was illegible.'

'So you hadn't even translated them?' said Nina, surprised. When she had been in charge of the IHA, such work would have begun immediately upon the texts' arrival. 'Oh, I see. Nothing obvious to reverse-engineer – sorry, *undergo deep systemic analysis*.' Her voice dripped with sarcasm. 'So they went on the back-burner.'

'Every artefact receives full attention in due time, based on our assessment of its importance,' was Hoffman's snippy response. 'In this case, perhaps we underestimated.'

'Just a bit,' Eddie rumbled. 'Since the other stuff they nicked looks like weapons and armour, and they were willing to kill some poor sod for it.' He cocked his head as a thought occurred. 'You said these hadn't been translated yet, and you haven't even announced you've got 'em?'

'That's right,' said Hoffman.

'So how did the robbers know about them?'

Seretse drew in an unhappy breath. 'Unfortunately, we cannot rule out the possibility of a leak from within the IHA itself. The investigation has so far produced no suspects, but . . .' He shook his head. 'That the raiders took those specific items while leaving others of greater apparent value suggests inside knowledge, both of the IHA's archive system and of the purpose of the artefacts. They knew exactly where to find them – and seemingly their nature.'

'Even though you *don't* know,' said Nina.

'Precisely. Which, as you can imagine, is a serious security threat. And why we asked for your help. If you can determine why these particular artefacts were taken . . .'

'It'll help you find who took them,' she concluded. 'Okay, so what else do I need to know?'

'It wasn't just that things were taken,' said Hoffman. 'Something else was *destroyed*.' He headed to the exit. 'I'll show you.'

They left the conference room and continued through the

archive. A hefty vault-like door stood in its rear wall – but Nina and Eddie's attention instantly went to the large, ragged hole beside it. 'Christ, looks like a bank robbery,' said Eddie. 'What do you keep in there?'

'Something I think you'll recognise,' Hoffman told them. He ducked to pass through the opening.

Nina regarded its torn edges as she followed. The wall was thick concrete reinforced with steel rebar. Yet it had been utterly pulverised. 'Did they blast this open with the baraka they stole?'

'No,' he said. 'We're certain it was unusable. They brought something of their own.'

She was alarmed. 'They had an earth-energy weapon?'

Hoffman gave her a grim look. 'It's what they used to kill the security guard. The biggest part left of him was his foot.'

'Jesus.' She entered the vault – and froze.

She did indeed recognise what the room contained. It was the *vimana-kal*: a flying craft built by the Nephilim, which used earth energy to levitate, pushing against the earth's magnetic field forcefully enough to overcome gravity. The flattened egg of golden metal was the length of a semi-trailer, around fifty feet, and thirty at its widest. Despite that, it was a mere tender for its much bigger parent craft, a floating fortress that had laid waste to a Chinese city before being destroyed. The mysterious powers of earth energy, including an invisible shield against physical attack, had ultimately been unable to withstand twenty-first century weaponry. The Nephilim had used the smaller craft to escape.

But now the vimana-kal had also been destroyed. Its crystalline front windows were blown out, the once-smooth hull ruptured from within. 'What happened to it?' Nina asked, the question followed immediately by: 'And how did you get hold of it?'

'The Australian government agreed to turn it over to the IHA for analysis,' said Hoffman.

'Under pressure from the US government, no doubt.'

His lack of a response told her she was correct. 'The intruders planted a bomb,' he said instead. 'An explosives team estimated four kilograms of C4.'

'Bloody hell,' exclaimed Eddie. 'Why'd they use so much?'

'Because they wanted to make sure the IHA – and its paymasters – would never be able to duplicate the technology,' Nina realised. 'They took the baraka, and the other artefacts, but this was too big. So they destroyed it instead.'

'They did that, all right,' Hoffman confirmed glumly. 'Anything we could use was completely obliterated.'

'Not necessarily a result I disagree with,' was Nina's pointed reply. 'But their methods . . .' She glanced towards the hole in the wall. 'They killed one security guard. Were there any survivors?'

'Yes,' said Seretse. 'Another man is recovering in hospital.'

'There were only two blokes watching this whole place?' said Eddie, incredulous.

'Most of the security is electronic, run from a hub in Lisbon,' Hoffman explained. 'The entire perimeter is covered by CCTV and motion trackers. If anyone had tried to enter, the police would have been here within five minutes.'

'But I'm going to guess . . . they weren't?'

The IHA director shook his head, aggrieved. 'The alarm wasn't raised by the security hub until several external CCTV cameras had been taken out.'

'How did they get to the building without being detected?' asked Nina.

'The same way they got out.' Hoffman went back through the hole, the others following. He pointed at the ceiling. 'There.'

The couple looked up. There was a rent in the roof, covered by a tarpaulin to keep out the elements until repairs could be made. Nina blinked. 'That must be thirty feet high. How the hell did they get up there?'

'Must have come in that way,' Eddie offered. 'Parachuted onto the roof, blew a hole through it and rappelled down, then went back up using powered ascenders.'

'No, they came in through the main door,' said Hoffman. 'The guard was killed right outside. They entered the archive the same way we did.'

'So, what?' Nina demanded sarcastically. 'They *flew* out?'

Hoffman and Seretse exchanged looks. 'I told you that the surviving guard's account of events was difficult to believe,' said the latter. 'But it is the only account we have, so we must pay it heed. However impossible it may sound.'

The group started back towards the conference room. 'What did he say?' Nina asked.

Hoffman took over. 'He and Braga, the dead man, saw a light in the sky that they thought was a drone and went to investigate. He was knocked out by an attacker; he said the weapon that hit him resembled a yo-yo.'

'A trikan?' Nina said at once. Another Atlantean weapon, which in capable hands could be lethal.

'That's our assumption, yes. But it's who, or rather *what*, he said was wielding it that's the difficult part to believe.'

'What did he say?' Eddie asked. 'Space alien? Elvis?'

Hoffman gave him a disapproving look before replying. 'He said his attacker was . . . an angel.'

It took Nina a moment to process his words. 'An *angel*? As in, servant of God, wings, halo – that kind of angel?'

'Yeah,' said Hoffman. 'And before you ask, he was given a full test for drink and drugs at the hospital. He was clear.'

'Well, obviously it wasn't really an angel,' she said as they reached the conference room. 'Maybe it was a drone rigged with lights to *look* like an angel. The guard sees it, is so startled he freezes – then someone tasers him.'

'You could rig a drone to shoot a stun gun,' Eddie added.

'The medical examination confirmed he was knocked

unconscious by a physical impact to the skull rather than a shock weapon,' said Seretse. 'And then there is the issue of the second guard being killed by something with the same effect as a baraka.'

'A grenade could do that. And we know they had explosives with 'em.'

'There were no traces of explosives where Braga was killed,' said Hoffman. He brought up something new on the screen: a video, shot by a security camera. 'And then . . . there's this.'

He started playback. Nina and Eddie watched for several seconds. The view was unchanging, covering a floodlit exit from the building. 'Okay,' Nina said uncertainly, 'what are we meant to be—'

A flash from the top of the frame – and a figure dropped from the sky on glowing wings. Its head was obscured by a bright sphere of light. It turned towards the camera, one arm snapping up – and something shot at the screen in the split-second before it went blank.

'Fucking hell!' Eddie exclaimed, startled.

Nina was just as shocked. 'What the – can you wind that back?'

Hoffman did so. Again, the figure dropped down to the ground, its body masked by a heat-haze shimmer, and the camera was destroyed. Another replay, and this time he paused it to freeze the intruder as it landed.

Eddie stared at the undeniably angelic figure. 'You know, it would have saved a lot of time if you'd showed us that first!'

5

Despite his injury, Fausto Carvalho insisted on coming to the IHA rather than have the investigators visit him. Nina suspected it was more out of the urge to prove he was telling the truth than merely not wanting to be confined to bed.

'I saw light in sky,' the Portuguese told his audience in Hoffman's upper-floor office. His English was not fluent, but his determination to tell his story made him entirely understandable. 'I radio Guilerme, then I hear a noise. Camera broken. I look for who did it – and then I see angel.'

Carvalho seemed entirely sincere, as far as Nina could tell. 'What did it look like?' she asked.

'It had wings,' he replied, frowning as he brought the traumatic encounter from his memory. An adhesive bandage covered a wound on his forehead.

'Like a bird?'

'No, no. They did not . . .' He searched for the English word, settling for imitating the motion of a bird's wings with his hands.

'Flap?' Eddie suggested.

'*Sim, sim,* yes,' Carvalho said, nodding. 'They were still, like an airplane. But not solid. Made of light, *luz néon.* I see through them.'

'Could you see their face?' asked Nina.

'No. The halo cover it.' He made the shape of a circle around his head. 'His arms, legs, hard to see too. Like . . . *névoa de calor.*'

'Heat haze,' Hoffman translated for the visitors.

Carvalho nodded again. 'Yes, yes. All I see through it is armour, gold metal.'

'So then what happened?' Nina prompted.

'I . . . I freeze,' was the embarrassed admission. 'You know, I see an angel! Big surprise. Then he hold something up, like a yo-yo. It start to spin, he throw it at me, and . . .' A nervous half-laugh as he indicated the bandage. 'Then I wake up in hospital.'

'Is this what he told you before?' Seretse asked Hoffman.

The IHA director nodded. 'Same story. However improbable.'

'It happen, Dr Hoffman, it happen!' Carvalho insisted. 'I tell truth. What I see, it look like angel!'

'We're not saying you're lying,' said Eddie. 'But even if it looked like an angel, it can't really have been one. Angels don't use C4.' He turned to Nina. 'And what he got hit with definitely sounds like a trikan.'

'Yeah,' she agreed. She had seen several variants of the disc-shaped Atlantean weapon; all had retractable blades that when charged with earth energy could slice through almost anything, and the ability to change direction in mid-flight at the mental command of their user. 'Lucky the angel decided not to extend the blades, otherwise Mr Carvalho would have more than a headache.'

'Or less than a whole head.'

Nina turned back to the guard. 'Is there anything else you remember? Did it talk, was it carrying anything apart from the yo-yo?'

'No, no talk,' said Carvalho. 'I did not see it carrying anything.'

'And you didn't see a second angel?'

'No.'

'There must have been one, though.'

'How do you know?' asked Hoffman.

'Because whatever killed the other guard wasn't a trikan. So we're dealing with at least two intruders – presumably with the same abilities.'

'Including flight?' Hoffman's scepticism was clear.

'We know earth energy can be used to levitate objects. You have – you *had* – an example right here, the vimana-kal. Maybe these people have some artefacts from Atlantis or one of the precursor races that can levitate an individual person rather than a whole craft.'

'Which would make this a matter for the IHA even if they hadn't forced the issue with a pre-emptive attack,' mused Seretse.

'You have to find them,' said Carvalho. 'They killed Guilerme. He was married; he was my friend. If they are angels, you have to ask, why they would do this? If they are not, if they are just men . . .' Anger entered his voice. 'You have to make them pay.'

'We *will* find them,' Hoffman assured them. 'Thank you for coming, Fausto. Take all the time to recover that you need.'

'Thank you,' Nina added. Carvalho nodded in appreciation, then departed.

'So,' said Eddie, 'what now? If somebody's got Atlantean stuff that even the IHA doesn't know about, that's pretty bad news – especially since they seem to know what *you're* doing.'

'They know what the IHA's doing – and are trying to stop them from finding out more,' said Nina. 'The texts from Uzbekistan hadn't been translated at all?'

'Only the first page,' Hoffman told her, 'and that was after the raid. The photo I showed you is all we have. But it doesn't contain anything helpful.'

'What does it say?'

'It's largely an inventory, taking stock of supplies and animals. Either in preparation to travel, or having just done so.'

'Charlie's mates wouldn't have nicked the rest unless they knew something about what it said, though,' said Eddie.

'Who's Charlie?' said Hoffman, puzzled.

'As in *Charlie's Angels*?' Blank looks. 'Oh, come on, I'm not that bloody old, surely. There were films! In this century!'

'This century's a third over already,' Nina pointed out. 'But you're right: the raiders *had* to know what the rest of the texts contained. There was something that made them important enough to steal – important enough to stop the IHA from learning.'

Seretse nodded. 'But how to find out what that might be?'

'I need to go to the source.' She addressed Hoffman. 'Do you have Dr Zaidi's number?'

Dr Salman Zaidi lived in Jordan, but modern technology made him as accessible as if he were in the next room. Hoffman let Nina use a smaller office to contact the Arab archaeologist, one equipped with the latest in augmented-reality screens. It was considerably more advanced than anything she'd previously used, with a glasses-free 3D display of almost startling realism.

In all honesty, she would have been happy with a simple video link, or even a telephone call. A smile: she could almost hear Macy's disapproval of her Luddism. But Dr Zaidi was apparently as technologically savvy as her daughter, using the same gear as Hoffman. The 3D effect made Nina feel as if she was peering through a window into his study. 'Good morning, Dr Zaidi,' she said.

'It has just turned afternoon here, but good morning to you too, Professor Wilde,' Zaidi replied with a smile. Jordan was two hours ahead of Portugal. The other archaeologist was in his forties, thin-faced and balding with thick-framed spectacles. 'It's a great pleasure and honour to speak to you in person. Well, more or less. I would shake hands if I could.' He extended a hand towards his own screen, making it seem to protrude from Nina's.

She smiled back. 'It's good to speak to you too. I've read some of your papers, and John's updated me on your work in Uzbekistan.'

'It is what we found in Uzbekistan that you wish to discuss, yes?'

'Yes. Did he tell you what happened here in Lisbon?'

The humour vanished from his face. 'Yes. Tragic – and very worrying.'

'The texts you found – did you make a full translation?'

He shook his head. 'Regrettably, I am not yet fluent in the Atlantean language. That is why I sent the plates to the IHA immediately after export permission was granted by the Uzbek government, so our experts could work on them. I managed a very rough translation of the first few pages, but that is all.'

'Anything you have may help us figure out why someone would want to steal them.'

'Of course. I have my notes here . . .' He tapped at his trackpad, then looked off to one side, his screen overlaying the document upon the video call. 'The text seems to be an account of a period of the Atlantean diaspora's movement eastwards through Central Asia, and their dealings with the various locals. Some they subjugated, others they fought.'

'Standard procedure for the Atlanteans, unfortunately,' said Nina. Although they had sent explorers out across wide swathes of the globe, the most legendary being a man named Talonor, the Atlanteans had always used the knowledge gained for conquest and exploitation. 'But similar texts have been found before. So what made this one in particular worth killing for?'

'I do not know,' said the Jordanian glumly. 'As I say, I did not make a proper translation.'

'There are no other photos?'

'Only of the plates as they were being excavated. The inscriptions are obscured by dirt.'

'And nobody took pictures after they were dug out?'

Zaidi thought for a moment, then suddenly straightened. 'Anwar!'

'Anwar?'

'My son. He was on the dig with me. He took some after the plates were removed from the ground. If he still has them, we may be able to see more of the words. Wait one moment, please; I will find him.'

Anwar Zaidi, when he arrived, turned out to be around Macy's age, his long dark hair in what Nina assumed to be a trendy style. 'It really is you!' he exclaimed on seeing her. 'Professor Wilde, I can't believe I'm talking to you.'

'Well, hi, here I am,' she said with a slightly embarrassed wave. 'With a reaction like that, I feel like a rock star.'

'Anwar has all your books,' said his father. 'You have been quite the inspiration to him. Perhaps even more than me!'

It was Anwar's turn to be faintly embarrassed. 'Father.'

Zaidi grinned. 'Now, Anwar, when we were in Uzbekistan, do you remember the texts we uncovered? The inscribed metal plates?'

His son nodded. 'From the ruined house. Yes, I remember.'

'You took some photographs of them with your phone. Do you still have them?'

To Nina's surprise, Anwar's expression turned to alarm: the look of someone caught with their hand in the cookie jar. 'I, ah . . .' he stammered, before trying to cover his dismay. 'I think so, yes.'

Zaidi regarded him suspiciously. 'Is something the matter?'

'No, no,' Anwar replied, a little too insistently.

'Then may I see them?'

Anwar reluctantly produced his phone, then issued a command in Arabic to its virtual assistant. He regarded the screen, then, with even deeper reluctance, handed it to his father.

Zaidi peered at the phone. 'These are all the photographs from the dig?'

'You heard me ask for them,' was the unhappy reply. Nina guessed he had told the phone to show all images from a specific geographic location. Zaidi scrolled through them. 'I see you have many pictures of Mariam. Did she know you were taking them?'

'Of course,' Anwar muttered.

'Perhaps I should check with her.'

The young man shifted uncomfortably, but Nina knew that wasn't what he was worried about. There was something else he hadn't wanted his father to see. Zaidi scrolled on – then his eyes went wide. 'When did you take *these*?'

'Just before they were packed to be sent away,' Anwar confessed.

'What are they?' Nina asked.

Zaidi turned the phone towards her. The 3D effect made it feel as if she could pluck it from his hand. Several pictures in the grid showed rectangles of tarnished metal. They had been mostly cleaned of dirt, characters legible even in the thumbnails. 'Are those the texts?'

'Yes,' said Zaidi, radiating disapproval. 'Anwar took photographs before they were sent to the IHA. Even though they had been declared classified!'

Anwar hung his head. 'I'm sorry, father.'

'You *know* you shouldn't have taken these! If they had leaked, they could have been used to loot other Atlantean sites before we could secure them!' Anwar's head bowed even lower.

'It's okay,' said Nina. 'The main thing is that we have the photos, and should be able to read a lot more of the text. And nobody else has seen them.' Anwar's flinch told her she was wrong. 'Have they?' she asked probingly.

Zaidi's questioning was more direct. 'Answer her, Anwar! Have you showed these pictures to anyone else?'

He couldn't meet his father's eyes. 'I . . . sent them to a couple of my friends on Uzz.'

'*What?*'

'I tagged them as "For your eyes only"! Uzz uses facial recognition so only the person they're for can look at them. You can't even take a screenshot; you just get a blank picture.'

'You could take a photo with another camera and send *that* to someone else,' Nina suggested.

'I sent them to my friends!' Anwar protested. 'Why would they do that? Who would they send them to?'

Zaidi gave him a cold look. 'We will discuss this later, Anwar. For now, send all these pictures to *me*, and I will send them to Professor Wilde and the IHA.' He returned the phone to his son.

'Yes, Father,' was Anwar's miserable response.

Zaidi turned back to Nina as the young man slunk away. 'I cannot apologise enough, Professor Wilde. My own son, doing such a thing – a terrible security breach!'

'I'm sure he didn't mean any harm,' she replied. 'And if the only people who've seen them are Anwar's friends, it's unlikely they're the source of the leak.'

'We shall see,' said Zaidi firmly. 'But much more of the text is readable in these pictures. You should be able to translate most of it.'

She nodded. 'I look forward to receiving them.'

'Ay up,' said Eddie as he entered the office.

'Hi,' Nina replied, barely looking up from her phone.

'Brought you some lunch.' He put a bag on the desk.

'Ooh, McDonald's!' she said in faked delight. 'You shouldn't have, you're really spoiling me.'

He chuckled. 'This part of town doesn't exactly have a deli on every corner. So what did you find out from this bloke?'

'Quite a lot. Although technically, it was more from his son.' She showed him the image on her phone; one of the metal plates excavated in Uzbekistan. 'There's some very interesting stuff here. Specifically, about a group of powerful Atlantean warriors . . . who could fly. Sound familiar?'

'Just a bit. So whoever robbed this place really was using stuff from Atlantis?'

'So it would seem. And look at this.' She flicked back to one particular photo, and zoomed in: not on words, but a picture. 'Does that remind you of anything?'

The inscribed image was of a human figure, its head hidden within a blank circle from which lines radiated, borne upon extended, stylised wings. 'Is that what Carvalho saw?'

Nina nodded. 'Just like he described. But I've seen this picture before, or ones very similar to it – and none of them were connected to Atlantis. At least, that we know of.' She gave him a look that she knew he knew: she now had questions, and would not stop until she had answers. 'I guess I need to start researching angels.'

6

France

By mid-afternoon, the city of Nice was bakingly hot beneath the remorseless sun. Macy didn't need to check the temperature on her phone: the many pharmacies had electronic signs outside, scrolling updates of the time, the date . . . and the forty-five degree heat. That was Centigrade; an instant mental conversion told her it was a searing 113° Fahrenheit. 'Are you seeing this?' she asked, aiming her phone at the sign.

'Oh, man,' said Zoe Reese, from New York. 'Rather you than me. It's only eighty-five here.'

'Yeah, but it's also only nine o'clock there,' Macy reminded her.

Zoe made a despairing sound. 'I think I'm just gonna sit in front of the AC all day.'

Macy laughed, then tilted her phone down. Rain's avatar appeared on the screen. The French woman made a face. 'Hey, Techno-girl. I'm right here,' she said.

The redhead lowered the phone to see her friend in the same spot as her digital counterpart. 'Sorry,' Macy replied with a giggle. Her friends an ocean away also laughed. 'Force of habit.'

'Is Techno-girl your superhero name?' asked Lily.

Macy smiled. 'Oh, didn't I tell you? I've had a secret identity for a while now.'

'I thought that was Rich-girl.'

Again, her friends back in New York laughed, but this time Macy didn't join in. Was there a hint of jealousy in Lily's voice?

'Hey, show us the street,' said Zoe. Macy obliged, sweeping her phone around to capture her surroundings. She and Rain were exploring Nice's historic heart, a maze of narrow streets and little plazas amongst warmly coloured old buildings. 'It looks beautiful there. I'd love to visit Europe.'

'You'd enjoy it,' Macy told her. 'Maybe sometime we should—'

She broke off as an Uzz notification popped up. She was being called by someone she didn't know; did she want to accept it? The caller's name was—

'Oh, my God,' she gasped. 'Oh my *God*! It's Rafael Loost!'

'What?' said Rain, startled. Her other friends expressed similar shock. 'Really?'

A green circle with a swooping tick accompanied the caller's name: their identity had been verified by Uzz. 'I think so, yes!'

'Are you going to answer?' asked Zoe urgently.

'Yeah, yeah,' Macy replied, flustered. 'Hold on, guys, let me take this – let me see if it's really him!'

She tapped the screen to accept the call. The view of the French street and her friends' avatars was replaced by the face of a spiky-haired man in his late thirties. She recognised him immediately; Rafael Loost was, after all, someone she followed on Uzz, and one of the most famous people in the world. He was also the richest – the first ever *trillionaire*. 'Uh, hi?' she said.

'Hi, I'm Rafael,' said the Canadian. 'Are you Macy?'

'Yeah, yes, that's me.'

He smiled. 'Will you be my friend?'

Out of context, the question could have sounded childish, even somewhat pathetic. But in this case, it was something that billions of people would love to be asked. Loost was, amongst his numerous other business ventures, the owner of Uzz, the planet's most popular social network. One of his habits – the more cynical, like Macy's mother, would have said 'gimmicks' – was that every day, he contacted a random Uzz user and asked if they would be his friend. Accepting not only got the lucky recipient five minutes of the business icon's time, but also a massive boost in followers and Uzz's virtual currency. 'I will, yes!' she gabbled. Another notification appeared: a friend request from Loost. She stabbed at it, a trilling ping signalling acceptance.

Loost smiled. 'Hi. Nice to meet you! So, I have five minutes to chat. What would you like to talk about?'

'Okay, okay,' said Macy, struggling to think of any questions. Rain's excited hopping at the edge of her vision did not help her focus. 'Uh . . . okay: what's it like living in space?'

Loost turned the camera. A large circular window came into view – beyond which was an incredible sight. The earth, as seen from orbit, an arcing sweep of vivid blue and green. 'Well, that's the view from my office,' said Loost. 'It's pretty awesome. There are some inconveniences to living on your own space station. But that makes up for them.'

Macy recognised the coastline of the Gulf of Mexico as it rolled below the orbiting habitat. Loost's unimaginable wealth had enabled him to do what mere billionaires had dreamed of but never achieved: leave the world behind. Although she knew there were reasons other than vanity. 'Does being up there help your health?'

'It does.' Loost adjusted the camera again to reveal he was riding an exercise bike in a small, white-walled chamber. 'Do you know what I suffer from?'

'It's a blood disorder?'

He nodded. 'Beta thalassemia intermedia. My blood doesn't carry enough oxygen. Not that long ago, I would have been dead by now – sufferers didn't live long into adulthood. But there are treatments that can extend longevity; chelation therapy, blood transfusions. Plus, I calculated that zero gravity would help minimise the symptoms. It turned out I was right. I usually am.' He grinned.

'I knew about the blood transfusions,' she said eagerly. 'I would have donated for you when you asked on Uzz a while ago, but I didn't have the right type.'

'Thank you,' he said, with an appreciative smile. 'Luckily, I have plenty of followers who do, who are just as generous as you.'

She felt her cheeks warm at his praise, still awed even to be talking to him. Other people apparently felt the same way; the bottom of the screen was alive with notifications of new followers, and that she was earning kudos as a result. Anyone friended by Loost would gain immediate online fame. 'Do you get lonely up there?'

'I have all the friends in the world just a call away – friends like you, Macy. And I have my nurses here. There would normally be three, but one had a family emergency. I consider myself a pretty decent boss,' an immodest smirk, 'so I let her go home in the reserve capsule.'

'Isn't that dangerous? What if something happens and you can't get back to earth?'

He shrugged as he continued to pedal. 'The odds of anything bad happening before the replacement capsule arrives with a new nurse are pretty tiny. Besides, the girls here can handle any medical situations. I won't need a blood transfusion for another month, and it'll arrive on a supply rocket before then. So, I feel perfectly safe. Safer than on earth.'

One of Macy's pet hates was the reductive use of 'girls' by men to describe adult women, but on this occasion she let it pass. 'That's amazing,' she said instead. 'And you run all your businesses from up there?'

He nodded. 'I ran businesses on different continents for years. My rockets are built in America, the launch site is in French Guiana, my quantum computing centre is in Switzerland, aluminum-ion car battery factories in Malaysia and Australia. And Uzz's headquarters are in California, of course. But in terms of communications, being five hundred kilometres up is no different from being five hundred kilometres across.'

'Amazing,' Macy repeated, wondering what to ask next. The question that jumped to mind was: *I recently became rich; how do I stop all that money screwing up my life?* But that seemed far too personal. Instead, she came up with: 'I want to make the world a better place. What should I do?'

Loost's eyebrows rose. She guessed it was a question he had not expected. 'I . . . think that depends. Everybody has their own vision of a perfect world. What's yours?'

'A fairer one,' she said. 'One where people work together to deal with the problems we're all facing, rather than only taking care of themselves. We've got to stop using fossil fuels and burning up the planet, for a start.' She and Rain had moved into a building's shade, but even out of direct sunlight the day was still drainingly hot. 'You're helping with that, making better batteries for electric cars. But I can't build a battery factory; I can't make other countries stop burning coal and oil.'

'Maybe not personally,' Loost told her. 'But you can find other people who think the same way. One person can't change the world on their own. Even if they're the leader, there are always other people behind them. You have to find the ones who'll follow you.'

She nodded. 'But even if you're doing something that's obviously making the world better for everyone, there are always people who'll fight you. All they care about is getting more for themselves. How do you deal with that, especially when they're the ones in power?'

'That's a very good question,' said Loost. 'Maybe . . . think of it like the Emperor from *Star Wars*. He was untouchable – until he wasn't. People *can* change the world. *One person* can change the world, make it better. They just have to work for it. It takes time.

But when people like you, your generation, take charge, you'll make it a much better place.' He glanced at a corner of his screen. 'Okay, I have about a minute left. Is there anything else you'd like to ask?' A wry smile. 'Something easier.'

'Oh, I don't know,' she said. 'How about . . . what's *your* vision of a perfect world?'

Loost laughed. 'I said easier! My vision? Okay . . . one where conflict isn't settled by violence and war, but negotiation. If there's something you need, you don't take it by force – you make a deal. Maybe it's because I'm a businessman, but that seems like the way things should work.'

'That sounds sensible,' Macy agreed. She now felt more confident about talking to the trillionaire, and her earlier question returned. 'One more thing. I came into some money recently – quite a lot of money. I want to do good with it, but there are so many deserving causes, and I don't know which to choose! How do I decide who gets my help?'

'You're really giving me the hard ones,' Loost said, amused. 'I would say . . . what's the first cause that springs to mind? Don't think about it, just answer.'

'I, uh – climate change,' she stammered, the words emerging almost unconsciously.

'Good call. It's one of my big concerns too; I've already set up a geo-engineering company to try to fix it.'

She hadn't known that. 'I've donated to Cool the Planet before. But I don't only want to help just one—'

'You don't have to,' he cut in. 'But that's where you start. After that, see where you go. I think you'll find the right way.' He looked briefly wistful. 'I'm a little jealous of you, Macy.'

She was surprised. 'Why?'

'You've got so much energy and idealism. Success tip: never lose it. Because I know from experience that you have to work really hard to maintain it as you get older.'

'I'll do my best,' she assured him.

He smiled. 'I'm sure you will.' Another glance at his clock. 'I've gone thirty seconds over! That never happens. You must be someone special. Great to meet you, Macy, and I hope we can stay friends.'

'I hope so too,' she replied. 'And thanks for helping me decide what to do. Maybe we should both donate,' she added, half-jokingly. 'I think you'd make a lot more difference to the world than I could!'

A thoughtful look crossed his face, then he nodded. 'Bye, Macy. Do what you need to do.' The call ended, the street scene reappearing.

Other avatars were now visible: more of her friends, including Curtis Seretse, peering expectantly at her. Notifications whizzed by so fast she couldn't read them. 'Oh, my God!' she gasped. 'The richest man in the world just friended me!'

Her existing friends responded with an overlapping chorus of amazement, congratulations and pouting that they hadn't been chosen. 'I can't believe it,' said Rain, flapping her hands excitedly. 'It really was him!'

'I know!' Macy squealed. 'And he gave me some really good advice, as well. About how to make a difference to the world. Isn't that incredible? He's got all that money, he lives in a frickin' *space station* – but he still found the time to talk to me. That is so cool!'

'Are you going to tell your parents?'

'I . . . don't know,' she admitted. 'They're probably busy with this IHA thing.'

'Your mom's working for the IHA again?' asked Curtis, surprised.

'Yeah. Some favour for your dad, in Portugal.'

'Really? He's over there too.'

'Huh. Small world.' She looked back at Rain. 'But to be honest, I doubt they'd care. Mom thinks Uzz is a colossal waste of time, and Dad doesn't like Rafael. "'Ow come I 'ave to pay bloody taxes and that ponce gets to dodge 'em by living in a space station?'" she said, in a decent attempt at her father's accent. Those who had met him laughed in recognition. 'No, if they ask, I'll tell them. But I doubt they'll ask.' She changed the subject. 'So, Rain – shall we find somewhere good to go out in Nice *ce soir*?'

Rain nodded. 'Absolutely. Will you be drinking this time?'

'No, no,' said Macy shaking her head. 'Well . . . maybe just *one* glass. I mean, I've got to celebrate making friends with the world's richest man, right?'

7

Portugal

Eddie wandered in from the hotel suite's bedroom to find Nina working on an IHA laptop. 'You still at that, love? It's late – we should get some dinner.'

'I'll just order from room service,' she replied in a faraway voice, which Eddie knew from long experience meant she was completely fixated on whatever she happened to be researching. 'You can go out if you want.'

'No, I'll have something in here too. Ozzy's paying! So, found out anything about these supposed angels that raided the IHA?'

'Not as much as I'd like. I've learned a lot more about angels in general, though.' She turned the laptop towards him, revealing one of the pictures Anwar Zaidi had taken of the Atlantean texts. 'This is an account of the movements of the Atlantean diaspora eastwards across Central Asia.'

'Diaspora is like refugees, yes?'

'Sort of. People who've been driven from their homeland, for whatever reason.'

'Having it sink underneath them's a pretty big reason.'

'Yeah. It's all interesting from an archaeological and anthropological point of view. But . . .' She brought up a different photo, zooming in to reveal the text inscribed on the metal sheet. 'There's one particular section that seems very relevant to what happened at the IHA.'

Eddie pulled a chair closer and sat. 'What does it say?'

'There's nothing specific about angels in the sense that we think of them, but that's an Old Testament term given a Greek name. *Angelos* means "messenger". But the text *does* talk about a group who seem to be some kind of elite soldiers. The name for them is here.' She indicated a word on the screen. 'It's an Atlantean term I've never seen before. But it seems related to others I do know. The closest translation would be something like "knight". They're described as using "the armour of the gods" that lets them fly, and they have weapons with the power of the Atlantean gods as well.'

'Like trikans, and those Nephilim zap-guns.'

Nina nodded. 'Exactly. They were sent on a mission to retrieve . . .' She found another section of text. 'The staff of the rebel king.'

'What, like his butler? He must have made a really good cup of tea.'

She laughed. 'I think they meant the stick kind of staff. But I'm not sure. Not all the text is legible, and even the parts that are were written with the assumption that anyone reading would already know the background. Like who the rebel king actually *is*, for instance. I haven't found anything that would confirm his identity, historically speaking. All I know is that he had a stronghold somewhere between the archaeological site in eastern Uzbekistan, and the Caspian Sea. Which is a pretty big area, like France and Germany combined.'

'So there's nothing that'll help us track these buggers down?'

'Not in the Zaidi texts, no. But I've been doing related research. Look at this.' She brought up the image of the plate inscribed with a winged figure. 'I knew I'd seen this before.' She switched programs, bringing up a tab on an internet browser. 'This is the Winged Sun of Thebes. From Egypt, circa 3000 BC.'

Eddie regarded the image. A circle at the centre, representing the sun, was flanked by wide, stylised wings. 'Looks a lot like your angel picture. Except it's got a circle rather than a bloke in the middle.'

'There are variations with figures rather than the sun. Thebes was another name for the Egyptian god Horus. The son of Osiris – you might remember him.'

'Oh, yeah,' Eddie said, nodding. 'That bloody cult.' The couple's encounters with a fringe religious group had led to the discovery of the Pyramid of Osiris beneath the Egyptian desert.

'Anyway, this was how the symbol was represented five thousand years ago. Go forward one millennium, and we get . . .' She switched to another tab. A new image appeared, similar to the first overall, though the details differed. 'This is from Meso-potamia, now modern-day Iraq. East of Egypt,' she added meaningfully.

Eddie noticed several more browser tabs. 'Going to guess you've found more of these things.'

'Yeah. From Mesopotamia we go east again, jumping forward another thousand years, and we find . . .' She clicked on the next tab. 'The symbol of the Faravahar, a keystone of Zoroastrianism – and don't start with the Zorro jokes, please.'

Eddie suppressed a grin and took a closer look. 'Okay, that's a proper angel. You've got a bloke with wings, and he's carrying . . .' The figure in the symbol held a disc in one hand. 'That's probably not a Frisbee.'

'It could be a trikan. But it's essentially the same symbol as the winged sun – two thousand years and two thousand miles apart. And then,' another tab, 'we have the winged celestials in Indian Buddhist art, and,' still another, 'again from ancient China . . . You see the pattern?'

Eddie nodded. 'It's moving east over time.'

'A lot of time, literally thousands of years – but it's the same image. Winged figures, surrounded by light. And the timescale matches the movement of the Atlantean diaspora, or at least one of its branches – the one that built the redoubt we found in the Himalayas. But this,' she brought back the picture from the unearthed texts, 'proves it originated in Atlantis.'

'So angels come from Atlantis?'

'The image of them, yes. The most familiar image, at least. There are some wild descriptions of God's messengers in the Bible – like the statues of the cherubim we found in the Garden of Eden.'

Eddie scowled. 'Oh, yeah. The things with four faces that tried to kill us with glowing swords.'

'Swords charged with earth energy. Everything ties together. Whoever these Knights are, they're in possession of Atlantean artefacts and weapons, developed from the creations of the Veteres and the Nephilim.'

'And now they're stealing other stuff like that from the IHA. Great, just what the world needs.' He rubbed his bald head. 'There's nothing else that would tell us how to find these arseholes?'

Nina shook her head. 'I've read as much of it as I can, and no. But the dig where the texts were found is almost three thousand years old.'

'Bit out of date.'

'Yeah. And I've exhausted all the IHA's sources of information – they don't have anything more.' She sat for a long moment, thinking – then her gaze flicked towards Eddie. 'But I know someone who might.'

'You do?'

She reached for her phone. 'I need to arrange a flight. Or rather, I need Oswald to arrange a flight. This is IHA business, so they can pay for it.'

Eddie smiled. 'Took twenty-five years, but I finally got you thinking like a Yorkshireman.'

'Aye, love,' she said, in an approximation of his accent.

'So who are we seeing?'

She scrolled through her contacts. 'Think about it: who has more intelligence on the Atlanteans than their enemies?'

* * *

A new day, and Macy felt happy.

The French town of Menton was a few miles along the coast from Monaco, just short of the Italian border. Macy had driven there on a whim after Rain received an unexpected call from her parents: some family matter. She explored the pretty streets for a while before enjoying a coffee and croissant in a tree-shaded square called the Place aux Herbes.

While she ate and drank, she checked Uzz. Since leaving the villa, she had amassed another *three thousand* followers and friend requests, on top of the insane number gained after befriending Loost the previous day. *Look at me, Ms Popular!*

Faint irritation moved in like a cloud over the sun. Once again, people were interested in her not for herself, but because of who she was connected to. First her mother, now Loost. Was that all she was ever going to be, an adjunct to someone more famous?

Further thought was interrupted by her phone. Speak of the devil; it was her mother. 'Hi.'

'Hi, honey,' Nina replied. 'Are you okay? Doing anything fun?'

'I'm good, thanks. Just having a coffee. On my own, for once. Rain's talking to her mom and dad about something.'

Concern entered Nina's voice. 'I hope it's nothing serious.'

'I don't think so. Why?'

'It's still the middle of the night in New York! It can't even be four o'clock yet.'

The six-hour time difference hadn't occurred to Macy. 'Huh, you're right. But Rain didn't seem worried. I wonder what's so urgent?'

'I'm sure she'll tell you,' said Nina. 'But I'm calling because there's something I have to tell you. Your father and I have finished what we were doing in Portugal.'

'Are you coming to the Riviera, then? Because I really don't mind if you and Dad visit me. I'm . . . I'm sorry if I—'

'No, we're not coming to France,' said Nina, speaking over her hesitation. 'We're going to Rome – to meet the Brotherhood of Selasphoros.'

It took Macy a moment to draw the name from her mental files – and when she did, she was shocked. *'What?'* she exclaimed. 'But – those are the assholes who tried to kill you, to stop you finding Atlantis! Why would you want anything to do with them?'

'They could have information about what I'm investigating. And after I *did* find Atlantis, they had to cooperate with the IHA or face jail. Besides, that was twenty-five years ago. All the senior figures within the Brotherhood who made the decisions back then are now dead.'

'It doesn't change what they did,' Macy said unhappily. 'They tried to kill you and Dad – and they *did* kill *your* mom and dad. They murdered them!'

Nina didn't reply for a moment, and when she did, her tone was one of forced unemotionality. 'They have something I need. So we're flying to Rome, to find out what they know.'

'And then what? Are you coming here?'

'I don't know. We might still have time to visit you; we'll see.'

'Okay,' was Macy's sullen response. 'Well, let me know.'

Her mother didn't seem to pick up on her distaste at the situation. 'We will. Okay, honey, I have to go – we're heading for the airport. You keep having a good time, okay? I love you.'

'Love you too,' she replied, ending the call and leaning back heavily, emotions swirling. What the hell was her mother thinking? Why would she voluntarily deal with people who had wanted her dead?

Her damn *obsession* striking again, Macy knew. Once Nina Wilde became involved with some archaeological riddle, everything else became secondary. Even her own family.

She needed to take her mind off it. Had Rain finished whatever she was doing? She checked Uzz. Her friend wasn't currently available, so presumably was still talking to her parents. She put away her phone and continued exploring the sunlit town.

An Uzz call came thirty minutes later. Macy was in a clothes store; she raised her phone. 'Hi,' she said, seeing Rain was in a car. 'Where are you?'

'Coming to meet you,' Rain replied. 'Uzz said you were in Menton, so I got a taxi. I'll be there in about fifteen minutes.'

'Okay, cool. Is everything all right with your parents?'

'Yes. Why?'

'My mom reminded me that it's still the middle of the night in New York. I thought it must have been something urgent.'

'No, they were already up,' Rain said quickly. 'They're visiting Europe soon, and we were talking about whether I'm coming with them.'

'You're already here,' Macy pointed out with a grin. 'How very convenient.'

'Yes, yes.' Rain's brief look of concern made Macy wonder if she hadn't understood her correctly. That was a very rare thing: the French-Vietnamese woman's English was perfect. Macy had once ribbed her father about how Rain was more comprehensible to Americans than him. 'Where are you? It looks like . . .' Her hand danced below her camera. 'Not far from the marina?'

'Yeah. I'm in a store.' Uzz allowed trusted friends to track the user's location, to within about fifty feet. Macy knew the app could do so with far greater accuracy, but except in certain specific circumstances its makers had chosen not to for privacy and legal reasons. 'There's a nice little square not far away. I'll meet you there.'

'You spoke to your parents, then? Have they finished in Portugal?'

'Yes – but they're not coming here,' Macy told her, exasperation returning. 'They're going to Rome.'

'Why?'

'There's this group called the Brotherhood of Selasphoros, a kind of secret society. They should be the last people Mom would want to talk to, because they once tried to kill her! But they have information she needs, so she's going, and that's that. Once she gets something in her head about archaeology, that's all that matters to her.'

'But she's usually right, isn't she?' said Rain. 'I'm sure she knows what she's doing.'

'She *thinks* she does,' was Macy's begrudging reply. She brought up a map, zooming out. A pulsing dot revealed her friend rounding Monaco's northern end. 'Okay, I'll send you the place. It shouldn't take you long.'

'See you soon,' said Rain, smiling.

Macy ended the call and found the Place aux Herbes on the map. She held her fingertip upon it. Options popped up; a couple of taps, and she had sent the location to Rain. That done, she left the store to head for the square herself.

A dishevelled man was looking in the neighbouring shop's window as she exited. She paid him no attention; he was just another tourist. But his eyes tracked her reflection in the glass as she passed – then once she was far enough away, he followed.

Macy found another table in the Place aux Herbes and waited, flicking between Uzz's latest funny videos and the map to see Rain getting closer and closer. Before long, her marker was almost at Macy's. She looked towards the square's northern end to see her friend searching for her between the trees and tourists, her black bob's metallic blue tint strong in the sunlight.

The place was busy, noisy with conversation and music from the cafés, so shouting to catch Rain's attention was pointless. Instead she touched the screen to bring up another Uzz option. It was effectively an electronic shout of 'Here I am!', pinpointing her position to within just a few feet. She watched as Rain reacted to an alert, held up her phone and turned to locate it – then beamed and waved as she spotted Macy.

'There you are,' said Rain when she arrived. 'It's so busy! I don't know if I would have found you if you hadn't sent that ping.'

'You would have heard me going, "Hey! Over here! Are you blind?" eventually,' Macy replied. They both laughed. 'What would you like?'

The shabby man had taken a table a discreet distance from the two young women. He pretended to peruse a menu, watching as Macy and Rain did the same. He waited for them to give their order to a waitress, then brought up his phone with thick, nicotine-stained fingers and made a call.

'It's me,' he said on getting an answer. His accent was Scottish, voice gravelly and world-weary. 'Aye, I'm watching them now. No, of course the lass hasn't seen me. I know what I'm doing.'

He listened to the reply, drumming his fingertips on the table. 'I agree,' he finally said. 'Time we gave Macy Wilde Chase her surprise package.'

8

Portugal

A big benefit of the IHA's paying for her air travel, Nina mused, was the airport's first-class lounge. It was an oasis of calm in the busy terminal's bustle, with luxurious reclining chairs and unlimited snacks and drinks. She had been tempted by an offer of Champagne, but restrained herself. It was still some way short of lunchtime.

Another benefit was the expedited check-in procedure. Rather than having to arrive three hours prior to departure, she and Eddie had only needed to reach Humberto Delgado an hour before. 'Maybe you *should* go back to the IHA,' Eddie suggested. 'First-class travel everywhere? I could get used to it.'

'Don't you remember what it was like when I ran it?' said Nina. 'I had the UN's accountants breathing down my neck the whole time. They would never have allowed it. Business class, maybe, but not first.'

'You weren't trying hard enough. I mean, you browbeat 'em into paying for all this, because they need you. You should make yourself just as valuable again. I mean, who'd be the better boss? You, or that snotty dickhead Hoffman?'

'I suspect the IHA has exactly the boss the governments funding it want,' she said. 'I certainly wouldn't let them use it as an R&D department for weird science. But thanks for the moral support.'

'Always here when you need me, love. How long before we have to go to the gate?'

She glanced at a departure screen. 'About ten minutes.'

'Good. Enough time for a piss.' He stood and started for the bathroom.

'Glad you could announce that to the world!' she said. He grinned, then exited.

Nina sat back in her recliner. Would the trip to Rome actually be worthwhile, in terms of both the IHA's money and her time? She had exchanged emails the previous evening with one Corso Benenati, the current head of the Brotherhood of Selasphoros. He seemed open to providing assistance, but whether he would remained to be seen—

Her phone rang: an incoming video call. The display listed the caller as unknown. Normally she would have ignored it, but it could be someone from the IHA, or even Benenati. She answered. 'Hello?'

The man who appeared was not someone she had ever met, but he was still familiar. It would have been impossible *not* to have seen him in the news over the past few years.

Rafael Loost.

'Hello?' he said. 'Professor Wilde?'

'Yes?' she replied, uncertain – and suspicious. Why would the world's richest man be calling her? For that matter, was it even him? She had first-hand experience of real-time deepfakes being used for deception.

'Hi,' said the Canadian. 'I'm Rafael Loost.'

'I know,' she said, still not convinced. 'Or at least, you seem to be.'

Her caller seemed faintly affronted by the suggestion that he might not be who he appeared. 'If you were using Uzz, my identity would have been verified automatically,' he told her. 'But you don't seem to have it, so you'll have to take me at my word.

Although maybe this will help convince you.' He tipped the camera – to reveal that he was floating in mid-air above a curving, pristine-white floor. 'I'm calling you from space, Professor Wilde. Right this second, there are not many people who can say that. Although . . . Can I call you Nina?'

'I guess you've convinced me,' she admitted. 'And yes, you can.'

He smiled. 'Hi, Nina. I'm not really a formal kind of guy.' He attached the camera to a mount, stabilising the view. 'I'm surprised you don't use Uzz. A lot of very high-profile people do, all over the world.'

'My daughter uses it,' Nina told him. 'My daughter's rarely *not* using it. But it's not for me. It's too manic and pushy and loud. I don't use social media much in general,' she clarified, not wanting to seem to be singling out his company in particular. 'Too many ads, too much hate speech.'

'It's more than a mere social media app – my ambition is for it to be the only one anyone needs.'

'With you taking a cut of everything.'

'Only a small percentage. And there is no hate speech on Uzz,' Loost added firmly. 'My AI scans every message, every conversation, in real time. Anything that violates our terms of service – or the law of its country – is flagged and reported, to the authorities if necessary. That's one reason why Uzz is so popular. It's not a toxic cesspool like other social media. Everything is based around earning kudos – social credit. It's a positive environment for everyone.'

'That's an admirable goal,' Nina admitted. 'But how can you monitor everybody? Doesn't it have two billion users?'

'Close to three billion,' said Loost proudly. 'But one of my other companies is the world leader in quantum computing. A whole division is dedicated to Uzz. And it's not even working at a tenth of its potential. Everybody on the planet could use Uzz simultaneously, and my AI would keep them all safe.'

An interesting way of saying it could spy on all of them at once, Nina thought, but she kept it to herself. Instead she asked, 'So . . . Rafael. What can I do for you?'

'It's more what I can do for you,' Loost replied. 'I want to offer you a job!'

She was startled. 'Really?'

'Yes. I'm creating a foundation to protect the world's cultural heritage – kind of a private version of the IHA. The intention is to digitise historical records, make 3D scans of important sites, rebuild ruins in augmented reality . . . basically make sure all information about our past is available for everybody, for ever.'

'For free?'

'Well, there'll need to be some way to stream revenue. But I don't plan on charging directly for it. There are other models, as Uzz proves. But,' he became more animated, 'you are at the head of my shortlist to run it. You're the world's top archaeologist; you have experience in leading a similar organisation; and, from reading your books, you're motivated to keep bringing new discoveries to the world. You tick every box – you are the perfect choice for the job.' He smiled. 'So, what do you say?'

'Why are you watching that twat?' Eddie had returned from the bathroom, and chose that moment to look over Nina's shoulder. 'Thought Macy was the one who liked that tax-dodging cockwomble.'

'Eddie,' said Nina through a fixed grin, 'I'm on the *phone*.'

He leaned closer. 'Really?'

Loost's own smile was just as immobile, but failed to fully mask his offence. 'Hi. You must be Nina's husband. Eddie Chase, I believe?'

'That's right,' Eddie replied. 'I'll let you two carry on, then. Don't mind me.' He returned to his seat, stifling laughter.

Nina shot him an irritated glare, then looked back at the screen. 'I'm sorry about that. My husband is, ah . . . vocal in his opinions.'

'I've heard worse,' said Loost. 'But anyway: do you want the job? The headquarters will be wherever you want to base them. The salary will be multiples of what you're earning as a professor. Your travel and expenses budget will be effectively unlimited. And, unlike the UN when you were in charge of the IHA, I absolutely will not be on your back about how the foundation is run. I've set the goal; you choose the path to reach it. Are you interested?'

He clearly expected her to say yes immediately. But she would still have had caveats even had she been sufficiently enthralled as to accept – which she was not. 'I'm very flattered, thank you,' she said. 'But I'll have to think about it. I have commitments to my faculty and my students, I have research ongoing for the university . . . and to be honest, I'm not sure I'd have the energy to devote to a start-up.'

'You would have all the resources and staff you need,' Loost went on, still in hard-sell mode. 'Whatever you want, it's yours.'

'That's extremely generous. But like I said, I need to think about it. I'm in the middle of something right now that could occupy me for a few days, for instance. So I'd like to get back to you when I'm done, and we can discuss it in more detail. Is that okay?'

Loost said nothing for a moment, face oddly blank. She suspected he was not used to being turned down. When he spoke again, it was with an exaggerated airiness. 'That's fine, sure. I understand. The offer will stay open, of course – when I said I had a shortlist, I wasn't joking. It's a very, *very* short list. But you can call me any time to talk about it. You've got my number.'

She was about to say he hadn't given it to her, then remembered her phone would have a record. 'Okay, thank you. I'll consider it, definitely – once I've finished what I'm doing.'

Eddie stood again. 'Our gate's opened,' he said, nodding towards the departure board. 'We need to get moving.'

'Sorry, but I have a plane to catch,' she told Loost. 'I'll talk to you again soon.'

'Have a safe flight,' he replied. Before Nina could say anything more, he terminated the call.

'So what was that all about?' Eddie demanded as he donned his black leather jacket. 'He was offering you a job?'

'Yeah,' she said. 'He's setting up something like the IHA, and wants me to run it.'

A dismissive grunt. 'Bet it's another bloody tax dodge. Are you going to take it?'

'I don't know. Like I told him, I need to think about it.' They picked up their hand luggage. Both were experienced travellers, with only a small backpack each. 'And I need to know more about what he wants this foundation to do. It seemed like . . . well, everything! Which is a pretty broad remit.'

'If he wants you to do everything, maybe he should pay you enough to afford your *own* space station.'

'I can't think of anywhere worse to live.'

'New Jersey?'

The lifelong New Yorker laughed. 'I would even choose *New Jersey* over a tin can four hundred miles up where you have to wait weeks for food deliveries and drink your own recycled pee.'

'When you put it that way, it does sound a bit crap,' said Eddie, amused. 'You all set?'

She nodded. 'Let's see what the Brotherhood of Selasphoros knows about angels.'

9

Italy

Nina and Eddie arrived in Rome after a three-hour flight. Seretse had arranged another car, which drove them to their destination. Nina had been to the Brotherhood's headquarters near the Vatican before; her reception back then had been begrudging at best, outright hostile at worst.

Things were different this time. 'Professor Wilde, hello, *buon pomeriggio*,' said Corso Benenati. The new head of the once-secret society was younger than she'd imagined, around forty. He wore a smartly tailored blue suit with an open-collared shirt, which with his stylishly tousled hair gave him the look of an up-and-coming businessman – far more informal than the old men who previously controlled the Brotherhood. He extended both hands to grasp hers. 'And Mr Chase, welcome to Rome!' Eddie received the same exuberant physical greeting.

'And you,' said Nina, out of ingrained social courtesy rather than any genuine pleasure. As Macy had reminded her, a quarter of a century might have passed, but the Brotherhood of Selasphoros – the name meaning *the light-bearers*, a self-appointed Illuminati dedicated to keeping anyone from rediscovering Atlantis – had still tried to kill her. And it *had* murdered her parents. Its archives might contain information she needed, but she didn't trust its members in the slightest. 'Did you get my emails?'

'I did, yes. We have found everything relevant in our archives.'

'Everything?' She was surprised. 'In such a short time? There can't be that much of it.'

'No, no, there is quite a lot.' Benenati was unable to keep still, stepping from side to side as he spoke. Too many espressos, or was he naturally overflowing with nervous energy? 'Ah, you think the archives are the same as when you last came here.'

'They aren't?' The ones she had visited were a vast catacomb of cellars and tunnels, storing a collection of stolen and suppressed knowledge of Atlantis dating back several millennia.

Benenati smiled. 'No. We have gone digital!' He led his guests from the reception area – which itself had been modernised – into an airy conference room. A laptop waited at the head of the table. 'It is a very big project, ten years and still going. But we will scan every book, every parchment. With very high security, of course,' he added, gesturing for her to sit at the laptop. 'The digital archive is not connected to the outside world. Nobody can hack into it.'

'Or access it legitimately without coming all the way to Rome,' Nina complained as she took her place.

'I am sorry for the inconvenience. But you of all people know the need to protect the secrets of Atlantis from those who would use them for conquest and war.' He regarded her questioningly. 'Which I believe is why you are here. Your Mr Hoffman did not tell me much, only that there has been some sort of incident.'

'You could say that,' she said, wondering how much Benenati and the Brotherhood needed to know. She decided to give him a minimalist précis. 'An IHA facility was raided about a week ago. The robbers killed a security guard and stole several Atlantean artefacts, including weapons. They also took a newly discovered ancient text – one that hadn't even been translated, so they shouldn't have known anything about its contents. Yet apparently they did . . . because what the texts described was connected to the raiders.'

'From what you have asked to see, I assume it was about angels?'

'Yes, amongst other things. I translated the texts myself, and got everything I could from them and the IHA's databases. But it occurred to me that as a group which followed the Atlantean diaspora after the sinking of Atlantis, you might have another perspective.'

He indicated the laptop. 'Everything we have is available to you. There are computer translations into English, but the original languages are there if you can read them.'

'Ancient Greek?'

'In most cases, yes. And also Latin.'

'Then I should be fine.'

Benenati bobbed his head in approval. 'If there is something you need which is not yet digital, or is a physical artefact, we can show you in the real archives.'

'I'll ask if I need anything,' she said dismissively, opening the laptop.

The Italian took the hint. 'Then I shall let you work.'

'How long'll this take?' Eddie asked.

Nina scrolled through the list that had been compiled for her. 'Quite a while, by the look of it.' She took out her notebook and pen. 'Maybe you could take our stuff to the hotel.'

'Then what?'

'I don't know! We're in Rome, it's a beautiful day – go look at things, eat gelatos, buy a nice suit.'

Eddie shrugged. 'Okay, bit of free time in Rome – I can cope.' He turned to Benenati. 'You got any suggestions?'

The Italian smiled enthusiastically. 'Oh, I have so many, you will want me to shut up. You should rent an electric scooter; it is a good way to get around the city. Come, I will show you.' He went to the exit, signalling for Eddie to follow. The Yorkshire-man gave Nina a joking *Help me!* look as he collected their bags, then left with Benenati.

Nina turned back to the laptop. 'Okay,' she said, 'let's see what you've got . . .'

She arrived at her hotel room over five hours later. 'You all done?' said Eddie as he let her in.

'Not even remotely,' Nina replied, flopping onto a couch. 'I'm going back tomorrow. Have you eaten yet? I'm starving.'

'Had a gelato like you suggested a while ago, but no, I was waiting for you. We'll find a restaurant.' He started a search of the locality on his phone. 'So what did you find out?'

'Some very interesting things,' Nina said, sitting up. 'The Brotherhood had information in their archives about these so-called angels – who are anything but supernatural beings. They're human: a group of seven elite warriors, the "Knights of Atlantis". Which happens to be the same as the number of archangels in Biblical mythology. This could be another case of legend being derived from reality.'

'Seven? That guard from the IHA was lucky only two of 'em turned up.'

'Yeah. They didn't have a reputation for mercy. They wore what the ancient Brotherhood described as "magical" armour, but from the description, it's clearly using earth energy. And yes, they had wings, just like the image from the Zaidi texts.'

Eddie paused in his search. 'So they both say the same thing?'

'Yes, but the Brotherhood's account is from an adversary's point of view. These Knights were considered a major threat. The Brotherhood travelled extensively, looking for allies to help fight them. They thought that if the Atlanteans established a solid seat of power in the Middle East or Central Asia, they would conquer all the other civilisations in the region, just as they did from Atlantis itself. The Brotherhood was trying to prevent that. The problem was that the Knights were effectively invincible. Whatever this armour of theirs was, conventional weapons of the time couldn't penetrate it. At all. An army could fire everything it had and not cause a scratch . . . and then the Knights would retaliate with earth-energy weapons. We've seen what they can do.'

He grimaced. 'So they're as powerful as that Nephilim UFO we saw in China, except it's been miniaturised into a suit of armour that looks like an angel? Fuck me. You wear it and you can fly, nothing can hurt you, and you've got weapons that can splat people into raspberry jam or chop 'em into salami. And there were seven of them. At least two of which are definitely still around. Yeah, that's not worrying at all.'

'I know,' she said. 'Which begs the question: are the two that attacked the IHA the only ones still active – or are there five more we haven't seen yet? If so, where are they, what are they doing, and what do they want?'

'The Brotherhood didn't have anything that helps?'

'Nothing yet. I did find something, though. There was one time the Knights were defeated.'

Eddie sat beside her, intrigued. 'Who by?'

'The Turanians. They lived in what's now Turkmenistan,' she explained. 'They were enemies of the Persians – the ancient Iranians.'

'I know where Persia is, love. It's got a big gulf and everything.'

'Sorry,' she said with a small smile. 'But the Turanians had a king, Afrasiab. Now, in Zoroastrianism, Afrasiab was very much a villain, one of the religion's most feared and hated figures. But you remember that the symbol of the Faravahar in Zoroastrianism is practically identical to the other angelic symbols over thousands of years? It made me wonder if they were one of the peoples dominated by the Atlanteans.'

'Were the Persians and the Zoroastrians the same lot, then?'

'The Persians were the people of the region. Zoroastrianism was one of their religions. But either way, they considered the Turanians, and Afrasiab especially, as their greatest enemies.

Which is why I think they were connected to the Atlanteans, because the Brotherhood went to a lot of effort to try to make an alliance with Afrasiab: "my enemy's enemy", and all that. They sent envoys to his desert fortress – and here's where things get really interesting.'

The rising enthusiasm in her voice warned Eddie to expect some great discovery. 'Go on, then,' he said. 'What mad bloody legend have you worked out is real this time?'

'Well, since you asked . . .' They both laughed, then she continued: 'Afrasiab's fortress was called Hankana, or the Iron Palace. I've heard of it before; it features in several classical Persian texts like the *Shahnameh* and the *Aogemadaeca*, a sermon from the *Avesta* – the holy book of Zoroastrianism. It's described as a huge underground chamber a thousand times taller than a man, lined with metal and lit by an artificial sun.'

'An artificial sun? Doesn't sound very likely,' he scoffed.

'We're talking about angels, and *that's* the bit you don't believe? But the Brotherhood's records described it in more detail – far more than anything else I've seen. They said they entered it through a deep cave in the desert, and inside it was illuminated by countless flames behind shapes cut into the metal walls – the sun, moon and stars. Now, if it really was somewhere in Turkmenistan, that country has some of the world's largest reserves of natural gas. Maybe Afrasiab or whoever built the Iron Palace tapped into the gas to light the place.'

He wrinkled his nose. 'God, the place must have stunk worse than curry farts.'

'No, natural gas is odourless,' Nina corrected. 'They add hydrogen sulphide so people can tell when there's a leak. But the important thing is that the Brotherhood made a written record of visiting the Iron Palace – and they weren't the types to fabricate something like that. Which means . . . it really existed.'

'So what's that got to do with these Knights?'

Nina leaned closer, face alight with the excitement of revelation. 'According to the Brotherhood, Afrasiab was the only person who ever defeated them.'

Eddie was impressed. 'How? I mean, if they're so powerful, and normal weapons can't get through their armour . . .'

'I don't know. But the Knights attacked his fortress, thinking they could trap him inside and kill him. Only it didn't go as planned. According to the Brotherhood, once they were inside the Iron Palace, Afrasiab's magic made their armour just . . . stop working. They were as vulnerable as any normal person. As a result, some were wounded, or even killed, by the defenders. The survivors managed to escape, taking the bodies with them, but it was a crushing defeat for the Knights. The Atlanteans took that as a bad omen and moved on from the region soon after.'

'So what happened to Afrasiab?'

'It depends which account you prefer. But the most commonly accepted one is that he fled after the Turanians were defeated, following the Battle of the Twelve Faces, and was eventually captured while hiding in a cave. The Persian hero Kay Khosrow beheaded him.'

'Live by the sword, die by the sword – literally,' said Eddie. 'But did the Persians ever find the Iron Palace?'

Nina shook her head. 'The Brotherhood knew where it was, or at least the route to reach it, but obviously they kept that from the Persians. Besides, their priority was keeping tabs on the Atlanteans, who had moved eastwards. Probably into modern Uzbekistan, where Dr Zaidi found those texts.'

Eddie leaned back thoughtfully. 'So are the guys who raided the IHA trying to find the Iron Palace?'

'Maybe. Or they're trying to stop anyone else from finding it. If there's something about it that renders the Knights' powers use-less, that would be a serious threat to them. But there's something else,' she went on. 'They weren't the only ones with what the

Brotherhood considered magical weapons. Afrasiab had one too. A staff, that supposedly let him control the weather.'

'You said about a staff before.'

'Yeah. "The staff of the rebel king." Afrasiab could well *be* the rebel king. There were suggestions in the Brotherhood's accounts that he was a renegade Atlantean who turned against his own people, taking the staff with him.'

'How could he control the weather with a staff?'

She shrugged. 'You got me. Some earth energy effect, maybe. We know it can be manipulated from great distances: Earthbreaker could cause an earthquake anywhere in two continents. And the Nephilim almost destroyed New York from Australia. But in mythology, Afrasiab was always portrayed as a figure who could control the weather. He inflicted a drought that lasted for years upon Persia – while also bringing rain to his own people. The *Bundahishn*, a Zoroastrian text, says he created rivers in the desert so his people could settle there.'

Eddie frowned. 'Sounds a bit hocus-pocus to me.'

'I would have thought so too. Except . . . he gave the Brotherhood a demonstration.'

His eyes widened. 'He did, did he?'

'I wrote it down; hold on.' Nina retrieved her notebook. 'Here. "Afrasiab led us from the cave to open sands some five stadia distant. He used the staff to summon a storm from a clear sky, of such magnitude we feared the deluge would sweep us away. He then dismissed the clouds as quickly as they came." He also had a bit of fun with his guests. "He called down bolts of strange lightning around us, so close their thunder was deafening. We crouched in terror, afraid of being struck, but Afrasiab stood tall, laughing. Afterwards, we saw that the sands where the bolts had landed were turned to glass."'

'That definitely sounds like earth energy,' said Eddie. 'We've seen things like that before.'

'Yeah, too close for comfort.'

'So the Knights aren't just looking for the Iron Palace. They're after this staff!'

'Maybe. I still have more of the Brotherhood's records to read. I'm hoping I can work out the Iron Palace's approximate location, which would help the IHA find and secure it. The Brotherhood said they travelled northwards through a desert to reach it. If any of their other records name a starting point or a landmark, I can use that to find a north-south search axis.'

'Still a lot of ground to cover,' Eddie said sceptically. 'Mostly *empty* ground in that part of the world.'

'I know. But the Zaidi text also gave me an east-west axis, remember? Between the Caspian Sea and Zaidi's dig site. So put the two together . . .' She extended the fingers of both hands and put them together in a cross shape.

'That'd narrow it down, yeah. You told Ozzy and Hoffman yet?'

'No; I want more info before I go back to them. And it's a bit late in the day now.' She stretched, suppressing a yawn. 'Have you heard from Macy?'

'No. She's probably still pissed off at us.'

Nina tutted. 'I *told* her why I needed to visit the Brotherhood. It's not as if I'm having a job interview.'

Eddie raised his phone again. 'We could call her.'

She considered it, then shook her head. 'You know what she's like: she needs a cooldown period. We'll talk to her tomorrow. Besides,' sarcasm entered her voice, 'I wouldn't want to interrupt her partying.'

10

France

After driving back from Menton in their Renault 5 rental car – Macy had wanted something compact, cute and electric – she and Rain spent the afternoon sunbathing and swimming in the villa's pool. Only when the sun dropped behind the western hills did they consider plans for the evening. 'Where shall we eat?' Macy asked, drying herself. 'Menton? Somewhere in Monaco? Or we could go to Nice.'

Rain clambered from the pool and went to get her own towel. 'I don't know. Perhaps somewhere we haven't been bef—'

She broke off with a yelp as her phone dropped out of the towel. She snatched frantically at it, catching it just before it hit the tiles at the pool's edge. 'Ah! *Merde, merde!*'

Macy cringed. 'Ooh, that was close!'

Rain carefully put the phone on her sunbed. 'I thought I would have to jump back in after it!'

'Good catch. Although maybe you shouldn't have forgotten it was there, Scatterbrain Rain.' Her friend treated her to a rude gesture. Macy laughed. 'We could go over into Italy. It's not far, and Ventimiglia looks nice—'

Her own phone rang; someone was calling via Uzz. Not her parents, then. She checked the caller's name – then stabbed at the button to accept the call. 'Hello! Hello?'

Rafael Loost smiled at her. 'Macy, hi. I hope you're well?'

'Yes, yes, everything's great, thanks,' she gabbled. Rain hurried over to see. 'My friend and I are about to go out for the evening. What about you?' She winced inwardly. What *was* there to do on a space station?

But Loost merely nodded. 'I won't keep you. I just wanted to tell you that I thought a lot about what you said the other day.'

'You did?'

'Yes – about helping people. So I decided to put my money where my mouth is. I'm donating ten million dollars to Cool the Planet. And you inspired me to do it, Macy.'

She was briefly speechless. Finally: 'You gave *ten million* dollars?'

'I can afford it,' he said, with a faux-modest shrug.

'That's . . . that's incredible! Oh, my God! I can't believe you've done that. Thank you. Thank you so much!'

He smiled. 'What's the point of being the richest man in the world if I can't make a difference to it? Anyway, I'm glad you're pleased.'

'Well, of course I am! Wow!'

'You go enjoy yourself; you deserve it. Bye.' A nod, then he was gone.

Rain gripped her arm. 'Did I hear that properly?'

'Yeah,' said Macy, still stunned. 'He gave ten million dollars to a cause, because I suggested it. *Ten million!* I'm . . . I just . . . whoa.' She let out a dumbfounded breath. 'Damn. That makes anything I could do seem . . . worthless.'

'Don't say that!' Rain gripped Macy's hand. 'If someone does a thing to help others, it's *never* worthless.'

Macy smiled. 'Thanks. You always make me feel better.'

'What are friends for?' She stepped back. 'So what are we doing now? Do you still want to go out?'

The redhead looked down at the lights of Monaco. 'Absolutely, yes. I want to celebrate!'

* * *

Some hours later, a taxi hummed to a stop outside the villa. Macy got out, regarding Pluc's home. The lights were on. A blind twitched; the landlord was checking on them. 'Shh!' Macy said, walking on exaggerated tiptoes. She wore the same dress as two nights prior; she was not nearly so drunk, but still more than a little tipsy. 'We need to be super-quiet so we don't wake Monsieur Pluc!' Rain giggled. With an almost audible huff, Pluc disappeared again.

The two women went to their own house. Rain unlocked the door. '*Amelie? Allume les lumières, s'il te plaît.*' The lights came on.

Macy smiled as she took off her shoes. 'It's cute, the way you always say please.' She sniffed. Could she smell cigarettes?

Rain didn't seem to notice. 'It never hurts to be polite.'

They entered the lounge. 'Or do you just want to be on the good side of the robots when they take—' Macy stopped abruptly.

A box, about a foot square, sat upon the coffee table. It had not been there when they left. She looked around in alarm. Nothing else had changed. 'Someone's been in here.'

'Perhaps it was Pluc,' Rain offered.

'He doesn't seem the kind to leave us a fruit basket.' She went cautiously to the table. The box was a varnished dark wood. A small card sat upon its top, bearing a single word: *Macy.*

'It could be a gift from your mom, to apologise?'

'You have *met* my mom, right?' The handwriting didn't belong to either of Macy's parents. Deeply suspicious, she cautiously opened the box's lid.

A gasp of shock as she saw what was inside.

A trikan.

The ancient disc-shaped weapon was nestled in its handgrip, an arcing wedge of orichalcum and gold. She had seen similar items before – *used* them before. Even before first seeing one in the flesh, she had owned a toy version, a copy of a prop from one of the movies based on her mother's books. That had been merely a fancy yo-yo. But she had become adept with it, and when circumstances led to her using one for real . . .

She had discovered – to her shock – that it was no mere yo-yo. She could control it, guide its movements with nothing more than the *desire* to send it in a particular direction. The Atlantean artefact responded to her will.

Not that anyone had believed her, even her father. That dismissal of what she knew to be true sparked a stubborn desire in her younger self to prove she was right. By the time she was ten, she was a self-taught expert at performing yo-yo tricks and stunts. When she finally used another authentic trikan, the knowledge saved the lives of herself, her parents, and countless others.

That trikan had been abandoned beneath the great red rock of Uluru in the Australian outback. She had never expected to see another, except in a museum. But now somebody had presented one to her. It was different from the others she had used: smaller than those created by the ancient race of giants, the Nephilim, a crystal set into its centre. Where had it come from? And more importantly, what was it doing here?

'That's a trikan, isn't it?' said Rain, moving beside her.

'Yeah.' Macy hesitantly touched the handgrip. A little static-like jolt made her flinch. Earth energy, either pent up inside the trikan or transferring from her to the weapon; she didn't know. But it told her it was the real thing, not a fake. Slipping her fingers into the grip, she lifted it out. The crystal shimmered with an eerie light. 'It's genuine. But I've never seen one like this before. Who brought it here?'

'That,' said a voice from the kitchen, 'would be me.'

Macy jumped, instinctively drawing back her weapon arm. The trikan sprang to life in response, spinning inside its holder – ready for action. Rain flinched. Standing in the doorway was a middle-aged man with messy sandy hair, his clothing rumpled despite seeming brand new. 'Who the fuck are you?' Macy demanded.

'My name's MacDuff,' said the man. His accent was Scottish. 'Euripides MacDuff.'

'Euripides?' she scoffed in disbelief.

He sighed, apparently used to the reaction. 'I was cursed with parents who were great fans of the Classics.' He glanced at the still-spinning trikan. 'You don't need to keep that thing whizzing around. I'm not here to hurt you.'

Macy kept the weapon active. 'What do you want?'

'I'm a genealogist,' he explained. 'My job is to seek out people of Atlantean descent who can channel earth energy to activate ancient artefacts. Like that one.' Another flick of his eyes towards the trikan. 'I've been watching you for some time.'

She frowned. 'Have you now?'

'No, wait, that came out all creepy,' said MacDuff, hastily raising his hands in apology. 'What I meant was, I was certain you had the power, probably extremely strongly. And I was right.' He waved a finger at her weapon. 'Your being able to use that proves it. So if you could, ah, power down the thing that could cut me in half so I can tell you more . . . ?'

Somewhat reluctantly, Macy did so. No specific mental command was needed; the trikan simply responded to her bidding, stopping with a faint metallic *clink*. She lowered her arm, but kept the trikan at the ready.

'Aye, that's grand,' he said, with clear relief. 'Now, because your ma has . . . a *history*, shall I put it, with artefacts from Atlantis, it was almost certain, genetically speaking, that you'd be able to do everything she could, and possibly more. As it turns out, there's no possibly about it. Why, I'm not sure. There's something in your DNA I havnae been able to explain.'

'Like what?'

'I don't know. All I do know is that before you were born, your ma resigned from the IHA and basically put her affairs in order. Like she didn't expect to live for much longer. Except . . .

something happened to her.'

'What?'

'How would *I* know? She's your mother – ask her! But whatever was wrong with her *stopped* being wrong with her. It was cured, and she's been in perfect health ever since.'

'Mom never gets ill,' Macy reluctantly acknowledged.

He nodded. 'And nor do you.'

'How the hell do you know that? And how did you get hold of my DNA?'

His gaze flicked between the two women; Macy could tell he had no intention of answering. 'Let me tell you why I'm here,' he said instead. 'I work for a group of very special people. I find potential new members. People like you. They want to invite you to join them.'

Macy gave Rain a confused look before turning back to MacDuff. 'What people? What do they do?'

The dishevelled man's chest swelled with pride. 'We protect the world.'

'From what?'

Before he could answer, a warbling chime came from the television. Like the villa's other screens, it was linked to the digital assistant. 'Oh, for fuck's sake,' Macy muttered, knowing who was calling. 'What's he complaining about *now*? We were quiet!'

'Just ignore him,' said Rain.

But the sound continued. 'Goddammit,' Macy sighed, hiding the trikan behind her back. MacDuff sidestepped out of view. '*Oui, connectez!*'

Pluc appeared on the TV, scowling. 'Did you not remember that I gave you a warning? I told you what would happen if you had a party.'

'We're not having a party!' she protested. 'We just came back, on our own. You saw us!'

The Frenchman's expression became one of smug triumph.

'Then why can I see six men walking towards your door?'

'*What* six me—' Macy broke off and whirled to face MacDuff. 'They with you?'

His bewilderment was plain. 'No.'

Past experience had taught her that unexpected arrivals during already bizarre circumstances rarely heralded good things. '*Fin!*' she snapped. The call terminated, cutting off Pluc mid-word. She darted to the nearest window – seeing that there were indeed several men in dark clothing marching up the path. One saw her and shouted something. The group broke into a run. 'Shit!' she gasped. 'We've got to get out!' She hurried back to her startled friend—

The front door was kicked open.

Macy grabbed Rain's hand and pulled her towards the kitchen, where there was another exit. But the intruders were already pouring into the lounge. Weapons came up. Her father's training let her identify them instantly. Not firearms, but stun guns: electrolasers, using powerful beams to ionise the air and deliver paralysing bolts of electricity without the need for a Taser's darts and connecting wires. Whoever the men were, they were here to capture, not kill.

A green line of light snapped onto Macy from the leader's stun laser. She froze, yanking Rain to a halt beside her. The targeting beam was only low-powered – but if he pulled the trigger, it would flick to full intensity, hundreds of thousands of volts following.

MacDuff meanwhile had also bolted for the kitchen. 'Oh, *shite*!' he gasped—

Another man locked onto him. The green dot danced across his back – then flashed almost blindingly. A miniature crack of thunder echoed through the room as a bolt of electricity shot from the staser. The Scot's limbs flailed, and he tumbled through the doorway to crash down on the kitchen floor. Another point of light found Rain.

Keeping his laser fixed upon Macy, the leader advanced on the two women. He was older than his companions, head shaved to a stubble, face lined with the stress of violence – inflicting more than receiving. 'Is there anyone else?' he demanded. His accent sounded Eastern European, but Macy couldn't identify which country.

'No, no,' she said, breathing heavily in her fear. The trikan was again behind her back, but there was no way she could throw it before the man could fire. 'Just me and Rain.'

He glanced at MacDuff, who was sprawled unmoving except for his twitching fingers, then nodded. 'You come with us.'

'Who are you?' demanded Macy, with a defiance she was definitely not feeling. 'What do you want?'

'We are the Brotherhood of Selasphoros,' he intoned. She felt a new surge of fear: *Mom and Dad!* But she had no time to act upon it as he continued, even more chillingly: 'What we want, is you . . . Macy Wilde Chase.'

11

Macy froze, shocked. The intruders were after her, specifically: why? It had to be linked to MacDuff's revelation – but how did they already know about it?

Finding out could wait. She needed an escape route.

There were none. The nearest door was to the kitchen, fifteen feet away. MacDuff hadn't made it; nor would she. The trikan was heavy in her hand, but with a laser spot upon her chest, making any move would get her zapped . . .

The leader addressed his men. 'We take them all with us. I don't want resistance. Stun them.' The man targeting Rain nodded, about to carry out the order—

Macy gripped Rain's hand more tightly – not in fear, but in readiness to move her. '*Amelie,*' she snapped, '*éteignez toutes les lumières!*'

The lights went out.

Macy instantly dropped, pulling Rain down with her. *Now* she whipped up her arm, the trikan already spinning, and flung the metal disc at the leader's head. She didn't extend its blades, but the weapon still delivered a painful blow with a ringing *clunk* of metal against bone. He stumbled back in the darkness.

Macy was about to tell Rain to run, but to her surprise her friend was already moving. They both made a break for the kitchen. The trikan clacked back into its handgrip as if pulled by a magnet. Unearthly green lines jittered across the room behind them, hunting for targets.

One danced across Macy's side. She released Rain and dived –

as a lightning bolt seared above her, hitting a wall. A staser took about ten seconds to recharge, she knew, but other beams were still searching for her. The first shot had acted like a camera flash, revealing her position. A second laser swung towards her—

Macy hurled the trikan again, willing it to follow the beam back to its source. Metal struck plastic, knocking the green line across one of the other men. Another flash and clap of localised thunder, and the luckless intruder flew backwards and crashed to the floor.

The trikan returned to Macy as she hurried for the kitchen. A low glow came from the lights illuminating the swimming pool outside. Rain pulled the dazed MacDuff upright. 'Help me with him!' she said.

Macy hesitated – the jury was very much out on his trust-worthiness. But she *could* trust her best friend. She grabbed MacDuff's other arm and levered him to his feet. A look back. Nothing was visible in the lounge except skittering laser lines, but they were already steadying, the attackers regrouping—

The trill of another incoming call from Pluc came from the kitchen's screen. Macy was about to ignore it – then realised it could serve as another distraction. '*Oui!*' she said, helping Rain bring MacDuff towards the exterior door.

The kitchen screen lit up – as did the one in the lounge. The house's digital assistant knew which rooms were currently occupied and opened channels to all of them, the image splitting. Pluc's angry visage filled one window. 'Hey! *Que diable*—'

His words were drowned out by a thunderclap as one man instinctively fired his staser. The television exploded with a shower of sparks. The other intruders flinched back, shielding their eyes.

But they quickly recovered. By the time Macy and her companions reached the outer door, the green laser lines were hunting for them again. 'Get him outside,' she ordered, releasing MacDuff.

'What are you doing?' Rain asked in alarm.

'Slowing them down. Go!'

Rain opened the door – Macy was sure she had locked it, but had no time to think further – as the trikan spun up once more. The half-light from outside let the American pick out the hob. She sent her weapon at it – and this time deployed its blades. They popped out with a sharp *snick*, the silvery metal gleaming with earth energy. When charged, they could cut through almost anything—

The whirling blades ripped through the hob's steel top plate – and severed the pipes to the burners. Gas hissed out.

Macy hurried to the door after Rain and MacDuff as one attacker reached the kitchen entrance. His staser came up, beam finding her—

Macy threw herself through the doorway as he fired. The crackling electrical bolt hit the door – but also ignited the gas jetting from the ruptured pipes.

The kitchen exploded.

Macy shrieked as flames burst from the doorway behind her. The man who had caused the conflagration screamed more loudly as the fireball caught him face-on, searing his skin and setting his hair alight.

'Macy!' Rain cried.

'I'm okay,' Macy replied, scrambling to her feet. The kitchen windows had been blown out, scattering glass. Fires danced inside the wrecked room. Would they spread to the whole villa?

That wasn't a concern right now. All that mattered was escaping. 'Come on,' she said, quickly rounding the pool. She gasped as a sliver of glass stabbed into her bare sole, but again, there was no time to think about it. 'Get to the car!'

A gate beyond the pool led to the little drive where their rented Renault was parked. Both women still had their handbags. Macy groped in hers for the keys and thumbed at the fob. Lights flashed beyond the fence as the car unlocked.

MacDuff finally recovered enough to stay upright. 'What happened?' he asked blearily.

'Macy blew up the house,' was Rain's disbelieving reply.

'Oh, aye? Takes after her parents, then.'

'Come on, quick!' Macy said as she hurried through the gate. She threw open the rear door for Rain and MacDuff, then took the driver's seat as they piled into the little car. 'Are you in?' she asked, tossing the trikan onto the passenger seat. Sounds of confirmation came from behind her. 'Okay, hold on!'

She jammed her bare foot down on the accelerator – and the Renault 5 surged from the drive with a skirl of motors.

Macy immediately made a hard turn to swing the car downhill. A dark van was parked outside the villa, presumably their attackers' transport – and she saw Pluc running from his own house, bellowing and gesticulating after her. 'I think we'll need to find somewhere else to stay,' she said.

Rain looked back. The fire had spread to other rooms, orange light flickering in the villa's windows. 'Oh no – all our stuff is still there!'

'We've got our phones and passports – that's all we need for now,' said Macy. She glanced at the mirror. Pluc was still roaring abuse after them – but then she saw another figure rush from the burning house. The leader.

He thrust a hand into his jacket—

'*Gun!*' Macy yelled. 'Get down!'

MacDuff and Rain ducked as Macy hunched as low as she could. She heard no gunshots, the weapon silenced – but something struck the car's rear with a harsh clank. MacDuff let out a startled curse. A moment later the rear windshield shattered. Macy yelped, swerving the Renault to make it a harder target. Another round twanged against the rear bodywork, but then she rounded a corner, blocking the man's line of fire.

'Is everyone okay?' she said. 'Rain, are you all right?'

'Yes, yes,' her friend gasped. '*Mon dieu! C'est fou!* Macy, you – you saved us.' Admiration in her voice. 'How did you know what to do?'

'I've done this before,' Macy told her, more dismayed than boasting. The road turned repeatedly back on itself as it zigzagged down towards Monaco. A sharp bend loomed ahead. 'Hang on!'

She braked, swinging the speeding car around the turn – and misjudging it. The front bumper clipped a stone wall, grinding against it before a chunk of the plastic fender was ripped away. Macy yipped in fright. 'Goddammit! Sorry, didn't mean to do that.'

'You're drunk!' Rain pointed out as she fumbled to fasten her seat belt. 'You shouldn't be driving!'

'You can't drive at all! Who else was going to do it?'

'I can,' MacDuff offered.

Headlights flared in the mirror. The van was pursuing – and gaining fast. 'Oh, great, then I'll stop so we can switch seats!' was Macy's sarcastic response.

Another hairpin loomed. Macy braked again, this time harder, and threw the Renault around the curve. Its tyres scrabbled noisily over the dusty asphalt – but she made it around without another collision. 'If we can reach Monaco, there'll be a lot more cops,' she said. 'Those assholes won't dare follow us.'

'They might arrest you for drunk driving, though,' MacDuff pointed out.

'I'm willing to take that chance!'

A car was parked outside a gate on the next bend, restricting the space available for the turn. Macy knew she needed to slow right down, but the van was closing. She braked as much as she dared, going wide to cut more tightly through the apex. 'This is gonna be close—'

She had misjudged. Her car's front wing caught the other's side, the impact throwing the Renault against the obstructing vehicle. Macy's window shattered, metal crunching as she accelerated again to wrench the two cars apart. Debris clattered along the road behind as she continued downhill. 'Why the hell would you park *there*?' she cried. 'You're just asking to have someone crash into you!'

Her point was proven seconds later as the van also rounded the hairpin too fast. The other car was smashed into the gate as the heavier vehicle pounded it aside. But any hope that the collision would slow their pursuers vanished as the van surged after them again.

'How far to the main road?' said MacDuff.

The route looked very different to Macy at night and after several drinks, but she was fairly sure she knew where they were. 'Two or three more turns. Then if we—'

She broke off as headlights dazzled her. A car was coming uphill. More parked vehicles and dumpsters along the roadside left no room to get past it. '*Merde!*' said Rain. 'We're trapped!'

Macy glimpsed something off to the left – another route downhill. It was not intended for cars, but she had no other options. 'Hold tight!' she yelled, swinging the Renault onto a steep footpath.

The first few metres of their new route consisted of concrete steps. The car's suspension was hammered to its limit, its occupants yelling at the fearsome impacts. Then the slabs gave way to dirt. The wheel abruptly slackened in Macy's grip as if she were driving on ice. A wall to the left, trees to the right; she used the former as a guide, deciding it was better to grind the car's side than have it plough head-on into one of the latter.

Bumps and ruts tossed her about in her seat – then suddenly the car slammed down on the next leg of the switchback road. Macy mashed the brake, but it had already careered across the narrow thoroughfare onto another section of the footpath. More steps pounded the suspension, the little Renault bounding uncontrollably down the slope. 'Stop it, stop!' Rain shrieked.

'I'm trying!' Macy's foot was hard down on the pedal, but the car was spending as much time in the air as on the ground. A wall loomed ahead on the right – channelling her inexorably towards the road. She struggled to remember what was there. The last leg before the main road below: narrow, steep—

A high drop on the other side.

'Oh, shit!' she gasped as the car's front wing crunched against the wall. The tyres finally found traction, but too late—

The car hit the asphalt nose-down, smashing what remained of its front bumper, before rebounding upwards. Macy caught a split-second flash of a low wall in the headlamps. She hauled at the wheel as hard as she could. But they had already vaulted across the narrow road. A horrific slam of impact and breaking metal as it hit the wall . . .

Then the Renault rolled over it – and fell.

12

Macy screamed as the Renault plunged—

It smashed down on top of another car. Its roof collapsed, absorbing some of the impact, but the car's airbags fired all the same. One hit Macy in the face. Then it deflated, job done, but the hatchback still hadn't reached the ground. It toppled like a felled tree, rolling from the crushed vehicle to land heavily on its own roof. All the windows blew out as the support pillars buckled.

Macy opened her eyes. Dizzied, it took her a few seconds to make sense of what she was seeing. A car seemed to be floating above her, ground and sky inverted. Then she realised she was upside-down. Pain pulsed in her thighs. Her legs had wedged against the steering wheel, keeping her from falling. She gripped the wheel and clumsily slid her legs free. In her shaky condition her arms weren't strong enough to hold her entire weight, and she fell with a startled gasp onto the damaged roof.

MacDuff was crumpled behind her. 'Ow, shite, what happened?' he mumbled.

'We crashed,' was the best response Macy could manage. 'Rain, are you – Rain?' Sudden panic: where was she? 'Rain!'

'I'm okay.' Macy twisted painfully to see her friend suspended from the rear seat, hair hanging down and brushing the roof lining. She fumbled with the seat-belt release. 'I'm stuck, I can't open the belt.'

Her weight was trapping it, Macy realised. She tried to reach her, but there wasn't enough room between the seats and the roof – the cabin was now several inches lower, flattened by its landing.

'You, Macbeth, whatever you said your name was – get her down. We've got to move. It won't take those assholes long to catch up.' As if in confirmation, she heard a screech of rubber as the van skidded around another hairpin.

Muttering 'MacDuff,' the Scot awkwardly moved to help Rain. Macy meanwhile squeezed through the side window. Their landing had been lucky, she saw, even if it had felt anything but. The wall the car had fallen from was over fifteen feet high; their fortune had come because the space along its foot was a parking area. Rather than pay the outrageous fees in Monaco, canny visitors could leave their cars here for free and walk the few hundred metres into the principality proper.

One of those visitors would regret that decision tonight. But Macy didn't have time to leave a note on their windshield. She stood, wincing as tiny cubes of safety glass dug into her feet, and pulled the Renault's rear door handle. It released – but the door didn't open. She tugged harder. Still no result. The bent pillars had jammed it shut.

She crouched to look inside. Rain was still upside-down, struggling to writhe free of the belt. 'Get her out of there!' she told MacDuff.

'I'm trying!' the Scot protested. He jabbed his thumb furiously at the release button, to no avail. 'Rain, try to lift yourself up, take some of the weight off!' Rain put her palms flat against the cabin's roof and pushed herself higher.

Macy waited with nervous impatience – then looked up at another shrill of skidding tyres. Their attackers would be here in seconds. 'They're coming! Hurry up!' Ignoring the pain in her feet, she hurried around the overturned Renault to try the other rear door.

It opened. The bent frame rasped against the road surface, but she was able to pull it wide enough for those inside to get out – if they could.

'Nearly got it,' rasped MacDuff as he battled with the recalcitrant release. 'Just a bit higher, Rain – *there*!'

The belt buckle popped free. Rain fell heavily from the seat. MacDuff shuffled backwards, pulling her with him.

'Come on, come on!' Macy cried. The intersection where the steep road joined this one was a hundred feet away. Lights washed over dumpsters at its foot, getting brighter. 'They're almost here—'

They arrived.

The van braked hard and swung onto the main road, then powered towards the wrecked car. *Run*, Macy's mind told her, but she couldn't leave her friend – and there was nowhere to go—

Something bright rushed overhead like a meteor.

A flare of light, a glowing line cracking like a whip – and the van's front end was sliced apart, a diagonal chunk including one of the front wheels and part of the engine suddenly tumbling along the road as the rest of the vehicle veered out of control behind it. Macy stared in disbelief as it crashed into another parked car and slewed around, blocking one side of the street.

But it was what had *caused* the crash that her eyes struggled to accept.

An angel.

A figure hovered above the road, soft light shimmering around its body. A brighter glow encircled its head – a *halo*, was the only word she could find to describe it. Wide wings extended sidelong from its upper back, bright neon filaments taking on the form of stylised feathers. In its right hand was a whip, also aglow, curling and twitching like an irate cat's tail. She watched in paralysed astonishment as the floating being regarded the wrecked van.

The crash had not eliminated its occupants. Two men stumbled out from its passenger door. Macy recognised one as the leader. The rear doors opened, disgorging more of her attackers.

One saw the luminous figure and retreated in fearful shock. Another man, though, instinctively whipped up a handgun and fired—

Five shots left the gun. None reached their target. Rippling pulses of light flowed over the being's chest where they impacted – or rather, Macy saw, millimetres *before* they impacted, an invisible barrier halting them.

She had seen an identical effect before. A shield. The Nephilim had used the same force to protect their floating fortress. Fear overrode her awe. The giant monsters from her childhood had returned—

But the figure was no giant. And it was not threatening her. The same was not true for her attackers. The whip cracked, the glowing tail changing direction mid-flight to home in on the gunman's outstretched hand. A flash of contact. The gun, chopped in two, clattered to the ground – along with some of the man's fingers. He screamed.

Another blur of light – and a *second* angel swooped from the sky to interpose itself between the van and the overturned Renault. It too held a weapon, but not a whip; Macy at first thought it was a spear before its head sprang apart to turn it into a trident. Only the two outer tines were spiked; the middle one was shorter, a truncated bulb at its tip. The new arrival pointed the trident at the van.

The leader fired first. More bullets smacked against the angel – again, to no effect. Macy heard the flattened rounds clink to the road below the figure's feet. Then the angel retaliated. The air in front of the trident's central tine seemed to ripple and tear, a booming shockwave erupting from the weapon – then the standing men were blown off their feet, the van behind them flipping onto its side as if struck by a wrecking ball.

The second angel turned and glided towards Macy, feet not touching the ground. Its companion followed. She backed up against the car, a primal fear of the unknown, of the *divine*, almost overpowering . . .

Both figures stopped before her. The second to arrive held out its arm – and spoke. 'Macy.' The voice was male, accented, oddly echoing. 'We're here to help you.'

That the beings knew her name sent another surge of cold, instinctual fear through her. She stared at them, unsure how to respond—

Then saw movement behind them. Another man crawled from the van – holding a sub-machine gun. 'Look out!' Macy cried, dropping flat. '*Gun!*'

Both floating figures whirled as the man opened fire. His gun was set to full auto, spitting out a stream of bullets. They smacked against the angels' shields, striking with enough force to make the one who had spoken flinch.

The first angel's whip lashed out again. It extended, stretching across the gap between its wielder and the shooter. Another flash – and the gun dropped to the road, the man's arms up to the elbows still gripping it. He gawped at the blood-spurting stumps of his limbs, then collapsed to his knees with a disbelieving scream.

The leader recovered. A shouted command, and the other attackers fled across the road. They vaulted a wall and dropped out of sight into the trees beyond. The leader turned as he reached the wall – and fired three silenced shots into the mutilated man's back. He slumped forward, dead.

Macy regarded the corpse in horror, then looked back up at the two glowing figures. They descended, feet touching down. Their faces were featureless shadows inside the bright haloes. She finally found words. 'What are you?'

'The Knights of Atlantis,' came the second figure's reply. His wings suddenly retracted, the extended filaments rapidly shrinking with a faint metallic *kli-kli-kli* before disappearing entirely.

'*Atlantis?*' Macy gasped. A million questions whirled through her mind, but before she could ask any, the luminous angel was suddenly gone, replaced by a man. A man wearing golden armour – but in moments that too vanished, metal scales crawling and retreating over his body and limbs until nothing remained but thick bracelets, anklets and a torc necklace. Of all the impossible things she had just witnessed, that was the one her mind most struggled to accept, a CGI transformation from a movie somehow made real. 'What – *what*?' were the only words she could produce.

The man smiled. He was black-haired, in his mid twenties, Hispanic with handsome if rough-edged features. 'We'll explain everything,' he said. His hand was still extended; he lowered it, inviting her to take hold. Numbly, she did so. He helped her stand. 'But we must get out of here. The police will arrive soon.'

The other angel also became a man in a couple of bewildering seconds. He was perhaps five years younger than the first, Caucasian, intense grey eyes below brown hair worked into a small quiff. His now-vanished armour had covered ordinary clothing; he took out a phone. 'Jari, we're at the bottom of the Chemin de la Turbie Supérieur,' he said when his call was answered. His English was more fluent than the first man's; was that a Dutch accent? 'We have Macy. Euripides and Rain are here too. Come and get us.'

The older man looked into the Renault's rear. 'Rain? Rip? Are you okay?'

'I've been better,' MacDuff groused as he clambered from the wrecked car. 'Some bastard tasered me!'

'The Brotherhood,' the younger man said grimly, glancing at the armless corpse. 'I was right. They *are* a threat.'

'More than we thought,' said his companion. He reached into the car. Rain gripped his hand; he helped her out. 'Hey, Chiquita,' he said, with evident affection. 'Are you hurt?'

'I'm okay,' she replied, smiling, before turning to Macy with concern. 'Are you all right?'

'Yeah. I think,' was Macy's numbed, confused reply. 'What the hell is going on?' She stared at her friend, realisation dawning as she recovered from her shock. 'You *know* them?'

'Come with us and we'll explain,' the Hispanic man reiterated. He looked around at an approaching vehicle. 'It's Jari.'

'Please, Macy,' said Rain, imploring. 'Trust us. Trust *me*.'

'Okay,' Macy finally said. 'For now.' A memory: she peered into the car. 'The trikan!' It lay amongst broken glass on the roof lining. She brushed the fragments aside and picked it up. Partly because it was a priceless relic of Atlantis – but also because if anything else happened, it would be her only weapon.

Rain glanced at her feet. 'Oh! The glass.'

The younger of the two angels stepped closer, glinting cubes crunching under his shoes. 'I'll get her.' Before Macy could react, he had effortlessly scooped her up in his arms, bringing her clear of the scattered glass.

The oncoming vehicle, a Land Rover Discovery, arrived. 'Hoy, hoy,' said a large bearded man through the open driver's window. 'Come on, gotta go.'

The SUV was a seven-seater; MacDuff clambered into the back row, followed by the younger 'angel'. 'Go on,' Rain said to Macy as she hesitated. The American took a deep breath, then entered and slid across. Rain got in beside her.

Macy's other rescuer took the front passenger seat. 'Go,' he ordered. The driver swung the Discovery around and powered away as sirens rose in the distance.

106

13

The bearded driver headed away from Monaco, joining an autoroute. Macy initially stayed quiet, partly to let her shock subside, but also to listen to the others in the SUV.

Her rescuers were a mish-mash of nationalities. The man who had lifted her up was indeed Dutch, his fellow 'angel' Spanish. The driver, while taciturn, sounded when he made a short phone call to be from a Scandinavian country. English was used as a common language between them, though Rain also spoke in Spanish to the man who had helped her from the car. Macy was fluent; she hadn't known the same was true of her friend.

But it seemed Rain had kept more than her linguistic skills from her.

'So,' Macy finally demanded, 'who are you people, and what the *fuck* is going on?'

'As I said, we are the Knights of Atlantis,' announced the Spaniard. 'I'm Fernando. Fernando Cruz.' He nodded towards the Dutchman. 'That is Emilian, and my hairy friend is Jari.' The driver gave her a grunt of acknowledgement.

'Emilian Dekker,' said the other 'angel'. He turned in his seat, offering his hand to Macy. She regarded it suspiciously. 'Hey, we're the good guys. We rescued you. What do you say?'

'Macy, it's okay,' said Rain, seeing her reticence. 'We really are the good guys.'

'"We", huh?' Macy replied pointedly. But she gave Emilian's hand a perfunctory shake. 'Thank you.' He responded with a thin smile.

'We suspected the Brotherhood of Selasphoros had taken an interest in you,' Fernando continued. 'When you came to France, we realised you would be more vulnerable than in New York. So we came as well, to watch over you. It is a good thing we did.'

'The Brotherhood weren't the only ones with an interest in me,' said Macy, a cold anger rising – a deep feeling of betrayal. She glared at Rain. 'I've known you for three years. I thought we were best friends. But you were working for these guys all along?'

'We *are* best friends!' said Rain, hurt. 'And I'm sorry I couldn't tell you about this before. But we wanted to wait until you were eighteen – an adult, who could make your own decisions.' She paused, hesitant. 'And . . . I don't just work for these guys. I *am* these guys. I'm one of the Knights.'

'Wait, you're – an *angel*?'

'Not an angel,' said Fernando. 'But it is where the image comes from.' He held up an arm, revealing the bracelet around his wrist. At first glance, in the freeway's flickering lights, it appeared plain – but on closer examination the golden metal bore a faint pattern, as if made from thousands of tiny interlocking leaves. 'The armour is an Atlantean artefact. Like your trikan, it responds to the will of the wearer.' He did nothing visible, but the bracelet changed shape to extend down his forearm, the little paper-thin scales sliding over each other with quiet clicks like the chitter of insects. Macy flinched, startled. As if in apology, the process reversed, each individual piece returning to its original place.

'But only if the wearer has something very, very special in their DNA,' added MacDuff. 'These lads, and this lass, do. And so do you. You're descended from the Atlanteans – but not just *any* Atlanteans. A direct line from the high priestesses. Men can use the power, if they have it – but women are stronger.'

'We mere men can fight okay,' said Emilian sarcastically.

'Aye, you can use the armour, and the weapons,' MacDuff

told him. 'But to go beyond that? That's what the priestesses could do.'

'They went *way* beyond that, according to my mom,' said Macy. 'Atlantis sank because one of the priestesses took things too far. She tried to destroy one of Atlantis's enemies, but ended up dropping the entire island into the ocean.'

MacDuff's face crinkled with wry humour. 'True . . . from a certain perspective. But your ma wasn't there, and the records she found don't tell the whole story. There's more to it.'

'You know that for sure?'

'We have the records,' said Fernando. 'The original accounts of the Atlanteans, dating back nine thousand years. And we have the records they made after they *left* Atlantis – the story of the survivors.'

Macy's surprise was quickly joined by another emotion: curiosity, a hunger to know more. She hurriedly tried to suppress it. *Damn it, Mom, that's all on you!* 'What do you Knights actually do, then?' she asked. A glance at MacDuff. 'He said you protect the world – that's kind of a wide-ranging brief.'

Fernando smiled. 'Yes. But it is what we do. We protect the world by protecting the secrets of Atlantis – so nobody can use them for bad purposes.'

'Isn't that the IHA's job?' From their reactions, it seemed the International Heritage Agency was not well regarded. A sign for Nice's airport rolled past; not the first she had seen. 'Are we going to the airport?'

'Yes,' said Fernando. 'Then to Portugal. We have a jet waiting.'

Macy remembered the driver's phone call, which had seemed official in nature. 'Not something you can arrange on the spur of the moment. You must have had it on standby. Expensive. I guess you guys have a lot of money.'

Emilian nodded. 'As much as we need, whenever we need it.'

'Just like the Brotherhood.'

That brought genuine outrage from Fernando. 'We are *nothing* like the Brotherhood! For thousands of years they have been hunting us, trying to wipe out every last person with Atlantean blood. They tried to kill your mother – they *did* kill your grand-parents.'

'I know,' Macy replied stiffly, unnerved at having her own earlier argument directed back at her.

Her reaction seemed to soften the Spaniard. 'We are not killers,' he told her, more gently. 'We defend ourselves, yes, and we do what we must to protect others. But we *are* protectors, not attackers. We keep the secrets of Atlantis safe.'

The driver, Jari, angled down an off-ramp. 'We are almost there,' he reported.

Emilian glanced back at Macy with a half-mocking smile. 'You do have your passport, don't you?'

Macy clutched her bag, to her relief feeling her phone and passport within. 'Yeah. Luckily for you, or we'd have to take a detour via the US consulate for a replacement.'

'What about you, Chiquita?' Fernando asked Rain.

'I – yes, yes, here,' she said, checking her own handbag in a sudden fluster. 'Got it.'

Her little moment of panic was somehow reassuring to Macy: her supposed best friend might have been planted to keep watch on her, but she was still the same person beneath. But her goodwill was short-lived. She had been lied to for three years, by someone who had worked her way into her life . . .

Her gaze snapped back to Rain, accusing. 'I asked how he,' nodding towards MacDuff, 'got hold of a sample of my DNA,' she said. 'Was it you?'

The other woman couldn't meet her gaze. 'I . . . would rather not talk about that.'

Macy's response was as cold and hard as stone. 'Oh, you wouldn't, huh?'

Fernando stepped in. 'We'll tell you everything in Portugal,' he said. 'No secrets, okay? But first we have to get away from here. The Brotherhood won't be able to follow us.'

'Okay,' said Macy, reluctantly accepting his words. She sat back, arms folded, not giving her former friend so much as a glance.

Even a flight in a private jet did nothing to improve Macy's mood. The aircraft was ready as soon as the group cleared Nice airport's security checks. She noticed that the Knights' various Atlantean artefacts, including the trikan, were sent through the scanners as valuables, put into custom-made cases. The paperwork Fernando presented when they were x-rayed was apparently sufficient to keep them from further scrutiny.

She spoke very little to her fellow passengers during the journey. Part of her silence was due to exhaustion: it was late, and she had been through a frightening and stressful experience. But she also didn't *want* to talk to anyone – especially Rain. The French woman sensed her hostility and, clearly upset, sat in a different part of the cabin.

The flight to Lisbon took two and a half hours. Despite her tiredness, Macy still noted the irony that her parents had left the same airport less than twenty-four hours earlier. Two cars were waiting. Rain got into the first; Macy pointedly entered the other. Jari drove her again, Emilian the only other passenger in her vehicle. 'Now where are we going?' Macy asked.

'We have an estate,' Emilian told her, 'between here and Fatima. It's very nice.'

'I'm sure it is,' was her sullen reply.

He turned in the front seat to look back at her. 'You don't like that Rain kept secrets from you.'

'That's putting it mildly.'

'I'm sure she didn't either. But she had no choice. We couldn't let you know about us until the time was right.'

'And what makes you sure the time *is* right?'

'Some bad guys tried to kill you. I would say the time was perfect.' He said it with humour, but her dark expression did not change. 'Okay, you're pissed off. I understand. When they first found me, I was not happy about the way it happened either. But, you know? Once they explained who they are and what they do, and what *I* could do, then I got it. And I'm sure you will too.'

'And if I don't?' she said. 'Will I be free to leave?'

'I'm not going to force you to do anything,' was the Dutchman's reply. It didn't fully answer her question. But she was in no mood for further discussion.

It took under an hour to reach their destination. Macy saw a high wall enclosing an expansive compound, an automatic gate rolling aside to let the two cars enter. Ahead was a mansion, picked out by spotlights. But rather than go to the large house, they stopped outside one of several bungalows in the grounds. 'We're here,' Emilian announced.

Rain's car had also halted. She got out, but instead of coming to Macy, she went to the bungalow. The redhead was startled when she saw Rain's parents emerge to greet her. *Of course*, she realised, *they had to be in on it too*. Moving a fifteen-year-old girl to the States to act as a spy wouldn't have happened without parental involvement. More betrayal: she'd liked the Belcourts.

Emilian exited the car. Fernando emerged from the other vehicle and opened Macy's door. 'We thought it would be best if you stay with people you know for the first night,' he said.

'Jury's out,' she muttered. As well as Rain's parents, one other person was waiting: a man in his mid sixties, tall and broad-shouldered with a trim greying beard. She immediately spotted a resemblance between him and Fernando, which was confirmed when the two men embraced, greeting each other warmly in Spanish.

112

A brief exchange, then the older man turned to her. 'Good evening, Macy. I am Mateo Cruz.' Fernando's father, as she'd thought. 'I am delighted to meet you – but I am sorry about the circumstances. We had hoped for a more gentle introduction.'

'No shit,' she replied.

A faint flicker of surprise at her bluntness, but he nodded. 'Again, I apologise. Tomorrow, I will answer all your questions. But for now, you should rest.'

Rain and her parents came to them, her father walking with his characteristic limp. That hadn't been faked, at least. 'Macy!' said Hana Belcourt, Rain's mother. The little French-Vietnamese woman was genuinely pleased to see her – and shocked by what had happened. 'Are you okay? Are you hurt?'

'I'm fine,' Macy told her.

'We were very worried,' Lucien Belcourt added, regarding her in concern. 'We're both glad you are safe.'

'Come, come,' said Hana, returning to the bungalow. 'We have a bedroom for you.'

'I don't want to impose,' was Macy's subtly cutting reply. Rain's parents didn't seem to pick up on it, though their daughter did.

'We will prepare a place of your own tomorrow,' said the elder Cruz. 'If you decide to stay. For now, please, accept this hospitality.'

Macy begrudgingly nodded. 'Okay. Just for tonight.' Hana smiled.

Cruz nodded. 'Then I will see you again tomorrow. Fernando?' He and his son moved away, talking quietly. Emilian hovered nearby.

The Belcourts ushered Macy into the bungalow. 'Here,' said Hana, leading her to a bedroom. 'If there is anything you need, ask us.'

'Thanks,' Macy said. The room was small but well kept, the bed welcoming in her tired state.

'We will see you in the morning,' said Lucien. Rain's parents retreated, but Rain herself paused at the doorway.

Macy glanced back at her. 'What?'

'I . . . I'm sorry I couldn't tell you everything. I really am. This isn't how I wanted you to find out about us.'

'Uh-huh.'

The non-response was intended as dismissive, and Rain took it correctly. She backed away, then paused. 'Can we talk about this tomorrow?'

Macy turned her back on her. 'We'll see.'

'Oh. Okay.' Defeated, Rain closed the door, leaving Macy alone with her dark and overwhelmed thoughts.

14

Despite her exhaustion, Macy's sleep was brittle, disturbing. A warped version of the previous night's events kept repeating: weapons pointing at her, laser lines bright as spotlights. Even when her rescuers arrived, they were frightening figures, filling her with as much dread as awe. They loomed over her, shadowed faces drawing closer and closer—

She jolted awake. A sound had roused her, a quiet knock. 'Macy?'

Rain. 'Yeah?'

'Are you awake?'

'I am now,' was her pointed reply.

'Oh. Sorry. I'll . . . come back later.'

'No, I'll get up.' She rolled out of bed. Her thighs ached where the overturned Renault's steering wheel had dug into them. No hangover: the adrenalin rush from the attack had blown the alcohol clean out of her system. Her only clothing was her green dress. No point asking to borrow anything of Rain's, as she was a good four inches shorter. With a sigh, she put the dress back on and opened the door.

Rain was outside, in light casual clothing. 'Hi. Are you okay?'

Macy shrugged. 'Been better.'

She took in the redhead's outfit. 'We'll get you some more clothes. Shoes, too. Would you like breakfast?'

'I'd like *answers*. But yeah, I'm hungry. Being chased from the house by gunmen and finding out your best friend is actually spying on you for some kind of Atlantean secret commando group does weird things to your appetite.' She brushed past Rain to head down the hall.

'I *said* I was sorry,' Rain replied, following. 'It wasn't exactly something I could tell you on the first day we met.'

Macy didn't reply. She entered a large combined kitchen and dining room. Rain's father was absent, but her mother greeted their guest. 'Macy, good morning. Are you okay? Sit down, sit. Have some breakfast.'

A little reluctantly, Macy did so. Rain hovered uncertainly before sitting beside her. Hana brought bread and butter, jam and pastries. Macy started to eat, but without enthusiasm. Any conversation was brief and stilted. She was relieved when, after five minutes, a doorbell rang.

Hana answered it, returning with Fernando and Emilian. Neither, Macy noticed, wore the pieces of the Atlantean armour. 'Macy, hi,' said the Spaniard. He presented her with a boxed pair of sneakers. 'I thought you would need these. Rain told me your size.'

'Along with other things, apparently,' the redhead replied.

Emilian took the seat on Macy's other side. 'Hey. Are you okay?'

'Everyone keeps asking that,' she said tartly.

'It's because we want to be sure you are,' Fernando told her, with sincerity. He reached over Rain's shoulder and took a piece of bread from her plate. She jabbed at his hand with a fork. 'Ah, Chiquita! I'm hungry.'

'Get your own breakfast,' she said, grinning.

He smiled back, then sat beside her. 'So, *are* you okay?' he said to Macy.

'I think so,' she said, uncomfortable at all eyes being upon her. 'Just cuts and bruises. But I need to call my mom and dad. I have to let them know I'm okay – and know that *they're* okay. What if the Brotherhood went after them too? Mom went to their headquarters in Italy. What if this whole thing was a trap, to get me *and* them?'

'It's possible,' Fernando said. 'Okay. Call them. But,' he added, 'be careful what you say.'

'Why?'

'Someone else might be listening.'

'The Brotherhood?' Macy's alarm rose. 'You think they might have taken them prisoner?'

'Perhaps. Or . . .'

'Your mom did go to see them voluntarily,' Rain pointed out.

Macy shot her an angry look. 'What's *that* supposed to mean?'

'She didn't mean anything,' said Fernando, placatory. 'But we need to find out what your parents know about the Brotherhood. Can you put your phone on speaker? And if they ask, tell them you're still in France.'

'I suppose.' It wasn't what Macy wanted, but now the seed of worry had been planted, she knew she had to be careful.

She returned to her room to get her phone, Fernando, Emilian and Rain in tow. Her call was quickly answered. 'Hi, honey,' said Nina. 'Are you okay?'

'Yeah, I'm fine.' Her mother didn't sound stressed, quite the opposite. Macy recognised her tone as a work-related fugue state, diverting just enough of her attention to attend to some lesser task. It was something she had come to resent on numerous occasions.

But what did it mean now? Were her parents all right – or was there something hidden behind it? 'I just wanted to see how you and Dad were doing in Italy,' she went on.

'Oh, we're fine. I'm researching something, and your dad's touring Rome on an electric scooter. I'm almost tempted to have a go myself when I'm finished.'

'What are you researching?'

'This thing for the IHA.' Was that hesitation, or evasion, before her mother spoke? 'I've been going through the Brotherhood's archives. They have a lot of material here – things I had no idea about.' Another note Macy recognised came into her voice:

enthusiasm. Her mother had once again become obsessed with unearthing the past, to the detriment of anything else.

'So . . . you're working with the Brotherhood?' she asked, trying to conceal her unease.

'They're helping me, yes.'

Macy gave Fernando a brief look of dismay. 'What are they helping you with?'

'Finding out more about an ancient group who called themselves the Knights of Atlantis. It seems they have a modern-day equivalent who stole several Atlantean artefacts from the IHA in Lisbon. A nasty business. A security guard was killed.' Silent shock from those with her. 'I'm trying to track them down before anyone else gets hurt. They might be trying to find something from Zoroastrian mythology, a staff with strange powers. If you'd told me that last week, I wouldn't have believed it, but after the things I've learned . . .'

Macy saw Fernando firmly shaking his head, mouthing words: *It wasn't us*. He seemed genuinely outraged at the accusation. 'What artefacts did they steal?' she asked.

'That's classified for now, I'm afraid. But nothing we'd want on the loose.'

'"We"? You and the IHA, or you and the Brotherhood?'

'The IHA. Don't worry, I'm not going back to work for them. Or anyone else,' she added. 'You won't believe this, but I had a job offer from—'

'Mom,' Macy cut in, 'can I ask you something?'

'Sure, honey. What?'

'It's about the IHA, and you. Why did you leave, and what happened to you afterwards?'

There was definite hesitation this time. 'Why are you asking?' Nina said.

'I was . . . chatting to Rain about our families, and it came up. I just thought it was weird that you never told me about it.'

118

'There's not much to tell. I left because I was pregnant with you.'

'No, you left before I was conceived. I worked out the dates.' No reply. 'Mom,' Macy said, voice hardening, 'I thought we weren't keeping secrets any more. You remember how badly that worked out last time? When you finally told me about the *other* Macy, the one you named me after?' That Macy, one of Nina's friends, had been murdered.

When Nina spoke again, her voice was a conflicted knot of guilt and restrained anger. 'Okay. I didn't tell you why I left the IHA, because – because I didn't want to scare you. I had a terminal disease, an infection from *eitr*.'

Macy knew the word. 'From Norse mythology? The source of all life?'

'Yes. Except it's also the source of all *death*. It's real, an incredibly powerful mutagen. On a cellular level, it causes rapid, uncontrolled mutations. On a personal level . . . it's basically concentrated cancer. One drop on your skin is enough to kill you, within months.'

'Oh, my God.' A cold horror ran through her. Her mother had almost *died*? 'So how did you survive?'

'It's a long story. One I try to avoid thinking about.'

'Because of your friend?'

She heard Nina swallow. 'Yeah. But the people who killed her were searching for the Fountain of Youth. We found it first.'

'The Foun— Jesus. That's real too?'

'Yes. It healed me.'

'Were you pregnant with me?'

'No, this was before.'

'How long before? Like, nine months before I was born?'

'I . . . think so.' Awkwardness, then: 'Why are you asking about this?' It was more demand than question.

'It felt important. I wanted to know.' The tension in the room had reached breaking point – and she was inwardly reeling from the confirmation of what MacDuff had said, that something about her was different. Had the combination of eitr and the Fountain of Youth somehow affected her conception? She searched for an excuse to end the call. 'Okay, I've got to go, Rain's just come in – we're going to, uh, Cannes. Tell Dad I said hi, okay?'

'Okay.' Her mother's dismay at the conversation's abrupt conclusion was obvious. 'I love you.'

'Love you. Bye.' Macy hurriedly ended the call.

Fernando immediately said out loud what he had been mouthing. 'We haven't stolen anything from the IHA – or killed a security guard!'

'The Brotherhood,' said Emilian. 'They're trying to frame us.'

The Spaniard nodded. 'And your mother is working with them, Macy. She might not even realise it,' he quickly went on, raising a hand to forestall her protest. 'But they could be using her as a way to find you – and us. They didn't get you in France. But they sent all those men to kidnap you. They won't give up.'

Emilian regarded Macy's phone. 'You should block your parents.'

'What?' she protested. 'Why?'

'Only temporarily,' he qualified. 'Until this is over. But that way, the Brotherhood won't be able to make them call you and threaten to hurt them to make you surrender.'

As much as she disliked the idea, Macy saw his point. She had been used as leverage to force her parents to reveal themselves before. They would not, she knew, want the reverse to happen. 'Okay,' she said, reluctantly going into her contacts and selecting, then blocking, MOM and DAD.

Emilian nodded. 'All right. That's done.'

'Now, we need to figure out what the Brotherhood want,' said Fernando.

'A staff with strange powers?' said Rain. 'That has to be the Staff of Afrasiab.'

Macy recognised the name. 'Afrasiab was a king, wasn't he? Persian, or – no, Turanian.'

'Turanian,' Rain echoed at the same moment. They exchanged amused looks – but the moment was instantly crushed as Macy remembered her friend's lies. She scowled, Rain looking away.

'The renegade,' said Fernando. 'The rebel king.'

'You know about him?' Macy asked.

'He was one of us, an Atlantean,' Emilian said, 'until he betrayed us.'

'There's a lot of that about,' she said, with another pointed glare at Rain. 'What else do you know about him?'

'There's more in our archives. But you can see that later. The Brotherhood have now attacked you, *and* the IHA. They've become a major threat. We need to be ready for them. So do you.'

'What do you mean?'

'If you're going to become one of us, you need to know what we can do. What *you* can do.' He turned to Fernando. 'We have to start training her. Right away.'

The Spaniard looked uncomfortable. 'My father wanted her to meet everyone first, and to tell her our history.'

'History can wait – it's not going anywhere,' Emilian insisted. 'It's the future we need to worry about.'

'I think he's right,' said Rain. 'The Brotherhood found us in France. What if they find us here?'

'Okay,' Fernando finally said, with reluctance. 'My father probably won't be happy, but . . . the sooner you know how to use your powers, Macy, the safer you will be.'

'My powers?' Macy echoed. 'You make it sound like I'm gonna be a superhero.'

'In a way, you will.' He went to the door, gesturing for her to follow. 'Have you ever wanted to fly?'

15

Italy

The Brotherhood's computerised archives were an impressive repository of knowledge spanning millennia. But even after a decade of work to digitise the ancient records, the job was incomplete. Nina eventually found she needed to read a physical text from the underground catacombs; part of her had hoped that would be the case.

She had entered the maze of tunnels before. Her hosts then had been deeply reluctant. Now, Benenati seemed almost as keen as she to visit the labyrinth. 'You like it down there?' she asked as they headed for the elevator.

The Italian tried to hide a smile. 'There is always something new to discover. I know the Brotherhood of old used violence to reach their goals,' he said, becoming more solemn, 'and that violence was directed at you and your family. For that, I am truly sorry. But they were thorough and accurate in their record-keeping. I could spend weeks down there, discovering and learning. But unfortunately I have to eat, sleep – all the other human weaknesses.'

'I know what you mean,' Nina agreed. 'And . . . thank you for the apology. It won't change what the Brotherhood did, but I know you, personally, had no part in it – and that the Brotherhood seems to have changed.'

'The moment you found Atlantis, the old Brotherhood died,'

Benenati told her. 'It had failed in its purpose. But like a dinosaur, it took some time before the rest of the body realised the head was dead.'

They made their way down a hallway. 'This has changed,' Nina observed. The entrance to the archives had previously been hidden, what appeared to be a cleaning closet actually a disguised lift. Now, it was a modern, perfectly ordinary elevator.

'We do not need to hide any more,' said Benenati. They entered, then descended into the secret society's private under-world.

This, somewhat to Nina's relief, was little changed. After going along a tunnel and through a vault-like security door, they entered the archives proper. A large room, retrofitted with climate control systems, contained stacks of old wooden drawers: a card index system. The cards themselves had been amongst the first things digitised, allowing the exact location of any record inside the miles of catacombs to be found in a moment. The actual pro-cess of locating items not yet in the database would take somewhat longer.

She was looking forward to it. Archaeology, she firmly believed, could only be done properly hands-on, and the same was true of finding information. Working to obtain something was intrin-sically more valuable than merely being given it. *Maybe that's why Macy thinks I'm a plodding old fart* . . . 'So where are we going?' she asked.

Benenati had already looked up their destination. 'The second gallery, twelfth cubiculum. This way, Professor Wilde.' He started down one of the tunnels leading from the library. Nina followed. The catacombs had originally been burial chambers; niches in the walls, once housing bodies, were now home to all manner of containers protecting the Brotherhood's centuries of records. She had to fight the urge to stop and browse. They descended narrow stairs and marched through more tunnels until they reached a vaulted octagonal chamber. Benenati switched on the lights. Ranks of ornate niches, *loculi*, greeted them. 'It should be . . .' He counted around the room, then up to one particular slot. 'Ah! Here.'

Nina watched with rising anticipation as he lifted out a wooden box. When opened, it revealed several parchments preserved between glass sheets.

'Can you translate them?' Benenati asked. She nodded. 'I can bring them to a reading room.'

'This is fine,' she said. The chamber's lights were bright enough to show the ancient Greek characters. 'Let's see what we have here . . .'

Translating the ancient text did not take long. Analysing what it revealed was more involved.

After she had taken copious notes, Nina and Benenati returned to the Brotherhood's building. She needed to see a map. What she had just read was not so much historical in nature as logistical, an account of what had been needed to support the ancient Brotherhood's trek to meet the Turanian king Afrasiab. The reason the seemingly mundane text had become so important was that unlike the record of the actual encounter, which focused on Afrasiab himself and the wonders in his possession, this described the journey the Brotherhood had undertaken to get there.

If she could locate the landmarks it mentioned, it would show the northwards route the Brotherhood had taken into the Karakum desert. Where that intercepted the eastward path the Atlanteans had followed from the Caspian Sea to Dr Zaidi's dig in Uzbekistan . . .

It would reveal the location of the Iron Palace.

Only approximately, she knew. But it would provide a search area. Perhaps a few dozen square miles; more likely hundreds. But considering that the Karakum was larger than the entire desert state of Arizona, narrowing it down at all would be a major achievement.

She switched her attention between a map on a laptop and her handwritten notes. 'There's a reference here to the highest mountain peak to the south,' she said, tapping her notebook with a pen. 'They must have travelled along the northern flank of the Kopet Dag,' the pen moved to the laptop's screen, sweeping over the line of mountains marking the border between Turkmenistan and Iran to its south, 'because there's nothing about their actually crossing the range.'

Benenati nodded. 'That makes sense. That route would become part of the Silk Road, centuries later. It is the easiest way to travel east.'

'But then they turned north to reach the Iron Palace – so that mountain was a landmark. The tallest peak in the Kopet Dag is . . .' She typed a query into a search engine. 'Mount Rizeh. Which is . . . here.' She zoomed in on the map, finding a summit not far south-west of Turkmenistan's capital Ashgabat. 'So that was their starting point.'

'You said they stopped next at an oasis.'

'Probably long gone.' She switched the map to a satellite view. North of the gnarled browns and greys of the Kopet Dag range was a thin strip of green, the sprawl of Ashgabat a pale paint-splat within it . . . then beyond that, nothing but hundreds of miles of empty sand. 'But there are some dried-up lakebeds about thirty miles north of the city.' She noticed other details nearby. 'That route's actually not far off the only modern-day way north through the Karakum. There's a highway and a railroad line. Where do they go?' She scrolled. 'Dashoguz on the Uzbekistan border, eventually . . . ah, and the gas fields.' She pointed out tiny dots of human activity in the heart of the blank desert. 'My daughter's told me about these – she's very much into environmentalism. The Turkmenistan government opened them up over the last few years. They want money, and Europe wants gas that doesn't come from Russia, so there you go. Never mind that every year gets hotter than the last one.'

'My son is also very . . . how can I say? *Loud* about these things,' said Benenati. 'Perhaps there is a chance for the future yet.'

'Let's hope. Anyway,' she went on, 'the Brotherhood headed north from their starting point to reach the Iron Palace. Even if we assume they could have wandered twenty miles in either direction off a hypothetical centreline, that gives us a relatively narrow band where the Iron Palace might be located.'

'And we know how many days they took to reach it. It is too bad we can only guess how far they travelled each day. If we knew, we could work out exactly how deep into the desert they went.'

'Yeah.' Nina felt a pang of guilt. She had deliberately not told the Italian that Zaidi's finding had given her an east-west search axis. Partly for security: the fewer people knew, the less chance of a leak. But her distrust of the Brotherhood of Selasphoros was just as responsible for her silence. Only now, after working with Benenati, had she been unfair to tar him with the same brush as the society's operatives of a quarter of a century before? He had been nothing but polite and helpful, giving her free access to what used to be jealously guarded secrets. And . . . she had come to like him. 'Say, Corso . . . it'll be lunchtime soon. Would you like to join me and Eddie? Our treat.'

He was surprised, but pleased, by the offer. 'I would enjoy that very much, Professor Wilde. Thank you.'

'Nina,' she said, smiling. 'Call me Nina. You're not one of my students.'

'When it comes to Atlantis, everyone is one of your students.'

She grinned. 'That's very kind of you. Now, I'm sure you know somewhere good to eat in Rome?'

'It is hard to find a bad place! But yes, I do. It is near the Piazza Navona – it will take us twenty, twenty-five minutes to walk there. Or we can get a taxi.'

The Piazza Navona was not far from her hotel, a long plaza near the ancient concrete dome of the Pantheon. 'It's a nice day. I'm happy to walk,' she said – before an idea came to her. 'Although, there's something else I wanted to try . . .'

'Ay up,' Eddie called out as he saw Nina and Benenati approaching. 'I don't think much of this electric remake of *Quadrophenia*!'

'We both speak English, but sometimes it feels like you're talking a totally different language,' said Nina as she slowed her e-scooter. The little machines had been common in New York for over a decade, but she had never felt any urge to ride one, the city's extensive mass transit system and ubiquitous yellow cabs handling any transport needs beyond her own two feet. There was also something innately childish about them. But the atmosphere of Rome had softened her resistance. Eddie had enjoyed using one, so why not have a turn herself?

'Tchah! But look at you, having fun on two wheels. Maybe we should both get Harleys.'

Nina stopped beside him, Benenati following suit. 'I'd rather get a migraine. Besides, parts of the ride were fun. The parts where I had to go through traffic, though? Terrifying.'

Eddie chuckled. 'We're in Rome. The traffic'd be terrifying in a bloody tank.' He glanced at Benenati. 'No offence.'

The Italian shrugged. 'I have lived here all my life. I cannot argue with you!'

'So, where are we going? Am I grabbing a scooter as well?'

Benenati dismounted, tapped his phone to his machine's dashboard, then took it to a parking bay nearby. 'No, we can walk from here.'

'At least Macy will finally get off my back about trying one of these things.' Nina stepped off her own vehicle and stood it beside Benenati's.

Eddie nudged her. 'You forgot to tap out, love. You're still paying for it.'

'Oh, whoops.' She touched her own phone against the scooter's dash. A bleep of confirmation, then the word *Libero* appeared on a display. 'C'mon, it's my first time. And probably my last.'

Benenati watched with amusement. 'This way.'

Nina and Eddie followed him. They waited at a crosswalk, buses, mopeds and more e-scooters zipping by until a red light forced them to stop. Even then, a couple of straggling two-wheelers kept going, horns bleating as they weaved around those crossing. A small piazza greeted them, pavement cafés at its perimeter and street artists drawing and painting in its centre. Nina tried to take in the scene, but Benenati was already leading them down a side street. 'This way,' he said. 'My friend makes, no lie, the *best* gelatos in all Rome.'

'I bet everybody in Rome says that about their mate,' said Eddie.

'But in my case, it is true!' They picked their way through busy, narrow streets in a convoluted shortcut to another little square. 'Here we are,' Benenati told them, heading for a large ice cream cart in one corner. Business appeared brisk, a line of people waiting to be served. 'What would you like?'

'I thought I was buying *you* lunch,' said Nina.

'This is not lunch. This is an *aperitivo!*'

She smiled, then checked the options. At least twenty flavours were on offer; she decided on strawberry. Eddie went for mint chocolate chip, while the Italian engaged in banter with his friend before settling on a cone topped by a gelatinous tricolour tower. 'You sure you'll have room for any food after that?' Nina said to Benenati, teasing.

He licked a drip from the cone. 'I will be okay.'

Nina tried her own. Whether it was the best in Rome she couldn't say, but it was certainly a cut above the typical super-market product. 'This is really good. How's yours, Eddie?'

Her husband was already halfway through his. 'Not bad,' he said in understated approval.

'Tell your friend that's British for "excellent",' she said to Benenati. 'Thank you.'

'My pleasure.' They moved clear of the cart to let other people join the line.

'By the way,' said Nina, 'I owe you an apology.'

The Italian gave her a quizzical look. 'For what?'

'For the way I treated you. I was . . . kind of a jerk. I assumed I was going to get the same reception as the last time I visited the Brotherhood, so I treated you like I thought you were going to treat me. I'm sorry.'

'It is okay, Prof— Nina. I understand. The old Brotherhood spent their whole lives thinking the people of Atlantis and their descendants were their enemies. Then, after you found Atlantis, they felt under pressure from the IHA. My father thought that way: "If we do not do what they say, we go to jail." They resented it.'

'But you didn't feel the same?'

'I did,' he admitted, 'for a time. But eventually I realised . . . things are different now. Our purpose has changed. We can no longer hide Atlantis from the world. But we *can* help protect its secrets.' He stepped closer, facing her. 'The IHA is not our enemy. And nor are you. You have saved the world, more than once. We do not need to worry about your loyalties. So now we must prove ours. I hope we have done so.'

'I would say . . . yes, you have,' she told him, appreciating his openness. 'Thank you.'

'Again, my pleasure.' He smiled, Nina returning it. 'Now, I have to finish this before we reach the restaurant!' Another lick of his cornet, then he started towards a side street, crossing in front of her—

Benenati's ice cream exploded.

The three flavours splattered over him, wet gobbets flying into the air. Nina flinched as droplets hit her cheek. The Italian staggered backwards. 'What the fuck was that?' said Eddie in sudden alarm.

Benenati turned towards them, his expression stunned incomprehension. His chest was covered in dripping ice cream. But something else was running down his clothing.

Blood gushed from a bullet wound to his heart.

16

Nina gasped as Benenati crumpled backwards, unblinking eyes staring at the sky.

Fear gripped her – and adrenalin, instincts gained from long and unwelcome experience kicking in. Where was the shooter?

Sixty feet away, outside a store. A man of around thirty, close-cropped hair, glaring at her. A newspaper draped over something in his right hand, smoke wafting from beneath the pages—

Eddie pulled her behind the cart as the man fired again. This time she heard the shot, a muffled *thwack* like a cane striking a cushion. Soda cans leapt from the cart, contents spraying as the bullet ripped through them.

Screams rose at the sight of Benenati's body. The tourists waiting for ice creams scattered in panic, the cart's owner also fleeing as another round exploded a stack of cones into wafer shrapnel. A man zipping through the square on an e-scooter lost control and fell off as terrified people ran across his path.

Eddie hunched down and pushed Nina against the cart's front end, shielding her. 'You okay?'

'Yeah!' She realised she was still holding her ice cream and hurriedly discarded it. 'What the hell is going on?'

'Told you you'd jinxed it about someone trying to kill you!' He risked a peek around the cart's side. Cover blown, the gunman had discarded the newspaper and was now advancing, suppressed gun held out in a two-handed grip. 'Shit! He's coming.'

Nina looked around. There was nothing between them and any of the piazza's exits. 'If we leave cover, he'll shoot us.'

'Then we won't leave cover!' The cart could be towed like a trailer, two wheels towards its rear end. A fold-down stand supported its front. Eddie grabbed the hitch and with a grunt lifted it higher, raising the stand off the ground. 'Stay with me.'

'What are you doing?'

'Ice cream to go!' He sidestepped, wheeling the cart around – then thrust it into motion towards the gunman. 'Which way's he going?' Eddie panted as he picked up speed, Nina scurrying beside him. 'Left or right?'

She glanced out from the cart's right side, seeing their attacker moving to get a clear firing angle. He spotted the red-head and unleashed more shots as she ducked back. 'Right!' she cried, bags of potato chips and water bottles bursting open above her.

Eddie swung the cart to the right. Now it was his turn to take a glimpse. The gunman's cold determination had changed to uncertainty as he became a target himself. He broke into a sidelong jog, no longer trying to get line of sight on his opponents but simply to avoid being mown down by the gelato juggernaut.

The Yorkshireman wheeled the cart around still harder, homing in. More suppressed rounds cracked against its flank. He flinched as one punched through the trailer's sheet-metal body mere inches from his shoulder, but kept going, now almost at a run. Nina snatched cans from the cart and hurled them like grenades. The gunman jinked to dodge them as they rained down.

But Eddie was running out of room to manoeuvre. He glanced out again, seeing their attacker running clear to their right – and a shop window on the left. 'In there!' he shouted to Nina, making an abrupt course change towards the clothing store. 'Go!'

He released the hitch. The trailer dropped back down onto its stand, which screeched over the cobbles – before ripping away. Unbalanced, the cart tipped backwards, catapulting its wares into the air as the hitch hit the ground.

But Nina and Eddie were already running alongside it as its momentum carried it onwards—

The cart's raised tail smashed through the shop window. The couple leapt through the newly gaping opening as dummies toppled and display stands collapsed.

Nina clambered over a fallen clothes rack into the store proper. Eddie followed, emerging in front of a horrified sales assistant. 'Ay up,' he said to her. 'Don't mind us, just browsing.'

Nina peered back through the window. 'Is he coming?'

The rail on the overturned rack had come free of its supports. Eddie slid all the hangers off and wielded the metal pole like a baseball bat. 'The bugger'll get clouted if he does.'

They waited, listening for footsteps crunching over the scattered glass outside – but instead heard new cries of fear from the square, farther away. 'He's running,' Nina realised. Eddie ducked outside, taking his makeshift weapon with him. 'Where the hell are you going?'

'After him,' he replied. 'Need to find out who he is and why he tried to kill you.'

She reluctantly followed. The square was almost empty, a few nervous laggards watching from doorways. 'My money's on these Knights of Atlantis – the same ones who raided the IHA.'

'Let's find out from him, shall we?' He peered warily around the crashed cart. No sign of the gunman in the piazza – but shouts of alarm revealed which way he had gone. A running figure pelted down a street, making a sharp right turn at an intersection.

Eddie's eyes snapped to the shortcut they had taken with Benenati to reach the square. He might be able to intercept their attacker—

'I'll cut him off!' he shouted as he sprinted across the piazza. 'Get somewhere safe!'

'Eddie, wait! Eddie – God *damn* it,' she called after him as he disappeared around a corner. Benenati was on his back in the middle of the square. She hurried to him, but already knew she was too late. The Italian was dead, blood from the chest wound pooling around him. She gave him a saddened, helpless look, then retreated, not knowing what to do . . .

The fallen e-scooter lay nearby. A light on its dash told her it was still active. Its rider had fled without tapping out—

She picked it up – then rode off in pursuit of her husband.

Eddie raced through the narrow streets, weaving between pedestrians. The alarm from the square hadn't yet reached this far, some people aware that something had happened nearby but not knowing what.

His route met a wider street ahead. He remembered it from earlier. Going right would take him back to the piazza with the artists—

The gunman sprinted across his path. Going right.

Eddie pushed harder, rounding the corner. His target was about twenty metres ahead. The gun was no longer in his hand, the man not wanting to raise new panic that would draw the police to him. But the Yorkshireman didn't imagine for a moment that he had abandoned his weapon.

He adjusted his grip on his own weapon as he closed in. A knot of tourists entered the street from the piazza ahead, forcing the assassin to slow. Eddie closed the gap. Into the square, past the first of the pavement cafés. The man still hadn't realised he had a pursuer, swerving between the tables and easels of the artists. Five metres between them, four—

The assassin finally registered running footsteps behind him. He glanced back – and saw Eddie.

He slowed, snatching the gun from his jacket as he turned—

Eddie swung the rail. The gunman's reflexes were fast enough for him to jerk his head clear, but the blow still struck a solid blow to his shoulder. He reeled back, crashing into a display of paintings. The artist shouted in angry protest, only for it to become fear when he saw the gun.

Swinging his improvised bat had unbalanced Eddie. He straightened, about to draw it back for another strike – but the assassin had also recovered, younger and faster. His gun arm came up—

No time for a swing. Instead Eddie tossed the rail at his face. The man instinctively raised an arm to deflect it away. The Englishman used the moment of distraction to lunge, shoulder-slamming him backwards before gripping the wrist of his gun arm with one hand – and driving a punch from the other into his abdomen.

The man gasped, flinching. But he had tensed his stomach muscles just in time to avoid being winded. Eddie nevertheless pressed his attack, sending an uppercut at the assassin's jaw. Again, the younger man twisted away, Eddie's knuckles only clipping his chin. Before the Yorkshireman could deliver another blow, the gunman grabbed his leather jacket's sleeve and threw himself sidelong, spinning Eddie with him. They both crashed into another rack of paintings, spilling the artworks to the ground.

The collision shook loose Eddie's hold on the man's wrist. The gun immediately swung towards him. Attack was his only defence: he pounded a brutal headbutt into the assassin's face. But the dull crack of bone on bone hurt him almost as much as his opponent. Squinting through pain, he saw the other man staggering back, blood on his lips. He clamped his hand around the fat tube of the gun's suppressor and tried to wrest it away—

The assassin's other hand found something on an artist's table. He snatched it up, swung – and a bottle smashed against the side of Eddie's head. He lost his hold on the suppressor and fell. Dizzied, he blearily looked up . . .

The man aimed the gun down at him.

Eddie cringed, expecting a gunshot—

Instead he heard the shrill beep of an e-scooter. The assassin looked around in surprise – and Nina leapt from the speeding scooter to knock him bodily to the ground.

Nina herself made a heavy, painful landing, at fifty-three youthful bounce and resilience long gone. It took her a few seconds to recover—

The assassin stood before her, already back on his feet.

Their eyes met. Nina saw angry satisfaction in his gaze. She was the person he had been sent to kill, and now he would eliminate his troublesome target—

Eddie jumped up, grabbed the scooter by its handlebars and spun like a hammer-thrower – hurling thirty kilograms of metal and batteries at the killer's back.

The impact knocked the gun from his hand, sending it flying into the road. Its owner almost tripped over Nina as he stumbled forward. She yelped as the scooter crashed down beside her.

The assassin regained his balance, grimacing in pain, then spotted his lost weapon. People nearby had backed clear of the fight, giving him a clear path to the road. Eddie ran after him, but was still ten feet short of the kerb when the other man reached the gun. He snatched it up, whirling to face his targets with a triumphant sneer—

A bus slammed into him.

The driver braked hard, the bus's tyres shrieking as it skidded. But its front wheel still rode over the tumbling gunman. A *whump* from its suspension as it hit the fleshy speed bump, then it finally jolted to a stop.

Nina hurried up behind Eddie. 'Jesus!'

'That was a bit *Final Destination*-y,' he replied, staring at the crushed corpse – then hurrying to it before anyone could react. '*Medico, medico!*' he called out, dragging the body from under the bus and quickly searching it. No wallet or phone – but the dead man *was* wearing a smartwatch. Gambling that it was one which could work without needing to be paired to a phone, he pulled it off the assassin's wrist – then held up the dead man's arm, aware that he now had an audience of shocked onlookers. '*Miraculo! Miraculo!*' he cried. '*Ha il polso!*' He pocketed the watch and signalled for Nina to move. She ran into the gathering crowd. '*Chiama un'ambulanza!*' he shouted as he followed.

'What the hell was that?' Nina said in surprise as he caught up. 'You don't speak Italian!'

'I said, "It's a miracle, he has a pulse!"' he told her as they ran. 'Jason Mach did it in one of the movies based on your books.'

The highly – to Nina, ridiculously – fictionalised cinematic versions of her adventures had petered out after five instalments. The money she'd made from them was welcome, but the liberties they took with historical accuracy was, considering her job, positively embarrassing. 'He did? I suppose I should have watched them to see how stupid they got.'

'Hey, I liked them.'

'Well, you would – they made you into the main character!' she complained as they rushed into the labyrinthine back streets of Rome.

It took a few minutes for Nina to recover her breath after she and Eddie stopped running, ducking into a small coffee bar half a mile from the scene of Benenati's murder. 'We'll have to talk to the police,' she said.

'And tell 'em what?' Eddie asked, fiddling with the smartwatch. '"I'm Nina Wilde, world-famous archaeologist and trouble magnet. Somebody tried to kill me, yet again. No, we don't know who, or why, except it might be something to do with angels. Wait, get away from us with those straitjackets!"'

'I am not a trouble magnet,' she said irritably. 'It's been three years since anything like this happened.'

'Most people go their entire *lives* without anything like this happening!' His phone was on the table, showing troubleshooting tips for the particular model of smartwatch. He tapped at the little screen, but to no avail. 'Bollocks. I can't get through the biometrics. Maybe I should have popped out his eye as well.'

Nina made a face. 'Gross. He didn't have any ID on him?'

'Not the kind of thing you carry around when you're trying to assassinate someone. Makes it a bit easy to work out who you are and who you're working for if you get caught.'

'Or hit by a bus.'

He nodded. '*Grazie, Italia.*'

'So what do we do now?'

'Get out of Rome, for starters. You should warn the Brotherhood, in case Benenati was another target instead of accidentally catching a bullet.'

'Good idea,' said Nina, taking out her own phone. 'Damn. Poor Corso. He had a family; I'll—'

Ominous martial music came from the smartwatch: a ringtone. Eddie twitched as it buzzed in his hand. 'Shit. Someone's calling.'

'Answer it!' said Nina. 'It might be whoever sent him after us.'

He regarded the screen, seeing the caller's name. 'Anton Granit?'

She was startled by his reaction: recognition. 'You *know* him?'

'No. But the name's familiar – don't know where from, though.' Below the name, a button pulsed on the screen. He hesitated, then tapped it, aiming the watch up at the ceiling in case it was a video call.

To his relief, it wasn't. 'Konstantin,' said a deep voice.

The single word was only enough to tell Eddie that the caller sounded Eastern European, but that could have encompassed anywhere from the Czech Republic to Russia. He gave Nina an uncertain glance, then improvised with a noncommittal grunt of, 'Yuh?'

'*Készítse el jelentését,*' said the caller. '*Megölted Nina Wilde-ot?*'

Nina felt a chill at the mention of her name. She had no idea what the man was saying, or even the language, but knew the call's purpose. 'If that means, "Have you killed Nina Wilde?" then nope, he hasn't,' she said.

Silence for a long moment. Then: 'Who is this?'

'Who do you think, dickhead?' said Eddie. 'Your man fucked up. He caught a bus – with his face.'

The reply was controlled, cautious. 'Where is he now?'

'Probably being scraped off the road with a shovel. He won't need a coffin; an envelope should do.'

Another pause. When the man spoke again, there was barely contained emotion behind his words. Anger – and more. 'Konstantin . . . was my *brother*.'

'My condolences,' Eddie said sarcastically. 'Where should we send the flowers?'

'You have made a very big mistake, Mr Chase. Mr *Edward Chase*.'

Now it was Eddie's turn to feel unsettled, but it quickly passed. It was far from the first time he had been threatened. 'I'm supposed to be scared because you know my name? Because I know yours too, *Anton*. Anton Granit.' He took the lack of response as Granit being startled by the revelation. 'And I've heard your name before somewhere. Shouldn't take me long to work out where. When I do, maybe I'll pay you a visit.'

'You will not get the chance,' Granit snarled. 'You will be dead. Both of you. I will send more of my men after you, right now. Make your peace with God, because you will soon meet Him.'

'Good to know we'll be going up, not down,' said Eddie, but the call had already terminated. He tapped the smartwatch's screen. 'Balls. Thought it might have let me in after I answered.'

A cold fear still clung to Nina. 'He said he had more men. Maybe he's a mercenary. Could that be how you know his name?'

'Might be. Mercenary, or private security. I'll call some of my old mates, see if they—' He broke off as the watch buzzed again – this time flashing a warning message. 'Shit!'

He showed it to Nina: REMOTE WIPE ACTIVATED. A progress bar filled with alarming speed. 'Oh, crap! Can't you stop it?'

'I don't know, I've never used one of these before!' He hurriedly scrolled through the troubleshooting page. 'Hold on, ah, er . . .' The watch's screen went black – then a moment later flashed brightly with an animated welcome banner. The device had been reset to its factory default. 'Buggeration and fuckery! I guess not.'

'He's deleted everything?' Nina said, dismayed. 'So even if we give it to the cops, they won't be able to get anything from it.'

'No. Arse!'

'We definitely need to get out of Rome, then.' She stood. 'Great, someone wants to kill me – *again*!'

17

Portugal

Portugal was as drought-stricken as southern France, Macy saw as Fernando led her, Rain and Emilian across the grounds. The grass was parched and yellow, even the stands of hot-climate trees like olives and carobs desiccated.

The walled estate was expansive, multiple acres of gently rolling land adorned with ornamental ponds and more bungalows like the Belcourts'. Her destination was the mansion she had glimpsed in the darkness. In daylight it resembled a castle, blocky towers at each corner rising above the three-storey wings connecting them. The building, clad in distinctively Portuguese ceramic tiles of seafoam turquoise, shimmered in the sun. It was beautiful, a historic structure that had been carefully – and expensively – maintained.

Fernando brought the group to a broad portico. Macy noticed a relief set into the lintel. It was one she recognised in part, long, stylised wings extending outwards from its centre, but where she would have expected to find an image of the sun or a human figure she instead saw an elaborate coat of arms. Symbols stood within it: a ship, a trident . . . angels.

'The sign of the Order of Behdet,' Fernando explained. 'Our cover. A charity, providing assistance to sailors, and the families of those who have been lost at sea, for over two hundred years.'

Macy knew the name; it was the same organisation Rain's

father worked for. The design of its logo prompted a question that had not previously occurred. 'Behdet – as in, another name for Horus? The Egyptian god?' He nodded. 'There was an Atlantean called Behedet,' she emphasised the small variance in spelling, 'a warrior called "the guardian of the empire".'

'They were the same person,' said Rain. 'A lot of Egyptian mythology was adapted from Atlantean.'

'Yes, I *am* aware of that,' Macy replied, snippy. 'I do know a bit about Atlantis. Since my mom *discovered* it.'

Rain looked away, hurt. Emilian, however, asked a question with a hint of challenge. 'Do you know as much as you think, though?'

His smirk brought a glare from Macy. 'Maybe you'd better tell me what I'm missing. Like exactly *what* secrets of Atlantis you're protecting?'

'Please, there is no need to be angry at Rain,' said Fernando, placating. 'But if you want to know the secrets of Atlantis . . . come this way.'

He opened the doors. Still frowning, Macy entered. The air inside was pleasantly cool. Fernando led the way down a wide hallway. More doors at its far end opened into a sunlit central courtyard, but she was brought to a stairwell halfway along the hall, leading downwards.

A heavy vault-like door awaited at the bottom. Fernando first put his hand on a biometric reader, then entered a code into a keypad. Locks released, and the barrier slowly swung open. He gestured for Macy to go through.

She entered the dimly lit room beyond. An odd sensation immediately struck her; the same still, quiet feeling as inside a museum or library, or even a church. Somehow, this was a place that evoked – required? – reverence.

She saw why as the lights slowly rose.

Glass cabinets contained treasures from the past, gleaming in gold and silver and every colour of gemstone. They would be worth tens, even hundreds of millions of dollars – but Macy knew they were kept here for more than their mere financial value. They were artefacts from Atlantis. Some she recognised, having seen similar items recovered from the lost civilisation. Many she did not.

One, though, was not merely recognisable. It was chillingly familiar. She had not only seen it before, but held it – *used* it. It had almost caused her death.

Earthbreaker.

The dagger, carved from a green jade-like stone, had been buried beneath the Pyramid of the Sun at Teotihuacán in Mexico for millennia. Unearthed by archaeologists, it was stolen by descendants of the cult that once controlled an empire by using its power: to cause earthquakes. When touched to a map sculpted from the same rock, a quake would occur in the corresponding spot in the real world. Macy wasn't sure how: something to do with 'quantum resonance' was her closest understanding. All she knew was that it worked, it was deadly . . . and she herself had the ability to use it.

She and her parents had tried their hardest to recover the dagger, but it had been lost, swept over a Guatemalan waterfall. Or so they thought.

Except here it was, in a secret museum an ocean away. 'Where did you get *that*?' she demanded.

'I retrieved it,' said Fernando, matter-of-factly. 'Earthbreaker was an Atlantean artefact we thought was lost for ever. When we realised it had been discovered again, we knew it was too dangerous for anyone else to control. So I went to Guatemala after your parents were rescued and searched the river. It took two days, but eventually I found it, before the IHA arrived.'

Macy remembered the location in the depths of the jungle. The search could not have been easy. 'How?'

'My armour helped me. It gives me a . . . *connection* to other Atlantean artefacts. Like using a metal detector, maybe. A sense of where something is.'

She understood what he meant from her own experiences. But she was more concerned about the dagger itself. 'You have to give it back.'

'To who?' said Emilian. 'The Mexicans? The Guatemalans?'

'The IHA.'

'So they can analyse it, and turn it into a weapon for America?'

'This is what we do, Macy,' said Rain, more softly. 'What we've been doing for a long time. We make sure nobody can use things from Atlantis for war. Like this.' She indicated an item in another case: a sword. 'Do you recognise it?'

Macy regarded it more closely. The weapon's blade was polished, almost shining, while two intertwined snakes were inscribed into its otherwise plain hilt . . . 'Oh, my God,' she said. She had never seen it in person – but knew it from its description. It had featured prominently in one of her mother's books. 'That's *Excalibur*! But – but how? Mom said it was lost at sea . . .' An officer from the US's Defense Advanced Research Projects Agency had tried to use the sword as the key element of a shipborne earth-energy weapon, and Nina as its human component – much as, two decades later, someone tried to do with herself and Earthbreaker. *Like mother, like daughter . . .*

'I'm afraid she didn't tell you the truth.' Rain's statement was made apologetically, as if trying not to give offence. 'My father found it in England, before I was born. The Order of Behdet once helped a sailor who was on the ship that rescued your parents. He said they had a sword with them – it hadn't been lost. So my father visited everywhere they went after they returned to England to look for it. He was there for almost a month. But he found it, at the bottom of a lake.'

'Appropriate,' was Macy's surly reply. She wasn't sure if she was more mad with Rain or with her parents for once again lying to her. 'So all these things are weapons?'

'Not all,' said Fernando. 'But they could be misused. That is what we protect here. The Knights of Atlantis once used their powers to fight wars. Now, we use them to preserve peace.'

'How, exactly?'

'We will show you.' He gestured towards the exit. The others filed out, Macy following. She gave the Atlantean treasures a last look as Fernando lowered the lights, the glimmer and sparkle fading to darkness as the heavy door closed.

The group headed back upstairs and continued down the hallway. Macy heard activity outside in the courtyard, but rather than enter it, Emilian stopped at a door near the passage's end. A keypad was set above its handle. 'We call this the "Batcave",' he told her with a smirk as he tapped in a code, then opened it and went through. Fernando gestured for her to enter.

She had expected the room beyond to be dark and forbidding like the underground vault, but it was bright and airy, two large windows flanking a door into the courtyard. At first she thought the windows made the security measures pointless – anyone wanting to get in could just smash them – but then noticed they had a faint blue tint. The glass was toughened, even armoured.

She saw what the room protected. Seven tall stands lined the room's rear wall. Upon four hung familiar pieces of golden jewellery: torcs, bracelets, anklets. Weapons were displayed before them.

She went to the one with which she was intimately familiar, the trikan, and regarded the metal bands above it. 'I assume these are meant to be mine?'

'Yes,' said Fernando. His reply had a hint of uncertainty. It occurred to Macy that they had once belonged to someone else. A friend of his? If so, where were they – and what had happened to them?

She put that thought aside as she examined the gleaming items more closely. All had the same fine scale-like pattern. She touched the torc – and flinched. 'Whoa.'

'Are you okay?' said Rain, concerned.

'Yeah. It didn't hurt. It's just . . . weird.' She touched it again, this time holding her finger in place. The sensation returned, as much in her mind as physical, a feeling of . . . *connection*, as Fernando had said. She ran her fingertip over the metal, feeling its faint texture. But even though she had seen with her own eyes how the armour had transformed and shrunk into the pieces of jewellery, it still didn't seem possible. 'So how does it work? I mean, for a start – how do you get this over your head?' The torc was a single unbroken hoop, with no seams or hinges that would allow it to open.

Emilian stepped closer. 'It opens when you want it to. You just have to *want* it to.'

'Like controlling a trikan?'

'Exactly,' said Fernando. 'It responds to you. It becomes a part of you.'

'Okay,' she replied, understanding – she thought. 'Then . . . open.'

She pulled her hands apart, *willing* the necklace to split – and it did.

She gasped, to her companions' amusement. There was no hinge, but the metal band behaved as if there were. The individual tiny, paper-thin scales slipped and slid over each other in response to her movements. Like iron filings reacting to a magnet – or the more organised group actions of ants? The idea that the inanimate flecks of metal were somehow given agency by her will was unsettling.

The others watched expectantly. Still hesitant, she brought the band around her neck, then slowly closed it. The two ends joined together with a faint tinkle. It felt heavy against her skin. She rubbed the metal. There was no trace of a seam.

'Now the others,' said Emilian.

Macy repeated the process with the two bracelets, then the anklets. She paused . . . but nothing happened. 'Okay, now what? Is there a catchphrase? "By the power of Atlantis!" or something?'

Fernando grinned. 'If you want.'

'I used to say *"Transformez-moi!"*,' said Rain. 'From my favourite cartoon as a kid. But only quietly.' A little laughter from the others, but when Macy didn't respond, the smile left the young woman's face.

Emilian collected a set of jewellery from another stand and went to the room's centre. 'I'll show you.' He donned them, the metal bands seeming to fold around his limbs and neck. 'All you need to do . . . is *want* the power.'

He stood with his feet apart, arms out from his sides . . .

Then he became an angel.

The transformation took under a second. The bands around his wrists and ankles *flowed* up his limbs, countless tiny metal leaves running over his clothing in a seeming race to join with the other glinting scraps descending from the torc. In a blink, his whole body was covered – then a shimmering distortion surrounded him, a luminous halo flaring into existence around his head.

Macy stepped back, startled. It was extraordinary and awe-inspiring even for her; she could only imagine the effect such a vision would have had thousands of years ago. 'Okay, I'm impressed. But where do the wings come from?'

Emilian made a half-turn, revealing a bulge in the armour running down his spine. Then in another impossibly rapid transformation it was gone, the glowing feathered wings extending outwards to each side. The bulge *was* the wings, the individual scales of metal forming them stacked together until needed. Looking closer, she saw the 'feathers' were more like filaments, extrusions from the wing's thicker top. 'Are they dangerous?' she asked. 'Can they cut through things like a trikan?'

'No,' said Emilian, voice rendered hollow and echoing. Air molecules could pass through the halo, it seemed, but were still affected by it. 'You can touch them if you want.'

'I'll . . . take your word for it.'

'They can bend if they hit something,' said Fernando, 'so they don't get damaged. But they are very strong.' He donned his own armour, which swept over his limbs and torso before his shield and halo appeared. In the light from outside, Macy saw the ranks of scales making up the golden covering varied in colour, producing a faint tiger-striped effect. 'Almost nothing can get through. Feel.'

Macy gingerly reached up to touch his chest. Something stopped her, a rippling sensation, not quite solid – but still impenetrable to her hand. 'That's weird,' she said, withdrawing. 'What *can* get through?'

'Earth energy. Our weapons are charged with it,' said Emilian. 'They can cut through the shield. So we are very careful.'

Rain also donned and powered up her armour. 'And we can get through as well.' She extended a hand to prod Fernando's cheek. He swatted it away with amusement. Where their shields intersected, Macy saw a jarring interference pattern.

'The armour doesn't turn you into a superhero,' Fernando said. 'You aren't any stronger. You can't breathe underwater or walk through fire. But it protects you from almost anything else that might hurt you . . . and while you are wearing it, you can do *this*.'

His own wings extended – and he rose effortlessly from the floor to hang six feet in the air.

Macy yelped in surprise, then blushed, embarrassed. Her brain refused to accept what her eyes were seeing: *It's a trick, it has to be!* But it was real, however impossible it seemed. As if to hammer the point home, Emilian took off as well, circling around her. 'Why don't you try it?' he said.

The suggestion was both exciting and scary. 'How?' she asked.

'I told you,' he replied. 'You have to *want* the power.'

'Okay. I can do that.' She stepped into a clear space. *Maybe I need a catchphrase after all*, she thought, having no idea what she was doing. None sprang to mind, except Rain's offering. Well, if it worked for her . . .

She took a deep breath, closing her eyes. *Want* the armour to change. *Want* to become invincible. She summoned her will. *Transform me—*

It did.

The feeling was electric, momentarily frightening before exhilaration took over. The torc and bands split into thousands of glittering rectangular scales, as thin as gold leaf yet far stronger, clinging magnetically to each other while simultaneously sliding almost frictionlessly towards where they somehow knew they needed to be. They rolled over her dress, drawing tight as each wave joined together. All that remained of the once thick necklace was a narrow wire encircling the base of her neck; a surge of power, and a sphere of light swelled from it to surround her head. She had expected to be dazzled, but could see perfectly clearly. 'Oh, my God!' she cried. Her voice sounded oddly echoing. 'I did it!'

'Of course you did.' Fernando landed in front of her. 'You are descended from the high priestesses of Atlantis. You have the power. It is part of you.'

Macy took a couple of tentative steps, flexing her arms. She had thought the armour would be restrictive, but it moved easily with her. 'So how do I fly?' She raised an arm, balling her fist. 'Up, up and away!'

Nothing happened. 'Come outside,' said Fernando, amused. 'We will show you what you can do.'

Emilian also returned to the ground, his wings retracting before his armour chittered back into its original separate items. He collected the coiled whip, then the trikan. He gave the latter to Macy, a wolfish smile spreading across his face. 'We will show you *everything* you can do.'

18

Still in her armour, Macy stepped into the courtyard, blinking in the bright daylight. Although it contained some small trees and bushes, it was not a purely ornamental space. A large square immediately beyond the Batcave's door put her in mind of an arena, benches for an audience surrounding it. Past that was what looked like a military obstacle course, large rocks and sandbags and scarecrow-like dummies—

One of the figures exploded.

Macy jumped. 'Jesus!'

Pieces of the luckless mannequin rained down, revealing another of the Knights of Atlantis behind it. This one wore heavy golden gauntlets, spiked guards like oversized knuckledusters visibly glowing even in the sunlight. The blast must have been a release of earth energy, Macy realised, delivering a punch with the force of a hand grenade.

It was not the only devastating weapon in the courtyard. Another, larger Knight raised a massive hammer high in a two-handed grip, the metal head shimmering with power – then with a yell of *'Haista vittu, variksenpelätin!'* smashed it down on another dummy with such force that a crater was blown into the gravel and dirt beneath the now-obliterated figure. The noise of the blast echoed off the surrounding walls, making Macy flinch.

'Hey, hey,' Fernando called, signalling for the two 'angels' to cease. They did so, detransforming. Macy recognised the larger man as the driver from the previous night. The other was in his mid twenties, wiry yet full of pent-up energy like a coiled spring. She guessed him to be North African: Moroccan or Algerian, perhaps?

The other Knights had also dispelled their armour. Feeling weirdly self-conscious, Macy tried to power down her own. Luckily, it responded to her will with the same alacrity as when she first transformed. Her halo vanished, and the metal scales pulled back into their original solid bands. The sensation was still odd and unsettling in reverse.

'This is Idris Benichou,' said Fernando, indicating the rangy man. He still wore the gauntlets, raising one in cheery acknow- ledgement. 'And you met Jari Halko last night, but he didn't say much. He's very shy.' Amusement from the others, the bearded man nodding to Macy with a half-smile. The Spaniard looked around. 'Where's Leni?'

'I'm here!' came a cry from above. Macy looked up to see a young man climb from an upper-floor window. No sooner had she taken in the sight than he jumped, plunging spread-eagled towards the ground three storeys below. She screamed—

Light flared, metal shimmering – and glowing wings snapped into existence, catching the falling man just above the earth. His fall turned into a swoop, weaving between trees before he gained height with a cry of adrenalin-fuelled delight. He held what Macy thought was a spear or long-handled axe – but rather than swing it at the dummies, he flipped it over to aim its bulbous foot at them. A flash and ripple of tearing air, as she had seen from the trident in France, and another unfortunate mannequin was blasted into fragments. Before all the pieces even hit the ground, the flying man touched down in front of Macy, striking a pose as he detransformed to reveal Slavic features. 'Hi,' he said, a grin with a prominent overbite splitting his face.

Macy let out a gasp. '*Not* funny.' The new arrival did not seem apologetic.

'This is Leni,' said Fernando, with a hint of exasperation. 'Leni Pobra. He likes to show off.'

'Yeah, I got that.' Her heart was still thumping.

'You should see me do a barrel roll,' said Leni, smile undiminished. His weapon resembled a *guandao*, or moon blade; an ancient Chinese polearm with a long, curved blade at one end, though the hook Macy would have expected at its base was replaced by the baraka's head.

'So now you've met us all,' Emilian said, stepping past her. 'And you've seen what some of us can do. Let's show you the rest.'

He transformed mid-stride, armour flowing back into place, and launched himself from the ground. Before Macy could fully take in the still-shocking sight, he climbed to head-height and accelerated towards the dummies, unfurling his whip in a single fluid motion. The metal coil glowed, lashing out, homing in – and one of the stationary figures was dismembered, limbs plopping to the ground around it. The whip snapped back, returning to a coil. He returned, landing and detransforming. 'Your turn,' he said to Fernando.

The Spaniard shook his head. 'Macy saw this last night,' he said, indicating his trident. 'There's no need to wreck any more dummies.'

'Cheapskate,' said Emilian with a half-smile. 'But she hasn't seen what Rain can do.' He turned to the French woman.

Rain held a weapon of her own: a sword, long and thin like a wasp's sting. She gave Macy an uncertain look, as if afraid to draw attention from the friend she had betrayed. 'I – it's a sword,' she said. 'It cuts things. I think Macy knows what it can do.'

'She doesn't know what *you* can do,' Emilian insisted. 'Go on. Show her. What are you afraid of?'

Rain's reluctance was obvious, but she went to one of the remaining dummies. Another almost embarrassed glance at Macy, then she transformed, the flaring halo surrounding her head. She raised the sword, paused as if in silent apology to the figure – then almost faster than Macy could follow, swung the blade in a

whirling zigzag. For a moment it seemed nothing had happened
. . . then the mannequin broke apart, splitting into precision-cut
chunks. '*Je t'ai eu*,' said the Frenchwoman, almost to herself.

Even though she remained mad at Rain, Macy was impressed.
'I didn't know you could do that!'

'I practised,' Rain replied, detransforming. 'Even before I met
you – before I officially became one of the Knights. I knew what I
was going to do one day, so I got ready for it.'

'She's good,' said Fernando. 'You will be too, Macy.'

'Being good at chopping up dummies is one thing,' said
Emilian, with a little sarcasm. 'But we have to be able to fight as
well. Which Rain's never done for real.' Rain reacted with surprise,
then her face fell. The Dutchman ignored her. 'I hear you have
though, Macy.' He pointed at her trikan. 'Why don't you show us
what you can do?'

Macy picked up on his undertone of challenge. Was he negging
her, implying that as a woman she wasn't up to the task? If so, she
would make him look like an ass easily enough. 'Well, I haven't
had as much practice as you guys,' she said, advancing and letting
the trikan slowly drop down from its holder before languidly rising
back. 'I only held this thing for the first time last night. But I can
do—' her arm whipped up, flinging the ancient weapon, '—*this*!'

Even as she threw it, she realised bravado might not be enough.
She focused, all her attention on controlling the spinning trikan,
her mind *forcing* it to go where she willed. A tug on its thin wire to
control its speed and direction, but the weapon itself was doing as
much of the work in response to her bidding, banking and turning
towards its target. *Targets*, she corrected; if she was going to give a
show, it would be an impressive one. The blades sprang out,
neatly decapitating one dummy. Another turn, sharper, the trikan
homing in on another figure – which split in half as it was bisected
from shoulder to hip.

But now her weapon was angling towards the ground. *Pull up*, *pull up*, her mind cried – and it did, kicking up gravel before sweeping back upwards to carve through a third dummy from its groin to the top of its head. Its two halves toppled apart as the trikan whirled back to her, clanking firmly into its holder and spinning to a stop.

She gave Emilian a mocking look. 'Was that good enough for you?'

He didn't reply, but Leni let out a whoop. 'That was great!' Some of the others applauded.

Emilian nodded. 'Pretty good.'

'*Pretty* good?' Macy echoed sarcastically. 'What would I have to do to get an *actually* good, spell out my name in dismembered dummies?' His cocky smirk returned.

Fernando smiled. 'That would be impressive. But I think you've proved your point. Now, how about I show you what I promised: how to fly?'

'I'd like that,' she said, intrigued – and also a little nervous.

He put down his trident. She did the same with her trikan and its holder, then followed him to the centre of the arena.

'So, what do I do?' Macy asked, facing him. 'Power up the armour?'

'First, yes,' he told her.

'Okay. I can do that.' This time, she didn't even need to concentrate on her transformation; the mere desire was all it took. 'What next?'

'Spread your wings,' said Fernando encouragingly. 'You just *want* it to happen – and it will.'

That concept was harder for her to imagine. But she took a breath, fixing the idea in her mind. She could feel the subtle weight of the metallic bulge over her spine. The wings were in it; *were* it. All she had to do was unfold them, spread them wide . . .

A shift in her balance, something moving – and suddenly . . . she had wings. She turned her head, regarding the glowing

155

'feathers' with astonishment, then twisted at her waist. The wings moved with her. They weighed almost nothing, but she could still feel their presence, as if her senses had expanded beyond her own body to encompass them. 'Oh, wow,' she said. 'And I didn't even need any Red Bull. So how do I fly?' She remembered what Emilian had done, and jumped into the air – only to drop straight back down.

Emilian laughed. 'It's like everything else. If you want something to happen, you have to *make* it happen.' He transformed, wings springing outwards, and he rose a foot from the ground, holding out his hands. 'Hold on to me.'

'The Flying Dutchman, huh?' The joke raised some chuckles. She reached up and took his hands. The rippling interference reappeared as their shields intersected. 'All right,' she said, visualising herself – no, *making* herself – rise into the air. 'Up, up, and away . . .'

Her feet left the ground.

It was not the graceful movement she'd hoped for. She'd imagined it would feel like being lifted from below, as if on an elevator platform. Instead, the armour around her body took her weight like a harness, hauling her clumsily upwards. The metallic sheaths over her limbs also unexpectedly lifted her, leaving her flailing. 'Ah! Whoa, wait! Put me down!'

'I'm not lifting you.' Emilian tightened his hold. '*You* are. You're in control.'

'It's okay, Macy,' Rain assured her. 'It will do what you want it to. You just have to learn how to use it.' A rueful smile. 'The first time I tried? I crashed into that tree.' She nodded towards a nearby olive.

Macy battled to straighten her legs, stabilising herself. She looked down. Her feet were several inches clear of the ground. Her body was still being hoisted by the armour, putting pressure under her arms, around her waist and between her legs – but her initial discomfort was already easing.

156

'It's like riding a motorbike,' said Emilian. 'You have to go with the movement, not against it. Try to fight it and you'll fall off.'

'I've never been on a motorbike,' she told him. Her mother in particular would be horrified at the mere idea.

'I'll give you a ride on mine. But first,' he released her hands, 'follow me.'

He drifted away from her, rising higher. Macy felt another moment of panic as she was left hanging helplessly . . . then overcame it. She *wasn't* helpless. If the other Knights could do this, if Rain – Scatterbrain Rain – could, so could she.

Deep breath, then she focused, and gradually rose. Making the armour obey her will wasn't a matter of giving it mental orders. It was no different from walking or picking up a cup: not a mechanistic series of specific commands to her muscles, but something that just *happened* semi-autonomously in response to the desire to do so. The armour was an extension of, not addition to, her body. She applied the realisation. *Stop.* She hovered, facing Emilian, who gave her an approving look. *Backwards. Down.* A slow reverse drift, descending. Then back up to her original position. This time, the thoughts were almost subconscious. The results were the same. 'I can do it,' she said, almost surprised at herself. 'Oh, my God. I'm flying! I'm a frickin' superhero!'

Fernando took to the air alongside Emilian. 'See if you can follow me.'

He tipped forward, gliding at jogging pace along the courtyard. Macy hesitated – the training wheels were coming off – then found resolve and followed suit. A new discomfort as gravity pulled her torso down inside the armour, but it quickly passed.

Fernando was already at the courtyard's far end. 'Turn,' he told her, smoothly banking to head back along its other side.

'Turning,' she said, willing herself to do so. The result was not what she'd hoped. 'Okay, turn, *turn* – ah!' She went wide, one wingtip bending as it scraped along the tiles. 'Crap! That could have been better.'

'You just need to practice,' Fernando reassured her. 'Keep trying. You can do it.'

She did so. Over the next half-hour, her abilities improved almost exponentially, the other Knights demonstrating what was possible. Her fear of falling evaporated; as long as she *wanted* to remain in the air, she would, as little conscious thought required as standing upright. That led to a question, though. 'What happens if I fall asleep when I'm flying?' she asked as she hovered thirty feet over the courtyard. 'Or if I crash into a telephone pole and get knocked out?'

'You fall,' was Emilian's blunt reply. 'So stay awake, and don't crash into telephone poles. Or birds.'

'They hurt if you hit them at sixty kilometres per hour,' added Jari from the ground. 'And it's not good for the poor birds either!'

She wasn't sure if he was joking. 'You can go that fast?'

'Faster,' said Fernando. 'But you have to be prepared. You need thicker clothes. Wind-chill gets very cold. And glasses or goggles help. A speck of dust in the eye at that speed *really* hurts.'

'I thought things couldn't get through the shield?'

'They can't, usually,' said Rain. 'But air can, and sometimes dust comes with it. We don't know why.'

'A bird won't get through the shield,' Emilian added. 'But you *will* feel it. It's like a bulletproof vest. It stops the bullet – but you still get bruised.'

'Good to know,' said Macy, grimacing. 'Okay, avoid birds, telephone poles. Sound advice.' She looked up into the clear sky. 'How *high* can I go?'

'How high do you want to go?' said the Dutchman. 'I've gone at least two kilometres up. But it's cold, windy.'

'Maybe not that high, then. But I'd still love to get a drone's-eye view.' She started to climb vertically, one arm extended ahead like Superman, gaining speed—

A chorus of 'No!' followed her. She stopped just above the mansion's rooftops, the parched countryside spreading around her. 'What's wrong?'

'Come back down,' said Fernando. It wasn't quite an order, but still firm. She landed and detransformed. 'We can't risk being seen.'

'But you showed yourselves in France.'

'To save you. And that was at night. Flying out from our headquarters, in broad daylight, would be . . . unwise.'

'I see your point,' was her sheepish reply.

'I think maybe that is enough for now. My father wants to tell you more about us.'

'Okay,' she said, disappointment plain.

'It sounds like you don't want to finish,' said Leni.

'Well, no,' she admitted. 'I'm just getting started! You've shown me how to fly, but I want to know more. What else the armour can do, how to fight . . .'

Emilian floated above her, arms folded. 'I think learning to fight is a bit advanced for your first day.'

Even with his face hidden by the halo, she knew he was smirking. Again, she got the feeling he was prodding her to provoke a response. Well, if that was what he wanted . . . 'I already know how to fight. My dad taught me; he was in the SAS. And I've been getting into life and death situations since I was ten! I've abseiled from a collapsing skyscraper. I fought the Nephilim. I've had special forces soldiers try to kill me. Plus, y'know, I'm from New York! I can take care of myself.' She treated the Dutchman to a mocking smile of her own. 'Can you?'

Leni and Jari both made *ooh!* sounds at him. He spread his hands, giving Macy an exaggerated shrug. 'Okay,' he said. 'Show me.' He gestured towards her trikan.

'Emilian,' said Fernando, in a subtle but clear warning tone. 'We have more important things to do.'

'We can spare a few minutes. Besides, you know what Euripides thinks, about how powerful she might be. Don't you want to see for yourself?'

'"She" is right here,' said Macy acerbically, picking up the trikan. Emilian might be handsome, but he definitely needed to be taken down a notch. 'So, what do you want me to do?'

Emilian backed into the centre of the arena. 'Try to hit me.'

Macy cocked her head. 'Isn't that from a movie?'

He shrugged. 'I'll make it easy for you.' A flutter of moving metal, and he detransformed. 'Go on.'

'I don't want to hurt you,' she objected.

His smirk widened. 'You won't.'

Jari sat on a bench, settling as if about to watch a football match. 'This should be interesting.'

Macy wasn't happy at being put on the spot. But on the other hand, Emilian was asking for it . . . 'Okay,' she said, slowly circling him, 'if you want to play? I'm ready to—'

She broke off mid-sentence, flinging the trikan at him.

The strike was only meant to scare him and wipe the smile from his face; she fully intended to divert her weapon away at the last moment. But he was somehow ready for her, transforming in a split-second and snapping up his whip. It struck the spinning disc with a sharp clang, knocking it away. Startled, Macy frantically yanked her hand back to regain control. The trikan wavered in mid-air, almost hitting the ground before the wire pulled it back.

Emilian showily coiled the whip back into his hand. 'That was okay. For a beginner.'

'Oh, was it?' said Macy. He *was* challenging her – and she was happy to accept. She grinned. 'Well, I'm a fast learner.'

'Macy, this is silly,' said Rain in alarm – but Macy had already transformed her own armour to begin the fight.

19

Macy resumed her circling of Emilian. With his face shrouded, it was hard to judge where his attention was focused. Was he watching her trikan, ready to respond to her next attack – or was he readying one of his own?

Some of her father's training came back to her. He had taught her how to deal with a threatening creep on the street: avoid him if possible, but if she couldn't, hurt him. She knew she could do that, in half a dozen ways. The problem here was that she didn't *want* to. This was – she hoped – just fun sparring. Could she knock Emilian down without inflicting pain?

There was also the issue of their weapons. She could disarm someone who came at her with a knife. A whip was another thing entirely.

This was all on her, then. Training could take her so far, but beyond that was uncharted territory—

Emilian made the first move.

The whip came at her, lightning-fast. She leapt sideways, frantically twisting to dodge it – but it caught her arm. The energy field surrounding her flared with the impact. It was as if someone had struck her with something weighty but flat, spreading the blow. There was no actual pain . . . but she still felt it.

The whip sprang back to its wielder. 'Hey, what the hell?' she demanded. 'You trying to cut my arm off?'

'I didn't charge it,' Emilian replied. He whirled the whip in a lazy loop above his head. It glowed with earth energy – then the light vanished, the weapon only inert metal for a moment before pulsing to life again.

Macy was startled. 'Wait, you can do that?'

Fernando nodded. 'We can adjust the power. It's how I used my trident to knock down those men in France rather than killing them.'

'Maybe you should wait until you know more before doing this?' Rain suggested.

Macy ignored her and let the trikan drop and rise, drop and rise – and with an effort of will extinguished the shimmering light within its crystal. Would it still respond to her commands, or was it now just a big yo-yo, dependent entirely upon her skill to control?

Only one way to find out—

She swung, sending the weapon at Emilian. It still obeyed her, arcing in mid-air to home in, but felt sluggish, hobbled. His whip lashed out to intercept it. Metal clanged against metal, the trikan wobbling off at an angle – and before she could recover it, he struck again, this time cracking the whip at her legs. It caught an ankle, snapping around it like a constrictor – and a moment later she was on her ass as Emilian pulled her foot out from under her.

Muted laughter came from a couple of the male onlookers. 'I think Rain's right,' said Emilian, casually coiling his whip. 'You need more practice.'

Macy jumped back to her feet. 'Oh, I'm just getting warmed up,' she said, setting the trikan spinning in its holder as she circled him again. Anger surged at her little humiliation – but it was tempered by excitement and anticipation. If that was how he wanted to play it, well . . . 'Like yo' momma after ten guys.'

The deliberately crude taunt produced amusement, surprise, even a little shock from the audience. The Dutchman, though, stiffened, annoyance – or more? – clear in his body language even beneath the armour. Had her joke touched a nerve?

It didn't matter. It had thrown him off – and given her an opening. She darted towards him, throwing the trikan. This time, she tempered the amount of earth energy flowing through it, keeping full control without turning it into a lethal weapon. Her attack caught him off-guard, but he just managed to dive and roll under it. Macy was impressed by his speed but didn't relent, bringing the trikan sharply back around. He sprang up and hurriedly snapped out his whip to deflect it again.

This time, Macy was ready. A jerk on the wire, sweeping the trikan into a spiralling motion – and it looped *around* the lashing metal tail. Emilian hurriedly yanked his weapon back, but too late—

Another flare of impact – this time from Emilian's armour, the trikan clipping his halo. He flinched away. Macy caught the disc, striking a triumphant pose. 'Told you I was a fast learner.'

More laughter from their audience. Rain still looked unhappy at the situation, but even Fernando had relaxed, appreciating that his guest was more capable than expected. Emilian straightened and faced her. His stance radiated contained anger – but his voice, when he spoke, was lighter. 'Then we need to see this through. It's two-one now. First to three wins. What do you say?'

'I'm up for that,' she told him.

'Okay. Then – *go!*'

His wings extended before he even finished speaking, and he shot upwards – sending the whip down at her. Macy threw herself sideways. The whip hit the ground beside her, kicking up dry soil and dust.

Macy ran around the arena. Emilian swooped after her. She knew she should fly herself to neutralise his advantage, but that was one area where he was definitely far more skilled. Thirty minutes of practice couldn't match the months or years he had spent in angelic flight. Instead she ducked beneath a tree, then sharply changed direction towards the dummies.

Her jink caught Emilian by surprise. He had flown on, expecting to catch her on the tree's far side. By the time he realised his mistake and turned, Macy had vaulted a bush to reach the little squad of motionless figures. She ducked behind one, readying her trikan.

He was already diving at her. The whip snapped out again—

The trikan intercepted the glowing lash. Its wire wrapped around the incoming whip, which squirmed – and *extended*. A supersonic crack, and the stuffed head flew from the mannequin's shoulders. Macy yelped as it tumbled past her feet.

The whip retracted, pulling out of the entangling wire to snap back to its owner. Emilian angled sharply upwards and circled around for another strike. Macy recovered, but in her moment of distraction had lost control of the trikan. She hurriedly recalled her weapon. The golden disc bounced off the ground before clanging clumsily into its holder. She looked up. Emilian rushed down at her again—

The trikan's awkward return had unbalanced her. She wasn't ready to throw it. Pure instinct took over instead – and she ducked and lobbed the dummy's severed head at the incoming angel.

The unexpected missile took Emilian by surprise. He swerved to avoid it – and *now* she flung the trikan. It flashed across the shrinking gap between them, homing in on his raised hand—

He rolled and jerked his arm downwards so it hit the whip instead. The impact jolted it from his grip. He was disarmed!

Macy rushed from her makeshift cover, already sending the trikan into a banking turn for another attack—

Emilian managed to catch the whip as it fell. He swung himself upright. Macy thought he was about to power straight upwards to get clear, steering the trikan to intercept – but instead he abruptly retracted his wings and dropped from the sky.

Straight at her.

Macy tried to jump clear as he fell like a human bomb. She didn't make it. He threw out both arms to tackle her, sending them both heavily to the ground.

Emilian had landed on top of her. He was already recovering, one arm passing through the shield with a frenzy of interference to pin down her torso. Where was the trikan? A thud nearby; it had hit the ground. A mental command and the spool of wire whirled, drawing it skitteringly back to her.

But Emilian's other hand was now coming up, the whip clenched in it. He brought it down towards her head. She grabbed his wrist with both hands, the trikan's grip hindering her, and tried to push him away. But he was stronger, forcing himself inexorably down onto her, down, down—

He twisted his wrist. The whip flopped down over her head, almost insultingly limp. Emilian's halo vanished as his armour de-transformed, revealing his broad smirk. 'I think I got you,' he said.

Macy scowled, still struggling to hold him off – then he released her and rolled back onto his haunches. She pulled the trikan back to her hand. 'You—' she began, but she knew, to both her annoyance and relief, that the fight was over. She had done her best, but still lost. She dispelled her own armour, which shrank back to its golden bands. 'Only just,' she told the Dutchman instead.

'I know,' he replied, the smirk becoming a more genuine smile. 'You almost had me. You're good. Some practice, and you'll be better.' He stood, holding out a hand to her. 'That was fun.'

Macy hesitated, then let him help her up. 'Yeah, it was,' she admitted. 'I'll get you in the rematch, though.'

'I can't wait.' They both laughed, tension broken. 'Are you okay? Did I hurt you?'

'No, I'm fine.' She had acquired a few bruises, but nothing worse. 'What about you?'

'Only my pride, the first time you got me. But I'll get over it.'

'I'm sure you will.' The smile he gave her in response was this time faintly bashful.

Fernando came to them. 'Well, now you've got that out of your system, Macy . . . my father wants to talk to you.'

20

The Knights returned their armour and weapons to the stands, then Fernando led the way through the great mansion. An attractive black-haired woman of around thirty awaited them at a large doorway. Macy guessed she was North African in origin, leading her to assume she was a partner or relative of Idris Benichou. That turned out to be wrong, as she instead greeted Jari Halko with a deep kiss, which was returned as he effortlessly scooped her from the floor. 'My wife, Naima,' he told Macy. 'We met in the Finnish Defence Forces during our national service.'

'Oh, that's, uh, great,' Macy said, deciding not to make any more ignorant assumptions based on appearance. The Knights of Atlantis was turning out to be a very cosmopolitan organisation.

Fernando opened the door. The spacious hall beyond bore the Order of Behdet's crest high on one wall. Chairs were arranged in a loose circle near the entrance. The people occupying them, five men and one woman, stood as Macy entered. She recognised half of the group: MacDuff, Fernando's father, and Monsieur Belcourt. The woman was well into her seventies, dressed in elegant black with her grey hair in a severe bob. The other two men had the air of military veterans despite their casual clothing.

Cruz stepped forward to greet their guest. 'Macy, hello. Did you sleep well?'

'I've had better nights,' she admitted.

'I am sorry to hear that. Hopefully they will improve from now on.' He indicated the old lady and Rain's father. 'We are the Elders of the Knights of Atlantis.'

'You're the bosses?'

'More like guiding hands,' said the woman, with a small smile. Her accent was cut-glass English, her penetrating eyes belying her age by decades. 'We were Knights ourselves, once. But eventually, one has to accept that your days of action are behind you.'

Macy regarded Belcourt with surprise. '*You* were one of the Knights?'

He gave her an apologetic shrug. 'I am sorry I could not tell you before. But you know now why we kept secrets from you.' He glanced towards his daughter. 'It hurt Rain to do it. But it was for the best reasons.'

She was still trying to grasp that the amiable, slightly bumbling Frenchman she had known for three years had once been some kind of superpowered guardian. 'Why did you stop being a Knight? Is that how you got your limp – were you wounded?'

The woman chuckled. 'Oh, yes, he was wounded. On the ski slopes at Val d'Isère!'

'I am afraid it's true,' Belcourt sighed. 'A tree was harder than my knee, and that was that. But Rain has the power stronger than I ever did, so she took my place.' He gave her a look of fatherly pride. She blushed.

'Diana Sayle,' said Cruz, of the woman, 'and you know Lucien, of course. As Diana said, we are not so much leaders as guiding hands. I have total confidence in Fernando to lead the Knights,' Cruz added. Fernando smiled pridefully.

'Seems a bit nepotistic,' Macy noted, dubious.

'We all trust him,' said Emilian firmly.

'And I see you have already met all the Knights,' Cruz went on. 'The *other* Knights, I hope you will soon call them. But that is why we brought you here, even if the circumstances were unexpectedly urgent. To see if you are ready to join them – and if you *want* to join them.'

'She's ready,' said MacDuff firmly. 'Like I told her, genetically speaking I've never seen a stronger candidate. And the lass saved *my* arse even without armour. I'd say she's up to the task.'

'She definitely is,' Emilian announced. 'We just had some . . . sparring practice.' One corner of his mouth curled into a surreptitious smile. 'She already knows how to fight.'

Cruz seemed unsure how to take that, but nodded, then introduced the other two men. 'James Renco,' the older of the two, a broad-shouldered man with a moustache that immediately made Macy think *cop*, 'and Oleksiy Meller.' The second was in his late thirties, but with a world-weary air that made him seem older. His name sounded Ukrainian; had he fought in the war there? 'They are in charge of security for the Order of Behdet – the charity that operates from here.' Cruz indicated the crest.

'Fernando told me about it,' said Macy.

'Then I do not need to explain again! They also,' he added, 'handle security for the Knights of Atlantis.'

'I would have thought they could do that themselves.'

'There are other kinds of security, which cannot be handled with armour and trikans.' He gestured for her to sit. 'So, Macy, you probably have many questions.'

Macy took the offered chair, the others sitting in the circle. She felt uncomfortable at all eyes being upon her. 'Thanks. Well, the obvious question is . . . why now? You've known about me for a long time,' her eyes flicked first to MacDuff, then more pointedly to Rain and her father, 'so why wait to show yourselves? Was there an unexpected vacancy?'

She had intended the remark light-heartedly, but it touched an exposed nerve. Glances were exchanged; Emilian was the one who gave her an answer. 'There were seven of us. My friend, Gael Adriano, was the other. He disappeared a week ago.'

'Oh, no,' Macy exclaimed, dismayed. 'I'm sorry.'

'Nobody knows where he went,' Fernando went on. 'But for him to leave without a word . . . it is not like him. Something bad has happened.'

'The Brotherhood got him?' she asked.

'I don't know. But it's possible. Especially after what happened to you last night.'

'So you want me to replace him? Even though you don't know what happened to him?'

'There are seven Knights,' said Cruz. 'There are always seven; there can only ever *be* seven. That is how many sets of armour were created.'

'They're not just armour, though, are they? They can change shape, have an earth-energy shield . . . they can *fly*, for God's sake. Were they created by the Nephilim?'

'That, I'm a little embarrassed to admit, we don't actually know,' said Sayle. 'I'm sure you know more about the Nephilim than we do. The armour is supposedly as old as Atlantis itself, and the Knights were its greatest warriors. Behedet, with whom I also expect you're familiar?' Macy nodded. 'He was once one of them. But most of our records date from after the fall – from the Atlantean diaspora.'

Cruz took up the story. 'The survivors of Atlantis moved eastwards after the island sank. Across Africa into Egypt, through the Middle East, then on into Asia. As conquerors, I am afraid.' He sounded genuinely regretful. 'They still had an army, and powerful artefacts, using earth energy. The Knights at that time were their most deadly soldiers. No weapon could harm them, and they struck terror into their enemies. But still . . . beneath the armour, they were just men and women. And there were only seven of them. It takes more than seven people to stand against the will of a people fighting a cruel oppressor.'

'They were defeated,' Macy realised. 'Driven out.'

Cruz nodded. 'Over and over, across thousands of years,

thousands of kilometres. The cycle was always the same. The Atlanteans moved in, conquered, controlled by force. But eventually, those they oppressed fought back. In their armour, the Knights were invincible. If caught unawares without it, they could be killed. And they were.'

'In brutal retribution,' Sayle intoned. 'Often deserved. The violence they had inflicted was returned, with interest.'

'And so the Atlanteans fled,' continued Cruz. 'They moved on. And the cycle began again. And again. Until even the Knights realised . . . it had to end. All the power they possessed was being used only for bloodshed and murder. For nothing! Atlantis was lost, and even though the leaders tried to rebuild it in new places, such attempts were doomed. Your mother discovered their final ruins in Tibet.'

Macy realised she had become intrigued by the tale despite herself. *Oh, God. I'm as bad as Mom!* 'What happened next? What did the Knights do?'

Fernando took over the story. 'They rebelled,' he said, pride in his voice. 'They stood against the rulers who ordered them to kill and conquer. They made a pledge: nobody, not the Atlanteans or their enemies, would ever again use the power of the Knights for war. They – we – have kept that promise ever since.'

'The Knights broke away from the other Atlanteans,' said his father. 'They took the armour and their weapons with them. We now only use them to keep Atlantean artefacts out of the hands of others – when we can. The IHA, as it is backed by major governments, has made that more difficult.'

'Macy's mother thinks we stole artefacts from the IHA, and killed someone to do it,' Emilian said.

Cruz reacted with shock. 'How would she even know we exist?'

'She's with the Brotherhood of Selasphoros, in Rome,' said

Fernando. 'They seem to have more about us in their archives than we thought.'

The old man frowned. 'I assure you, this had nothing to do with us,' he told Macy. 'We do everything we can to avoid harming others. Even if this means that sometimes . . . there are witnesses.'

'People have seen you?' Macy asked, before realising the implications. 'They don't see you – they see *angels*. You mean . . . all the supposed sightings of angels through history were actually you?'

'Not all,' said Sayle, with a wry smile. 'Just like UFOs, people see what they want to see.'

'But some were us,' Belcourt admitted. 'The angel sightings at Fatima here in Portugal, in 1916? That was one of the Knights showing themselves to help someone – even though we have very strict orders not to intervene.'

'You never intervene?' said Macy.

'Only when absolutely necessary,' Sayle told her. 'Until last night, the Knights hadn't acted that openly for decades. The risks today are greater than ever. Everybody has a camera with them at all times, and can put what they film on the internet in seconds. One clear, undeniable video would set governments and powerful private interests searching for us – to try to take what we're protecting for themselves.'

'Seems like someone already is.'

'The Brotherhood,' Emilian growled. 'They were always our enemy. They still are. Except now, they've somehow found out too much about us. Like: how did they know we wanted to recruit Macy?'

MacDuff spoke up. 'They must have tracked me, somehow.'

'But how did they know about you in the first place?' said Macy. Nobody had an answer.

Fernando stood. 'We are facing new threats,' he said, addressing the others as if making a speech. 'The Brotherhood tried to kidnap

Macy. They might come for us next. We need to be ready – or even go after them first.'

It was clearly an argument he had made before. Opinion, Macy saw, was divided. The Knights themselves were either on the fence or in agreement, while the older contingent disapproved, heads shaking. Cruz stood, facing his son. 'We will *not* take direct action – against the Brotherhood, or anybody.'

'We should be ready to defend ourselves,' Fernando insisted.

'We *are* ready. That is what you have trained for!'

Emilian stood alongside Fernando. 'We can't just sit here and wait for our enemies to find us.'

'We have other places we can fall back to,' said Renco. His accent was American.

'That's not what I mean. We shouldn't *have* to fall back.' The Dutchman gave Macy a meaningful look. 'The Brotherhood has attacked us – so we should retaliate.'

'No,' said Cruz firmly. 'We will not do that.'

'Then we should find allies, people who will help us,' said Fernando. 'The Order has connections in the Portuguese government. Maybe the Knights should make connections too.'

'Our secret is our secret,' the older man said. 'The more people who know about it, the greater the risk that we will be found. Do you want the treasures in the vault to be handed to the IHA? Or worse, stolen by a government that will use them for war? No! We *will* protect ourselves, but that is all. We are guardians, not soldiers. That is the end of it.'

'I agree,' said Sayle. 'Going to France, even to protect Macy, was risky enough, and we certainly didn't expect that you would end up in a gun battle. Actively seeking out confrontation is simply inviting disaster.' Belcourt agreed with a nod. Fernando and his father stared at each other, unspeaking, for a long moment, then the younger Cruz seemed to shrink a little. He returned to his seat. Emilian evidently had more to say, but angrily held it in and joined him.

The charged atmosphere made Macy feel even more uncomfortable. 'This has, ah, all been quite a lot to take in,' she said. 'I'm feeling a bit overwhelmed. Could we maybe pick this up later?'

The others accepted her excuse for wanting to leave. 'Of course,' said Cruz. 'We can continue when you are ready.'

'We have a guest suite for you upstairs,' added Belcourt. 'In the east wing. Rain, could you show Macy there?'

Rain was about to rise, but hesitated on Macy's chilly look. Emilian stood instead. 'I'll take her,' he said, before adding: 'If she wants me to.'

'Sure,' Macy decided. She followed Emilian to the door. Rain watched unhappily as they passed, but said nothing.

Emilian led the way to the next floor. 'Rain was only doing what she was asked to do. I think this has really upset her.'

'I'm not exactly thrilled about it myself,' Macy replied. 'The person I thought was my best friend was spying on me!'

'You're still *her* best friend,' he said. 'Whenever she came over here while she was living in New York, she would always talk about you. She really loved being with you.'

'Oh.' Unsure how to take the revelation, she instead changed the subject. 'Is that how you were recruited? They sent someone to befriend you and see if you were suitable?'

A pause before he answered. 'No,' was the eventual reply. 'But I wasn't in the same situation as you.'

'What situation?'

'Having a home and a family.' Before she could overcome her surprise, he stopped at a door. 'Here. It's a nice room, it should have everything you need.'

She opened it, seeing an expansive hotel-like suite beyond. 'Thank you. Aren't you coming in?'

'No, I'll let you settle in. You probably want to rest – after almost kicking my arse.'

'Only almost?' she said, with a sly grin.

'I did say you were good, for a beginner. Some more practice, who knows? Perhaps you will . . .'

'Beat you?'

'I was going to say manage a draw.' They both smiled. 'Say, if you want to talk more, I'll be in the archive this evening.'

'Not out cruising around on your motorbike?'

'Oh, I'll do that afterwards. I have a reputation to keep.' He became more serious. 'I know this is all strange and confusing. But I've been through it too. Maybe I can help.'

'I'd . . . like that,' she said.

He smiled again, this time more warmly. 'Then I hope I'll see you again later.'

'Bye,' Macy said as he walked away. A moment of uncertainty, then she entered her new room and closed the door.

21

Italy

Nina nervously looked up from her notes at the bustling bar's doorway as people entered. The new arrivals, Italian men and women ranging from their forties to their sixties, probably weren't international mercenaries out to kill her. But even then, she didn't relax.

She and Eddie had hurriedly collected their belongings and checked out of the hotel before finding somewhere to plan their next move. The bar had been chosen at random, in a part of Rome with lots of tourists – and police. While she tried to piece together her archaeological puzzle, Eddie worked on more immediate matters, making numerous phone calls to friends and associates. 'Thanks, mate,' he said, ending the latest before addressing his wife. 'I *knew* I'd heard the name Anton Granit before. Just spoke to Charlie Brooks in New York.' The Yorkshireman had sometimes worked as a security consultant, using his military expertise for the benefit of clients. 'Granit's in the same line of business.'

'Security?' Nina asked.

'Sort of.' He performed a search on his phone. 'He's Hungarian. Runs a PMC, private military contractor. GCM International – stands for Granit Contingency Management.' He showed her the company's web page, its logo a menacing black hexagon formed from the initials.

'Contingency Management? There's a worrying euphemism.'

'Yeah. Not so much the kind of security who keep clients safe with bodyguards, as the sort who pre-emptively stop anyone causing trouble for the client by beating the shit out of them. Or killing them.'

'And someone's hired him to "manage" us?'

'Probably more you.'

'Ah, that makes me feel so much better.'

He gave her a crooked smile. 'Like I said, you're a trouble magnet. So we need to work out who you're causing trouble for, and why.'

She tapped her notes. 'It has to be something to do with this. The IHA's raiders, these Knights of Atlantis, don't want anyone else to find the Iron Palace of Afrasiab.'

'You're sure it's that?'

'Nothing else fits. They must want the staff. If it's real – and based on the Brotherhood's records, I think it is – then being able to control the weather would give you a lot of power.'

'Then you need to work out where it is first. Once you do, you can get the IHA to secure it.' The door opened again. Eddie glanced up, but the middle-aged tourists who entered were unlikely to be threats. 'How close have you got so far?'

Nina had bought a physical atlas in a bookstore; she opened it on the map of Central Asia. 'The Atlanteans described setting out eastwards from an inland sea off what can only be the Caspian. Which has to be this.' She pointed at a blue bite out of the western coast of Turkmenistan, separated from the far larger waters of the Caspian Sea by a thin sandy line. 'The Garabogzaköl Basin, and yes, I'm sure I completely butchered the pronunciation. If you head due east from there, you end up in eastern Uzbekistan, where Zaidi found the texts.'

Eddie examined the map of the desert region. 'About six hundred miles of fuck-all between 'em.'

'Yeah. But somewhere in those six hundred miles, the Knights of Atlantis attacked Afrasiab's palace – where it all went horribly wrong for them. And,' Nina went on, 'knowing what I now do from the Brotherhood's records . . .' She located the Turkmenistan capital of Ashgabat. 'They headed north from around here. Where the two axes meet – *that's* the search area.' She used the side of her phone as a makeshift ruler, drawing lines running north-to-south and east-to-west, then circling where they intersected. 'Here.'

'Right in the middle of the Karakum,' Eddie observed. 'The fuck-all-iest part of fuck-all.' He checked the map's scale. 'Must be a couple of hundred square miles in that circle.'

'I've narrowed it down, though. The Brotherhood said they entered the Iron Palace through a deep cave. That suggests a rocky area rather than open desert, somewhere with enough elevation change to accommodate an entrance. So either hills, or a canyon. I looked at satellite images already. There aren't many candidates.' She raised her phone. 'I'll call Oswald. The IHA can carry on from here.'

Oswald Seretse was impressed by Nina's deductions. But to her dismay, there was little he could do to act upon them. 'An official expedition is, I'm afraid, out of the question,' he told her apologetically. 'The United Nations holds very little sway with the government of Turkmenistan. The IHA, still less. Arranging such an operation would require both time and a considerable amount of, shall we say, facilitation fees.'

'You mean bribes,' said Nina. The Turkmenistani regime was notoriously corrupt and authoritarian even by the region's standards, many of the former Soviet states having collapsed into despotism.

'I'm afraid so. And archaeological research is of far lower importance to them than resource extraction. Any expedition would be competing with the very deep pockets of gas and mining interests. At least,' he added meaningfully, 'any *official* expedition.'

Eddie was leaning close to his wife to hear the conversation; he and Nina exchanged glances. 'Wait – you're saying *we* have to find the bloody thing?' he complained.

'It would be very difficult for the IHA to organise an operation within Turkmenistan,' Seretse replied. 'But if two private individuals were to happen to visit the country, I could use my diplomatic and personal contacts to arrange transport and supplies.'

'Oh, you could, huh?' was Nina's unimpressed reply. 'I'm sure their border control would accept the world's most famous archaeologist turning up without notice as just a spur-of-the-moment vacation.'

'Might be a way round that,' said Eddie, to her surprise. 'Could get in via Azerbaijan, on the ferry. There's someone who owes me a favour or six who could get us through customs without any questions.'

'That's great, but, y'know, we're not going,' Nina said firmly. 'Oswald, there has to be some way you can twist some diplomatic arms. Like you said before, the US government is the IHA's biggest financial contributor. This affects them, or could do. Suppose someone unfriendly got the staff and used it to cause a drought in the Midwest? Or washed Florida off the map?'

'I will see what I can do,' said Seretse. 'In the meantime, any further deductions that might narrow down the precise location of the Iron Palace would be most helpful.'

'I'll see what *I* can do,' she replied, with a faint smile. 'But we need to leave Rome. Having someone try to kill you kinda takes the shine off of a place.'

'In that case, I will not detain you.' He seemed about to say goodbye, then remembered something. 'Oh, by the way, Curtis told me about Macy's new-found fame. Congratulations, if that is the most appropriate term.'

Another exchange of glances, this time in alarm. 'What fame?' Eddie demanded.

'Macy hasn't told you?'

Now Nina was worried. 'Told us *what*?'

'She was befriended by Rafael Loost, on Uzz. A source of considerable social cachet, according to Curtis.'

'Loost?' The name escaped Nina's lips as practically a gasp – of fear. 'Oh my God.'

'We'll call you back, Ozzy,' Eddie said urgently, thumbing the end-call button. 'Loost's been talking to *Macy*?'

Nina found herself breathing heavily. 'Loost offers me a job, I turn him down, someone tries to kill me right afterwards – and he's also made contact with our daughter? That's not a coincidence. He's going after her, too. Shit. Shit!' Hands suddenly shaking, she fumbled to call Macy.

Digital static, a single ring . . . then three abrupt bleeps terminated the attempt. She looked at Eddie in horror. 'I can't get through.' She switched to FaceTime. The video messenger was equally unresponsive.

Eddie tried to call with his own phone. 'Cut off after one ring – but it didn't go to voicemail. If her phone was off, it wouldn't have rung at all. Has she *blocked* us?'

Nina's disbelief mirrored his own. 'Why would she do that?'

'I don't know. She wouldn't. Unless someone made her.'

An idea came to the redhead. 'Wait – I've got Rain's number, I'll phone her,' she said, suddenly hopeful. The feeling lasted only as long as it took for her call to be cut off. 'She's not answering either!'

Eddie stared helplessly at his own phone – then hurriedly flicked back to Granit's corporate website. 'Charlie said Granit's got some big clients – oil companies, offshore investment firms, stuff like that. People who don't want anyone looking too closely at what they're doing, but also don't want to get their own hands dirty. I'm just seeing if he's got a list.'

'You think anyone who hired him would want their name made public?'

'The so-called respectable ones, yeah. He probably does genuine security work as well as the dodgy stuff – and the man's got to advertise.' A new page appeared. 'Let's see who's on there.' He read the list. 'Oil company, Gulf dictatorship, African dictatorship, capital management, some sheik – ay up!' He turned the phone towards her.

Her eyes widened as she saw the name. 'Rafael Loost,' she said, in fearful confirmation. 'He's behind all this.' The puzzle pieces suddenly clattered into place. 'I just realised: Zaidi's son sent the photos of the texts from Uzbekistan to his friends via Uzz. They were supposed to be in a mode that stopped them being shared any further . . . but Loost told me his company's AI scans everything that goes through Uzz. He already *had* the texts, and probably a machine translation too. They were stolen from the IHA to make sure nobody *else* could translate them. That's half of the information needed to find the Iron Palace.'

Eddie indicated her notebook. 'And that's the other half.'

'Yeah. Granit's brother was probably supposed to take it after killing me.'

'So what does a man who lives on a space station want with an ancient underground palace? I mean, the view's not going to be as good.'

'He wants the staff,' said Nina. 'Loost became this rich because he controls information. Imagine if he could control the *weather*.'

'He's already the richest man in the world, though. Not like he can go any higher.'

'It's not about money. It's about *power*. He might live in orbit to avoid taxes, but governments can still tax his businesses – or even shut them down. But if he had the Staff of Afrasiab? He could blackmail them into doing whatever he wanted. A country that has no rain for a year – or nothing *but* rain – is going to do whatever it takes to bring things back to normal. If that means giving in to Loost's demands, they don't have a choice.'

'Could Loost use the staff, though?' Eddie wondered. 'Even if it's real.'

'I'm sure he could afford to pay someone with Atlantean DNA to do so.'

'If he could find them.'

'He was bragging about how powerful his quantum computers are. I bet if they had a large enough genetic database, they could analyse it to find candidates in an afternoon. Shit,' she exclaimed, at another thought. 'He could probably do the same thing to find the Iron Palace! He has the Zaidi texts, so that's half the information he needs already – the east-west axis.'

Another glance at her notebook. 'No use without that, though.'

'I don't know. If his computers work out where the Iron Palace *can't* be, whatever's left is where it *can* be. And Loost has effectively unlimited resources. Even if he spent billions to search, it would be like us spending the change we find down the back of the couch.'

'We've got to tell Ozzy, then,' said Eddie. 'That should give him a bit more ammo when he's trying to persuade people to do something.'

'We don't have any proof, though,' Nina pointed out, frustrated. 'And like you said, Loost is *the richest man in the world*. That gives him enormous influence on the very people Oswald needs to persuade. As the saying goes, if you come at the king, you'd better not miss.' She stared at her notebook. 'We need to find it ourselves. Before he does.'

'No. We don't.' The firmness of her husband's reply startled her. 'We need to make sure Macy's safe, before anything else. I don't care if this fucking staff gives the bad guys mind control powers, she takes priori—'

'You're right, you're absolutely right,' she cut in, raising her hands. 'I'm sorry. Okay, we have to warn her. We can't get her phone, but we can still try email.'

'She hardly ever uses it,' Eddie reminded her sardonically. 'Too old-fashioned. Might as well expect her to check for a telegram.'

'We still have to *try*. Text too, just in case.' She brought up her email app and started typing. 'I've still got Loost's number. Maybe I should call him, tell him I know what he's doing – warn him off.'

Eddie was texting Macy. 'He won't admit to anything. Like you said, we don't have any proof. And we'd just be tipping our hand. We've got to make sure Macy's okay *before* we accuse him of anything.'

'Good point.' She sent her hurried email. 'Okay, what's the quickest way to reach her – fly, or drive?'

'I'll check out flights,' said Eddie, dispatching his text. 'You look for hire cars.'

A few minutes of frenzied searching yielded unwelcome results. 'Earliest flight out of Rome won't get us to Nice until about ten tomorrow morning,' the Yorkshireman reported. 'And then we still have to get to her villa. What about driving?'

'Most of the rental agencies in Rome closed at eight,' said Nina. 'The ones at the airport are open twenty-four hours, but it'll take us an hour to get there, and the drive to Monaco will take almost eight hours.'

'Still gets us there before a plane.'

Nina quickly packed up her belongings, then tied her hair into a ponytail. 'Okay. Let's go find our daughter.'

182

22

Portugal

The argument that had prompted Macy to leave was far from over, she found when she returned to the mansion's great hall, wearing new clothes that had been brought to her. She guessed Rain had chosen them, the jeans and top close to her usual style.

The divisions between the group's elder members and the current Knights of Atlantis were clearer than ever. 'If I hadn't gone to Guatemala, the IHA would have found Earthbreaker,' insisted Fernando. 'But I found it first – and because of that, we have saved two whole continents from the threat it poses.'

The senior Cruz wearily kneaded his temple. 'And if you had been discovered, you would have exposed us all.'

'But I wasn't. And the Knights have actively recovered artefacts in the past.' He gestured towards Belcourt. 'Lucien found Excalibur!'

'That was different,' said Belcourt. 'I found Excalibur the hard way, by searching, by detective work. You used your armour's powers. You could have been seen.'

'I was in the middle of a jungle!' said Fernando, annoyed. 'I took every precaution. And it *had* to be done. Someone had already used Earthbreaker, in Mexico. Thousands were killed in the earthquake. And others were going to do the same in Guatemala. Macy, you were there!' He faced the American. 'What do *you* think we should have done?'

'Me?' she said, unhappy at being put on the spot. 'I – I don't know. But I sure as hell wouldn't have wanted Earthbreaker to end up anywhere near the Temple of Skulls, where someone could use it again. No,' she decided, 'I think you did the right thing.'

Fernando nodded in satisfaction. His father was less enthusiastic. 'This is not a matter of simple black and white,' said Cruz. 'When governments are involved, things become more grey. We have to be very, very careful.'

'If we're too careful, we'll never do *anything*,' Emilian objected. 'While we *debate*,' the word sounded like a curse, 'the IHA – or worse people – will take things that should be under our protection.'

'This is why we should use the Order's influence with governments,' said Fernando. 'We have friends all around the world. They can help us – if we're willing to ask them.' Some of the other Knights, Rain among them, made sounds of approval.

'Fernando is right that we should take direct action,' agreed Emilian, 'but . . . we shouldn't wait for others to help us. If you try to change the system from inside, it ends up changing you. We all know we're doing the right thing. So why waste time arguing? If we see something that should be ours, by right – we take it. If someone threatens us? We stop them.' His eyes flicked towards Macy as if seeking support.

Before she could express any, or otherwise, Sayle spoke up in sharp-tongued annoyance. 'And what should we do if – no, when – our goals come into conflict with a world power, whether one with which we are allied or not?'

'She is right,' said Belcourt. 'We have survived for all this time by avoiding conflict. What you propose would encourage it. It is too dangerous!'

Cruz nodded. 'What should we do, hmm?' He was looking at his son, but the question was aimed at all the Knights. 'Suppose a country takes an action that we oppose. Do we fight them? Use the powers of the Knights to attack them? Remove their leaders? For centuries, we have prevented anyone from using the powers of Atlantis for war. Should we now start using them ourselves?'

A debate broke out, growing louder as it went on. Macy saw that not only was there a division between the older and younger generations, but also another within the Knights themselves. Rain and Jari backed Fernando's collaborative approach, while Idris and Leni were more supportive of Emilian's proactive posture. Renco and Meller, meanwhile, had apparently decided to sit the issue out and wait for consensus to be reached. 'What about you, Macy?' Rain finally asked. 'What do you think we should do?'

'I'm not sure,' she said. 'But . . . I think you have to do *something*. You only have to look at the state of the world to know it can't be left to the people who are in charge now. Authoritarian governments are on the rise everywhere – and you don't want them to get hold of Atlantean technology, because they *would* use it for war and conquest. My dad's got a saying: the Nazis weren't defeated by reasoned debate.' There was more to it – *but by putting bullets in their fucking skulls*, was how her father had once vehemently continued – but she felt the abridged version got the point across. 'You have to take action to stop the bad guys. And I know *that* from experience.'

'Forgive me for saying this, but you don't have as much experience as you may think,' clucked Sayle. 'You're only eighteen; you have . . . an *unnuanced* view of the world, shall I put it.'

Belcourt's response was more diplomatic and apologetic, but similar in feeling. 'I think that would be taking a dangerous path, Macy.'

'It would,' agreed Cruz. 'But so would *any* path that risked exposing us to the world – or our enemies. We are safe here, hidden. But the more unnecessary chances we take, the more likely eyes will turn upon us. And that is something we cannot afford.' He stood, hands on hips in a stance that announced further discussion was over. 'It is getting late. Macy, would you perhaps like to join us for dinner?'

She was still irked at being patronised. 'I'm good, thanks. I'll eat in my room.'

'As you wish. In that case, we will see you tomorrow. I hope you will have decided by then if you want to join us.'

'Or if you are ready to,' was Sayle's faintly waspish addendum.

Macy gave her an icy look. 'We'll see,' she said, standing and starting for the door.

Emilian quickly rose and followed her out. 'Thank you,' he said.

'For what?'

'Agreeing with me.'

'I just said what I thought. I learned a long time ago that you *have* to when you're dealing with someone who's already made up their mind.'

'Your parents?'

'Yeah. Well, more my mom,' she corrected with a small laugh. 'When it comes to anything connected to Atlantis, anyway.'

'You stood up for yourself. That's good. Just because someone is older, it doesn't mean they're always right.'

'Definitely.' She reached the next floor and was about to head for her room, then paused as Emilian continued upwards. 'Where are you going?'

'The archive. Top floor, north wing.' He gestured in the relevant direction. 'I'll be there for a while. If you want to find me after you eat . . .'

She gave him a half-smile. 'I might just do that.'

The archive took Macy a little while to find, even knowing roughly where it was. The door was unmarked, anonymous. But a thin line of light under its foot finally revealed it. She entered to find a long library with a window at its far end, the walls lined with packed shelves. More doors led to side rooms. 'Emilian?'

'Here.' She followed his voice to find him sitting cross-legged on the floor behind a protruding shelf unit. A large book sat in his lap. The pages were not paper or parchment but sheets of thin metal, held in frames to keep them from bending. A gap on a shelf told her it lived amongst several similar volumes.

'What are you doing?'

'Research,' he replied, tilting the book so she could see. Macy immediately recognised the text inscribed upon the hammered plate as Atlantean. 'I'm reading about the lost artefacts that we need to find. If Fernando and I had our way, we'd be looking for them already. Atlantean is quite a hard language to learn, though.'

She crouched beside him. 'I'm fluent in it. Do you want me to help?'

'I'd like that, thank you.'

'How far have you gotten?'

He pointed out a line halfway down the page. Macy looked back to the start to find the context. 'This is about . . . Rostam? He was a Persian hero, wasn't he?'

Emilian nodded. 'And also one of the Knights of Atlantis, for a time.'

The writing seemed to confirm that. Intrigued, Macy kept reading. *Mom would love to see this* . . . 'So the Knights were actually part of Persian mythology?'

Another nod. 'Their armour was known as the Babr-e Bayān. It means "tiger-skin pattern", something like that.'

She pictured the Knights' armour in her mind's eye. 'I can kind of see that? I suppose they look stripy in certain lights.'

'One of the Zoroastrian religious texts says that Rostam wore his armour in a fight against Afrasiab.'

'That should have made the fight pretty one-sided.'

'You'd think so. But Afrasiab had some tricks of his own.'

'You mentioned him earlier,' she remembered. 'The "rebel king". I only know the name from Persian mythology, but I guess the Knights have more about him.'

'Yeah. He broke away from the rest of the Atlanteans to set up his own kingdom. And he stole one of their weapons. A staff that could control the weather.'

'The Atlanteans could do that?' She then wondered why she was surprised. Past personal experience had involved Atlantean artefacts that could cause earthquakes or destroy cities with antimatter explosions. Which justified the Knights' reason for existing, she supposed . . .

'He used it to cause droughts for the Persians,' Emilian told her. 'It's something we should keep out of the wrong hands, don't you think?'

'Definitely, yes. If we can find it.'

'I've got some ideas where it might be. Afrasiab had a huge underground fortress, called the Iron Palace. A place full of *evil magic*, apparently.' He waggled his fingers sarcastically to indicate spookiness. 'It was somewhere in the Karakum desert.'

Macy had by now read on past the point Emilian had indicated . . . and found the text confirmed what he had just told her. 'Wait – you've already read this?'

A smirk rose. 'I said Atlantean was a hard language to learn. I didn't say I hadn't learned it.'

'Oh, you asshole.' They both laughed.

'That's why I come to read all the old records,' the Dutchman went on. 'To find clues that can tell us where all these things are. In the past, the Knights actually did go out to find them. Some of the things in the vault, they brought with them when they turned away from the Atlantean kings. But others, they tracked down and took from the people who had them. They haven't done that for a long time, though. Because they're scared of being discovered.'

'It *is* kind of a risk,' she pointed out. 'If someone sees you while you're flying around in your armour, there'll be media reports of angels the next day.'

'Which is why we have to be careful. But that doesn't mean we should be cowards.'

She nodded in agreement. 'So do you know where this palace is? Other than the middle of nowhere?'

'No. But there must be some way to find it. Maybe we need to look at what we have in a different way. New eyes might help.' His gaze fixed upon hers.

Macy felt her cheeks flush. 'How new are your eyes? I mean,' she added awkwardly, 'when did you join the Knights?'

'Euripides first found me four years ago,' he said. 'In Rotterdam.' He looked away; the memory was troubling. 'He'd worked out that both my parents had the Atlantean gene. He came to the Netherlands to find them. But my mother . . .' A pause, his expression becoming more grim. 'She had died. And my father . . . well, he abandoned me, the piece of shit. I had to survive on my own, on the streets.'

'Oh, my God,' Macy said softly – before cringing in appalled embarrassment. 'And I made a joke about your mom – oh, God! I am so sorry! I didn't mean to—'

'You didn't know,' he cut in. 'It's okay. I have heard a lot worse, from people who were *trying* to hurt me.'

'I'm still sorry. I shouldn't have said it.'

'It's fine, really. But anyway, when Euripides found me, I didn't trust him at first. An older guy, approaching a homeless kid on the street and saying he's been looking for me – you think he wants to fuck you, you know?' A twitch of his eyebrows. 'Sorry for the language.'

'I've heard worse,' she replied, managing a small smile.

'But eventually, he convinced me. I came here, met the others, started training. That part was easy, because I always had to fight,

189

my whole life. Trusting other people, working as a team . . . that was harder. But I got there. And you will too.'

'If I stay,' she said. 'Is this what I want to do with my life? I don't know.'

'I hope it is.'

She looked back at him in surprise. But before she could decide how to react, the archive's door opened. 'Is someone in here?' said a Scottish voice.

'We are,' said Emilian, leaning back to look past the shelves. Macy saw MacDuff in the doorway. 'Me and Macy.'

'Hello there, Macy,' MacDuff said. 'What're you doing in here? I thought your ma was the historian.'

'Archaeologist,' Macy automatically corrected. 'Emilian was showing me something about the history of the Knights.'

'Oh, aye? All stuff worth knowing, I suppose.'

'What are you doing this late, Euripides?' asked Emilian.

'A genealogist's work is never done,' said MacDuff, going to one of the side doors. He took out a ring laden with keys and unlocked it. 'Got some more genetic data, so I need to add it to the database and run an analysis. See if I can find more people like the two of you.'

He entered the adjoining room; Macy, now curious, followed, Emilian watching from the doorway. A high-end laptop was connected to a bank of black boxes that she guessed were servers or additional processors. But her attention went to a safe set into one wall. 'What's in there?' she asked MacDuff as he tapped at a keypad to unlock it. 'Porn stash?'

He gave her a small laugh as he pulled the heavy door open. 'No, this is where I keep my really important data. The computer's not connected to the internet, for security. Even so, I don't want this stuff left lying around.' He took out a blocky object protected by a rugged case of thick rubber: a hard drive. 'If our enemies got hold of this,' he said, 'they could use it to identify and hunt down people with the potential to become one of the Knights – people like you – all over the world. If they kill you, you can never pose a threat to them.'

'They already tried,' Macy noted unhappily.

'Aye, that they did.' He connected the drive to the laptop, then logged in. 'Which is worrying for more than just the obvious reasons. How did they find you? I'm certain they weren't following me. I might not be a soldier or a spy, but I know how to spot a tail. And I never discussed you with anyone outside this organisation. So how did they turn up at your villa right after me?'

'I don't know.'

'No, me neither. Which is a concern.' He inserted a flash drive into the laptop. 'Right. I'll back this up first, then get started.'

'We'll leave you in peace,' said Emilian.

MacDuff looked around at them. 'See you both tomorrow.' He turned back to his work.

'Bye,' said Macy, retreating. Emilian returned the large book to its place. He headed for the exit; she followed. 'So, what now?'

'I was going to go for a ride,' he said. 'Out into the countryside. It helps clear my head.'

'I could use some head-clearing right now,' she said ruefully.

'Why don't you come with me?'

'What, on your motorbike?' The idea prompted an instinctual rejection – until she realised it was coming from her mother, not herself.

'Sure,' he said. 'I have a spare helmet and jacket.'

Again, she almost turned him down automatically, but fought past the urge. 'You know . . . why not? If you're a safe rider.'

'I haven't crashed yet,' Emilian said, grinning. 'Do you want to?'

'Yes,' she decided. 'Sure.' They headed for the stairs.

'What Euripides said, about how the Brotherhood followed him,' he said as they descended. 'It means it's more important than ever that we're ready to take direct action. Whatever Fernando's father and the others say. They found you in France, somehow. They'll still be looking.'

'Yeah, that's a fun thought.'

'We can protect you. We just have to be ready for trouble – and willing to do whatever's necessary.'

'It'll be hard to do that when what you can do in training is so restrained, though,' said Macy. 'I mean, you can't even leave the house.'

They reached the bottom of the staircase. Emilian started for the main entrance – then paused, looking in the other direction . . . towards the Batcave. A sly smile spread across his face. 'Do you want to do something *unrestrained*?'

23

'Oh my God,' said Macy, looking back towards the villa as Emilian drove his motorcycle – with her riding pillion – down the estate's driveway. 'I can't believe we're doing this. They'll be *so* mad if they find out.'

'They won't,' Emilian replied, voice muffled by his helmet. 'They never have before – why would they now?'

Emilian was carrying the orichalcum bands of their armour in a messenger bag. Macy had been racked by fear when they entered the Batcave, certain someone would demand to know what they were doing, but the Knights were apparently granted total trust with the artefacts that granted them their powers. 'How many times have you done this before?'

'I'll just say . . . more than one.'

They neared the main gates. They were automatic, detecting a tag on the motorbike and silently opening just in time for it to pass through. Macy glanced behind, seeing them close again once the bike was clear. She also spotted numerous cameras keeping watch on the road. The Order of Behdet's security was focused outside rather than within.

She held on to Emilian more tightly as he swept onto the road and accelerated. Her instinctive thought as the bike tilted was that it was going to fall over, her mind screaming at her to straighten to balance it out. But she remembered his advice while training with the armour: go *with* the movement, not against it. It seemed to work. The bike's tyres maintained their grip, carrying them through the turn before rider and passenger came back upright.

She tried to relax, but found her gloved hands were still clenching the front of his heavy leather jacket. It reminded her of her father's usual choice of outerwear.

He felt her nervousness. 'Are you okay?'

'Yeah, yeah,' she replied. 'It's just – like I said, I've never done this before.'

'You'll be fine. Just leave everything to me.'

She had noticed forested hills surrounding the villa in the brief moment when she flew above its roof. Emilian took her into one of the swathes of darkened woodland. The road became more winding as they climbed, leaving behind the few scattered houses along the way. Macy maintained her hold on the Dutchman, glimpsing the road rushing through the stark beams of his headlights whenever she looked over his shoulder, but to her relief he had decided not to show off – or scare her.

Eventually the bike slowed, turning onto a dirt track through the trees. 'Where are we going?' Macy asked as they bumped along.

'My quiet place,' came the reply. 'Nobody can see it from the road. I come here so . . . so I can fly.'

He stopped the bike in a clearing and turned off its lights. It took Macy's vision several seconds to adapt. Stars appeared in a glittering blanket across the heavens. The moon was somewhere off to one side, pale highlights catching the edges of the trees. Cicadas chirped; it was still hot even after sunset. Emilian dismounted and removed his helmet, gesturing for her to do the same. 'Here we are,' he said, unslinging the messenger bag. He took out his own pieces of armour and slipped them on. 'These are yours.' He passed them to her.

She donned them. 'So, what do you do when you fly?'

'I fly. What more is there? It is . . .' Despite his excellent English, it still took him a moment to find a suitable word. 'Incredible. It's *freedom*, like nothing else. You'll see.'

He stepped back – and transformed, the glinting scales flowing over his clothing as his halo flared to life. In the darkness, it was bright enough to make Macy briefly squint. The glowing wings extended from his back. 'Your turn,' he said, voice made hollow.

'Okay . . .' She moved clear of the bike. Her borrowed jacket was too big for her, and she considered removing it, but then remembered Fernando's remark about wind-chill. Guessing that if the armour could cover somebody the size of Jari Halko it could also deal with an oversized leather jacket, she mentally readied herself . . .

And transformed.

The insectile sensation of the armour's tiny leaves scuttling and swirling over her body was one she was still not used to. But they adapted to her bulky clothing without difficulty, sweeping up from her wrists over the leather sleeves to join with the wave descending from the torc around her neck. She felt the shifting earth energy field enclose her as the armour completed its transformation, her own halo appearing. It gave off enough light to show the lines in her palm when she raised a hand. No wonder Emilian came all the way out here for his covert flights; the 'angels' were probably visible from some distance away.

Emilian rose from the ground, hovering in front of her. 'Don't forget your wings.'

A faintly embarrassed laugh. 'Yeah, I kinda need those, don't I?' Another effort of will, and she felt the luminous wings snap into place. 'Okay, I'm ready.'

'Then let's fly.'

He rose vertically, slowly at first but with increasing speed. She focused – and followed. The feeling of the armour taking her weight was still uncomfortable to begin with, more so with the extra thickness of the leather jacket under her arms and around her body. But she kept her limbs straight, using them to guide her movement rather than give in to the unnatural forces tugging at them. She climbed after Emilian, clearing the treetops . . .

The forest opened out around her.

She gasped, genuinely amazed. The moon, fat on the horizon, cast a raking light over the darkened canopy, picking out each tree with almost impossible clarity. She looked down. The clearing was an empty circle of black beneath her feet, shrinking with each passing moment.

Emilian slowly tilted himself towards the horizontal, moving out across the woods. Macy shifted her own weight to follow him. He picked up speed. After just a few seconds, she guessed they were moving at thirty or forty miles per hour, the shimmering carpet of trees rolling past a hundred feet below. She couldn't feel any appreciable wind on her face, the halo holding it off – but she *did* feel cooler. Enough air was passing through the energy field surrounding her to carry away her body's heat. 'Slow down,' she called – not out of worry, but more that she wanted to fully appreciate the experience.

He did so, turning in mid-air to face her. 'Are you okay?'

Macy brought herself to a slightly wobbly hover, still unused to the way the armour held her. 'Yes, I'm fine – I'm great! You were right. This *is* incredible.'

He made a sound of amusement. 'This is only the start. See what you can do.'

She surveyed the surrounding landscape. The lights of isolated houses on the forest's fringes stood out, larger settlements in the distance beyond. 'Are you sure nobody will see us?'

'We'll be fine,' he said. 'The nearest house is over a kilometre away. And there is hardly any traffic on this road.'

They had passed several cars along the way, so Macy wasn't entirely sure about that. But there were no headlights in sight at the moment. 'Okay,' she said. 'What *can* I do?'

She leaned forward again – and started to fly.

The trees slid past beneath, faster and faster. Wind started to whistle around her as she picked up speed. The barest sensation of a breeze now caught her face. A glance back. Emilian was following, a winged, glowing figure off to one side. The sight gave her confidence. She angled upwards, still accelerating. How fast could she go? How *high* could she go? The forest dropped away. She kept climbing, excitement rising with her. This was what it was like to be a bird, an eagle soaring high in the sky . . .

More than that. She was no mere bird. She was a *superhero*, breaking free of the restrictions of gravity, of earthbound mundanity. And she wasn't limited to the pages of a comic book or a movie screen. This was real. She could do the impossible. She could do *anything*!

She let out a long whoop of pure exhilaration, turning as she ascended to see distant towns and cities strung along the horizon like jewels. Only a handful of people throughout history had ever seen the world like this, not falling helplessly or using clumsy aircraft, but in total control of their flight. To prove the point, she changed direction with the swiftness of a bird of prey, banking this way and that, then showing off to Emilian by looping the loop in front of the spotlight of the moon. 'Oh, my God!' she cried, unable to stop smiling – then laughing. 'This is the best thing *ever*!' She stopped, hovering silently – how high up was she? A thousand feet, more? – in the air. It took a moment to realise she had unthinkingly struck a heroic pose, fists clenched, feet pointed towards the ground. 'I can't believe I'm *doing* this!'

Emilian joined her. 'It's amazing, isn't it?'

'It is! Why are you not doing this all the time?' Reality wormed its way through her enthusiasm. 'Apart from the obvious "bad guys would try to hunt you down and kill you for the armour", I mean.'

'That's one reason, yes,' said Emilian, amused. 'But I do this when I can.'

'I'd be doing it every fricking night!' Macy set off again, accelerating forcefully enough to make the armour pull uncomfortably hard at her body. But the reward was more than worth it. The wind rose to a thrumming roar as she dived back towards the forest. She let out another exuberant cry, adrenalin surging. Trees resolved themselves from the moonlit mass as she plunged towards them.

The thrill was suddenly leavened with concern: *okay, how fast can I pull up?* She tried to level out, but had built up so much momentum that she just kept going—

'Macy!' Emilian yelled as she disappeared into the treetops. He hurtled down after her, hearing cracks and crunches as branches snapped . . .

She reappeared, climbing considerably more slowly as shredded leaves and broken twigs showered from her. 'I'm okay!' she said, panting. 'Just a little unscheduled air-to-foliage interaction. Whoo!' The normally barely visible shield around her had flared and sparked brightly as it fended off branches during her brief journey through the forest's upper reaches. Most had been thin enough to bend or break as she hit them, but a couple of blows were solid enough to hurt. 'I guess I still need some more practice with steering.'

'You've got to be careful,' he warned. 'If you get knocked out, you'll fall. And if you're twenty metres in the air . . .'

'Yeah, that wouldn't have been a good end to my first time,' she agreed. 'Lesson learned. I'll be more careful.'

She began to ascend again, but Emilian called out: 'We should go back to the villa.'

'Really?' she said. The urge to keep flying was overwhelming, almost addictive. 'We were just getting started . . .'

'You had one near miss. I don't want to risk another. You're too important.'

She smiled despite her disappointment. 'Well, that's very nice of you to say.' A small sigh, then she looked around. The forest looked much the same in every direction. 'Where did we leave the bike?'

'Follow me.' He rose and made a sweeping turn to head over the trees.

Macy went after him. A moment of worry as she spotted lights on the road, but she and Emilian were too high up for anyone inside the car to see them. The driver was going excessively fast for the conditions, she thought; even with the headlights on high-beam, they wouldn't have much time to react if an unexpectedly sharp bend appeared in front of them.

Or another car. She glimpsed more lights through the trees half a mile ahead – coming the other way. It took her only a moment to calculate where they would come together. 'Uh, Emilian,' she said, watching with growing worry as the two vehicles closed on each other. 'I think there's gonna be a crash.'

Either he didn't hear her, or he chose not to respond. The speeding car didn't slow as it whipped around a bend. Concern rose to actual fear – had the drivers seen each other? The slower car had surely spotted the approaching high-beams, but she knew from the ride up that the road was narrow – was there enough room for it to get out of the way?

They were almost on each other. The speeder still hadn't slowed. 'Emilian!' she shouted, this time catching his attention. 'Those cars, they're going to—'

The slower car reduced speed, pulling sharply over to the roadside – but the oncoming vehicle kept coming. Only at the last moment did its driver spot the dimmer headlights in their path and swerve—

Too late. They collided, the second car's rear end swinging around wildly as the first smashed into it. The speeding driver stamped on the brake, their car slithering to a stop almost sideways-on across the road. But the vehicle it had hit was still spinning . . .

It slipped over the edge of an embankment – and rolled onto its side, sliding down the slope before slamming to an abrupt stop against a tree.

'Jesus!' Macy cried, horrified. She changed course, swooping down towards the scene of the crash. 'We've got to help them! Come on!'

'No!' Emilian shouted – rapidly moving to block her path. 'Are you crazy? We can't let them see us!'

Beyond him, Macy could see the overturned car, its lights still on – but also with a new, more ominous glow rising from its exposed underside. It was an older vehicle, gasoline-powered, and flames were licking from its engine compartment. 'It's on fire! For God's sake, we've got to get them out of there!'

The Dutchman hesitated. Muttering 'Fuck!' under her breath, Macy jinked past him and descended towards the crash site. The small hatchback had ended up on the driver's side. She saw the passenger door jolt upwards as someone inside struggled to force it open.

The flames spread to the tinder-dry grass. Macy glanced back. Emilian hadn't followed. She was on her own.

She hovered over the car and grabbed the door handle, pulling it open. 'Get out!' she shouted in Spanish, hoping it was close enough to Portuguese to be understood.

The driver, a small woman in her twenties with an oozing cut on her temple, got the message whether she comprehended or not. She hauled herself up onto the car's side. But she didn't drop down and run – and Macy knew why when a sound chilled her blood.

A baby's scream.

The driver tugged desperately at the rear door's handle. It didn't open. Macy moved to help her – and for the first time, the woman saw her rescuer. An initial shriek of shock was cut short by a gasp of fearful awe. *Now* she scrabbled back, falling clumsily to the ground and staring up at the angelic figure hovering over her car.

'No, no, it's okay!' Macy gabbled. But the mother was too stunned to move. The redhead also tried to open the door, but with no more success. The car's side had been caved in by the collision, jamming it. 'Emilian! Goddammit, I need your help!'

None came. Cursing, she dropped down at the car's rear. The hatchback was also stuck. Could she smash a window? She kicked at the glass, but it didn't crack. The baby's terrified wails grew louder. The fire was spreading, now lighting both sides of the overturned vehicle. Suddenly feeling utterly, horribly useless despite her new-found abilities, she stood helplessly by the wreck, so close to the baby yet unable to reach it—

Light flared above – and Emilian dropped from the sky on glowing wings.

The woman let out another fearful cry as he landed beside her. 'There's a baby in the back!' Macy told him. 'I can't open the door, it's jammed!'

Emilian looked between the growing flames and the rear door. His whip could slice precisely through the metal. But neither he nor Macy had their weapons. There was nothing they could do . . .

Even without being able to see his face, Emilian's body language suggested to Macy that he was deeply conflicted about his next course of action. Then he raised an arm – and to her surprise, the armour changed shape, the scales writhing and climbing over each other to extend out past his hand into a narrow, paper-thin blade. It shimmered with the eerie blue light of earth energy. Then he ascended and drove his new weapon into the door's rear edge. The blade sliced through the metal as if it were tissue paper. He gripped the handle and pulled—

The door screeched open, leaving the severed section of panel still caught on the frame. Macy ascended and looked inside. The baby, about a year old, was trapped in its rear-facing seat, held in place by the belts. 'Shit!' she gasped. She had never dealt with a baby seat before. She pulled at the clasp where the straps met across the baby's chest, but it didn't release. There had to be some way to loosen them—

Another strap hung down from between the baby's flailing legs. It was secured by a plastic bar across it. She pushed at it with her thumb. It hinged upwards, releasing the strap. She pulled at the belts again – and this time they slackened. 'Come on, come on,' she gasped, fumbling to open the clasp. 'Oh God, come on—'

The clasp finally released. The baby dropped, sliding sideways in the seat. Macy stifled a yell of fright and grabbed it, sliding a hand behind its body to support its head. Both its arms were still entangled in the straps. 'Come on!' Emilian barked. 'The fire!'

She didn't need to look to know that the flames had grown. The ever-brightening flicker of orange and yellow in her peripheral vision told her enough. She yanked at the straps, working the baby's arms free. 'Hurry up!' shouted Emilian.

A last, desperate tug – and the baby was liberated. Macy clutched it to her chest. 'Grab the mom!' she cried – then she shot upwards.

A shriek from behind told her that Emilian was lifting the baby's mother. Macy came about to land on the road and looked back—

A flat thump from the crashed hatchback as the flames finally met vapour escaping from the fuel tank – and the car exploded.

Macy yelped, turning her back to shield the baby. Luckily, the detonation was considerably less extreme than those in the movies based on her mother's books. The car bucked, pounding back down with a crunch of metal and breaking glass. A column of fire swirled from the ruptured gas tank and spread through the car's rear.

Emilian landed beside her, the woman in his arms. He deposited her on the asphalt, then regarded the burning wreck. 'We need to get out of here.'

'*Aquí está tu bebé*,' Macy said to the mother, again hoping that Spanish was similar enough to Portuguese to be understood. In this case, it was. She handed the squalling baby to her. The woman burst into tears as she reclaimed her child, babbling in gratitude. Macy nodded to her – then turned. 'Just something I have to do first,' she told Emilian as she took off again and flew the short distance to the other car.

The driver of the sporty electric SUV had left his vehicle. He was unsteady on his feet, a couple of drinks beyond the legal limit. He stared in shock at what he had caused – then his emotions were supplanted by fear as Macy dropped down right in front of him. '*¡Oye, imbécil!*' she shouted. '*¡Llame una ambulancia! ¡Y los bomberos!*'

He understood, fumbling for his phone with one shaking hand – while the other made the sign of the cross. She realised what had just happened from his point of view: an angel had just called him a moron for causing a car crash. Well, a bit of religious terror was the *least* he deserved . . .

'Come on!' Emilian demanded impatiently. He rocketed skywards, the woman staring after him in speechless astonishment. Macy took a moment to make sure that mother and baby seemed okay before following.

The flight back to the motorbike did not take long. Emilian detransformed, almost throwing his armour into the messenger bag. 'Come on, take those off,' he ordered as Macy landed. 'We have to get out of here before the cops arrive.'

'What are they gonna do, arrest us on suspicion of being angels?' she objected as her armour shrank into the golden bands.

'This isn't funny! We weren't just seen. We interacted with people!'

'We saved their lives, you mean.' She handed her armour to him. He shoved the pieces forcefully into the bag. 'That woman and her baby would be dead if we hadn't helped them! What should we have done, let them die?'

That question, he didn't answer. Instead, he said: 'This will be all over the news by tomorrow. It won't be hard for the rest of the Knights to work out what happened – and who did it.'

'You were the one saying we should take more direct action,' said Macy.

Even in the moonlight, she saw anger on his face – but it subsided as he took a deep breath. 'Maybe it *is* time to challenge them,' he said after a moment. 'But we'll see tomorrow. Come on. Put your helmet on. We need to get back.'

Macy complied. She mounted the bike and Emilian started its engine, guiding them back through the trees.

24

France

The overnight journey to the hills above Monaco had been one of the most tense and fearful of Nina's life. While Eddie drove, she tried again and again to contact Macy, Rain and even Rain's parents. None of the attempts succeeded. She had even done something she'd never thought she would – and now had very good reasons to resist – by installing Uzz on her phone in the hope of getting through on her daughter's preferred means of communication.

But despite the rigmarole of signing up and confirming her identity and even having her face scanned, that too proved fruitless. All she got was a sad emoticon telling her Macy was unavailable, with no further explanation. The knowledge that Uzz's owner was the cause of her fear made the little stylised image seem almost mocking.

'Not far now,' said Eddie, checking the satnav. 'Just up this hill and we're there.' He slowed the hire car. They had deliberately chosen a petrol-engined vehicle, despite the rental company pushing electric options; he hadn't wanted to risk running out of battery and spend a long time recharging along the four-hundred-mile journey.

Nina saw a narrow road doubling back to head steeply upwards. A parking bay before the junction was coned off, a wall above partly collapsed. She brought up a photograph Macy had sent of her rented villa as Eddie made the turn. 'It'll be on the right,' she said. 'Should be easy to find.'

That turned out to be the case – but not for the reason she had expected. After several switchback turns, the villa came into sight. Or rather, what remained of it. 'Shit,' Eddie said, horrified. 'What the fuck happened?'

He stopped the car, and he and Nina hurried out into the early morning sun. The building before them was a burned-out skeleton, only a couple of half-ruined walls still standing. Everything within had been reduced to firehose-soaked ash.

'Oh my God!' Nina cried, running up the drive. 'Macy! Eddie, where's Macy?'

'I don't know,' he said. 'Jesus!' He regarded the villa's blackened shell in dismay – then moved to check the driveway. 'Macy hired a car, didn't she?'

'I – I think so,' Nina managed to say.

'It's not here.'

'I can *see* that!' Her outburst was driven by pure desperation.

'No, I mean there's no broken glass, nothing burned. If it'd been here and caught fire, there'd be some wreckage.'

Sudden hope in her voice. 'So she got away?'

'Looks like it. At least, I hope to God that she did.' He surveyed the grounds. A swimming pool behind the villa, debris bobbing in the water, a scorched lawn at the front—

'*Hoi!*'

They turned at the shout, seeing a curly-haired man scurry towards them from a nearby house. '*Sors d'ici!*' he went on, gesticulating furiously for them to leave. '*C'est une propriété privée!*'

'Is this your villa?' Nina asked.

'*Quoi? Oui*, yes,' he said, switching to thickly accented English as he reached them. 'Get out of here!'

'No, wait! Our daughter rented this house. Where is she? What happened to her?'

The mention of Macy changed the squat man's anger from a general displeasure to something more laser-targeted. 'Your daughter? The American girl?'

'Yes, Macy! Where is she?'

'She burned down my house!' the Frenchman snarled. 'Parties, noise, every night. Against the rules. I warned her that if she did it again, I would throw them out. But she had another party anyway – and set the place on fire! Then she ran away. I have told the police. They will catch her, do not worry. She will pay for everything. If I have my way, she will go to prison!'

'She wouldn't burn down your house and run away,' Nina insisted, a protective anger of her own surging. 'Something else happened here.'

'I know what I saw!' the Frenchman snapped, stepping close enough for her to smell cigarettes on his breath.

She expected Eddie to intercede – but her husband instead climbed over the fence. The angry man saw him. '*Hoi! Hoi!* What are you doing? Get out!'

Eddie ignored him, crossing the seared lawn to collect something from the brown grass. 'She was having a party, was she?'

'Yes!'

He held up the object. It glinted in the sunlight: a small brass cylinder. 'Some fucking party. This is a cartridge casing! Someone fired a gun here, and I doubt it was Macy.' He vaulted back over the fence to face the Frenchman. 'Right, you – what's your name?'

'Auguste Pluc,' came the huffy reply.

'Okay, Monsieur Pluc, I want to know what *really* happened. 'Who was shooting, and where's my daughter?'

'I do not know,' said Pluc, eyeing the metal tube. 'I did not see anyone with a gun. The girls came back, making noise again, and then some men arrived and went into the house.'

'What men?' Nina demanded. 'How many of them?'

'Six – I know that for sure, I counted them. Six men, two girls. Huh!' His face creased with disgust. 'I knew I should not have let them rent my house.'

Eddie loomed closer to the Frenchman. 'You'd better not be saying what I think you're saying about my little girl, mate. These men went inside. Then what?'

'I called her to tell her to get out, but she cut me off. Then there were lots of flashes of light – and then a big bang! A fire, in the kitchen. The girls drove off in their car. The men went after them in a van. I call the fire department, and the police.' His gaze flicked away from Eddie as he recalled a memory. 'I heard next day there was a car crash, at the bottom of the hill. Somebody was killed.'

Nina's breath froze in her throat. 'Macy? Or her friend?'

'No, a man. Shot – and his arms chopped off! That is what I heard, anyway.'

'But you've no idea where Macy is now?' Eddie asked.

'No, no. But you are her parents, yes?' He stabbed a finger at the burnt-out wreckage, before wagging it in Eddie's face. 'Then you can pay for this! That house is worth two million euros. Your girl burned it down, so you can – aagh!'

Pluc's rant abruptly became a cry of pain as Eddie grabbed his hand in a crushingly tight hold, forcing him down onto his knees. 'You've really picked the wrong day to piss me off, mate,' the Yorkshireman growled. He nodded towards a large metal wheelie bin on the drive. 'Nina, open that, will you?'

She would normally have tried to persuade her husband to back down, but on this occasion was fully on board. 'Here,' she said, lifting the lid.

Eddie twisted Pluc's arm up behind his back and frog-marched him to the bin. 'What are you doing?' he gasped.

'Putting out the trash.' Before Pluc could protest, Eddie hauled him off the ground and threw him inside, slamming the lid shut.

'If I see your head pop out, I'm going to kick this bin down the road to Monaco – with you inside it. Got that?' He banged on the metal side with a balled fist for emphasis.

'Yes,' came the quavering reply.

'Good.' He started back down the drive, Nina going with him. 'I don't like this,' he told her.

'Understatement of the damn year,' she replied, feeling numbed and sick. 'Where's Macy? Did these men get her?'

'Maybe. But then who shot this bloke – and chopped his arms off?' They got into the car. Eddie finished the latest of several energy drinks he had consumed to stay awake, then started the engine. 'Check the local news, see if there's anything about what happened,' he said, heading downhill.

Nina used her phone's translation function to convert the search results into English. 'Whoa.'

'What?'

'It wasn't just some guy's arms who got chopped off. What the hell happened here?' A photograph showed a wrecked van – its entire front corner sliced off as if by a giant knife.

Even the brief glimpse Eddie gave it was enough. 'We've seen stuff cut up like that before.'

'Yeah. Something charged with earth energy did that. Not a trikan, though. This was something else.'

'That must have been the van that was chasing Macy. Granit's men, probably. So who attacked *them*?'

'Someone else is involved,' was Nina's grim conclusion. 'Maybe the same people who raided the IHA – these angels. Oh, God,' she said, with sudden despair. 'Where *is* she, Eddie? What's happened to her?'

'I don't know. But we'll find her. We *have* to.'

'You've got friends in high places – or low places, depending how you look at it. People in the intelligence services. Maybe they can help.'

Eddie shook his head. 'Alderley retired from MI6 a couple of years back. Jared got promoted, but I haven't spoken to him for a while. I can try him, though.' He quickly called Jared Zane in Israel – but got only his voicemail. 'Jared, it's Eddie Chase. Got a serious situation, and any help you can give me would be appreciated. Call me back, or email me. It's urgent.' He ended the call. 'Hopefully he'll get that soon, but . . .' A helpless shrug. The Mossad operative could be anywhere in the world.

Nina regarded her own phone. 'Somebody's got Macy. They must have, or she would have contacted us by now. But are they using her as leverage against me, or . . .' A deep breath – then she stabbed at the screen, launching the Uzz app. 'Fuck it. I'm going to call Loost – challenge him right to his face.'

'You sure that's a good idea?' Eddie said dubiously.

'No. But he doesn't know we've made the connection between him and Granit. It might shake him enough to give something away.' Uzz had hooked itself into her phone's contact list during the installation process; a tick beside Raphael Loost's name meant the social network had confirmed his identity. 'Let's see.'

She tapped his name. Seconds passed, a connection attempt in progress – then a woman answered. The screen showed only an animated icon, rather than Uzz's augmented reality avatars. 'The office of Mr Loost. May I take your name and the purpose of your call, please?'

'This is Professor Nina Wilde,' Nina replied, trying to keep her anger – and worry – out of her voice. 'I'm calling Mr Loost back regarding his job offer.'

'Please hold.' A lengthy silence, Nina and Eddie exchanging concerned looks – then the woman returned. 'Putting you through to Mr Loost now, Professor Wilde.'

'Thank you.' A shorter wait, then the icon was replaced by a familiar face, the earth a vivid backdrop behind him. 'Nina!' said Loost, smiling – too broadly, to her mind, forced. If he'd thought she was dead, the call would have come as a shock – and, like her, he would be probing for information. 'I'm glad you called back. Have you reconsidered my proposal?'

How to play it? Subtle, or direct? She decided on the latter. 'Where's Macy?'

'Macy?' Feigned bewilderment in the trillionaire's tone.

'My daughter. Don't tell me you don't know her. You befriended her on Uzz.'

'Oh, of course. I befriend a lot of people, picked at random. It took me a moment to remember her name.'

'Bull. *Shit*,' Nina growled. 'There are eight-point-seven billion people in the world, and you just *randomly* chose her – right before you offered me a job?'

'The offer still stands,' Loost said smoothly. 'If you want it.'

'Cram your offer. I don't work for people who've tried to have me killed.'

Any congeniality vanished in an instant. 'I would advise you to be very careful what you say, Nina,' he replied coldly. 'All my calls are recorded, and immediately available to my lawyers. I have some of the world's best on retainer in London to handle cases of libel or slander against me.'

'Oh, you're recording this?' she said. 'Good. I'll be sure to ask for it as evidence if *I* need it. Do you know Anton Granit?'

'Granit, Granit,' Loost said, clicking his tongue. 'Oh, yes. One of my security contractors. One of many,' he added. 'We employ dozens of companies around the world for such services.'

'How many of them carry out assassinations?'

His eyes narrowed. 'I don't think I like your insinuation, Professor Wilde.'

'It's an accusation, if that helps. Anton Granit works for you. He also sent a man – his brother – to kill me in Rome. Coming right after I turned down your offer and refused to step away from investigating the raid on the IHA, I find that very suspicious. And now Macy's missing. Where is she? Did you order Granit to kidnap her?'

Loost was silent for a moment. Then: 'I think this conversation has gone far enough. You'll be hearing from my lawyers very soon, Professor Wilde. Goodb—'

'I know you're trying to find the Staff of Afrasiab.'

Despite her earlier deductions, Nina was still not totally sure that was Loost's objective. But she now felt pushed into playing her trump card – her *only* card. From his reaction, though, she finally felt certainty. He was not merely surprised, but his eyes widened with momentary alarm, caught. 'I don't know what that is.'

'Then you won't be interested that I've narrowed down its location to an area of a hundred square miles. It won't take long to pinpoint it. Once I do, I'll make sure it doesn't fall into the wrong hands. By destroying it, if I have to.'

Again, his eyes betrayed concern. 'Preserving the past, not destroying it, was my foundation's goal, Professor Wilde. So perhaps it's for the best that you've turned down my offer. Now, as I said, my lawyers will soon be in touch. In the meantime, I hope you find Macy.' A small, cold smile. 'She's a very smart, passionate girl. I genuinely believe she has a great future ahead of her.'

'She's a woman, not a girl,' Nina said, seething. 'Where is she?'

The smile became an oily smirk. 'Goodbye, Professor Wilde.' The call ended.

Eddie's hands tightened on the steering wheel. 'If I ever meet that shithead in person, I'm going to hit him so hard his teeth'll end up in his ears.'

'I don't think you'll get the chance, unless you hijack one of his spaceships. What *is* it with ultra-rich guys and giant, thrusting rockets, anyway? Definitely compensating for something there.'

It was a measure of how seriously Eddie was taking the situation that he didn't even show a hint of a smile. 'So, what are we going to do? We still can't prove Loost's involved, so we've got nothing to give to Ozzy.'

'And we're no nearer finding Macy, either. All we know is . . . she's not here.' Nina looked grimly across the sun-scoured Riviera. 'Whoever has her, they haven't tried to use her to get to us – to force me to stop looking for the Staff of Afrasiab.'

'Or to get what you just told Loost you had,' Eddie pointed out. 'Its location.'

'Maybe that was a mistake, but I wanted to see his reaction. He *is* looking for it, I'm sure. But he hasn't found it yet. He was worried when I said I knew its location – and that I'd destroy it. He wants it. If we get it . . . we can trade it for Macy.'

'If he's the one who's got her. What if it's these angels? You saw what happened to that van. Maybe they took her. But did they rescue her, or are they holding her prisoner?'

Nina leaned back, kneading her forehead. 'They murdered that guard at the IHA, so I doubt they have lily-white motives. I think we've got two factions, both wanting to find the Iron Palace – and they're as bad as each other. We can't let either of them get the staff.'

Eddie gave her a sidelong look. 'So you're suggesting . . .' he said, with growing resignation.

'Yeah,' she replied. 'We have to find it first.'

25

Portugal

Macy sprang out of bed, fizzing with energy and excitement. The memory of her achievement the night before was still fresh and exhilarating. She had saved lives; she was a hero!

More than that. She was an honest-to-God *superhero*, swooping down from the sky to rescue a mother and her baby. It felt as if nothing was impossible. A whole new world had opened up before her. She was eager to explore it – and grasp the opportunities it offered.

She quickly washed and dressed, then hurried from her room. Her plan was to find Emilian and spend as much time as she could practising with her armour and trikan. Even knowing she would be restricted to the courtyard, she was still hungry to use her new-found powers again. And later, maybe she could persuade him into another moonlit excursion . . .

Someone was coming up the stairs as she descended. 'Oh, hello there,' said MacDuff. She had crashed through a tree the evening before, but he looked as if he had joined her. Did he *work* on appearing dishevelled? 'You seem perky this morning.'

'I had a good night,' she replied. 'Oh – could you tell me how to find Emilian's bungalow?' She had not visited it the previous night, instead being collected and dropped off outside the mansion so the Dutchman's neighbours wouldn't see the two of them riding together.

'Aye, sure. Go out through the main door and it's the second on the right after you pass Rain's place. Although,' he added, 'you should stop by on the way and see her.'

'Why? Is she okay?'

'I'm sure she's fine, physically. But . . . well, she hasn't said anything to me, and it's entirely her business, but I know her quite well – and I can tell she's upset. Heartbroken, even.' He gave Macy an apologetic look. 'She thinks her best friend doesn't want anything more to do with her.'

'Maybe if she hadn't lied to her supposed best friend for three years, that wouldn't be an issue,' was the redhead's cold reply.

'I know you're upset too. But Rain was doing what we asked her to. And I have to take the blame for that – I was the one who found you.'

Macy was keen to change the subject something less emotionally painful. 'How *did* you find me? With that genetic database you have upstairs?'

'That was part of it. But to tell the truth, everything your mother's done was a wee giveaway that you're both of Atlantean descent, even without a DNA test. I don't know whether your dad has the gene too; it's possible. But I suspect trying to get a sample off him would not be a good idea.'

'Probably not,' she agreed, amused at the thought.

'That was how I found Rain's family, though,' the Scot went on. 'Hard work, a lot of genealogical research. I traced how the Atlantean gene spread throughout the world, found family lines where it was especially strong. Like Hana's, Rain's mother. It's not a common thing in Vietnam, but there are still people who possess it. I tracked her family from Vietnam to France – they moved there in the 1950s – and found that she'd married Lucien, who was also from a strong Atlantean lineage. No surprise that when they had Rain, she had the potential to become a Knight too.

When she was old enough, obviously. It's not quite the thing for a baby.'

'You've known Rain her whole life?'

He nodded. 'Lucien joined the Knights before she was born. Hana had the potential to be one as well, but she didn't want to. Which is her choice; we're not going to force anybody to do something they don't want. Besides, once Rain came along, she considered raising her more important.'

She gave him a pointed look. 'So nobody forced Rain to keep tabs on me? It was her decision?'

'After the business with Earthbreaker, I was convinced you had the potential to join the Knights. But considering your ma's history, with the IHA and all, we were pretty sure she'd think we were the bad guys. So the original plan was to sound you out, as it were, see if you'd be open to us and what we do. Rain was only meant to be in New York for a few months. But then you became her best friend, and well, here we are three years later. And that was also Rain's choice. She wanted to stay with you . . . so we arranged things so she could.' A chuckle. 'Funny thing is, Lucien running the Order of Behdet's American arm was only meant to be a cover, but he turned out to be really good at it. You don't need special powers to help people.'

Macy covered her sudden unease; MacDuff couldn't possibly know what she had done the previous night. But the revelation about Rain had also thrown her a little. 'You let Rain stay in New York just so she could be with me?'

'There was some self-interest, I'll admit. We wanted to keep an eye on you. Like I said, you were very likely to have the Atlantean gene because of your ma – which could have drawn attention from people with not-so-good intentions. And that turned out to be the case, so . . .' He shrugged. 'But you might want to give Rain another chance. She's strong, but she's still only a young lass. Sometimes she needs a bit of extra support.'

'She's got her family.'

'I mean from her best friend.' He gave her an imploring look. 'Will you?'

'I'll . . . I'll think about it,' she said. 'I'm not promising anything.'

MacDuff sighed. 'Well, I tried. Anyway, I've got some more work to do. I'll see you later.'

'See you later,' Macy echoed.

She headed downwards, exiting the mansion. The sun was as intense as ever, even fairly early in the day. She started across the grounds, remembering MacDuff's directions. There was Rain's bungalow; Emilian's was beyond . . .

The door to the Belcourts' home was open. She heard voices coming from inside. One was Rain's. She slowed, trying to identify the other speaker, a man. They were talking in Spanish, so it was probably Fernando—

She heard her own name.

Macy froze, listening. The Spaniard had just said that Rain should talk to her. Rain's reply, after some hesitation, sounded almost fearful. 'But what if she doesn't want to talk to *me*? She's mad at me, and she has every right to be. I lied to her!'

'You were doing what we asked you to,' Fernando insisted.

'That doesn't change things. She's my best friend, but now I'm scared that I've lost her.' Fearfulness became tearfulness. 'What am I supposed to do?'

'You should talk to her,' came the reply. 'It's been a crazy few days, and Macy might not even have taken in everything that's happened yet. You've been best friends for three years. You can't give up on that just because you're worried how she *might* react. You have to find out for real.'

'I . . . suppose you're right,' came the reluctant reply, followed by a lighter, 'Ugh! I hate that about you.'

'What, that I always am?'

'That you *usually* are.' They both laughed. 'Thank you for this, Nando.'

'Any time, Chiquita. I always look out for you, don't I?' The door opened; Macy flinched, her tumbling emotions at learning Rain's true feelings abruptly replaced by embarrassment at being caught eavesdropping. Fernando stepped out, halting when he saw her. 'Oh! Macy, hi.'

'Hi, hi,' Macy replied, blushing. Fernando glanced back into the bungalow, subtly gesturing for Rain to come out. The Frenchwoman made it as far as the threshold, but froze on seeing Macy, expression conflicted. 'I was, uh . . . looking for Emilian. Which one's his house?'

'That way, second on the right.' Fernando pointed along the path. Behind him, Rain retreated. 'Rain, are you going to talk to – Rain?' He realised she was no longer there. 'Macy, I think you—'

'Sorry, I need to get moving,' said Macy, quickly walking on. 'I might come back later. Thanks.'

To her relief, he didn't try to follow her. She reached the bungalow, her knock on the door soon answered. 'Macy, hi,' said the Dutchman. He glanced around as if making sure she was alone. 'Come in.'

She entered. The bungalow's interior was different from the busy, homely atmosphere of the Belcourts', plain and austere not as a minimalist statement, but because its occupant considered the house a purely functional living space. If he had been on the streets not long ago, she mused, he might still have the subconscious mindset of owning as few belongings as possible in case he needed to move on in a hurry. The thought was a little sad; surely he felt he belonged here by now?

Just because he didn't have many possessions didn't mean he wasn't willing to spend money on those he had. A very large television in the living room showed a Portuguese news channel, the volume muted. She didn't have a chance to comment on it, though, as he spoke in a low, intense voice. 'Has anyone said anything to you about last night?'

'No,' she replied. 'I met Mr MacDuff in the house, but he didn't mention anything. What about you?'

'No. But it'll make the news sooner or later.' He glanced at the screen. 'We need to get our stories straight.'

'What's to get straight?' Macy asked. 'We went out to practise flying in an isolated spot, saw a car crash, saved a mom and her baby from burning to death. Besides,' she went on, seeing he was about to object, 'the guy who caused the crash seemed drunk, so nobody'll believe him, and the other driver hit her head. If she says she saw an angel, they'll blame it on a concussion. I don't think it'll even make the news.'

He made a faintly condescending sound. 'Maybe you're right, I don't know. But I still think the others will find out sooner or later. So what do we tell them?'

'Well, either we lie and deny everything, or tell the truth. You said yourself, it's time to challenge them about whether we should take direct action.'

He seemed outright displeased at the prospect. Had his opinion changed after having the night to think it over? Uncomfortable, she changed the subject. 'That's a big TV,' she said, indicating the screen. 'I don't think it would even fit in my room at home.'

'It's not just a television,' he said. 'I use it to talk to people on Uzz as well.'

'Oh, you're on Uzz? Me too. Well, who isn't? Apart from my mom.' She laughed a little. 'We'll have to friend each other.'

'Yeah, we will. If you're staying with us. But . . .' He gave her a probing look. 'I think you've already decided, haven't you?'

'What do you mean?'

'You said just now that "we" should take direct action. Like you're definitely going to join the Knights of Atlantis.'

'I—' She broke off, uncertain. She hadn't yet made a decision

– at least, not consciously. *Did* she want to join them? 'I don't know what I'm going to do yet,' she said. 'I mean, it's . . . a hell of a change from what I thought I'd be doing with my life.'

'Which was what?'

'I dunno – go to university, get my degree . . .' Except she'd already had her doubts about that path. It was what was *expected* of her; specifically, by her mother. But her inheritance meant she no longer needed to worry about following a traditional career pathway. And now, a thrilling new world was on offer . . . 'I don't know,' she repeated. 'I need to think about it.'

'Then while you're doing that, why not carry on from yesterday? Not out in the forest,' he quickly added. 'But practising with your armour and your weapon. Learning *how* to be a Knight.'

'Maybe having a rematch?' she asked, with a sly smile of challenge.

'If you want to lose again, sure.'

Her smile widened. 'Oh, it's *on* now.'

He grinned. 'Then let's do it. Then if you decide what I think you've already decided . . . you'll be ready.' He spoke to the television in Dutch, which responded to his command and switched off. 'Shall we?'

The prospect of regaining her powers, even within the limited arena at the mansion, was impossible to resist. 'Yeah. Let's go.'

26

Azerbaijan

Eddie stifled a yawn as he and Nina exited customs at Heydar Aliyev International, the airport serving the Azerbaijani capital of Baku. They had been lucky with their timing: a flight from Nice brought them via Istanbul to arrive while the sun was still above the horizon. The tickets were expensive, but Seretse had – reluctantly – covered the cost, as well as arranging transport in Turkmenistan. The Englishman had used the trip to catch up on sorely needed sleep.

But now he needed to be awake and alert. Not so much for threats posed by Granit's mercenaries: the person he had come to meet was slippery enough. 'There he is,' he told Nina, spotting a figure leaning against a pillar. 'Just keep an eye on him. Give him half a chance and he'll nick your watch.'

'Boy, I do love it when you introduce me to your friends,' she said, amused.

'He's not a friend. He owes me, but he's definitely not a friend.'

'What does he owe you for?'

'Not killing him on two separate occasions when he deserved it, for a start.' They cleared the small crowd waiting for family and friends at the gate and went to their contact.

Even when standing in the open, Gurban Gasimov seemed to be lurking. The Azerbaijani was around Eddie's age but looked considerably more weathered. He wore a long, shapeless coat that gave him the appearance of having no shoulders; Nina's immediate thought was that he resembled a disreputable penguin.

'Eddie, Eddie Chase!' he proclaimed, smiling broadly to reveal a mouth glinting with gold teeth amongst equally yellow natural ones. 'It has been a long time, eh?'

'Yeah, and I bet you wish it'd been longer, Gurban,' Eddie replied.

'Oh, you hurt me. But I know we are really friends. After all, I am always ready to help the man who saved my life.'

'How did you save his life?' Nina whispered.

A dark chuckle from her husband. 'See previous answer.' He turned back to Gasimov. 'So, can you do what I asked? Bloody well better, seeing as I've come all the way out here.'

Gasimov sniffed with wounded pride. 'Of course. I have passage on a fast ship to Turkmenbashi, for you, me and your lovely wife.' He gave Nina a belated bow of greeting, then before she could refuse took her left hand and kissed it. 'I have also spoken to my friend the customs officer on the other side, and even found you the supplies you asked for. All I ask is a modest payment, to cover costs.'

Eddie stared stonily at him. 'How much?'

'Ten thousand dollars.' The Yorkshireman's gaze turned even harder. 'But for you, Eddie? Only four thousand!'

'I'll give you three.'

'Done!'

'Arse,' Eddie muttered to Nina. 'I could probably have got away with two. By the way, you still got your wedding ring?' She hurriedly checked, to her relief finding it still on her finger. 'All right, Gurban, let's get moving.'

Gasimov drove them not to the port in Baku, as Nina had expected, but the town of Alat some sixty miles south. 'Today's ferry from Baku has already gone,' he explained. 'But a cargo ship sets off in two hours. It will get us to Turkmenbashi early tomorrow afternoon – if there is room in the port. If not, that is why Eddie asked me to get supplies.'

She was not reassured. 'Something I should know about?'

'Timetables aren't really a thing in this part of the world,' Eddie told her. 'Ships go when they're loaded, and arrive when they get there. If there isn't a space to dock, they just have to wait.'

'That is how we met,' Gasimov said, grinning. 'We were waiting on the same ship for two days!'

'Said I was unlucky,' Eddie remarked. He turned to regard a canvas holdall beside Nina in the back of the Azerbaijani's elderly Renault 19. 'Did you get me a gun?'

'Yes, yes.'

Nina sighed unhappily as he collected the holdall. 'Oh. Great. A gun.'

'If we get into any trouble, I want more than a clothes rail and a scooter this time.' He opened the bag, producing an automatic pistol and magazine. 'Fuck's sake. This the best you could find?'

An offended little huff from Gasimov. 'You want better? Give me more time. And more money.'

'What's wrong with it?' Nina asked.

Eddie frowned as he gave it a rapid, professional examination. 'It's a Pakistani knock-off of a Chinese copy of a Soviet Tokarev that's older than my dad. Piece of crap.' He racked the slide to make sure the chamber was empty, then listened carefully to the click as he pulled the trigger. 'Nothing's rattling around loose, I suppose.' He loaded the magazine and chambered a round, again listening to the mechanism.

'It will work,' Gasimov insisted. 'I have a reputation to keep.'

'You've got a reputation, definitely.' He glowered at the gun, but applied the safety and slipped it inside his leather jacket.

By the time they arrived at the port of Alat, the sun had set. There was little there beyond container cranes and a few buildings;

it was oriented towards cargo rather than passengers. Gasimov stopped at a checkpoint and engaged a bored official in brief conversation. The man went to a nearby cabin, an older, more senior official emerging. He was clearly friends with Gasimov, or at least part of a mutually beneficial arrangement. A surreptitious exchange of banknotes for folded paperwork, then the Renault was waved through.

'You see?' Gasimov said, driving across a vast concrete expanse towards the floodlit dockside. 'All good. That is our ship, there.' He pointed out a hulking, grimy freighter.

'What about customs checks?' Nina asked.

'That *was* the customs check! We can go straight aboard.'

He pulled up alongside other cars near a low building, then got out, taking the canvas bag. Nina and Eddie collected their belongings, then the trio went to the ship. Another official met them at the gangway. Gasimov handed him the paperwork, more banknotes tucked inside. A nod, and the arrivals were waved aboard.

'So is *everyone* on the take here?' Nina asked as they ascended the gangway.

'This is a Free Economic Zone,' Gasimov said, the term tinged with sarcasm. 'Everyone makes lots of money – except the workers. I help to spread the wealth around.'

'You're a regular socialist hero,' Eddie told him with a mocking chuckle.

A crew member greeted them on the deck. Gasimov spoke with him, then they were led into the ship's superstructure and brought to a cramped cabin. Nina was taken aback to find that one of the four bunks was already occupied, an overweight bearded man blinking up at them. 'Nearly all ships take passengers,' said Gasimov. 'Extra money.' He checked his watch. 'We go in half an hour, if we leave on time. We probably won't.' He put down the bag. 'I got food, water, first aid kit, insect spray, as you asked,' he told Eddie, opening the holdall. 'And also . . .' He

224

triumphantly took out a roll of toilet paper. 'The most important thing!'

'Cheers, Gurban,' said Eddie. 'A gun and bog roll. I'm sorted.'

Nina took the top bunk across the cabin from their fellow passenger, not wanting a stranger staring at her all night – or to have to climb over him to reach her bed. Eddie flopped into the bunk below her. 'What the hell are we doing here?' she sighed. 'I was supposed to be writing about the twenty-fifth anniversary of discovering Atlantis. Instead I'm racing against the world's richest man and some murderous angels to find a mythical underground palace containing a staff that can control the weather!'

'I dunno,' said Eddie. 'Seems appropriate. You stopped one rich nutter from destroying the world back then; you're doing it again now.'

'So this is my frickin' encore?' She dropped her head heavily down onto the pillow. 'God, I hope Macy's okay. It's killing me, Eddie. I feel sick. I don't know where she is, what she's doing, if she's safe . . .'

'I know, love.' He sat up, reaching up to take a reassuring hold of her hand. 'I know. We'll get through this. She'll be fine.'

'But what if she isn't?' Her voice cracked with emotion. 'What if – we never see her again?'

'We will,' was all he could say. She gripped his hand more tightly, husband and wife – mother and father – as close together as they could be.

Gasimov's prediction that the ship would not leave on time was correct, but the delay was only half an hour. A mournful blast from its horn, and the freighter lumbered from the dock, setting out on its overnight journey across the Caspian Sea.

27

Portugal

Macy's training session lasted for most of the day, with breaks only for food and other biological requirements. Emilian was her main tutor and sparring partner, but most of the other Knights dropped in and out for workouts of their own. Rain, though, was conspicuous by her absence. Macy once spotted her through the Batcave's tinted windows talking to Fernando, but she never entered the courtyard, despite her earlier conversation with the Spaniard.

The redhead wondered what her friend was feeling – was she really so afraid of rejection that she didn't dare speak to her? – but lacked the spare mental capacity to give it her full thought. She was focused on learning how best to use the Atlantean artefacts. The more she practised with the trikan, the more she realised how clumsy and unfinessed her earlier attempts had been. Throwing it like a yo-yo was only the beginning of the story; it was capable of so much more. Or rather, *she* was capable. It responded to her commands; the greatest limit on what it could do was how much she could envision.

Her use of the armour was more restricted. She tested it as far as she dared by ascending to the rooftops, going just high enough to catch tantalising glimpses of the surrounding land-scape before dropping again. But it was only a fraction of the rush she had felt the previous night, flying free over the forest. How did the others not all sneak off into the dark to do the same?

That brought her mind back to Rain. Macy wondered how old she had been when she learned she had a destiny, a future she would be expected to follow. Had she ever wanted to rebel and find her own path in life? Or was becoming a Knight of Atlantis like her father and friends all she had ever wanted?

If so, she had hidden it well for the past three years. The smart, diligent, caring, sometimes goofy and dorky young woman she knew – she *thought* she knew – did not seem like a member of an ancient order of superpowered guardians. But nor had her personality changed following the revelation; Scatterbrain Rain was not an act. She was who she was – there was just more to her than met the eye . . .

'Macy?'

There *was* Rain, finally entering the courtyard. The arena was now lit by spotlights, Macy only belatedly realising that the sky had turned a bruised purple as the sun went down. She was hanging twenty feet in the air, Emilian beside her as she practised hitting pinpoint targets on the ground with her trikan. Jari Halko was also working out, his wife watching as he performed fast and intricate striking and blocking moves with his great hammer. 'I'm here,' she called.

Rain advanced a few paces, then stopped, looking up at her. 'Can I talk to you?'

She had finally plucked up the courage, then. 'Back in a minute,' Macy told Emilian, before landing in front of Rain and detransforming. 'What is it?' Even having initiated the conversation, Rain seemed hesitant. Macy decided to break the awkward moment with a question of her own. 'So, you and Fernando. Are you . . . a thing?'

Rain was surprised – then almost appalled. 'What? No, no! That would be . . . weird. I've known him since I was little, he's like my big brother. Nooo!'

'Okay, glad we got that settled,' Macy said, amused. 'So what's on your mind?'

She thought she knew what the topic would be. She was wrong. Rain lowered her voice. 'Macy, did you, ah . . . do something last night?'

A chill ran through Macy. 'Like what?'

'Like go for a flight in the forest with Emilian?'

Oh, shit. She was about to deny it, but her friend knew her too well. Instead, she whispered, 'Yeah, I did. I'm sorry, but I just wanted to see what it was like.'

'I know; I understand. I've done it too.'

She was surprised, and a little impressed. 'You have?'

'Yes, I've been out with Emilian a couple of times. I wouldn't have done it without him, but he can be . . . persuasive.'

She glanced at the Dutchman, who had touched down not far from her. 'Yeah, he can. But how did you know?'

Rain brought up her phone. 'You're on the news.' She tapped the screen, and a video started playing.

Macy's stomach dropped towards her feet. The view was from a stationary car's rear dashcam – the car that had been speeding along the forest road. The overturned hatchback was out of sight on the slope below, but the flames rising from it lit the trees beyond. The drunk-driver came into view at the side of the frame . . .

And an angelic figure, wings aglow, dropped from the sky to land in front of him.

'Oh . . . buggeration and fuckery,' Macy muttered as her recording harangued the man in Spanish.

'Yeah,' agreed Rain. 'Macy, what have you done?'

'I saved a baby!'

'I know!' She wound the video back. The baby's mother, now with a bandaged temple, excitedly recounted events. 'The mom said they were rescued by an angel – an angel who spoke Spanish with an American accent. That would be a big giveaway even if I *couldn't* tell it was your voice!'

Emilian dispelled his armour and joined them. 'What's wrong?'

'We're blown,' Macy told him bluntly. 'We got caught on camera. Or I did, anyway.'

His face tightened. 'I *told* you not to get involved.'

'Well, it's too late now, isn't it? So what's going to happen? Do the others know about this yet?'

An answer came as Fernando entered the courtyard, expression serious. 'Macy. We need to talk to you.' By now, the Halkos had also taken an interest, Jari powering down his armour.

'I don't suppose it's about which bungalow I'm getting?' Macy asked, trying to cover her sense of dread.

He didn't respond to the joke. 'Can you come with me? Everyone else, too. It concerns all of us.' He gave Emilian a pointed look. 'Especially you.' The Dutchman put on a show of affronted confusion.

'Oh, give it up,' Macy groused. 'All right. Let's get this over with.' Fernando led everyone from the courtyard.

High overhead, unseen, a hovering drone watched them enter the house.

Macy's feeling of imminent doom only intensified when she entered the hall. Previously, the chairs had been laid out in a loose circle. Now, she could only think of their arrangement as a courtroom. She had no doubts about who was on trial.

All the Knights were there, as were the 'elders': Mateo Cruz, Diana Sayle and Lucien Belcourt. MacDuff and the Order of Behdet's security team, Renco and Meller, were also present, plus several people Macy didn't recognise; she assumed they were related to the others. 'Macy, sit down please,' said Cruz, gesturing at a chair.

It was on its own, facing the rest. 'Should I ask for a lawyer?'

Again, the attempt at humour fell flat. She bit her lower lip and took the seat, putting her trikan on the floor beside it. Emilian and Jari also laid down the weapons they had brought in. 'I think you know why you are here,' said Cruz. 'But to be sure everyone knows exactly what has happened . . .' He tapped at his phone, then made a swiping gesture to send the image on it to a screen on one wall. It was a freeze-frame from the dashcam footage: Macy in her angelic armoured form descending towards the stunned driver. Some of the audience apparently hadn't yet seen it, reacting with surprise and dismay. 'This was filmed last night, in the Serras de Aire. It made the news in Portugal today. By tomorrow, it will be all over the world. One of the Knights of Atlantis has been caught on camera – and our enemies have been told where we are to within a few kilometres.' He faced Macy again. 'What do you have to say?'

She took a deep breath before replying. 'What do you *want* me to say? Yes, it's me. But I saved the life of a baby and its mother. What was I supposed to do, watch them die?'

'You shouldn't have been there to watch them at all,' snapped Sayle, her voice ice-cold. Her gaze turned to Emilian. 'I don't need to ask if she was out there alone, do I?'

'I don't know what you mean,' was his tight-lipped, sullen reply.

'No? Grant us *some* credit, young man. The security cameras at the gate recorded you riding away with her on your motorcycle less than an hour before this happened. What were you thinking? You should know better than that!'

'It was my idea,' said Macy. 'I wanted to see what it was like to fly, properly. We went somewhere totally isolated. I didn't know there was going to be a car crash!'

'Was it really your idea?' Fernando asked quietly – and meaningfully. Emilian shot him an angry look.

'Anyway, you're overestimating how big a story this will be,'

Macy continued, dismissively indicating the angelic image. 'I mean, look at it! People will think it's fake, it's CGI. Nobody will believe it. The only reason it's made the news at all is because it's something different. If somebody claimed they had a video of a UFO, it would be ignored because everyone would think they were a crank. This'll be forgotten in a few days.'

'Not by the people who know the true nature of angels,' Cruz intoned. 'Like the Brotherhood of Selasphoros. They were already hunting for you. Now, they know where to start searching – for all of us.'

'Perhaps we made a mistake in considering you to join us?' said Sayle. She glanced towards MacDuff, who shifted uncomfortably.

'The question is,' Cruz said, 'what are we going to do now? You've broken our greatest rule – that we never show ourselves to the world. We have to decide what action to take.'

'Are you going to kick me out?' Macy asked, dismayed.

'You haven't even joined us yet,' Sayle pointed out archly. 'And there is also the security of the organisation as a whole to consider. You've already broken our trust once. Can we be sure you'll hold your silence about us if we decide to reject you? Especially since your own mother is currently working with the IHA *and* the Brotherhood. Two organisations whose goals are diametrically, and in the latter case violently, opposed to our own.'

'My mom is not one of the bad guys!' she protested.

'That remains to be seen.' Sayle straightened, addressing the whole room. 'We need to discuss Macy's future – all aspects of it. In private,' she added, to Macy. 'If you would wait outside?'

The *all aspects* part sounded worryingly like a threat, and her being curtly dismissed like a schoolgirl only served to make the redhead angry. 'What, don't I get to speak in my own defence?'

Cruz's expression was apologetic, but no less serious. 'I think you have said as much as you need to. I am sorry, but we will call for you soon.'

Lips clenched, Macy stood and marched for the exit. 'Macy, wait,' said Rain. 'This isn't fair! She saved people's lives – she saved a baby! Isn't that what we're supposed to be doing, protecting people?'

'That is what we are going to discuss,' said her father. 'What is our priority? Protecting the whole world, or individual people in it?' From his unhappy attitude, he clearly expected there to be no good answer.

Macy gave Rain a brief look of gratitude. 'I'll be out here, I guess,' she said, exiting. She shut the door and slumped against the wall beside it. 'Goddammit,' she sighed, emotions heavy on her heart. A new world had opened up to her – but now it was almost certainly going to be taken away. Even though she knew she had done the right thing, that apparently wasn't enough. Feeling alone, she waited for the decision that would affect the rest of her life.

'Hold position.'

The order was growled into a throat-mic by the leader of the men approaching the walled estate across the dry, sparse woodland to its north. The black-clad mercenaries, spread out widely to cover the full span of the compound ahead, hunched down in the darkness and readied their suppressed weapons.

The leader also crouched. His name was Anton Granit, head of the private military company Granit Contingency Management. The Hungarian wore a pair of what looked like sleek protective goggles, curved to fit his hard, battle-lined face. A tap at one of their arms, and the lenses lit up. They were advanced augmented reality glasses, superimposing data over his vision as if he were watching a screen floating before him.

The overlaid image was tinted red to minimise the impact on his low-light vision. It looked almost like a satellite photo – but it was a real-time feed, coming from the drone hovering high above the mansion.

One of the drone's functions was the automatic identification and tagging of human figures. Tiny icons marked where it had lost track of people it had been following. They were clustered around the main house.

Granit frowned. That could complicate his mission. The intel he'd been given suggested that by this hour, the residents would mostly be in their own individual bungalows. He tapped at his smartwatch. A couple of commands, and the warble of a call via Uzz sounded in his earpiece.

It was answered almost immediately; his client was keeping close tabs on the operation. 'We're outside the grounds,' Granit reported. 'But the drone's shown that lots of people have gone into the main house. Do we proceed?'

He listened, taking in an intelligence update, and his orders. 'Understood. Proceeding.' He ended the call, then touched his throat-mic again. 'The primaries and targets are now inside the house,' he told his men. 'We continue as planned. The security station is currently unmanned, but the cameras and motion detectors will still be shut down for one minute on my mark. Everyone get to their positions.'

Another touch on the goggles' arm to dim the head-up display, then he cautiously advanced across the thin woodland until he reached a point fifty metres from the wall. The effective range of the sensors inside the grounds, he knew, was thirty metres. He would not be seen even if anyone was watching the monitors.

He brought back the overlay. He was now inside the drone's wide field of vision; new tracking markers showed himself and his team, forming a dotted line parallel to the estate's boundary. Even had they been hidden by trees or inside a building, he would still be able to see his men's positions to the metre: all had military-precision GPS tags. Nobody was moving inside the grounds.

'Overriding cameras in three, two, one . . . mark.' His pay-master had somehow obtained access to the estate's security system; he tapped his watch again, this time to send a message: *Ready*. He waited, tension rising . . .

A reply flashed up in his vision: *Go*.

'Move!' he snapped, rising and hurrying to the wall. It was old, brickwork cracked and chunks of mortar missing. It took only moments to scale. None of his men had any difficulty in climbing the obstacle. The HUD told him all were inside the grounds with thirty seconds to spare. 'Move to entry positions,' he ordered. 'Tag and identify any hostiles before engaging. Remember that the two primaries must not be harmed. Anyone else is a valid target.'

Bent low, he scurried across the grounds, guided towards his destination by a pulsing yellow marker in his AR glasses. His team were following similar beacons in their own goggles, spreading out around the mansion to cover all the ways in . . . and make sure nobody got out.

Macy raised her head as the door opened. It was Rain. 'Hi,' said the American, butterflies in her stomach.

'Hi,' Rain replied. Her defeated tone did not inspire confidence. 'They want you to come in.'

Macy followed her into the hall. Everyone inside was seated; the feeling in the air was now not so much courtroom as funeral. She was sure that in a similar situation her father would have made a smart-ass comment, but nothing came to her mind. Rain led her to the isolated empty seat, then took a place beside Fernando.

The Spaniard's father was now flanked by Sayle and Lucien Belcourt, Renco and MacDuff also in the row with them. The senior figures of the Order of Behdet – and the Knights of Atlantis. They faced her, faces grim.

'Macy,' said Cruz, standing. 'Thank you for waiting.'

'I didn't have any place else to be,' she offered lamely. 'And . . . I suspect I'm not going to be here for much longer, am I?'

He couldn't quite meet her eye for a moment, but then drew in a slow breath and regarded her gravely. 'I'm sorry to tell you this, but . . . no. I'm afraid you've shown you are not a suitable candidate for the Knights of Atlantis.'

Even having expecting this, hearing the words out loud was crushing. Macy forced herself to remain still and expressionless. MacDuff, meanwhile, appeared stricken. She felt a pang of sympathy for the scruffy Scot; he was the one who had considered her more worthy than any other potential candidates, and she had immediately – literally the next day – let him down.

'It wasn't a unanimous decision.' She looked around as Fernando spoke up. 'Some of us wanted to give you another chance.'

'You saved a baby's life!' added Rain. 'You were a hero. That was the right thing to do.'

'Maybe it was,' said Sayle, cutting. 'But the circumstances that led to it were entirely wrong.' Her gaze locked onto Emilian, who sat slightly apart from the other Knights, posture tight and defensive. 'Rest assured that we discussed Emilian's actions as well. They were wrong too, and we still need to decide how to react to them. But even then, he had the good sense not to reveal himself to the public – especially not on camera!'

'So that's it?' said Macy, a glimmer of outrage pushing through her dismay. 'I'm done, I'm gone?'

'Not quite.' Cruz seemed uncomfortable about what he was about to say. 'There is still the question of, ah . . .'

'Of whether or not we can trust you to hold your silence,' Sayle finished for him. 'You know who we are, where we are, what we do and how we do it. That information in the wrong hands would be infinitely more damaging and dangerous to us than what you've already done.'

'So – what?' Macy said in sudden alarm. 'You're going to *kill* me to keep me quiet?'

'Of course we're not!' said MacDuff firmly, before the old woman could reply. 'Nobody even considered that. *Did* they, Diana?'

'That would have been a rather extreme solution,' Sayle replied, after a moment.

'Yeah, no kidding,' said Macy. 'Look, if you want my word that I'll keep your secret, then absolutely, I'll give it.' She turned towards the Knights. 'Rain will vouch for me, I'm sure . . .'

'Yes, of course I will,' Rain told her – but Macy's attention was caught by something behind her, outside one of the tall windows. The lights in the hall meant that nothing but blackness was visible beyond, but just for an instant, she thought she saw a tiny, pin-sharp flash . . .

'I have eyes on hostiles inside the house,' said a voice in Granit's earpiece. One of his men, Voronin, was covering the western side of the building. The mercenary leader looked in that direction, his AR glasses revealing the GPS-tagged positions of Voronin and his companions despite the darkness. 'At least sixteen people. I've identified one of the primaries; tagging her.'

A new icon appeared in Granit's computer-enhanced field of vision, a blue triangle. The 3D effect of the glasses made it seem to be inside the mansion, despite its walls blocking any direct view. 'Tag the other primary if you see him,' he ordered. 'And as many targets as you can.'

'Yes, sir.' More icons blinked into existence. Most were red circles, but another blue triangle appeared amongst them. The AR system calculated how far they were from his position, ranges in metres appearing above each new subject. Granit assessed the situation. All were relatively close together, the two blue pings amongst the reds . . .

Several of the circles were in a line, a gap separating them from the two primaries – those his employer insisted had to be kept alive. He tapped the glasses again, then raised a hand and swept his forefinger over the line of floating icons, highlighting them. The same effect would appear in the AR vision of the other team members. 'Can you put a grenade behind these targets, so they'll shield the primaries?'

'Yes, sir,' came the confident answer.

'Fire on my mark. Everyone else – prepare to move in!'

'That's good,' said Cruz, in reply to Rain, 'but we will need more . . .' He paused. 'Macy?'

Macy hurriedly turned back towards him. 'Sorry, I thought I saw—'

She broke off at another minuscule flicker of light – this time inside the room. The little dot, no larger than a pinprick, briefly appeared on Cruz's shoulder. It reappeared a moment later on Renco's chest . . .

A laser. Someone outside was shining it through the window.

Dawning horror as she realised what it was doing. Like the low-powered beam on the stasers used against her in France, it was targeting people in the hall . . .

She jumped up. 'Shit! Everyone get out, somebody's about to—'

One of the windows shattered.

Something small and cylindrical arced through the room, hitting the polished wooden floor and skittering across it behind Cruz, Sayle and the others—

The anti-personnel grenade exploded.

28

Macy had instinctively covered her face and ducked just before the grenade detonated. Metal pellets ripped through the room, one catching her arm like a searing needle. But the people sitting before her took almost the entire force of the blast. Sayle and Renco were killed instantly, shredded by hundreds of hot steel fragments. Cruz caught more of the storm in his side as he jumped up from his chair. Belcourt and MacDuff were farther from the explosion, mostly shielded by their fellow elders, but still fell as pieces of shrapnel tore through their clothing and the skin beneath.

Macy recovered from the sense-pounding detonation, finding herself on the floor beside her overturned chair. Her arm burned where the pellet had caught her. The Knights had also been knocked down by the blast, equally dazed. 'Rain!' she cried, seeing her friend sprawled nearby. She scrambled to her. 'Oh my God, are you okay?'

Rain dizzily rose. 'What happened?'

Before Macy could answer, she heard Fernando's desperate cry of, '¡Papá!' She turned to see the leader of the Knights stumble towards his fallen father. Grey smoke wafted around him. Through it, Macy glimpsed the torn bodies of Sayle and Renco, and gasped in involuntary horror.

The younger Cruz crouched beside the elder. The wounded man was still breathing, but was covered in blood. 'Someone help me!' Fernando yelled.

'Get out, get out!' someone else shouted. Macy looked through

238

the dispersing haze to see one of the people she didn't know, a black-haired man, running for the exit—

Another window shattered – and he fell, two ragged bullet wounds in his back.

'Macy!' Emilian pulled her to her feet. He seemed unhurt. 'Jari! We've got our armour – we need to power up so everyone else can get out!'

He was already holding his whip. Macy saw her trikan on the floor. She hurried to pick it up. By the time she had, Emilian and Jari had transformed and readied their weapons. 'We need to block their fire,' called Emilian. 'Everyone, stay behind us and get to the door!'

Macy jumped up, willing her armour to activate. The metal scales seemed to flow over her body faster than ever, as if knowing the situation's urgency. 'Rain! Get everybody to somewhere safe, then get your own armour!' She joined the other two angels, standing between them to form a protective wall.

Her gaze went to the windows. Their attackers – the Brotherhood, it had to be – were somewhere outside. Did they have line of sight on them?

The answer came a moment later as Jari flinched, the shield around his armour flaring as a bullet was caught in front of his chest. Another ringing strike, then a third—

A pane of glass shattered – and a fourth bullet hit Macy.

Her armour halted it, but the impact was still forceful enough to knock her back. She gasped, then braced herself, ready for more incoming fire.

'Go, get out!' Jari shouted. 'Naima, run!'

His wife hesitated, not wanting to leave him, but then ducked into the cover of the angelic barricade before running for the exit. The others in the room followed her. Belcourt called out to Rain as he joined the exodus. 'Your mother's still in the bungalow! I'm going to find her!'

Rain was helping Fernando pull his father towards the door. 'Dad, no!' she shouted. 'Wait!' But he had already gone.

Meller ran to join them, regarding Renco's body with horror before assisting. Blood trailed along the floor behind the wounded Cruz. 'No, no,' the Spaniard rasped. 'Leave me. Get out, get out!'

'I'm not leaving you!' Fernando protested. The others had by now fled into the mansion; the little group reached the doors, shielded by Macy, Emilian and Jari.

'You have to,' said Cruz. He gripped his son's hand. 'You have to lead the Knights – protect everyone else. Go, go!'

Fernando looked down at him helplessly, then his expression became one of determination. He hauled his father into the hallway. 'Get him to the security office,' he told Meller. 'If anyone who isn't one of us comes in, shoot them!'

'I will,' was the Ukrainian's grim promise. Fernando reluctantly rose, leaving his father as he and Rain ran after Leni and Idris towards the Batcave.

Macy looked back, glimpsing them through the doorway. 'They're clear!'

'We'll have to fight,' warned Emilian. 'Are you ready?'

She raised her trikan. 'No, but I don't have much choice, do I?'

'It doesn't look like it. Jari, what about you?'

The Finn brought up his hammer in both hands. 'Let's kill these bastards!'

Fear speeding her breathing, Macy searched for the best exit route. The shots had come through two particular windows. Others at one side of the room had only been damaged by the grenade explosion, not bullets. 'Nobody's shooting at us from there,' she said, gesturing. 'If we go out that way, we'll be able to get clear.'

'No, we attack them head-on,' countered Emilian. 'Our armour can take it.'

'Not for ever, it can't! If they concentrate their—'

'Stop talking and move!' boomed Jari. He ran, extending his wings to rush in flight across the room – and swung his hammer at one of the bullet-wrecked windows. The metal head glowed with earth energy, releasing it in an explosive pulse that blasted wood and glass into splinters. He hurtled through the debris and rocketed out of sight.

Emilian started after him. 'Follow me—'

Macy had already chosen her own path, running for the side window. She threw her trikan to smash it and vaulted through the falling glass into the darkness outside before extending her wings and taking flight—

Bullets pounded against her armour. The impacts felt harder with each successive hit. She flinched, momentarily breathless. *Shit! Stay focused, or you'll lose the shield!* She fought to recover control. The sky rolled above: freedom, safety. Another effort of will, and she surged upwards, the mansion dropping away below her. Floodlights suddenly came on, casting a stark light all around it. Had Meller used them to dazzle the attackers?

One last round caught her, then the gunfire aimed at her ceased. She levelled out, circling the building two hundred feet up. The Brotherhood hadn't all been shooting into the hall. Another group was running towards an entrance on the mansion's opposite side – and muzzle flashes from the grounds told her there were at least another two groups of attackers. It wasn't a raid to capture a couple of young women, as in France; this was an all-out assault.

Where were Emilian and Jari? She looked back. Jari was easy to spot, wings alight as he swooped down at more muzzle flare behind some bushes. A flare from his swinging hammer – and the gunfire instantly stopped, two broken figures cartwheeling into the air amidst an eruption of soil and stones. The Finn whirled his weapon, then took off again. Flashes came from his shield as other intruders tracked him with their guns.

It took her a moment longer to spot Emilian. There: sweeping around behind trees at low level. He must be heading to attack someone—

Another flick of light, much closer. A laser spot on her arm. She'd been targeted again!

Wait – she was looking *down* at her arm. Something didn't make sense—

She had no time to think about it. More bullets struck her armour. The laser had told the intruders where she was. She accelerated, crossing above the villa. The illuminated rectangle of the courtyard passed below her. Figures ran out from the building into the central space.

Relief filled her. The other Knights had reached the Batcave and retrieved their armour and weapons. One, two, three, four angels took to the air, rapidly rising to meet her.

'Macy!' called the smallest: Rain. 'Are you okay?'

'Yeah,' she replied. The burning pain in her arm was all but forgotten in her adrenalin rush. 'What about you?'

'I'm all right. Where are Jari and Emilian?'

Macy pointed. 'Over there.'

'Then let's help them,' said Fernando, rising up alongside Rain. He readied his trident, the prongs opening with a sharp clack to expose the baraka between them. Leni flipped his moon blade over to power up its own bulbous pod, while the spiked knuckles on Idris's gauntlets surged with energy. Only Rain was left; she hesitated, then drew the sword from her back. 'Okay. Let's go!'

The group swept down towards the grounds. Macy decided to stay with Rain; the others split up to target different groups of attackers. The two men with ranged weapons were the first to strike back, Fernando and Leni unleashing their barakas. Crackling pulses of energy distorted the air as they tore through it. One intruder exploded with a wet thump as Leni's bolt hit him, ripped apart as if dynamite had detonated inside his body. The sound gave Macy a split-second nightmarish flashback to beneath the great red rock of Uluru in the Australian desert, when the leader of the Nephilim had used a baraka to kill a man trying to help her.

She forced the memory away, concentrating on the now. The second energy blast narrowly missed another black-clad attacker, but the force of its detonation on the ground still sent him tumbling over a bush. He did not have time to be thankful for his luck, as Fernando homed in on him. A swing of his trident – and the man's head was lopped from his shoulders.

'Shit!' Macy gasped. She had witnessed death before, too many times, but that did not make it any less shocking.

Rain seemed equally horrified, angling away from the scene. Macy followed, but still saw more of what the Knights were capable in battle. Idris dropped from flight as a man fired at him to roll beneath the spray of bullets, then launched himself into a twisting parkour somersault – and punched his target with one of his crackling gauntlets. Physical body armour was useless against the raw power of earth energy, the man's torso exploding. Idris rolled and jumped again, launching himself back into the air.

Other members of the Brotherhood opened fire on the newcomers, setting their shields strobing from multiple bullet impacts. Leni drew the brunt of the assault as he ascended, visibly flinching as the force of the strikes increased – then he abruptly veered and spun into a tree with a crunch of breaking branches.

'Rain!' cried Macy, alarmed. 'Leni's down!'

'I saw!' Rain changed course – heading for the cluster of men who had brought the Knight to earth. Macy did the same, suddenly scared that her friend was on a suicide mission and accelerating to back her up. She threw the trikan, guiding it to a target as she had in France – but this time deploying the blades. The weapon struck home, a man falling with a choked scream as it sliced into his chest. A moment later, Rain swung her sword – the glowing blade slicing cleanly through the trunk of the tree the attackers were using for concealment. The top half of the carob crashed down onto them.

Macy realised Rain had deliberately avoided making a directly lethal attack. But this was not the time to criticise or commend her restraint, as she saw Jari send another man flying with an explosive strike from his hammer – only to reel back as a blazing burst of bullets struck him. He staggered towards the mansion, shield visibly weakening as it took the rapid-fire onslaught . . .

The shooting stopped. Macy guessed the gunman had emptied his magazine in his full-auto fury. 'Jari!' she shouted. 'Take off now, while—'

Another member of the Brotherhood opened fire – but not with bullets. The grenade from his rifle's underbarrel launcher exploded against the villa's wall just below the eaves, ripping out a great chunk of brick and tile and cement—

The debris plunged to the ground – smashing down on top of Jari.

Even with his shield, the falling masonry hit hard enough to break one of his legs. He screamed. The heaviest piece of the wall was on top of him, pinning him down, the armour's energy field flaring as it tried to resist the crushing weight – then the light abruptly vanished. The hunk of brickwork dropped again, crushing flesh and bone. Jari let out a final gurgling rasp before he fell silent.

Macy gasped in horror, then climbed to escape the other guns that would now be hunting for her. How many men had the Brotherhood sent? There must be twenty, or more—

Another pinprick of light caught her, reflecting off the shimmering scales covering her arm. Again, she was looking down when she saw it – on the *upper* side of her armour. That meant it had to be coming from above . . .

She looked into the night sky. Nothing was visible. But there had to be something up there acting as a spotter—

'They're tracking us with a drone!' she yelled, accelerating upwards forcefully enough to make her armour pull painfully against her body. 'I'm going to take it out!'

Granit reached a side entrance to the mansion, two other men with him. 'Team one in entry position,' he said. 'Team two, are you ready?'

'Team two in position,' came the reply, but markers in his AR glasses had already told him the four men had reached their own ingress point. He quickly looked around to make a virtual survey of the grounds. Where were his opponents?

It was easy to pick them out from the assault group even without the differences in icon shape and colour. They were *flying*. After the unexpected encounter with the . . . whatever the hell they were, in France, he had demanded answers from his employer. The explanation, that his opponents were using advanced jetpack technology and experimental body armour, seemed increasingly implausible the more he saw of what they could do. They looked like *angels*, for God's sake! But he had demanded, and received, more money as compensation for the increased threat level; once GCM took on a job, it was seen through. Whether technological or supernatural, his targets would still be eliminated.

At least one already had been, it seemed. The drone providing overwatch had replaced one tracking marker with a blinking symbol signifying loss of contact. Granit had heard a grenade explosion moments earlier. Maybe the 'angel' had been returned to heaven – in pieces. Another was motionless some distance from the action. The mercenary leader briefly considered ordering the nearest men to find it and finish the job, but the ongoing battle required everyone's attention.

How many threats were left? Five tracks in the air, and a couple of additional targets were now fleeing across the grounds. Again, the latter were a lower priority, but once the other objectives were met, mopping-up would follow—

A sudden change in the AR overlay. Two of the fliers turned from red – in the confusion following the initial attack, the tags had been lost and everyone reclassified as hostile by the drone when reacquired – to blue. Momentary surprise, then he remembered his employer also had access to all the tactical data, and had just identified the primaries he wanted left unharmed. How he had determined that, Granit didn't know, but it wasn't important. 'Primaries have been tagged,' he warned. 'Fire on targets only.'

Confirmation came in from his men. One last check of the situation – one of the blue markers was making a wide circle clear of the house, the other ascending as if trying to flee – then he nodded to his companions. 'Team one, team two – go!'

One man covered the entrance with his suppressed gun as the other kicked the door open. Nobody was visible within. Had anyone been, they would have been dead moments later. The trio rushed inside.

Granit knew his objective's location: the top floor. The rear stairs, he'd been told, were to his right. The information was accurate. The three men hurried up through the mansion.

29

Fernando grunted as more bullets struck his armour. The shield took most of their force, but they still felt like punches to his gut. He swept down behind a stand of trees to break the gunmen's line of sight, but somehow they were still tracking him, another round tearing through foliage before hitting home. How many were attacking – and how could they still target him even when he was hidden?

'Fernando!' The Spaniard looked around as Emilian arrived alongside him. 'I just saw some of them going into the house. They must be trying to break into the vault!'

He swore. 'We can't let them take anything. Where are the others?'

'Leni got hit and went down somewhere near my bungalow. And – Jari's dead.'

Fernando drew in a shocked breath. The big Finn had always seemed invincible, even without his armour, but now . . . 'If they're going for the vault, there's only one way in and out – we can trap them.' The pair dropped lower, flying behind a bungalow. The muted rattle of suppressed fire finally stopped. A moment of respite, but Fernando knew it wouldn't last. 'Split up. You find Idris, I'll get Rain – and Macy.'

'Macy's up there,' said Emilian. He pointed above the villa.

Fernando saw her glow ascending high into the sky. 'What the hell is she doing?'

Macy kept climbing, coldness washing over her as she picked up speed. She didn't know how high up she would have to go, or even if her plan would work. But surely the best place for a drone to observe the entire estate would be directly above the mansion, giving it the widest field of view . . .

She could only guess her altitude as she looked down. Five hundred feet, six hundred? The villa was a hollow black rectangle below, the floodlights on its outer walls brightly illuminating its surroundings. But it was the central courtyard's glow that dominated her attention. She slowed, bringing herself over its centre. If the drone was beneath her, it would be revealed as a silhouette . . .

There. A dark spot, exposed by its parallax shift against the background.

She dropped towards it, readying her trikan. The spot took on form, a large diamond-shaped quadcopter. This was no toy, but a professional-grade piece of equipment. It hovered perhaps four hundred feet above the villa. From there, its Gorgon stare would have a view wide enough to take in the whole grounds, while still being able to pick out details – and track individual people, software spotting movement, identifying humans, and using a laser rangefinder to tag their range and position. That was how the attackers could be so accurate: they must have AR gear that let them see the drone's overwatch from their own perspective . . .

Not any more. She threw the trikan, deploying its blades – and smashed the quadcopter to pieces. One of its ruptured battery packs sprayed out a fizzing burst of sparks, flaming debris dropping towards the courtyard.

That should help even the odds. Now, she had to help the others.

Granit and his two men reached the top floor. He knew which door to go to, and opened it. Beyond was a library. One of his mission objectives involved the room, but not yet. There was something else to do first.

He went to one of the side doors. It was locked, but a small explosive charge quickly took care of the problem. He forced the smoking door open. A laptop and what he assumed to be servers were the first things he saw, but again they were not his objective.

The safe, however, was.

He knew the model. Heavy, solid, fireproof; it would take several minutes to cut open. None of that mattered if he had the combination, though.

Which he did.

He tapped in the code, then pulled sharply down on the handle. His employer's information was again accurate; the combination worked. He opened the weighty door. Inside was a hard drive in a rugged protective case. He could have simply taken it, but for whatever reason, his client had other instructions. He put the drive on the desk beside the laptop and took out a small, blocky device with a high-speed USB connector attached. The cable's other end, he attached to the drive. A red LED on the gadget lit up, flickering rapidly as data was copied onto it.

'Urgan, watch the corridor,' he ordered. 'Tarlev, set the firebomb. You know where to put it.'

Both men acknowledged and left the room. Granit turned his attention back to his own task, impatience growing as the seconds passed. The longer this took, the more risk of the defenders regrouping and fighting back—

Some of the symbols in his AR glasses suddenly vanished. He could still see the positions of his men via their GPS tags, but the overlay showing their targets had gone. He immediately knew what had happened. Someone had realised they were being tracked by a drone – and destroyed it.

The leaders of the other teams reported the same loss. No matter. Every GCM operator was an experienced soldier, able to perform without the high-tech crutches some armed forces had come to rely upon. 'Continue as planned,' he ordered. 'Take out any targets you see.'

'Sir, we can't tell the primaries from the targets any more,' one of his men replied. 'What do we do if—'

'If you're attacked,' Granit cut in firmly, 'defend yourself. With all necessary force.'

Rain shrieked as she came under fire, bullets smacking against her shield. She instinctively flew faster, ducking and swerving through trees as she made a wide loop around the mansion. A few last rounds whipped past her, then she was clear.

Where was everyone else? She climbed, searching. A glimpse of a halo through trees – but then she saw someone running along one of the footpaths, picked out by the little lights along it.

Cold fear hit her. She instantly recognised the man's limping gait.

Her father.

He was trying to reach their home, to find her mother. But from her elevated position, she could see something he couldn't.

Black-clad figures were moving through the trees towards him.

'Dad!' she cried. But he was too far away to hear. She changed direction, desperately chasing after him. '*Daddy!*'

The four men in Team Two clattered down a flight of stairs. A heavy vault door awaited them at the bottom. They had reached their objective.

One man taking up position to cover the stairs, the others quickly assembled the pieces of equipment they were carrying into one device. It was a thermal lance, a high-powered cutter capable of slicing through even the toughest steel. The mercenary holding the long tube of the lance itself lit the oxyacetylene torch at its head, another man opening the valve on a cylinder of compressed oxygen. Molten metal sprayed from the tube's tip as the steel rod inside it ignited, the pure oxygen feeding the flame rapidly bringing its temperature to over four thousand degrees Celsius.

The wielder brought the lance to the door and began to cut out the lock, the metal barrier melting away as if it were nothing more than a sheet of plastic.

Macy dropped back towards the house, looking for the other Knights. She spotted Idris making a rapid withdrawal skywards, shield flashing as it took hits. His gauntlets might deliver a literally explosive punch, but that was little use if sustained gunfire forced him away from any targets.

Where were the others? She slowed her descent, surveying the grounds – and saw another Knight swoop towards the mansion's roof and clamber in through a top-floor window. Was it Emilian? She flew to follow him—

A panicked cry reached her. She instantly knew the voice.

Rain.

Rain flew across the gardens towards her home. Her father reached the door, calling out his wife's name. Hana hurried out to join him. Both ran along the path, heading away from the mansion and the men attacking it as fast as they could—

Not fast enough. Her father's injury slowed him, her mother quickly drawing ahead. She slowed to wait for him, looking back.

The path's lights picked them both out in the darkness. Rain could see them clearly.

As could others.

Two men burst from bushes near her parents, guns raised. 'Mom! Dad!' she screamed. '*Run!*'

But instead her parents instinctively looked towards her voice, only registering her warning a moment later—

The gunmen fired.

Each only unleashed a three-round burst. It was enough. Lucien and Hana Belcourt both fell, bloody wounds erupting in their torsos.

Rain screamed. The sound instantly drew the mercenaries' attention – and fire. Bullets struck her shield. She was flying towards the shooters, most of the impacts around her head and upper body. The blows jarred her with increasing force, punches to her skull – then, stunned, she fell, tumbling to a painful stop on a dry lawn.

The men ran towards her. Momentary hesitation at seeing she was only a young woman, but then their faces hardened, weapons fixing upon her—

One of the mercenaries blew apart in a gory blast.

The earth energy detonation knocked his companion to the ground. Wings aglow, Fernando swept down at the fallen man – and snapped his trident's points together before driving the weapon through his chest with such force that it burst from his back and stabbed into the soil beneath him. The man let out an animalistic screech, limbs flailing before he slumped into the stillness of death.

Fernando yanked out the trident. 'Rain!' he shouted, hurrying towards her. 'Get up, get out of—'

He staggered as a blaze of full-auto fire hit him in the back.

Three more mercenaries had followed him, now angrily avenging their fallen comrades. Bursts of light came from the shield as it stopped the bullets, but with each ringing strike they became weaker, the impacts upon him stronger—

The flashes stopped.

Even with a residual earth energy charge, once the shield was gone the Atlantean armour's paper-thin scales offered almost no resistance to high-velocity rifle rounds. The wings' glow vanished, metal filaments buckling and snapping as they were hit. Fernando lurched drunkenly forward as bullets tore through his body. He stumbled for a couple of steps, then dropped to his knees, looking directly at Rain in silent pleading for her to run as he raised his arms high . . .

Another round exploded from his heart, shredding the armour covering it. He fell forward, collapsing lifelessly to the ground.

Rain screamed his name. The mercenaries rounded on her, guns finding their new target—

A golden blur in the air – and one of the men shrieked as his right arm was sliced off below the elbow, blood spouting from the stump.

Macy hurtled down from on high like a bird of prey. Her trikan was already changing direction, swinging hard to its right to carve a four-inch-deep gash up through the next man's chest and throat before making another sharp turn to smack into the side of the last man's head, one of the glowing blades punching into his brain. She yanked on the wire to snap the trikan back to her as she flew over the attackers. Two of them crumpled, dead or dying; the one-armed man fought through his shock, groping for his gun and fumbling to shake his severed hand from the grip so he could take hold of the trigger with his other—

She threw the trikan again. The metal disc hit his face with the force of a baseball bat. He toppled nervelessly backwards, nose mashed into an unrecognisable pulp.

Macy retrieved the trikan and dropped down beside Rain. She was frozen, staring in horror at the bodies before her. Her friend – and her family. 'Rain,' Macy said, forcing down her own shock. 'We've got to go.' The French woman didn't move. Macy put a hand on her shoulder; she flinched. 'Rain!'

Rain looked at her, eyes wide and tearful. 'Macy, they – they . . .'

'I know. But we need to move.' She took hold of Rain's arm and gently but firmly lifted her to her feet. 'I've got to find

Emilian. I think these assholes are raiding the house – he went into it after them. Come on. I'll get you to somewhere safe.'

She rose from the ground, maintaining her hold on Rain's arm. Trembling, Rain finally tore her gaze from the scene of carnage and ascended with her.

30

Granit regarded the hard drive with growing impatience. How much longer would this take? There must be a hell of a lot of data being transferred—

The copying device's flickering LED turned a solid green. Finally! He disconnected and pocketed it, then put the drive back in the safe, leaving its door open. Again, he wondered why he had been ordered to copy the data when he could have just taken the whole thing, denying it to their opponents as effectively as burning it.

His not to reason why. He was being paid – handsomely – to do what his client wished. Speaking of whom . . . He tapped his smartwatch again. 'I've copied the hard drive,' he reported when the connection was made. A glance through the doorway; Tarlev gave him a thumbs-up to confirm the firebomb had been set. 'Everything's ready in the archive. The other team is still cutting into the vault – they should only take—'

His employer interrupted. Granit listened . . . with increasing surprise as he was given new instructions. 'You want us to *withdraw*?' he exclaimed. 'But we'll have the vault open in less than two minutes!'

'The database was the primary objective,' said the voice in his earpiece. 'Everything else is irrelevant. No matter what happens, I have what I need. Get that data to me, now.'

A new emotion rose inside the Hungarian: anger. 'You mean the vault is just a *decoy*? And what about my men outside? Some of them have died! Were they just decoys too?'

'Compensation will be paid as agreed,' was the dismissive reply. 'Now, get out of there. I want that data uploaded within the hour.' The call ended.

Granit clenched his fists, tempted to close the safe to protect its contents out of spite, but professionalism won. He spoke to his men. 'This is Granit. Withdraw, withdraw. Get to the rendezvous point.'

'Sir, we've almost cut open the vault!' protested Team Two's leader, Dutroux.

'You have your orders. Move!' He strode from the anteroom. 'Where's the bomb?'

'Here.' Tarlev went to one particular shelf. The incendiary device was nestled amongst large and heavy books.

'Good. Start the timer, and let's go.'

Tarlev flicked a switch on the firebomb. A small digital timer began to count down. Granit and his companions hurried from the library and clattered down the stairs.

A moment later, Emilian emerged from another upper-floor room and headed with purpose for the archive.

Macy and Rain touched down on a flat section of roof atop one of the mansion's corner towers. 'They won't be able to see you up here,' said Macy. 'Wait for me.'

She was about to take off again when Rain clutched her hand, the intersecting shields flickering. 'Don't go, please!'

'I *have* to. I'm sorry. I'll come back as soon as I can, but I need to find Emilian.' She squeezed her friend's hand, then pulled free. 'Stay hidden.'

She launched herself from the roof, flying to the open window she had seen Emilian enter.

The four men outside the vault abandoned the thermal lance and hurried up the stairs. None could guess why they had been ordered to withdraw moments before achieving their objective, but Granit's command was clear, so they obeyed. The mercenary leader engendered loyalty in the kind of men he hired – because he was exactly as ruthless and brutal as they were.

Dutroux led the way, reaching the ground floor. Gun raised, he swung out to cover the hallway beyond—

His torso blew apart as one of Idris Benichou's gauntleted fists pounded into his chest.

The blast and the shower of gore and smashed bone knocked the men behind him back down the stairs. The remains of Dutroux fell wetly to the floor as Idris vaulted over him, delivering another explosive punch to the second mercenary's head. Blood and glistening grey matter splattered the stairwell. The headless body crumpled. Idris slashed one gauntlet's spikes across the third man's throat, then jumped again. The last man recovered and aimed where he expected his attacker to fall, firing—

The bullets passed under his target. Wings extending with a snap, the Algerian broke free of gravity and hurtled onward, kicking the mercenary hard in the face. He fell backwards down the steps. A crack echoed through the stairwell as one of his wrists broke. He let out a snarl of pain—

Both he and the sound were short-lived. Idris dropped, another blow from his spiked fist smashing onto the top of his skull. Both gauntlets had expended their stored explosive power, but there was still enough earth energy surging through the metal spikes to punch through a few millimetres of bone. The final merc spasmed as if electrocuted, then slumped, twitching.

Breathing heavily, Idris regarded the ruined bodies, then hurried down the stairs. To his surprise, the vault door was still closed, a ragged arc burned almost all the way around the lock. Why had they withdrawn when they were so close to their prize?

Macy clambered in through the window. The room was an office, an open door leading to a hallway. She ran to it, about to call out to Emilian – then caught herself. There could be more intruders, and she had just seen first-hand that concentrated gunfire was lethal even against the Knights' armour.

Instead she peered warily out. No one in sight. She emerged and looked nervously around a corner.

She recognised the hallway from the previous night. The back staircase was not far ahead. Beyond it, she saw that the archive's door was open. Was Emilian inside – or were the raiders stealing something from the room?

Trikan ready, she hurried down the hall. 'Emilian! Are you there?'

A sound ahead, movement. She stopped, ready to throw her weapon – but the person who emerged from the archive was one of the Knights, face shrouded in light. 'Emilian?'

The figure detransformed: it was the Dutchman. 'Macy!' he said, surprised to see her. 'We have to get out of here – they've planted a bomb!'

She also powered down her armour to face him directly. 'What?'

'I'm going to try to defuse it, but it'll go off in less than thirty seconds. You, go!' He hurried towards her.

'Wait, thirty seconds? Don't defuse it, just get it out of here. We can *fly*!' She broke into a run.

'No, wait, it's too—' He moved to block her, but she jinked past him, rushing into the archive.

Where was it? Nowhere in immediate sight. She hurried towards the room's far end, seeing it on one of the protruding shelf units. A Thermos-sized metal cylinder had a small digital timer affixed to it – along with a slab of something she had a horrible feeling was explosive.

'Bad idea,' she told herself, even as she went to it. What did the timer say?

Seventeen seconds. '*Very* bad idea!'

But she had already grabbed the device. Too late, some part of her mind informed by her father warned that it might be booby-trapped. But she was still alive a second later. Fifteen to go, and now she had to get out, fast—

The window was closed. She ran at it all the same, willing her armour to activate. The bands and torc split into their component scales, chittering over her, joining. She felt its shimmering field of earth energy spring to life around her . . .

As she dived at the window.

The shield protected her – but the wooden frame and panes of glass still proved an unexpectedly tough obstacle, years of seeing people thrown through windows in movies not even remotely preparing her for the reality. She smashed through it, but lacked the momentum to make it all the way outside. Her stomach hit the sill, spikes of glass crunching and snapping under her. Only the Atlantean armour saved her guts from being ripped open. She rolled out, debris crashing around her.

And fell.

Windows whipped past. Macy gasped, too scared to scream – then panicked instinct as much as memory took control. Leni had caught himself from just as high a drop—

Her wings deployed almost before she had consciously finished the thought. The armour suddenly strained around her body and limbs as it tried to halt her fall. But she was still dropping, the floodlit ground rushing at her . . .

She twisted, changing direction as well as orientation – and skimmed over a lawn for a moment, tearing up grass, before ascending.

There was no time to exult over her survival. She focused, picking up speed as she flew straight up into the night sky. How long did she have left? She raised the bomb. Her halo gave off enough light to show the timer.

Four seconds. Three.

Shit!

She threw the device upwards – then turned away as hard as she could—

The bomb exploded.

The blast hit as hard as if she had fallen onto concrete. Stunned, she desperately battled to stay airborne—

Agony seared through her leg.

Macy screamed, twisting to see why – and finding a roiling fireball in the air behind her, liquid incendiary streaks arcing towards the earth. One had caught her. Flames lashed in her slipstream, intense heat seeping between the armour's scales. She swatted desperately at them, trying to snuff them out, but succeeded only in scorching her hand. *Get it off me, get it off,* her dazed, panicking mind cried—

The armour obeyed her will – and detransformed.

The part covering her leg retreated to reform the band around her ankle. The flames didn't vanish with it. They instead caught her jeans, searing the fabric – and the skin beneath. She screamed again, the pain almost overpowering the sensation of falling . . .

Almost. She was plunging towards the ground, wind whipping through her hair. She had to transform. Transform! But nothing happened, her mind overpowered by the terrible burning—

A rushing light in her peripheral vision – and the breath was knocked from her lungs as someone slammed into her.

Arms clenched tightly around her body. One of the Knights had caught her. But the impact had been like a football tackle, winding them both. And she was still falling. Her rescuer had only been able to slow her, not stop—

Water exploded around her.

Her saviour had guided her to one of the ponds in the grounds. Macy choked and spluttered as she went under. The Knight released her. She rolled, kicking and flailing, finding the bottom of the pond and bringing herself upright. The water was chest-deep. She stood, sweeping wet hair from her face, and wiped her eyes.

She had expected her rescuer to be Emilian. But it was Rain. The French woman clumsily pulled herself up onto the pool's edge. 'Macy,' she gasped. 'Are you okay?'

'Yeah,' Macy said automatically, solely on the grounds that she was still alive. 'Actually, no,' she corrected as pain pulsed excruciatingly in her leg. The fire was out, but the damage it had done remained. 'Oh, God, that hurts.'

She crawled from the pond, flopping down on her side – then jerked back up as she remembered they were far from out of danger. 'Oh, shit! Where are the Brotherhood? We've got to get out of here, find somewhere safe—'

Rain put a reassuring hand on her arm. 'The bad guys ran off. I think they're all gone.'

'What?' Macy frowned. 'Why? They wouldn't have done all this just to put a bomb in the archive—'

The answer came to them both simultaneously. 'The vault!' Rain gasped. 'They must have come to raid the vault!'

Macy forced herself to stand, scanning her surroundings for any sign of more gunmen. But her friend was right; nobody was there. 'We've got to get back to the house.' They started unsteadily towards the villa. 'Are you all right?'

It took a moment for Rain to answer. 'No,' she said, voice quavering. 'But – but I can't think about it right now. We need to find the others.'

Macy put an arm over her shoulders, to support herself physically – and Rain emotionally. 'I'm with you,' she said. 'I'll stay with you.'

The reply was little more than a whisper. 'Thank you.'

Macy was still on full alert as they crossed the grounds. But the Brotherhood had indeed withdrawn. An armoured figure emerged from the villa's main entrance as they approached. 'Idris!' called Rain. 'What happened? Where are the others?'

'Oleksiy is with Mateo in the security office,' the Algerian told them. 'Some of the others managed to hide. I haven't found everyone yet.'

They entered the building. 'What about the vault?' Macy asked. 'Did they steal anything?'

Idris shook his head. 'They tried to cut the door open, but left before they finished.'

'Why would they leave when they almost had what they wanted?'

'We drove them away.'

'We didn't, though,' Macy told him. 'They were kicking our—' She stopped, not wanting to appear disrespectful. 'I . . . have some bad news.'

Idris's halo disappeared, his armour shrinking away as he looked her directly in the eye. 'What has happened?' he asked, voice quiet and controlled.

'Jari's dead. And so is Fernando.' She felt Rain tense. 'Leni might be hurt; I don't know. And . . . other people have been killed too.'

He remained statue-still for several seconds. Rain started to quiver. Macy held her more tightly, trying to comfort her. Finally, Idris spoke. 'We must tell Mateo,' he said, jaw clenched. 'Come with me.'

He led the two women through the house. Macy looked around at the sound of running footsteps. Emilian hurried down the stairs to them. 'Macy!' he said. 'Are you okay? You could have been killed! You should have—'

'That doesn't matter right now,' she told him firmly.

His eyes widened in momentary anger, but then he nodded. 'Yes, okay. Where are the others?'

Before Macy could reply, Idris reached a door and called out to those beyond. It opened, revealing Meller. The Ukrainian held a sub-machine gun. He regarded the group with concern. 'They have left the grounds,' he said, glancing towards a bank of security monitors. 'Is everyone all right?'

'No,' said Macy. MacDuff and one of the people she didn't know were in the room as well. She guided Rain to a chair, then came around a desk. Cruz was lying on his back behind it, a rolled-up jacket acting as a makeshift pillow. Blood from the multiple shrapnel wounds had seeped through his clothing to the floor. 'Oh, God! We need to get him to a hospital.'

Cruz weakly turned his head towards her. 'It is too late for me,' he whispered. 'And we cannot let the authorities know what has happened here. There will be . . . too many questions.'

'But people have died!' she protested. 'You can't just cover that up!'

'We have to,' was Meller's grim reply. 'I will take care of the bodies. I have experience, from the war.'

Macy knelt beside Cruz. 'I have to tell you something,' she said. 'One of the people who died was . . .' Her voice cracked with emotion. 'It was Fernando.'

Cruz's whole body sagged. 'Fernando? Oh, no, no . . .' His trembling lips clenched tight, a tear running down his cheek. '*Mi hijo* . . . But I will soon be with him again. Oh . . .'

Macy also started to cry, clutching his hand. His skin felt cold. 'I'm so sorry.'

Emilian knelt beside her. 'Jari is dead too,' he told the Spaniard quietly. 'And Lucien, and Hana. But . . . Macy saved Rain's life. And she saved the whole history of the Knights. They planted a bomb in the archive. She got it away before it exploded.'

Cruz looked across to the huddled Rain, then back at Macy. 'You . . . saved Rain?'

'I tried to save everyone,' Macy whispered, shame at her failure welling within her. The image of Fernando and Rain's parents, sprawled dead on the darkened lawn, came unbidden to her mind. 'I . . . I couldn't.'

He seemed to sense her feelings – and gripped her hand with surprising firmness, despite his injuries. 'No, you did . . . you did everything you could. And . . . you saved a child as well. You did *more* than the rest of us would have. You are a hero, Macy – you are a *Knight*. I was wrong. You are more than worthy of joining us. If . . . you will forgive us for doubting you.'

Macy squeezed his hand, feeling tears roll down her cheeks. 'Of course I will.'

He managed a faint smile through his pain. 'Good. Emilian?'

The Dutchman lifted his head. 'Yes, Mateo. I'm here.'

'With Fernando and Jari gone, you are now the . . . the most experienced of the Knights. You are their new leader. Protect them – and protect our legacy.'

Emilian reacted with startlement, then uncertainty. 'Me? But – I . . . will do my best,' he said.

'I know you will.' Cruz closed his eyes. 'We have taught you all we can. Honour us . . . remember . . . us . . .'

Each word was quieter than the last, his final utterance a mere whisper. Then he fell silent. His hold on Macy's hand went slack. 'Oh, God,' she said, as the awful reality sank in.

A sharp breath told her that Rain had also realised it. 'Is he . . . ?'

Macy looked sadly at her friend. 'I'm sorry. I'm sorry . . .'

Rain shuddered, trying and failing to hold back tears, then hunched up more tightly into a ball of grief and loss.

Emilian stared at Cruz's motionless body for a long moment. Then he stood. 'We have to leave here – it isn't safe. We need to get to our fallback location.' He turned to MacDuff and Meller. 'Euripides, come with us, and bring your database – the Brotherhood tried to destroy it, so something in it must be very important. Oleksiy, secure the grounds, then . . . do what needs to be done with the bodies. I will take the rest of the Knights to Barreiro.'

'Are you sure that's the best course of action, Emilian?' MacDuff's question was gentle, but pointed.

The Dutchman's voice became more firm. 'You heard Mateo. I am the new leader of the Knights. I didn't ask for it, but . . . I have to protect everyone who is left.' He looked down at Macy, extending a hand to her. She hesitantly released Cruz from her grip and took it. He raised her to her feet. 'Macy, help Rain. We have to go.'

Macy went to her friend, comforting her as Emilian issued more orders.

31

The Knights' fallback location was a far cry from the splendour of the villa. To Macy, it looked like a factory, one that had been abandoned for some time. It occupied a stretch of largely derelict industrial waterfront in the town of Barreiro, across the estuary from Lisbon. 'Here we are,' said Emilian, getting back into the SUV after unlocking a gate. 'It might not look nice, but it has everything we need.' He drove into the darkened outer grounds, heading through a short tunnel in one of the factory's walls to enter a long central courtyard. A second SUV, driven by MacDuff, followed. The two vehicles parked, and everyone got out.

Emilian deactivated a security system and led the way into one of the building's wings, switching on lights. 'There are living quarters upstairs,' he told Macy. 'Go with the others and find a room. I need to talk to Oleksiy at the villa. Everyone come to me in the office when you're ready.'

'Okay,' Macy replied. She started up the stairs with Rain as the Dutchman continued into the building.

A large space on the top floor had been divided into smaller rooms, each containing two beds and storage facilities. 'Do you want to share?' Macy asked Rain. Her friend had barely spoken during the drive, alternating between blank-faced silence and fits of crying. The redhead had offered comfort when wanted, space otherwise. Neither felt like enough.

The French woman nodded. 'Thank you. I don't want to be on my own.'

Macy gave her a sympathetic smile. 'I'll help you with your stuff.'

There were enough rooms for the others who had also come from the estate – Idris, Leni, Naima and MacDuff – not to have to share. The place had been intended to house the families and support staff of the Knights as well as the guardians themselves. That there were empty spaces was a grim, silent reminder of their losses.

Macy and Rain put their belongings into one of the dorm rooms, then explored their immediate surroundings, finding a kitchen and bathroom facilities. The food stored in the former was canned, dried or deep-frozen, putting Macy in mind of television shows about Doomsday preppers, but it was reassuring in some small way that they wouldn't go hungry. Once everyone else was ready, they went in search of Emilian. 'Have you been here before?' Macy asked Rain as they headed downstairs.

'No,' she replied. 'I knew we had this place for emergencies, but I never came here. I suppose I hoped I would never need to,' she added, with a sigh.

Macy gave her hand a sympathetic squeeze as they reached the bottom of the stairs, then they went through a door with a hefty locking bar beside a large roller shutter, entering what had once been the old factory's main floor. It was a long, high space with a vaulted ceiling, catwalks running along the side walls at two higher levels with doors to both the building's wings. A row of large windows looked across the courtyard, several doubling as entrances. A few old and dusty machines of indeterminate function were still in place, but most of the floor space had been cleared. It was now a storage area, numerous crates and pallets covered by tarpaulins. She also saw a couple of similarly shrouded cars and what appeared to be a boat. Emergency equipment for the Knights, she assumed.

A door at the far end was open, lights on beyond. MacDuff

caught up with them. 'Through there,' he said. 'The office is on the top floor.'

'You've been here before?' Macy asked him.

'Aye, I keep backups of my work here.' He held up the hard drive from the archive. 'I hear you saved this, and a lot of other stuff, from being blown up or burned to a cinder. Thank you.'

'Thanks,' she echoed. 'Although . . .'

'What?'

'I don't know. It's just weird that those assholes left after planting the bomb, and didn't even bother to finish breaking into the vault. Like they thought destroying the archive was more important than stealing the Atlantean artefacts.'

'Why would they do that?'

'Beats me. Like I said, it seemed weird.'

They went through the door, MacDuff leading the way up more stairs. Voices came from a room along a hallway on the top floor. 'Emilian?' said MacDuff as he entered. 'We're here.'

'Good.' Emilian, still in his biker jacket, stood before a large screen, Meller's three-dimensional image almost as clear as if he were in the room as well. 'Oleksiy and some of the others are cleaning up,' he told MacDuff. 'They'll dispose of the Brotherhood.' He noticed that Macy and Rain had entered behind the Scot. 'But they'll . . . take special care of our people,' he said, somewhat awkwardly. The others filed into the room as well. 'You're all here. Good. Sit down. Oleksiy, stay on the line. You'll need to know the full situation.'

Everyone found seats. 'So, what *is* the situation?' asked Naima. Like Rain, she had been crying, but her grief over her husband's death was masked by a stony military professionalism.

'This is what we know,' said Emilian. 'We were attacked by a large group from the Brotherhood of Selasphoros. They tried to break into the vault, but didn't manage to cut through the lock.

They *did* plant a firebomb in the archive – which Macy got rid of just before it went off.' He gave her an appreciative nod, before turning to MacDuff. 'Euripides, you thought they'd done something else in the archive.'

'Aye,' said MacDuff, holding up the hard drive. 'They'd managed to open the safe – how, I don't know. That model should take hours to crack without the combination. They probably thought we'd think they opened it so this drive would be destroyed by the fire. But something felt wrong. I have a wee bit of OCD – I always put the drive back nice and square inside the safe. When I checked it, though, it was on the skew. Someone had taken it out – then put it back, not quite right. Now, I wondered, why would they do that? So when I plugged it in to my laptop, I checked the drive's access logs. Imagine my surprise when I saw they'd connected it to something – and copied *everything*.'

'They have your whole database?' Meller asked, alarmed.

MacDuff nodded. 'Every last byte. A perfect copy. And then they put the drive back, meaning to destroy it. If it hadn't been for Macy, we would never have known.'

'But you have a backup here,' said Rain.

'Aye. But it's not up to date. I only copy it every few months because, well, it's a pain in the arse coming all the way down here,' he admitted. 'That'll teach me to be lazy. And the Brotherhood would have the most recent version – while we wouldn't know they had it.'

'What could they use it for?' asked Macy.

'They could do what I do,' MacDuff told her. 'Find people with the Atlantean gene. People like you. There's decades of work in the database. All my genealogical records, DNA samples from all over the world. If you know how to analyse that data, you can track the movements of lineages over time, work out family connections . . . basically, locate people with strong enough potential to become a Knight.'

'And then kill them,' Emilian intoned.

Expressions of dismay filled the room. 'We have to get it back,' said Idris. 'Or destroy it.'

'But we don't know where they've gone,' Leni countered.

'Their headquarters, in Rome,' the Algerian insisted. 'We should go there, and attack – before they can be ready for us.'

'We don't know that they'd take it there,' said MacDuff. 'They probably have safehouses like this one.'

Emilian began to say something, then paused. 'What is it?' Macy asked.

'I just remembered something. The bomb they planted in the archive – it was the same section we looked at yesterday. About Afrasiab.' He looked at her in realisation. 'They were trying to destroy our records of Afrasiab! And we know your mother was also looking at the stories of Afrasiab for the Brotherhood – and no, I'm not saying she had anything to do with what happened tonight,' he said before Macy could interject. 'But it can't be a coincidence. The Brotherhood is trying to find the rebel king – and they tried to stop us from doing the same. All of this is about Afrasiab.'

'They're looking for the Iron Palace,' Macy realised, remembering what she had read. 'And Afrasiab's staff – the one that could supposedly control the weather.'

'*Our* staff,' cut in Idris firmly. 'Afrasiab stole it.'

'You know about him?'

'We all do,' said Rain. 'We've learned about the history of the Knights. There wasn't a record of the Iron Palace's location – not accurate enough to find it, anyway. But it might not be a place we want to find. Some of the Knights of that time died there.'

'Except . . . maybe now someone else can find it,' said Macy, with dawning concern. 'My mom's put the pieces together. The

IHA had something, the Brotherhood had something else – and now they've got your database too,' she said to MacDuff. 'Could they use that to figure out where it is?'

'Aye, I suppose,' he replied. 'If you identify enough of Afrasiab's descendants, you could track their genealogical history to follow their dispersion across the world over time. Keep going back far enough . . . oh, Christ.' He put a yellowed knuckle to his mouth, realising the full implications. 'They would move towards their point of origin. You can just follow the lines to where they intersect. With enough data, you can pinpoint where a particular genetic line came from to within a few miles; I've done it before. And I've collected a *lot* of data.'

'So now they can find Afrasiab's stronghold?' said Emilian. 'They can find the Iron Palace?'

'It's a definite possibility, yes.'

Emilian was still, thinking – then straightened. 'We have to find it first,' he said. 'They've done all of this because they want the staff of Afrasiab. They want to control the weather!'

The statement was greeted with stunned silence. 'You're right,' said Idris after a moment. 'We can't let them find it. Not after what they've done.'

'But . . . you're saying we should take direct action,' said Meller. 'Mateo and the others said we shouldn't do that.'

'Mateo changed his mind about Macy before he died,' Emilian said. 'He would have changed his mind about this too. The Brotherhood has attacked us. We can't just hide out in our nice estate any more. They didn't only kill Mateo, remember. They killed James – your friend. They killed Fernando, *my* friend. And Jari,' a nod to Naima, 'and Lucien and Hana.' Rain clenched her fists, nails digging into her palms. 'And the others too. They would have killed us *all* if they could.'

Meller looked uncomfortable, but nodded. 'All right. What do you want to do?'

'We do what I said. We find the Iron Palace before the Brotherhood.'

'And then we deal with them,' said Naima in a low, dangerous voice.

'Yeah,' the Dutchman agreed. 'We deal with them.'

Macy looked around the room, wondering if there would be any objectors. There were none; even Rain said nothing. She turned to MacDuff. 'So I guess you need to analyse your database. Can you track Afrasiab's descendants back to the Iron Palace?'

'Aye, probably,' he said. 'I'll need to compile a big enough sample size of potential candidates, then identify DNA matches, cross-check everything against the genealogical records, collate all the results as geographical vectors, and then work that back over time to locate the point of origin.' Sarcasm entered his voice. 'Shouldnae take me more than three or four months.'

His answer was not well received. 'We don't have three or four months!' protested Leni. 'Can't you do it faster?'

'If I had a faster computer, sure. But even if I had a super-computer, it would still take a couple of weeks. I'm talking a *lot* of very complex data . . .'

Macy jumped up in her seat with sudden excitement. 'There might be a way to speed things up,' she said. 'I know someone who owns the world's most powerful quantum computer . . .'

Macy had no idea whether Rafael Loost would respond to her call. It was entirely possible he had already forgotten her. But he had spent ten million dollars at nothing more than her suggestion. Trillionaire or not, he would surely remember *that*.

She went into her dorm room for privacy. Trepidation as she found his name in her Uzz contacts and tapped on it. He could be busy; he might turn her down; he might simply be asleep. It was well after midnight in Portugal, but when was night when you were in space, orbiting the planet every ninety minutes?

She expected someone to be screening his calls. So it came as a surprise when the man himself appeared on her phone's screen, the earth rolling beyond the panoramic porthole. 'Hello?' he said.

'Hi,' she said, trying not to seem taken aback. 'Sorry, I hope I'm not interrupting. I hope you don't mind my calling. I hope you even remember who I am!'

Loost smiled. 'Macy Wilde Chase, wants to change the world, convinced me to donate ten million dollars to Cool the Planet. You made an impression.'

'I did? Oh, ha, good.' She laughed nervously, but then the seriousness of the situation forced her back on track. 'I'm calling because . . . I'd like to ask a favour. And I'm sure people say that to you all the time, but I'm not asking for money!' she added, awkward again. 'It's a group I'm involved with, friends of mine: some genealogists. They help archaeologists like my mom with genetic research. They need to analyse some data. It would normally take them months to do it, but there's some time pressure, and they need it as quickly as possible. So I was wondering, and I know this is a big ask, but . . . you have the world's fastest computer. Is there anything you could do to help them?'

He regarded her quizzically. 'You want me to get my company to do a rush-job on some data analysis, jumping the line ahead of major corporations and governments, and probably for free, even though quantum computer time is charged at a million dollars per minute. Am I right?'

Embarrassment gripped her. 'Well, when you put it that way, I . . . look like an absolute idiot, don't I? I'm sorry for wasting your time.'

He laughed. 'No, no! Don't hang up.' She froze her thumb over the end-call button, having been about to do exactly that. 'I was just seeing how you would react. If this had been a grift, you would have expected me to say no, and already had some argument to try to convince me. But your motives were genuine; you were hoping I'd say yes, but just hadn't thought far enough ahead.'

She still felt foolish. 'I can pay for it,' she said, hoping that was true; how many minutes of computer time could she afford? 'But if there's any way you could make it an urgent job—'

Loost held up both hands. 'Don't worry. I'll do it.'

'Really?'

'There's a certain amount of downtime built into the system. Sometimes, clients need results before an unexpected deadline. And I won't even charge you. I already spent ten million dollars at your suggestion. What's a few million more on top?'

To most people, a lot, she thought, but decided not to criticise his generosity. 'Wow. Thank you. I didn't expect you to say yes.'

A wry grin. 'Yes, you did, or you wouldn't have called me.' He leaned back, slowly drifting in zero gravity. 'Now, what data do you need to analyse?'

The others had congregated in the kitchen; Macy excitedly rushed in. 'He'll do it!' she said.

'He will?' said MacDuff, surprised.

'Yeah! I've got all the details of how to send the data to his company; I'll forward it to you.'

'You didn't tell him about us, did you?' asked Emilian warily. 'About the Knights, or why we need to track Afrasiab's descendants?'

'No, of course not. I just said you were genealogist friends of mine. He didn't ask for more details. All he needs to know – or rather, what you need to tell his company – are the search parameters. He even said he'll do it for free.'

MacDuff raised his eyebrows. 'Really? Doesn't sound like any billionaire – sorry, trillionaire – I've ever heard of. They don't get rich by doing favours.'

'He's not like that,' Macy insisted. 'He gave ten million dollars to charity just because I mentioned it.'

'Oh, aye? He probably makes more back in interest in a day. And he'll get to claim the donation against his taxes.' A cynical snort. 'Assuming he pays any, which I doubt. I mean, the man lives in space! Who would he pay them to, Darth Vader?'

'It doesn't matter,' said Macy, becoming annoyed. 'He's agreed to do it, and that's what counts. So you need to send the database. The sooner you start, the sooner we'll get a result.'

MacDuff made a sour face at being told what to do, but nevertheless took out his phone. 'All right then, boss. Send me the info, and I'll get started.'

'How long will it take?' asked Rain.

'He wasn't sure,' Macy replied. 'It depends how it can be fitted in with other jobs. Oh,' she said, remembering, 'and I also asked him to tell me if anyone else came to his company with the same data. I said there was an academic prize involved, and you needed it quickly because someone hacked your servers and stole it, to try to beat you to the results.'

'Good thinking,' said Leni, nodding.

'This is great,' Emilian told Macy. 'Thank you.'

'I just hope it's enough,' she said.

'I'm sure it will be. Now, we should try to get some sleep.' His face hardened. 'Tomorrow . . . we fight back against the Brother-hood.'

32

Turkmenistan

Several blasts of the ship's horn jarred Nina from her unsettled sleep. 'Eddie?' she gasped, jolting upright. The cabin's only illumination was a faint emergency light above the door.

'I'm here, love,' came his voice from below. He swung out of his bunk and stood beside her. 'You all right?'

'Yeah. What time is it?'

'About one.'

'What, in the afternoon?' She was startled that she had slept for so long under the stressful circumstances. 'Are we there?'

'In sight,' he said. 'I went out for a look a bit ago. Could be a while before we dock, though. Depends how many ships are in front of us.'

'Great. I really want to be stuck aboard a rusty tin can that smells of diesel and feet.'

'I'll change my socks as soon as I can, I promise,' he said with a grin. 'Have some breakfast, though. You need to eat and drink.'

She was not in the mood to do so, but accepted that he was right. The bag Gasimov had provided was stuffed with provisions, including enough food – however junky and unappetising – to last for a few days, as well as several plastic bottles of water. Once she was done, she visited the nearby head to use the toilet and clean her teeth, then went with Eddie up to the deck. The sun was high overhead, the ship's steel structure giving off waves of nauseating heat. A long sandy spit to the west formed a natural breakwater, several ships waiting around them in the outer harbour.

Nina was concerned only with her phone, though. 'Shit,' she sighed. 'No reception.'

'We should get some once we dock,' Eddie assured her. 'I know – I want to hear from Macy too. Just hope she got our messages.'

'Yeah.' She regarded what lay ahead. Turkmenbashi stretched along the coast to the north, ragged brown hills rising beyond. She knew little about the country, or what to expect. 'Have you been here before?'

'Once. Not for long – I was heading through to a job somewhere else.' The Yorkshireman had embarked on a globetrotting career as a mercenary for a few years after leaving the SAS. It was a part of his life he rarely spoke about, and Nina knew better than to ask for details. 'Wasn't a fan. That was in the "mad dictator building massive rotating golden statues of himself and renaming April after his mum" phase, mind. Although I don't think it's got much better since. Just a normal corrupt dictatorship rather than the batshit kind. The ordinary people seemed fine, which is pretty much the case anywhere. It's the arseholes who work for the government we have to be careful of.'

'Which is pretty much the case anywhere,' she said, managing a faint smile.

They found shade beneath a walkway and waited, nothing else to do except watch the ponderous movements of ships on the shimmering sea. Eventually, their own vessel shuddered as its engines came to life. More warning blasts from the horn, and it started towards the grey slab of Turkmenbashi's seaport. The freighter was about a mile from shore when Nina thought to try her phone again. It had a bare minimum of reception, connecting to one of the local cellular networks. Dismay followed immediately, though: Macy had not responded to any of her messages. 'Me neither,' Eddie told her gloomily as he checked his own device.

'I still need to call Oswald,' she said. She brought up the diplomat's contact info.

Seretse was soon on the line. 'Good morning, Nina. Or is it afternoon? Where are you?'

'Afternoon,' she replied. 'We're just coming into Turkmenistan. We'll be docking soon.'

'Did you manage to make arrangements with the local authorities for entry visas and the like?'

'Ah . . . let's say one of Eddie's friends handled that side of things.'

'I see. Do try not to be arrested, then. I would hate for you to miss the anniversary event.'

'I'll do my best, Oswald. Did you arrange what I needed?'

'I did. One of my contacts will provide you with a vehicle and suitable equipment. He is presently in Dashoguz, near the northern border. The search area you located is about four hours' drive away. He just needs to know where to meet you.'

'I'll tell him as soon as I know myself,' Nina said, semi-apologetically. 'I need to check satellite imagery, but I haven't had an internet connection.'

'Keep me informed of your progress. And Nina?'

'Yes?'

'Do please be careful. You are below the radar, so to speak; I will not be able to provide help should you experience any difficulty with the Turkmenistani authorities.'

'I'll keep that in mind, Oswald,' was her rueful reply. 'Talk to you soon.'

She ended the call, then checked her phone again. An icon showed she had a data connection. It was not what she was used to: 6G networks had come online in the West in the previous few years, whereas Turkmenistan was still using the 4G standard of over two decades earlier. It would do. When she discovered Atlantis a quarter of a century before, she hadn't even yet bought her first iPhone. Access to information on the move was a luxury she had managed without, however crazy that might sound to someone of Macy's generation . . .

The thought of her daughter dampened her mood again. Why hadn't she replied? All manner of terrible scenarios presented themselves. She forced them back. Work would hold them at bay.

She looked to shore. The seaport grew slowly but steadily larger as the freighter plodded towards it. 'Okay,' she told Eddie. 'I'll get my notes. Then, I'm going to work out where the hell we actually need to go.'

The ship took over an hour finally to make port. Nina made good use of the time, the task becoming gradually less frustrating as her data connection improved. By the time the crew began to bustle with the relief of completing another voyage, she had found what she needed – more or less.

'I think it's somewhere here,' she said, showing Eddie a roughly V-shaped feature in the otherwise blank expanse of the Karakum. She had switched the map from satellite view to topographic, displaying the landscape's height. Most of the desert was practically flat, with variations measured in tens of metres at most, but what she had found was considerably higher, jutting out into the sandy plain like a dock into a harbour.

He regarded the image. 'Is that a canyon?'

'Kind of. The northern side is about a hundred metres higher than the southern – but there are parts in between that are genuine depressions, sixty, seventy metres below sea level. It's the only place with enough of an elevation change to allow for a cave entrance as big as the one the Brotherhood described.' She zoomed out the map. The contours of the canyon's northern edge stood out clearly, a dark tooth against the paler striations of the surrounding desert. 'The nearest railroad station is here – Ruhnama.' She indicated a marker she had placed earlier. 'There isn't much there. It must serve one of the new gas fields. If we meet Oswald's contact there, the canyon is only about fifteen miles away.'

Eddie rubbed the bristles on his chin. 'Can't help thinking that if there was a cave that big there, someone would have found it already.'

'The thought had occurred,' she admitted. 'It's actually a little outside the search area I worked out. But nothing else fits the bill.'

Her husband did not seem convinced, but if he had any alternative suggestions he kept them to himself. 'Okay. Well, you'd better tell Ozzy, then.'

'Right.' She brought up her contacts.

'Ah, there you are!' said Gasimov, rounding the superstructure to find them. He had his own phone in hand. 'Good news, Eddie. I have spoken to my friend. There will be no trouble getting you through customs. We will use the,' a small laugh, 'special VIP lane.'

'Good,' said Eddie. 'What about the train?'

'You have plenty of time. The sleeper train goes at six o'clock. It arrives in Ashgabat at eight, tomorrow morning. The train going north to Dashoguz leaves at nine.'

Nina sighed. 'Another whole day spent travelling. Great.'

'I drove overnight to get us to France, and I don't think my heart's recovered from all those energy drinks,' Eddie reminded her. 'I'm not bloody driving all the way.'

'The trains here are quite good,' said Gasimov. 'If you spend the money to ride at least in *kupe*. Below that? Not so much fun.'

'*Kupe*?' Nina asked.

'The class of bed. *Kupe* is next to the top; you get a cabin, with air conditioning. *Platzkart* is below that, like being in the army. Six beds, no door on the compartment. As for *obshye* . . .' He shook his head. 'I would spend the extra money for a *lyux* cabin. Just the two of you, and you can lock the door.' Another little laugh. 'You never know who has their eye on your luggage.'

'Speaking of which,' said Eddie, 'just going to get ours. I'll check through it. Make sure nothing's gone missing.' He gave the Azerbaijani a hard look.

Gasimov got the message. 'Eddie, Eddie, why do you insult me?' he said, with an exaggerated smile. 'You know I would not dream of doing such a thing. After all . . . you have not paid me yet.' The smile tightened. 'There is a bank near the railway station where you can get US dollars – and manats, of course. This country runs on cash.'

'Like you.'

A dismissive flick of one hand. 'Digital money? Pah. With cash, if someone wants to steal from me, they have to fight me for it.' He made a stabbing gesture. 'I would rather do that than lose everything to some kid with a computer on the other side of the world.'

'You may have a point there, Gurban,' said Eddie. 'All right, love,' he told Nina, 'I'll get our stuff.'

'I'll call Oswald,' she replied. 'Let's get started.'

To Eddie's relief – and Gasimov's – his and Nina's belongings were all present and correct. The trio trooped down the gangway along with the other passengers. Green-uniformed officials awaited the new arrivals at the bottom, directing them to a nearby cabin for inspection. However, one of the customs officers came to meet Gasimov and his companions; a quiet exchange, and they were led to another building close by. Rather than go inside, though, they slipped behind it, shielded from view by a container.

'So this is the special VIP lane, is it?' said Eddie. 'Smells a bit rank.' He kept his right hand unobtrusively high against his chest, ready to draw the gun inside his leather jacket should the situation take a dangerous turn. But despite his innate mistrust of the Azerbaijani, Gasimov seemed good to his word. Money changed hands and the Turkmenistani stamped the visitors' passports, then returned them along with some papers.

'All done,' the gold-toothed man said at last. 'You have your visas. Welcome to Turkmenistan!'

The customs officer peeked out to make sure nobody was watching, then gestured for them to accompany him. They rejoined the string of people following a marked route on the other side of the customs cabin, making their way through the commercial zone to an elaborate terminal building that would not have been out of place at an airport. Eddie kept a wary watch on their surroundings, considering every person in uniform a potential threat, but the officials seemed more concerned about finding shade under the searing sun than investigating the newcomers.

'We can get a taxi to the bank from here,' Gasimov finally said. 'Then, the station.'

'Great,' said Nina, but her mind was on more important matters. She made a phone call as the Azerbaijani headed for the cab rank. 'Please, baby, pick up . . .'

But her attempt to contact Macy again met with failure. She closed her eyes. 'God *damn* it. Where is she?'

Eddie put a comforting hand on her shoulder. 'We'll see her again soon. I know it.'

'*How* do you know?' The question was little more than a despairing whisper.

'Because she's our daughter. She's as smart as you, and as stubborn as me. Whatever trouble she's in, she's working on a way to get out of it.'

'I hope you're right. Oh God, I hope you are.' She pressed closer, wiping away a tear. He held her.

Gasimov returned. 'We have a taxi,' he said. 'Come, this way.'

'Okay.' She took a deep breath, then straightened. 'Let's get a ticket to ride.'

33

Portugal

Macy awoke to the sound of sobbing.

The room was dark, windowless, unfamiliar. She sat up in bed, needing a moment to remember where she was – and why she was there. 'Rain?'

The crying stopped, choked off. 'Macy?' came the hoarse reply.

'I'm here, it's okay.' A command to her phone lit up its flashlight, letting her see her friend in the other bed. She clambered from hers and knelt beside Rain. Various pains pulsed as she moved. Her injuries had been treated as best they could with the medical supplies at the hideout, but the painkillers had worn off over the course of the night. 'How do you feel?'

She had meant it physically, but Rain's pain was elsewhere. 'I . . . I don't know what to do. My parents, they . . .' She shuddered, curling up into a tight ball of grief. 'They died, right in front of me, Macy. And I couldn't do anything! I should have saved them. It's my fault, it's my fault . . .'

Macy felt her own surge of loss. 'Rain, it's *not* your fault,' she told her softly. 'You can't blame yourself. You did everything you could.'

'It wasn't enough!' Rain raised her head, cheeks wet with tears. 'And Fernando, he – he's dead *because* of me. I wasn't good enough, and he had to save me, and . . . and he died. It's all my fault!'

Macy leaned forward to hold her. 'Listen to me, Rain,' she whispered. 'I know how you must be feeling, and how terrible this whole thing is. But it *wasn't* your fault. Your mom and dad wouldn't want you to blame yourself. Nor would Fernando. They all believed in you. *I* believe in you. The Brotherhood did this, not you.' She hugged her reassuringly. 'I'm here for you. Whatever you need, I'll give it. I'll help you through this.'

Rain turned, taking hold of Macy. 'Thank you,' she said. The two young women remained unmoving for some time, offering and accepting comfort.

Then Macy's phone trilled. She looked; the caller's name was on the screen. 'It's Rafael!' she exclaimed. 'Hold on, I have to get this.'

Rain reluctantly released her. Macy quickly answered the phone. 'Hi, hello?'

Loost was in a part of his habitat she hadn't seen before, a cylindrical chamber with walls of pale plastic and stainless steel. She glimpsed a woman in form-fitting white overalls: one of his nurses? Her guess was confirmed when he shifted position, revealing intravenous lines connected to his left forearm. The transparent conduits were connected to a boxy machine affixed to a stand. 'Hi, Macy,' he said. 'Sorry about this; I had a few minutes while my chelation therapy is being set up.'

She regarded the machine curiously. 'It's something to do with magnets, isn't it?'

'It removes accumulated metal contamination from my blood. It only goes so far, though. I'll still need a full blood transfusion soon. But enough about me,' he said, smiling. 'I have some good news. My quantum computer finished its analysis. The result's been sent to your friend.'

'Oh, wow,' she said, impressed. 'You did it that quickly?'

An immodest smile. 'It's the most powerful computer ever built. There's nothing it can't crack. The more data it has, the quicker it can work, but it can still brute-force an answer millions of times faster than any regular supercomputer.'

'So what was the result?'

'I don't know. I didn't read it. It wouldn't be good for business if people thought I read their private data, would it?'

'I guess not. Thank you so much for this. You didn't have to do it.'

'Like I said, you've impressed me. Not many people do that. By the way, nobody else has asked us to work on this data. Your friends will definitely have it first.'

'That's a relief. Thank you again.'

The woman said something in the background; Loost nodded. 'Okay, I have to go. I'm pretty sure you don't want to watch my blood being drained.'

'Not before breakfast,' said Macy, managing a small smile.

He returned it. 'Nice to talk to you again. Bye.'

'Bye,' she said, as he disconnected. She lowered the phone. 'Oh my God, Rain. He might have found the Iron Palace for us!'

Rain's response was considerably less enthusiastic. 'That's good,' she said with a sigh.

'I'm sorry. I'll be right back; I have to tell the others.'

She left the room. A couple of the other dorm rooms were open; people were up. 'Mr MacDuff! Are you here?'

Naima appeared in the kitchen doorway. 'He went downstairs. For a . . .' She mimed drawing on a cigarette. 'I won't let him do it in here.'

'I'll go find him. I've got good news – Rafael came through!'

She hurried down the stairs, finding the outside door ajar. The stench of cigarette smoke told her that MacDuff was indeed there. She called his name.

'Macy? What's up?' he replied.

She went out into the morning sun, finding him leaning against the wall with a half-smoked cigarette in his hand. 'Rafael Loost sent you the results from your database.'

'Really? That was quick.' He fumbled his phone from a pocket. 'Oh, so he has. I'll check this on my laptop; it'll be easier to read.' He dropped the cigarette and ground it out. 'Didn't expect anything from him, to be honest, never mind this fast.'

'Maybe you were wrong about him,' she said, following him back inside.

'Maybe. Come on, let's see what it says.'

Word soon got around. Everyone, bar Rain, congregated in the office as MacDuff checked the results on his computer. 'Well?' Leni asked impatiently. The young man had been knocked out during the battle, but suffered no lasting injuries. 'What does it say?'

'Give me a chance to read the thing first,' the Scot complained.

He scrolled through what appeared to Macy to be an impenetrable list of numbers and dates, before reaching something she *could* comprehend: a map, overlaid with numerous arrowed lines pointing inwards from its edges. She tried to identify the region, but there were few landmarks: a line of mountains to the south, some lakes. 'Where is it?' she finally asked.

'Let me see . . . Turkmenistan,' he announced. 'The Karakum desert.' He zoomed in on the map, even the few landmarks disappearing to be replaced by nothing but flat emptiness. 'If your rich mate's quantum gadget is right, this area is the origin point for Afrasiab's descendants.'

Emilian leaned closer to see. 'That makes sense. Afrasiab came from that region.'

'So it's not telling us anything we couldn't already have guessed,' MacDuff said, pursing his lips.

'It's confirming it, though,' said Macy. She looked more closely herself. 'What's the scale on that map? How big an area are we talking?'

'About a hundred square kilometres.' That drew dismay from his audience. 'It hasn't really narrowed things down. And if the Brotherhood has information we don't, they have an advantage.'

'But we have information *they* don't,' said Emilian. 'In the archives. There was definitely a description of how the Knights got into the Iron Palace, even if it didn't give the exact location.'

'I read it,' piped up Idris. 'They went down into a deep cave. I can't remember the details, though.'

Emilian reached for his phone. 'I'll get Oleksiy to bring us the records from the archive.'

MacDuff reacted with surprise. 'Are you sure about that? Taking things out of the archive, I mean. It might not be safe for them.'

'That firebomb wasn't safe for them either,' Macy pointed out.

'Oleksiy is coming here anyway,' Emilian went on. 'I asked him to bring some of the artefacts from the vault. Our security has been compromised; the more dangerous items need to be kept somewhere safer.'

Again, MacDuff was less than enthused by the idea. 'You think here is safer?'

'Nobody knows about it. And the Brotherhood almost got into the vault at the estate. It's better that they're somewhere they haven't found.'

'Yet,' was the Scot's mordant addendum. 'But . . . well, you're in charge now. If that's what you think we should do . . .'

'It is,' the Dutchman said firmly. 'And I also think we need to plan a mission to Turkmenistan. As soon as we know where to find the Iron Palace, we should move – and beat the Brotherhood to it.' He raised his phone. 'I'll call Oleksiy. Euripides, narrow down the search area as much as you can. Everyone else, get ready to move out. We're going into the desert; we need to be prepared.'

The group began to disperse. MacDuff still appeared reluctant, but scrolled back to begin a more thorough reading. Emilian left the office, Macy following. 'Where's Rain?' he asked.

'In our room,' Macy replied. 'She's . . . not in a good place. She lost her parents *and* the guy who was like her big brother.'

'You should be with her,' he said. 'You're her best friend. She needs you. Go and help her.'

'Okay.' She gave him a small smile. 'Are *you* okay?'

'I'll be fine,' he said. 'I'm still in shock, but . . . I can't let it interfere with what I have to do. We *need* to stop the Brotherhood. Once we've done that, then . . .' A long, unsteady breath, emotion cracking through his stoic mask.

Macy squeezed his hand. 'I know. Don't worry. We'll be here for you when you need us.'

He nodded. 'Thank you.' Another squeeze, then Macy headed back through the factory to find Rain.

Emilian waited until she was gone, then entered a nearby room. It had once been an office, now home only to boxes of supplies. The door had a bolt. He quietly closed it, then raised his phone and made a call through Uzz.

It was soon answered. 'Well?' said Rafael Loost. The intravenous feeds were still attached to his arm, dark blood now being pumped through them via the chelation device. 'What's happening?'

Anger replaced Emilian's sadness. 'No, you tell *me* what's happening,' he growled. 'Your fucking mercenaries were only supposed to take out the elders – but they killed some of the Knights too! They could have killed me!'

Loost frowned at his tone. 'I didn't authorise additional lethal action.'

'You didn't prohibit it, either.'

'I didn't expect to need to. Their whole purpose there was to give you a pretext to search for the Iron Palace by seeming to want to destroy your records of it. Granit exceeded his orders. I'll penalise him for it.'

'You'll *penalise* him,' Emilian echoed in mocking disgust. 'That will make everything better, will it? Fernando is dead, and so is Jari. And it was only luck that Macy didn't get killed! That would have fucked everything up, no? Since she's so *special* and *important* to the plan.' His face twisted with bitterness.

'Fernando is dead?'

'Yes.'

A pause. 'I'm sorry about that. I really am. But . . . with the elders gone as well, that puts you in charge of the Knights, doesn't it?'

'Yes,' came the curt reply.

'So that actually makes things easier. You don't have to persuade Fernando or any of the others what course of action to take. You can decide on it yourself. Isn't that right?'

'I'm already doing it,' the Dutchman admitted. 'We looked at the data you analysed and found the Iron Palace's general location. I can use the information from the archive to narrow it down. I've got photos of the texts on my phone, but I'm having them brought here so it'll seem like we find the answer together. I've already told the others to get ready to travel once we know where to look.'

'That's excellent news,' said Loost, with an approving nod. 'That proves what I thought: you have initiative, intuition . . . leadership. That was why I approached you, rather than any of the other Knights, after my computers deduced that the Order of Behdet was the cover for something considerably more interesting. You have, to coin a phrase, the right stuff.' A small laugh from the man in orbit, which was not returned. 'But I could tell from everything you said and did on Uzz that we share the same beliefs, the same attitudes. The only time timid and complacent people grow a backbone is when they try to stop people like us doing what needs to be done. When we find the staff, we'll be able to do that. We'll *make* the world's corrupt governments change.'

'I know,' said Emilian. 'I know. I just wish . . . the others hadn't died.'

'I'm very sorry it happened. But it's the same as when you had to remove Gael, to make room for Macy. It's ultimately for the good of humanity. That's our goal, isn't it? To make the world a better place for everyone?'

'Yeah, it is. Yes.' The Dutchman took a deep breath, centring himself. 'We can do this. We can change the world.'

'We can indeed,' Loost assured him, with a patriarchal smile. 'Now, I have some influence with the Turkmenistan leadership. I'll get you free access to the country.'

'Good. Thank you.'

'There's one minor issue. Macy's parents are already there.'

Emilian reacted in alarm. 'They found the Iron Palace?'

'I'm not sure. But now her mother's installed Uzz on her phone, I can remotely access it whenever it's within range of a cell tower and track her – and also spy on her. The place she's going is slightly outside the search area I calculated from MacDuff's database. But just in case, I'm arranging to have her dealt with.'

He scowled. 'You're sending Granit to kill them?'

'You don't need to worry about it. But it will help our cause. If Macy is isolated, she'll turn to the Knights, to *you*, for support. And then she'll be far more likely to do what we need her to do, voluntarily.' A woman spoke in the background. 'My therapy's finished. I need to get back to work. I'll talk to the Turkmenistanis; you get ready to travel there.'

'Okay,' said Emilian. Loost ended the call. For a moment, the Dutchman regarded the phone with a conflicted expression – then determination took over. He unlocked the office and strode out.

* * *

Oleksiy Meller arrived in a van a few hours later. He brought with him several items from the mansion's vault, Macy concerned to see Earthbreaker and Excalibur among them, and also some of the large books from the archive. She was surprised to discover there was a small, concealed vault at the top of the stairwell by the living quarters, hidden behind shelves. Once the artefacts were secured in it, attention turned to the books.

'I'm certain there are things in here that will help us locate the Iron Palace,' said Emilian. 'We just have to find them.' He turned to the other Knights. 'Everyone who can read Atlantean, take a page. See what you can find.'

The books were taken to one of the unused offices and laid out on a desk. To the discomfort of some of his companions, Emilian cracked the spines on the old volumes to remove the individual glass-protected metal sheets. 'We'll work faster this way,' he said. 'We can repair the books later. Anything you find that could be a clue to finding the Iron Palace, make a note.'

Of the remaining Knights, Emilian, Rain, Idris – and Macy – could translate the ancient texts, though Idris admitted he was still learning the language. They set to work. Despite the task's urgency, Macy found herself becoming distracted, intrigued by other truths revealed in the old records. They provided a new insight into a civilisation from thousands of years earlier, what at the time would have been mundane book-keeping now providing tantalising glimpses of ordinary life . . .

She made herself stay focused. The Brotherhood had tried to kill her – *had* killed Rain's parents. She glanced at her friend. Rain was even more fixated upon the work than she, using it to force away awful, overwhelming thoughts. Macy gave the French woman a reassuring smile when she realised she was being watched, then returned to her own work.

With four people scouring the texts, it did not take long to collate every possible clue. 'It says here that the Knights flew over a river to the south of the Iron Palace,' said Macy, showing a map app on her phone. 'I checked a satellite view. There aren't any rivers anywhere in the search area now – but there are traces of where there used to be.' She zoomed in on a faint line weaving across the orange-grey sands. 'If they only crossed one river, then it has to be between this one, and another one a few miles to the north. So it must be somewhere in this band.' Zooming out again, she indicated a swathe of desert between the two long-dry riverbeds.

'That's still a big area,' said Rain. 'At least sixty square kilometres.'

Leni had not been able to contribute to the translation effort, but still stayed with the other Knights as they worked, compiling notes. 'It's smaller than what we started with, though.'

'It's good,' said Emilian. 'What else do we have?'

Rain and Idris had also found nuggets of information, but nothing conclusive. 'I might have something too,' said the Dutchman after noting the other findings. 'After some of the Knights were killed in the Iron Palace, the survivors wrote that they had to get outside, away from Afrasiab's evil magic, before they could fly again. But they also said they then carried the bodies *up* to get them clear. So the entrance might be at the bottom of a canyon.'

'There aren't any canyons where we're looking,' Macy pointed out. 'It's just a big flat plain. Maybe a sinkhole or something?'

'We'll have to search in person,' Emilian decided. 'I'll tell Oleksiy and Euripides to arrange for a helicopter.'

'We're just going to rock up in Turkmenistan and start poking around?' she asked, dubious. 'It doesn't exactly have a reputation as the world's most open and friendly government.'

'The Order of Behdet has connections,' he assured her. 'I'll handle it.' He stood. 'Okay. We know roughly where to look. We *don't* know if the Brotherhood have better information than us. So we have to make sure that if they find the Iron Palace first . . . they don't get away with the staff. Whatever it takes. Are we all ready for that?'

He looked at the others, one by one. Each confirmed in turn that they were. Rain nodded, despite her trepidation . . . then finally Macy did the same. 'Yeah,' she agreed. 'Whatever it takes.'

'Okay,' Emilian said. 'Then let's get started.'

34

Turkmenistan

Nina and Eddie took Gasimov's advice and paid extra for a private *lyux* cabin on the overnight train to Ashgabat. The fares did not break the bank: despite its vast energy reserves, Turkmenistan was a poor country, almost all wealth in the hands of the ruling elite. What was an unaffordable luxury for the vast majority of its population was an almost embarrassingly modest sum for the two Westerners.

Where a large chunk of the nation's riches had gone became apparent as the train arrived in the capital. Ashgabat was dominated by extravagant white marble towers, shimmering in the summer heat. Nina was immediately put in mind of a cemetery, the gleaming blocks precisely aligned like rows of tombstones. The image was exaggerated by the emptiness of the streets between them, broad multi-lane highways dotted by only the occasional ambling car or bus.

The train rolled into the city's central railway station. Like so many other structures, the terminal building was a massive white marble edifice, capped with blue tile roofs and golden spires. Despite its size, it did not actually have many platforms. 'Doesn't need 'em, I suppose,' Eddie replied when Nina noted it was not exactly Grand Central. 'Country's basically only got two lines. You can go across it, or up it.'

'And we're going up – into the middle of nowhere.' She

collected her backpack. 'I just hope Oswald's contact is waiting for us.'

'He's still got time to get there,' said Eddie, donning his own pack and picking up the holdall. Gasimov had stayed in Turkmenbashi, departing with a relieved golden smile after receiving his promised three thousand dollars. 'Even if the next train's on time, it'll take over five hours to reach where we're going.'

'Joy,' she sighed. The train finally shrilled to a stop. 'Okay, let's get ready for the next thrill-ride . . .'

They exited. There was life at the station, at least, people clustered in the shade of long blue arched canopies. 'Ay up,' Eddie muttered as he and Nina headed for the main building. 'Think we should avoid that lot.' One waiting group was around a dozen men in dark green uniforms; not military, but some kind of internal security agency. They appeared to be on their way to a new posting, all having baggage – as well as holstered sidearms on prominent display. The ordinary citizens nearby, consciously or not, had left a clear exclusion zone around them.

'What are the chances that they'll be on our train?' Nina wondered as they angled to pass behind them.

Eddie snorted. 'With our luck? A hundred and ten per cent.'

For now, the agents were more occupied with loud, macho bantering amongst themselves than scrutinising the other passengers. The couple slipped past and entered the main building. It did not take long to find the ticket office. 'All right,' said Eddie once they were done. 'Two *kupe*-class tickets to Ruhnama. You sure about not going first-class for this leg?'

'It almost feels like rubbing our money in their faces,' Nina replied. She had travelled extensively in poverty-stricken countries in the past, but Macy's recent vocal stance against global wealth inequality had made the issue more personal. 'Besides, we might stand out less if we're in a crowd.'

A humourless laugh. 'Not with your hair.'

'Okay, maybe I should buy a headscarf,' admitted the redhead. Not every woman in sight had their hair covered, but the vast majority wore colourful wraps. As in so many authoritarian states, the heavy thumb of traditionalism bore down predominantly upon women. 'How long before the train?'

Eddie checked a departure board. The destination names were in Cyrillic, but there were few enough options that working out which was Dashoguz, their train's final stop, was straightforward. 'Half an hour. Same platform we arrived on.'

They went back outside and found a bench well away from the security agents. Even in the shade, the heat became oppressive. It was a great relief when a bleating horn finally heralded a train's arrival, a blue and silver diesel locomotive towing ten carriages. Nina checked her ticket; their assigned compartment was in coach number five. They headed along the platform towards it. 'Oh, crap. They *are* getting on our train.' The uniformed men were also preparing to board.

'At least they're not in our carriage,' said Eddie, seeing them head farther forward. 'Just hope they're off-duty and don't decide to check through the whole train.'

'But we've got visas.'

'Dodgy ones. If they check with customs, they'll know we never even applied for them, never mind got approval.'

'Then let's pray for lousy cell phone coverage,' was Nina's unhappy retort.

But the group disappeared into the train's second carriage. The couple went to their own coach. An attendant regarded them quizzically on realising they were foreigners, but showed no signs of suspicion. He checked their tickets, then directed them to their compartment.

Kupe on this train saw them sharing the space with four other people: two women, a boy of about six and an elderly man in a black felt fedora. Again, the presence of obvious Westerners was greeted with mild surprise, but no hostility. One woman changed seats so Nina and Eddie could sit facing each other beside the compartment's door. Eddie found himself next to the boy, who regarded him with the anticipatory expression of someone who had just been given a new pet. Nina tried to hide a smile. Eddie gave her a small sigh of resignation, then greeted his new neighbour with a friendly nod. The boy took that as permission to open up, asking excited questions in Turkmen until his mother apologetically hushed him. 'It's okay,' Eddie told them with a grin. The boy held his silence for a good ten seconds before resuming his interrogation.

'Enjoy the trip,' Nina told her husband, amused.

The train's departure was late, as they had half expected, but not excessively so. The locomotive huffing out plumes of diesel fumes, it lumbered from the station to begin its long journey northwards.

The strip of fertile land along the northern flank of the Kopet Dag range was long, but not deep. It took barely half an hour for the train to clear it, irrigated farmland giving way to scrub and sand. There were no white marble edifices in the settlements beyond the capital, only run-down stone and concrete – and before long, there was nothing at all. 'Welcome to the Karakum,' Eddie said to Nina, regarding the dusty desolation rolling past the window.

'Karakum!' echoed the boy, whose name had turned out to be Serdar. A gabble of Turkmen was followed by a grinning, 'Mister Eddie.' The Yorkshireman had been unable to resist introducing himself to the cheerful child.

Nina checked her watch. 'Still about four hours to go,' she wearily reported. The compartment's seats were comfortable enough, but the train itself bumped and swayed along the track in an occasionally alarming manner. She was already attuned to a warning of impending instability. A distinctive metallic thunking from the coupler linking their carriage to the one ahead would be followed in moments by sudden rolling, like a ship in choppy waters. The sound came again; she braced herself for the inevitable sidelong lurch. 'Jeez,' she said as the carriage settled. 'The last thing I expected in a desert was to feel seasick.'

'At least we're not riding camels,' Eddie replied. 'Remember that time in Syria?'

'I'd tried my hardest to forget it.'

He grinned, then looked around as the door slid open. A uniformed attendant pushed a trolley bearing a samovar, a large steel water boiler heated by a gas burner. He peered into the cabin. '*Çaý, çaý?*' he asked. '*Kofe?*'

'Well, I've worked out the second thing,' Nina said. 'Shall we get something?'

'Sure,' said Eddie. 'Wouldn't mind a cuppa.' The three adult locals put in their orders, *çaý* turning out to be tea. 'Thanks,' said Eddie as he and Nina received steaming hot coffees. He handed over a fifty-manat note, the lowest denomination he had. The man's look of shock, then his hurried scrabble to find enough coins to return, told the Yorkshireman he had grossly overpaid. 'No, no! It's okay. Keep the change.' The attendant's reaction, disbelief turning into a skull-splitting smile, suggested it was the best tip he had ever received.

Nina laughed. 'Doing your part for wealth redistribution,' she said as the man pushed the trolley on. 'Macy would be proud.' Her humour vanished. 'I wish I knew where she was. I wish I knew *anything*. Just . . . that she's *alive* would be enough right now.'

'I know, love,' Eddie said gloomily. He reached across the cabin to hold her hands. 'I know.'

The train rolled on through the desert, hours slipping by even as the landscape barely changed. It occasionally stopped, a couple of times at small, isolated stations that Nina guessed served drilling facilities out in the empty wilderness, but also on intermittent stretches of double track to let long, clanking tanker trains go by in the other direction. She passed the time by reviewing her notes, searching for any clues she might have overlooked. Eddie, meanwhile, amused himself by teaching Serdar English – or at least, his own version of it. 'Ay up,' he said.

'Ay up,' Serdar repeated.

'By 'eck.'

'By 'eck.'

'Bugg—'

'Eddie,' Nina cut in.

The Yorkshireman laughed, all the more so as the young boy cried, 'Bugg!'

'I'm very, *very* sorry about my husband,' the redhead told Serdar's mother. 'Really. You have no idea.' The Turkmenistani woman smiled, understanding perfectly despite the language barrier.

The coupler's clunking warned of another approaching sway. The adults all braced themselves, but Serdar jumped from his seat to stand with arms outstretched as if surfing. The carriage rolled beneath him, pitching him onto Eddie as he shrieked with glee. It was his mother's turn to apologise. 'That's okay,' said Eddie, helping him back up. 'Used to do the same thing when I was a kid.'

'You still do when you ride the subway,' Nina pointed out.

Serdar's mother signalled for him to sit on her lap. He begrudgingly did so, looking out of the window. Something caught his attention. '*Eje!*' he called, pointing into the sky. '*Serediň!*'

Whatever he had seen was unusual enough to startle his mother. Nina and Eddie both leaned over to see for themselves – spotting a helicopter travelling parallel to the track half a mile away, overtaking them. The aircraft was flying low, no more than five hundred feet up, and they quickly saw it was descending. 'Is it in trouble?' Nina asked.

'Don't know,' Eddie replied, realising they were slowing. 'But

I'm getting a nasty little feeling that *we* might be.' He went to the window, looking ahead as best he could. The helicopter was already past the train, steadily dropping lower as it continued into the dusty distance. There were no signs of drilling rigs anywhere in the endless sands. He quickly left the compartment and looked out of the window in the corridor. The Karakum was equally empty on that side. 'If there's a station ahead, that chopper's landing there,' he said as he returned.

'You think they're after us?'

'I don't think it's been sent because one of those security guys left their packed lunch behind.'

'So what are we going to do? Jump off the train?' She gestured at the flat plain beyond the window. 'There's nowhere to hide out there. They'll see us!'

'I don't know. But we need to be ready to move. Or fight.' He surreptitiously checked that the gun was ready inside his jacket.

The train continued to slow. Nina went to the window. A single building stood ahead – and a drifting cloud of dust told her the helicopter had touched down near it. 'It's landed,' she reported. 'I think – yeah, I can see people getting out. They're running to the station.'

'They really, really want to catch this train,' said Eddie darkly. He went back into the corridor and hurried to the end vestibule. He'd suspected the exterior doors could not be opened manually, and that turned out to be the case: they were electronically controlled, by either the driver or guard. His eyes flicked up to the emergency cord, but he already knew that would be no help either. Pulling it would merely set off an alarm, rather than the Hollywood version of slamming on the entire train's brakes. Getting off the train before it stopped would require smashing a window – and even if he did, then what? As Nina had said, there was nowhere to hide in the empty wilderness.

And whoever had just landed was already one step ahead. He

glanced through the corridor window – to see that at least two men had run across the track, moving clear of the approaching train. Watching, in case anyone *did* try to make a desperate exit.

The train shook again as it went through points at the southern end of another passing section. He returned to Nina. 'Definitely trouble,' he told her. 'We can't jump off – they've got guys on both sides of the track.'

'What do we do?'

'Don't know yet – but they'll have to come and find us. That gives us a bit of time.'

'To do *what*?'

'Soon as I know, I'll tell you!' He joined her at the window. The approaching stop was the diametric opposite of Ashgabat's grandiose station, a lonely cabin on a stand of barren sun-baked concrete. The helicopter, he saw, was large enough to carry at least a dozen passengers – and from the number of men waiting for the train, it appeared to have been near capacity.

'Sit down,' he told Nina, retreating to his own seat. 'Don't draw any attention as we go past. If they don't know where we are, they'll have to search the whole train.'

Nina took his advice. Their fellow passengers regarding them with concern, she and Eddie watched sidelong as the train rumbled into the little station. The men on its platform slipped by. All wore dark military-style clothing, hair clipped short, eyes hidden behind sunglasses . . .

Except one.

He was older than the others, face weathered, eyes narrowed and menacing. Even though they had never seen him before, both Nina and Eddie felt a chill of recognition. Though there was around ten years between them, his features were almost identical to the man who had tried to kill them in Rome.

He was the assassin's brother. The man who had sent him. Anton Granit.

35

'How the hell did he know we were here?' Eddie demanded. 'More to the point, how are we going to get away from him?' countered Nina. 'We can't get off, they'll see us.'

'We'll have to hide.'

'Where?' The train stopped, the pneumatic grunt of its opening doors echoing through the carriage. 'They're coming aboard!'

'I dunno, we'll—' He turned to their fellow passengers, an idea forming. 'We need a disguise.'

Their companions' looks of concern revealed that they had realised the men at the station were people the Westerners desperately wanted to avoid. 'Hi,' said Eddie, raising his hands in what he hoped would be recognised as a gesture for assistance. 'I know you can't understand me, but we need your help. We need, er . . . how the bloody hell do I get this across?' Out of desperation, he raised one lapel of his leather jacket to conceal the lower part of his face.

Blank looks came in response – then Serdar let out a cry of understanding. 'Ah! Ah! Mister Eddie!' He pulled his own T-shirt over his face to hide it, then quickly spoke to his mother. Comprehension dawned around the compartment. Serdar's mother nodded, then indicated her headscarf before pointing at Nina.

'Yes, yes,' Nina said, relieved. 'Please, if you can?'

A sudden flurry of activity filled the cabin as bags and suitcases were retrieved and opened. Nina was offered another headscarf and a colourful traditional shawl, the elderly man passing his hat to Eddie. The Yorkshireman in return took out some money, only

303

to meet unanimous rejection. 'You sure?' he said, but the reaction was the same. 'Thank you.'

He and Nina hurriedly donned their new garments as the train set off again. Not all of the men at the stop had boarded, a few remaining on the platform. 'They must be flying on to the next station,' said Nina unhappily as she clumsily wrapped the scarf over her hair. 'They're going to wait for their buddies on the train to find us.'

'Let's make sure they don't.' Eddie adjusted the hat, then leaned back in his seat, tipping the brim to shade his face. As a disguise it was feeble, but if their new friends made them seem like part of the group, it might work . . .

Nina was still struggling to knot the scarf. Serdar's mother made a fussing sound, then reached across to do it for her. 'Thanks,' she said, with a faintly embarrassed smile. 'Can you see my hair?'

'Nope,' Eddie reported. 'It's all covered.'

'Good.' She draped the shawl over her other clothing. The men of Turkmenistan could wear whatever they wanted, whether traditional garb or more western outfits, but the women almost universally wore loose, body-covering embroidered dresses and trousers, a uniformity she suspected was enforced rather than voluntary. 'I still don't know if this is going to work . . .'

'Just have to run with it.' He closed the compartment door, then checked again that the gun was ready before settling into position – only for Serdar to clamber onto his lap. 'No, no,' he said, trying to shoo him off. 'Too dangerous. I can't risk—'

Serdar's mother interrupted with what seemed to be a passionate defence of her son's idea. 'They're not looking for anyone with a kid,' Nina pointed out.

'Mister Eddie,' Serdar insisted, grinning. 'Bugg!'

'*Definitely* bugg,' Eddie sighed. With deep reluctance, he gave the boy and his mother a nod. She passed a toy car from her bag to Serdar, who started playing with it, driving it up and down the Englishman's leg.

The other woman passed Nina a magazine. 'Thanks,' she said. The text was incomprehensible, but the pictures suggested it was a good housekeeping publication. Far from her normal choice of reading, but as an aid to her disguise it would do the job.

She hoped.

The train returned to its normal speed, thumping and swaying through the parched landscape. Nina and Eddie waited, tension rising. Some of Granit's men had definitely boarded – so where were they?

After several minutes, they heard sounds from the corridor. A compartment door opened, then after a few seconds closed again. Another door rumbled open – nearer to them. Someone was coming through the carriage, looking into each cabin in turn. Eddie slipped his right hand across his chest, fingertips mere inches from the hidden gun. Nina brought the magazine closer to her face, eyes fixed upon the Turkic text . . .

The door opened.

Nina risked looking up; not reacting at all could seem suspicious. A cold-faced man stood in the doorway, eyes flicking over the cabin's occupants. Another equally unfriendly figure peered over his shoulder. Silence for a long moment, nobody moving. Her fear rose. Had they been recognised? She was internationally famous – it was not as if photos of her were hard to find . . .

Serdar held his car up to the two men. 'Vroom, vroom!' he cried, smiling. One muttered something, then they moved on towards the carriage's rear, closing the door behind them.

Nina waited until she heard the next compartment open before lowering the magazine in relief. 'Oh, God,' she whispered. 'That was close.' She turned to her fellow passengers. 'Thank you.' They responded with appreciative nods.

'We're not safe until we're off the train,' Eddie reminded her.

She checked her watch. 'We're still over an hour from Ruhnama. Do you think they'll come back?'

Not even the hat could hide her husband's grim expression. 'They knew we were on the train. They know we didn't get off it. Yeah. They will.'

Anton Granit made his methodical way forward through the train, two of his men, Wesler and Ort, accompanying him. He had boarded the rearmost of the ten carriages, inspecting the occupant of every seat, every bunk, personally. Some of the first-class compartments had been locked; an officious rap had made those inside assume he was a ticket inspector, or worse, and open up. He would not stop until every square metre had been checked.

Somewhere aboard, he knew, were the people who had killed his brother.

Nina Wilde's phone had given her position away to his employer, the Uzz app automatically reporting in each time it made contact with a cell tower. Her journey had been tracked. A helicopter was waiting for his rapidly assembled team when they landed in Ashgabat: Rafael Loost's money oiled the wheels even in a country as authoritarian as Turkmenistan. Granit wondered how high up his client had gone. There was certainly no shortage of world leaders, democratic or otherwise, keen to curry the favour of the world's richest man.

It didn't matter, though. He was here – and he would make Wilde and her husband pay for what had happened to Konstantin. The thought of his little brother brought a surge of rage. Yes, they would *pay*.

Once he found them. He was near the front of the seventh carriage when he heard the connecting door to the sixth open, the grinding rumble of wheels on the track briefly louder before it shut again. Two more of his men, Qabbani and Hellinger, came into view at the corridor's end. 'Well?' he demanded.

'No sign of them,' Hellinger replied.

Granit scowled. There were only three compartments left to check in this carriage. A command, and the new arrivals opened the farthest, Ort and Wesler the middlemost. Granit himself pulled wide the door of the closest. The six seats inside were all occupied, surprised Turkmenistanis looking up at him. His eyes swept over each in turn, comparing their features to those of his targets. He didn't need to check against photographs; they had been burned into his memory.

No matches. Ort gave him a 'clear' gesture, but he still went to see for himself – then on to the last cabin, even as Qabbani signalled his assurance that his targets were not there. 'That's everywhere,' said Hellinger. 'They can't be on the train.'

'They're here,' snarled Granit. 'You didn't search well enough.'

'Sir, we checked everyone, looked in every compartment and bathroom—'

'You went through six carriages in the time it took me to do four. You rushed – you missed them! I don't tolerate sloppy work. You will be penalised – both of you,' he said to the American and his Syrian companion.

Hellinger drew in a sharp breath, but nodded. 'Yes, sir.'

Qabbani was equally crestfallen, but still made a report. 'Sir, there are eleven men from the State Border Service in one of the coaches. The rest of it is empty.'

'Nobody wanted to share it with the pigs,' Hellinger added.

Granit considered the news. 'Wilde and Chase wouldn't risk getting close to them. That means we have one less carriage to search.' He jabbed a finger along the train's length. 'Move it!'

Serdar returned to his seat, chatting to his mother. Nina and Eddie, though, remained tense, acutely aware their disguises

307

would not withstand a more intense inspection. 'They went towards the back of the train,' said Nina. 'Maybe we should move forward, find somewhere to hide.'

'Granit's brother's dead; he'll check every square inch of this train to find us,' Eddie replied. 'And those security goons are three coaches forward.'

'So what else can we do? Can we get on the roof?'

'Not without smashing a window, and that'd draw attention—'

He broke off at the sound of a compartment door opening. 'Do you think that's them?' Nina asked.

Another door opened, the heavy clump of boots moving closer. 'Safe bet,' Eddie rumbled. He tipped the hat to cover his face and brought his hand closer to the gun. Serdar spotted his change of attitude and again hurried to climb onto his lap. 'No, *no*,' Eddie insisted, trying to push him off – but before he could do so, the door handle rattled.

He froze, Nina burying her face in the magazine as the door rumbled open. A different man stood in the opening, eyes narrowing as he scrutinised the passengers. His gaze went to Nina, the other women, then back to her, uncertain. She ignored him, feigning disinterest. Again, Serdar's presence meant that Eddie was all but overlooked. The man retreated. They'd fooled him—

Another man pushed past to take his place. Granit.

He stared at each of the women in turn, the Turkmenistanis reacting with embarrassed worry. Finally, his eyes locked onto Nina. She focused on a picture with laser-beam intensity. He stepped into the compartment, standing in front of her. For a moment he was still. Then he put his hand on the top of the magazine, pushing it down. Cringing in fear, Nina tipped her head to follow it, unwilling to look up. He let out a brief grunt that could have been a sardonic chuckle. 'Professor Nina Wilde,' he said. 'We finally meet.'

She raised her eyes. There was nothing but hostility behind the gaze that met them. 'You have very pale skin,' he went on. 'You stand out among these people.' A glance towards his companions at the doorway – now four of them, she saw with alarm. 'That should have been *seen*.' Two of his men shuffled uncomfortably.

He pulled the magazine from her hands, then dropped it. 'Now. Where is Eddie Chase?'

'Right here, aiming at your balls.' Eddie gently but firmly pushed Serdar away with one hand – the gun in his other shielded from the other passengers' sight. The men in the corridor could see it clearly, though, hands darting into their own outer clothing. 'Ah-ah. Anyone draws, bye-bye boss's bollocks.' The concealed weapons remained so.

Granit stood still. 'Wesler. Show Mr Chase your other weapon.'

A man with a goatee beard slowly opened his dark coat. A sheathed combat knife was revealed within. 'If you shoot me,' the Hungarian continued, 'my men will not only kill you and your wife, but everyone else in the compartment. They will cut the throat of the boy's mother in front of him, then his too. Are you willing to sacrifice innocent lives for a pointless gesture of defiance?'

'If I shoot fast enough, I won't have to,' Eddie replied.

'Not even the SAS can shoot that fast. And you are an old man, Mr Chase. Almost sixty. My men are as well-trained, and half your age. Delta Force, KSK, Republican Guard – they will fire back before you can take your second shot. Is that how you want to die?'

'Two years off isn't "almost" sixty, you cheeky twat,' the Yorkshireman complained, covering his concern. Granit was right: for all his bravado, the chances of taking down all five men before being killed himself were near zero.

Nina knew the same thing. 'What do you want?' she demanded.

'Come with us. Quietly, without trouble. We will get off the train at the next station.'

'And then what?'

His lack of an answer spoke volumes. 'If you do not,' he said instead, 'your friends here will die.' The others in the compartment might not have understood Granit's words, but his tone made the threat clear. Serdar scrambled onto his mother's lap, and she hugged him protectively.

Eddie leaned sideways so he could see Nina past Granit. He gave her a questioning look: *What should we do?*

'I . . . don't think we have a choice,' she said, defeated.

'No,' he reluctantly agreed. 'Fuck. Sorry, Serdar,' he added. 'Don't copy *that* word.'

Nina stood, taking off the headscarf and shawl and handing them back to Serdar's mother. 'Thank you.' Granit moved aside and pushed her into the corridor. Eddie returned the elderly man's hat with a nod of thanks, then followed Nina. Granit came out behind them, gesturing to warn the Turkmenistanis not to follow before closing the door with a bang of finality.

The moment there were no longer any witnesses, the mercenaries drew their weapons. Most were silenced pistols, but an Arabic man produced a stun laser, fixing its green targeting beam on Eddie's cheek while Granit reached into the Yorkshire-man's jacket. He tugged out the ageing automatic, giving it an almost contemptuous look before pocketing it and gesturing with his own gun. 'Okay. Move. Wesler, Qabbani, go in front of them.'

The Arabic man lowered his staser and squeezed past Eddie and Nina, joining the American to lead the way forward. 'So where are you taking us?' Nina asked as she set off. 'To see your boss?'

'That would be difficult, since he lives in space,' Granit replied, following with his gun raised. The remaining two men were close behind him. 'But you will be going part of the distance to him. About three thousand metres up. Then, when I am done with you for what you did to my brother,' those words were said with a tight-lipped snarl, 'I will finish the job I was hired to do and return you to the ground. Without parachutes.'

'Done that before,' said Eddie. 'Managed okay.'

'Only because I *did* have a parachute,' Nina reminded him.

'Enough,' Granit snapped. 'Our helicopter is waiting at the next station. But if you try anything, I will shoot you both right here.' They neared the corridor's end. A dog-leg bend around the final compartment led to the door to the carriage's forward vestibule. He glanced at his watch. 'We will be there in—'

The door opened, the attendant pushing his tea trolley through.

Wesler stopped, everyone else halting behind him. Granit cleared his throat. The sound was a practised signal to his men, who rapidly hid their weapons. 'Remember what I said,' he warned his prisoners.

The attendant saw the people in his way. A grunt of exasperation, then he manoeuvred the trolley into the corridor's end corner, leaving just enough room for them to squeeze by. 'Move,' Granit ordered. Wesler turned to sidestep past the steaming samovar.

Qabbani started after him. Nina and Eddie began to follow – then heard a familiar sound. The clunk of the coupler—

Eddie shot Nina a look. She instantly knew its meaning: *Get ready*. They both braced themselves . . .

The carriage rocked.

The mercenaries, unprepared, staggered. Eddie, though, was already moving. He whirled, smashing his elbow into the side of Granit's head. Before the Hungarian could recover, he grabbed his arm, trying to wrest the gun from his hand.

Nina charged bodily at Qabbani. The impact slammed him against the samovar. Its lid came off, boiling water splashing his arm and face. He shrieked and staggered blindly back against the windows, clutching at his scalded skin. His staser clunked to the floor.

Wesler whirled, pulling out his pistol—

Eddie yanked Granit's arm towards him. 'Nina, down!' She dropped – and her husband clawed at the trigger. A flat *thwack* from the Hungarian's suppressed gun, and blood burst across the carriage's rear bulkhead as a round ripped through Wesler's upper arm. The American gasped in pain, dropping his gun as he stumbled against the wall.

Nina snatched up the fallen staser. She spun to aim it at Granit, but he was still grappling with Eddie. If she fired, she might hit the wrong person. But the same was true for the two men behind Granit, their boss blocking any clear firing line at the Englishman. 'Eddie, come on!' she cried, slipping past the trolley and dodging the startled attendant to dart into the end vestibule.

Granit fought back, trying to swing Eddie around so Hellinger could shoot him. Eddie kicked out, catching the frame of the last compartment door and propelling himself backwards – taking Granit with him. The Hungarian crashed into Hellinger, sending him staggering. Eddie bashed Granit's hand against the window. The gun was finally jarred free – but it glanced off Granit's arm, clattering down behind him.

The Yorkshireman knew trying to get the weapon would be suicide. Instead he elbowed Granit in the face, then broke away. He ducked past Qabbani and the trolley. Wesler was starting to recover. His wound was messy, but not life-threatening. It was far from painless, though – especially when Eddie punched the injury. The American screamed. Eddie looked for his gun, but it had ended up beneath the trolley. He instead snatched the combat knife from inside Wesler's jacket and ran after Nina.

She had already gone through the concertina-like connecting passage to the next carriage, waiting for him at its door. Her gaze flicked to his newly acquired weapon. 'You couldn't get his *gun*?'

'Like that bloody thing's much better!' he complained, seeing the stun laser. 'Let's go!'

'To *where*?'

'Wherever those arseholes aren't!' They rushed into the next coach, slamming the door behind them.

Granit retrieved his gun, head still ringing from Eddie's attacks. 'Get after them!' he roared.

Scalded face drawn into a tight grimace of pain, Qabbani squeezed past the trolley. The staser had been his secondary weapon; like the other mercenaries, he was also armed with a suppressed handgun. He drew it, to the attendant's horror, and threw open the vestibule door. Nobody was beyond. 'They're running,' he reported, before rushing in pursuit.

Granit went to Wesler. The American had a bloodied hand pressed to his wound. 'Can you still fight?' his leader demanded.

The reply came through gritted teeth. 'Yeah. I'm gonna kill that bastard!'

'Good. Move.'

Wesler exited. Granit turned to follow, seeing the attendant frozen in fear beside the doorway. He regarded him coldly – then snapped up his gun and shot him in the forehead at point-blank range. Red and grey slurry exploded over the wall behind him. The dead man crumpled to the floor. Granit didn't even give him a second glance. What mattered was that a witness had been removed and could no longer raise the alarm. 'Let's get them,' he ordered. His other men followed as he marched through the train after his targets.

36

The next carriage was another *kupe* coach, compartment doors closed. Nina and Eddie raced down the corridor. The train swayed as it passed over a small bridge, a concrete culvert beneath channelling water through the arid desert. Eddie almost stumbled, having to slow to steady himself.

The vestibule door behind him was thrown open. 'Go, go!' he told Nina, running again. She rounded the dogleg at the corridor's end. Eddie glanced back as he reached it, seeing Qabbani at the carriage's rear. The mercenary's gun came up—

Eddie flung himself around the corner. The bullet cracked against the bulkhead behind him. He thumped against the wall, momentarily unbalanced.

Qabbani ran after them. Nina hauled open the vestibule door and darted through. Eddie pushed himself upright and followed, but their pursuer had closed the gap—

Nina wasn't running. Instead she was waiting for him – with an almost expectant expression. 'What're you doing?' Eddie demanded as he slammed the door. 'Keep moving!'

'Just wait a second,' she replied.

'He'll be *here* in a second!'

'I know!' She raised the staser – and aimed it at the door handle, the green laser dot reflecting off the metal.

Eddie hurriedly moved clear. The handle turned—

Nina fired.

A savage electrical arc streaked along the line of ionised air – and passed through the metal to the man holding the other side.

Qabbani was still wet from his collision with the samovar, making him extra-conductive – and was blown backwards with such force that the handle was ripped from the door. He crashed unconscious to the floor, the handle still gripped in his paralysed hand.

Nina stared at the barrier. 'Think I got him?'

'Suddenly smells like a barbeque, so yeah,' Eddie replied. They rushed into the next carriage.

This was considerably more crowded and chaotic. It was a *platzkart* coach, open compartments with bench seats that could double as beds on one side of the gangway, single seats facing each other across small folding tables on the other. Bunk beds were mounted above the seats on both sides, limiting headroom. Every place was taken, people even sitting with their legs dangling down from the upper bunks. 'Glad we paid for the fancy seats,' said Eddie as they weaved along the aisle.

'There can't be many more cars left,' Nina warned. 'However we're going to get off this train, we need to figure it out fast!'

Several large bags and cases were precariously stacked on an upper bunk. Eddie yanked them from their perch as he passed, sending them tumbling into the gangway behind him. 'Sorry!' he said to the outraged owner, who jumped up with a shout. He dislodged more luggage a few compartments on, prompting other angry people to spill into the aisle. That would both slow their pursuers and prevent them from getting line of sight for a gunshot – assuming Granit was concerned about civilian casualties.

They reached the carriage's front end. Nina led the way through the vestibule and connecting corridor, the rubber bumpers squeaking and moaning against each other. She opened the next door—

And froze.

The new carriage was again *platzkart*, but considerably less crowded. She instantly realised why. Looking back at her from the aisle was one of the green-uniformed security officers from

Ashgabat station. The train's other passengers would rather endure cramped discomfort than share space with government agents who might be snooping on their every word.

The man's look of mild surprise became one of growing suspicion. Nina gave him a desperate smile and a wave, then hurriedly shut the door. 'Okay, car full of Gestapo,' she told Eddie.

'Shit!' he said – hearing a new commotion as Granit and his men forced their way through the passengers behind. A glance at the ceiling in the hope that there was a hatch to the roof . . .

There wasn't – but his eyes went instead to the connecting passage. 'Here,' he said, hurrying into it – and bringing up the combat knife. He stabbed its needle-sharp point into the top of one of the flexing bumpers and pushed hard, driving the blade deeper.

'What are you doing?' Nina asked.

'If I can cut through this,' he said, grunting as he used his weight to force the knife downwards, 'we can climb out.' The bumper, a sheet of thick rubber that had been folded back on itself to form a vertical tube, split neatly apart as the razor edge sliced through it.

'Is it big enough?'

'Should be for you.'

'But what about you?'

He didn't answer, instead crouching to carve through the bottom of the tube, before standing again and kicking hard at it. The ruined bumper flapped open, hot and dusty air blowing in along with the oily stench of diesel fumes. He glanced outside. Various connectors and pieces of equipment were built into the forward carriage's end – along with the small rungs of an access ladder. 'Get onto the roof,' he said. 'See if there's any way back inside the train so you can hide.'

Nina regarded the gap. She would be able to squeeze through, with effort, but Eddie was considerably more stocky. The only way for him to fit would be to cut away the other bumper – but there wasn't time. 'I'm not leaving you!'

'I'll get the Gestapo involved,' he said. 'Might be arrested, but it's better than being shot.' The commotion behind grew louder. 'Quick, go! They're coming!'

Nina gave him the staser to free up her hands before reluctantly pushing through the opening. 'I love you!' she called.

'Love you too – see you soon!' he replied, entering the next carriage.

She overcame her dismay and dragged herself outside. The remaining bumper ground against her with almost crushing force as the carriages rocked. But she managed to take hold of a protruding handle and haul herself through, finding a foothold on the ladder's lowest rung. A final pull, and she squeezed her hips through the gap – to leave herself clinging to the carriage as it clattered and swayed through the desert at fifty miles per hour.

'God *damn* it,' she gasped. 'Oswald, next time you can do your *own* investigation!' Still swearing under her breath, she clambered upwards.

Eddie pocketed the knife and staser in his jacket and entered the next carriage. That he was not Turkmenistani was obvious to its occupants, and the fact drew immediate suspicion, the two men standing in the aisle calling out an alert to their companions. Other faces peered from the compartments.

'Ay up,' said Eddie, walking urgently towards them. 'Anyone speak English?' The answer was evidently no. 'Bollocks. Okay . . .' He pointed back over his shoulder. 'Men, back there. They've got guns. Guns?' He held up a hand, putting his fingers into the shape of a pistol. 'Bang, bang! They're, er . . . selling drugs. Drugs!' Now he mimed injecting his arm with a syringe. 'Back there! You need to catch them. Quick!' He gestured for them to get moving.

The Border Service agents exchanged glances; some puzzled,

others hostile. One man, rank insignia suggesting he was the senior officer, marched up to Eddie and spoke in a stern, harsh voice. The Yorkshireman doubted he was even thirty years old. 'Sorry, don't understand,' he said. 'But go on, go, have a look. They've got guns.' More frantic charades. 'Fucking hell, you lot'd be useless at a Christmas party. Go and see!'

The officer finally comprehended at least part of his meaning. He issued an order, another man heading for the carriage's rear. Eddie started the other way, wanting to put as many of the agents between him and Granit's men as possible – but a sharp bark from the officer stopped him in his tracks. The man stabbed a finger at a bench seat, wanting him to sit.

'No, I really need to get going,' said Eddie. 'I need a pee. Toilet?' He mimed urinating – which prompted only a disgusted scowl from the officer. 'Look, I'll just be on my way, let you sort things out . . .'

He tried to continue along the gangway – but a sudden sway of the train pitched him against one of the agents, a slab of beefy muscle whose shirt collar strained to accommodate his thick neck. The man reacted with an aggressive shout, shoving him forcefully back against a divider. 'Oi!' Eddie said, instinctively bringing up an arm to ward him off. 'No need to—'

Anything less than immediate and total submission to authority was clearly unacceptable to those who wielded it in Turkmenistan. The hulking man smashed a balled fist into Eddie's stomach, bending him double. Before he could recover, his attacker and another agent threw him to the floor and pounded kicks into his chest and abdomen.

The officer snapped out another command. The assault ceased – but Eddie had no chance to catch his breath. He was dragged upright and thrown into a seat on the aisle's narrower side. A handrail was mounted on the divider beside the blue vinyl headrest. His left arm was forced against it – and by the time he realised what was happening, he had been handcuffed to the rail and rapidly searched. The officer glowered at the knife and staser, as if totting up the number of years they would earn the Englishman in prison.

Eddie twisted to look back down the carriage. The man who had been dispatched to investigate had paused to watch the one-sided fight; he now continued on his way. 'No, no, shit!' he said, yanking hard at the cuffs. Neither they nor the handrail gave way.

He was trapped – and Granit and his men would reach the carriage in moments.

Granit finally pushed past the last of the *platzkart* passengers and reached the vestibule door. He knew the situation had changed the moment he opened it. The metallic roar of the train's wheels was far louder than before, the stench of the locomotive's exhaust overpowering. He saw why as he stepped through. One of the rubber bumpers at the connecting corridor's side had been cut open, bright daylight streaming through the gap.

He rushed to it – just in time to see a pair of legs disappear over the top of the next carriage's roof. 'It's Wilde!' he growled. 'She's outside!'

'Where's Chase?' asked Wesler. The mercenaries had concealed their guns so as not to start a panic in the previous coaches, though his wounded arm had still drawn unwanted attention; he now drew his handgun again, holding it in his left hand.

'I don't know. We'll keep moving forward in case they've split up.' He assessed his men. 'Hellinger, can you fit through there?'

Hellinger was the slimmest of the team, with a triathlete's wiry build. 'I think so.' He quickly removed his jacket and started to squeeze through the narrow opening.

Granit continued onwards, readying his gun as he went to the next door.

* * *

The Border Service agent reached the vestibule door—

It opened.

Granit stood on the other side. Both men froze in momentary surprise. Then the Turkmenistani saw the new arrival's gun. He yelped a warning, his comrades reacting in alarm—

The Hungarian knew instantly that the game was up. He fired two bullets into the uniformed man's chest, dropping him, then sent another two shots down the gangway. The officer fell with a shrill cry. Granit rushed forward and ducked into the first of the open compartments. 'Kill them all!' he shouted.

Wesler hurried up behind him to take up position in the smaller compartment opposite. Ort remained in the doorway. His line of fire was restricted by the dogleg bend at its end – but the three mercenaries could between them still cover the carriage's entire length. All opened up at once, bloodily cutting down another agent as his fellows dived for cover.

'Jesus!' Eddie yelped, pressing himself against the window as bullets smacked into the divider behind him. One blasted a hole through it bare inches from his handcuffed arm, splinters stabbing into his hand. 'I fucking *told* you they had guns!'

The Turkmenistanis leaned out from the compartments to shoot back. Wesler ducked behind his own divider as rounds impacted around him. Eddie winced at the deafening cacophony of gunfire, but with only one hand free couldn't shield his ears. Instead he grabbed the cuff around his wrist and yanked at it, trying to break the chain or the handrail. Neither gave way.

The smaller of the men who had attacked Eddie shouted to his companions, then jumped into the aisle, unleashing a barrage of bullets as he rushed for the cover of the next compartment. A couple of the agents tried to give him covering fire. Eddie knew the attempt was doomed – the gangway was so narrow, the man was blocking their firing lines. The Turkmenistani was still a pace short of his destination when Ort put a round into his throat. He fell backwards, spewing a gargling fountain of blood as he clutched helplessly at his torn neck.

The big man was clearly his friend. He let out an incoherent roar of horror and rage, then lunged into the open to blast away at the mercenaries. Granit was forced to duck as bullets ripped through the wooden dividers. Ort also pulled back from the onslaught. Wesler fired a last wild shot, then retreated into concealment, needing to reload—

The Turkmenistani tracked him and kept firing. Holes exploded in the panel shielding the American – then a great burst of blood splattered across the rear bulkhead. The dead merc toppled into the aisle, the back of his skull blown open.

Granit swore – then, still crouching, swung back out into the gangway. The big man saw him and lowered his aim – but too late. Granit's first shot punched through his heart. Two more rounds hit beside it before the agent even started to fall. He slammed down on the floor just short of Eddie, a meaty barricade filling the aisle.

Eddie regarded the dead man – then remembered he was the one who had handcuffed him. If he could get the keys—

He dropped as low as he could, cuffed arm limiting his movements as much as the confined space, and reached out to claw at the corpse's jacket. More bullets flew in both directions above him. Another truncated cry of pain as an agent was hit. He closed his fingers and pulled. The dead man was too heavy to move, wedged against the gangway's sides – but his jacket's buttons strained before popping loose. Eddie hauled at the lapel, peeling the garment open. Another round blasted a hole in the wood close to his bound wrist. He flinched, then tugged at the jacket, trying to reach the inner pocket.

His fingertips slithered over the lining, then found something solid beneath the material. Where the hell was the top of the pocket? He risked peeking out. One merc down, but he could see both Granit and the man in the vestibule – and now they could see him—

He jerked his head back sharply as bullets shredded the blue vinyl seat above him. Another desperate yank at the dead man's jacket – and he finally found the pocket, feeling metal and leather inside. He grabbed everything he could and snatched his arm back into cover as a round tore into the corpse's chest.

The mercenaries switched targets back to the agents as the gun battle continued. Eddie stayed low, seeing what he had found. A State Border Service identity card in a shiny leather wallet; an actual wallet, out of which fell a folded clipping from a pornographic magazine—

Keys.

'Yes!' Eddie said under his breath. He quickly thumbed them around the ring, looking for the one for the handcuffs. House key, locker key, padlock key, old-fashioned long door key—

'*No!*' That was all of them. The handcuff key was in a different pocket. And he couldn't reach it without being shot. 'Fucknuts!'

He rose, planting his backside on the little table and twisting to kick at the handrail. In his awkward position he could barely get any leverage, weakening his strikes – and worse, he was partially exposed to the mercenaries' fire. He hurriedly abandoned another kick as Granit saw him, throwing himself sideways as far as he could go – which was not far. Shattered wood spat into his face as another bullet hole burst open beside his trapped hand.

Ort, meanwhile, concentrated his fire on the Turkmenistanis. A wet *smack* of lead hitting muscle and bone was followed by the thump of another body on the floor. A shout to Granit to call for covering fire, then the German rushed forward, vaulting the fallen Wesler to reach the compartment in front of him while his boss's shots kept the agents pinned.

The mercenaries were advancing on Eddie's position, cutting down the less well-trained Border Service men one by one.

And he had no way to escape.

37

Nina ran as fast as she dared back along the train, arms extended for balance. The gap between each swaying car was about five feet, the rubber bumpers of the connecting passages shrilling against each other. She vaulted over another, already halfway along the train's length.

A glance back into the gritty wind. One of Granit's men pulled himself up onto the roof. She forced herself to move faster, hunching down as she awaited the inevitable—

The sound of the silenced gunshot was lost beneath the diesel locomotive's throaty snarl – but the whipcrack as the bullet passed her was clearly audible. She flinched, dropping even lower. The train's constant, unpredictable shimmy had thrown off the man's aim. But the closer he got, the less chance that he would miss. She had to get inside.

Easier said than done. What she had thought was a hatch atop the rear of one car had turned out to be the blocky cover of an air conditioner, furiously thrumming against the remorseless desert heat. Nor did any of the connectors have an opening wide enough to fit through. The only possible entry point was the last carriage's rear door, and if it was locked, she would be trapped . . .

Not that she had any other choice. She hurried on. Another gap: only three more coaches to go. She made the jump—

A rattle and shrill from the couplers – and the train rocked.

The roof lurched sideways under Nina's foot as she landed. Unbalanced, she stumbled – and fell. The sun-seared metal burned her palms as she caught herself. She instinctively drew back her hands – only to slide down the curving roof towards its edge. She screamed as she clawed at the featureless surface—

A gutter, barely an inch deep, ran along the roof's edge. The toe of one shoe snagged it. She braced her leg, the metal strip catching her. Panting, hands searing, she dragged herself back up.

The mercenary was still coming. Nina scrabbled back to her feet and ran on. Another jump. This time she landed safely. Two more carriages . . .

And then she had nowhere left to go.

Eddie shielded his face with his free hand as another bullet smashed through the divider. Ort was concentrating his fire on the dwindling number of uniformed men, but Granit's only target was the man he blamed for his brother's death.

A horrible shriek told Eddie another of the Border Service men had been hit. At most, three of the Turkmenistanis were still in the fight, and a new voice warned that the numbers were now even as the recovered Qabbani caught up with the other mercenaries. The security agents wouldn't last for much longer – and then Granit would come for him—

Another shot tore through the divider, scant inches above his head – and the window shattered.

Eddie protected his eyes as the wind blew flying fragments into the carriage – then realised he now had more room to manoeuvre. He rose higher and leaned out of the new opening. Hot, dusty air hit him, but it was preferable to a bullet. He twisted, trying to bring his other foot as far back as possible . . . then kicked at the handrail.

The metal rang with the impact. He felt the jolt through the cuffs. It was stronger than his previous efforts. Another kick. Small cracks lanced across the divider as the rail's screws started to tear loose. He pulled at it as hard as he could. Kick, kick, wood cracking, the dull thud of another dead agent hitting the floor, kick—

The handrail broke free.

Eddie jerked backwards with the sudden release of tension – and toppled through the window.

He fell towards the blur of sleepers and stones below—

The handrail caught in the window frame's corner.

The other cuff was still locked around the metal bar. Eddie cried out as he jerked to a halt, the unyielding steel clasp grinding against his wrist bones. He flailed his other arm, managing to grab the bottom of the frame. The cuff cutting into his flesh, he started to pull himself up—

One foot clipped a mound of ballast on the trackside.

Even the light impact with the fist-sized stones almost tore him from the train. Again, the wedged handrail saved him. He dangled helplessly before once more swinging up his right hand. Fragments of broken safety glass ground into his fingers as he clutched the frame and dragged himself higher. A straining, painful sweep of his leg, and he hooked an ankle over the smashed window.

Only one gun was still firing forward of his position. A fusillade of near-simultaneous suppressed fire came from the carriage's rear – and the noise of gunshots abruptly ceased.

Eddie hauled himself up to take hold of the gutter. The handrail clattered loose from the cuff and dropped back into the coach. He stood straight and stretched his arms across the roof. His leather jacket blocked some of the heat radiating from it, but his palms burned on contact. Grimacing, he dragged himself onto the carriage's top. The hot metal seared his chest and belly; he hurriedly rolled onto his back, then sat up.

The fifty-mile-per-hour wind did little to cool him under the pitiless sun. He panted, trying to catch his breath – then realised he had no time for such a luxury.

Nina was at the train's far end. One of the mercenaries was closing on her.

He jumped up and started running back along the carriage's top—

Bullets ripped through the roof behind him.

Satisfied that all resistance had been dealt with, Granit reached the bullet-riddled divider. He whipped around it, gun raised—

His target was not there.

Thumps from above instantly told him where the Englishman had gone. Granit whirled and fired several shots into the ceiling, tracking the moving sound. But the pounding footsteps continued, rapidly fading.

He stabbed an angry finger back down the train. 'Find them!' he ordered. Ort and Qabbani ran back the way they had come as Granit climbed out of the broken window.

The railroad line came into view below, stretching away into the empty distance as Nina neared the end of the final carriage. She glanced back. The mercenary had just vaulted onto the penultimate car.

The last several feet of the gently arched roof were cut away to accommodate another blocky air-conditioning unit. She angled to its side, planting her soles firmly on the flat deck next to the rumbling machine and peering down. The car's rear was identical to the one she had first climbed up, another access ladder below.

She turned, starting her descent—

The man was already at the other end of the carriage.

His gun came up. She ducked – but wasn't far enough down the ladder to find full cover. The bullet struck the roof's edge, shrapnel spitting into her face. She flinched back – feet slipping from the ladder.

Falling—

One hand still had just enough of a hold to arrest her fall. Only for a moment – but in that split-second her foot hit a protruding electrical connector. The impact pitched her sideways against the connecting corridor. She clutched desperately at it, catching one of the bumpers.

Nina hung there, gasping in fear as the track rushed past beneath her. At this speed, a fall on to hard stone and concrete and steel would break multiple bones, even if it didn't kill her.

But she would be dead soon enough no matter what. Hellinger peered over the roof's edge. A shrug of mild surprise that she had wedged herself precariously in place – then he aimed his gun down at her.

She cringed, waiting for the shot—

More noises, rapid thuds – then Hellinger flew over her, arcing down towards the track. His startled scream was cut off as he hit the concrete sleepers head-first, skull and neck breaking with crunching snaps. His body tumbled along the line before stopping, dislocated limbs splayed grotesquely across the track.

Nina looked up again – and her heart filled with utter joy and relief at the sight of her husband above.

'Nina!' he said, breathing heavily from his run along the train's length to dropkick the mercenary off its end. 'Reach up, I'll grab you.' He crouched beside the air conditioner and stretched his arm down towards her.

She shakily brought up her free hand. Strong, rough fingers gripped hers. He pulled, letting her regain her balance and find a secure hold on the rungs.

Nina knew they needed to get inside the train, but all she wanted was to hold him and know they were both alive. She quickly scaled the ladder and hugged him. 'Thank God you're okay.'

'Close thing. My arm's fucking killing.' He raised his left wrist, revealing a set of handcuffs jangling from it. Blood oozed where the steel band had cut into his flesh. 'Still, stopped me from falling off the train, so I can't complain too—'

'Eddie!' Nina cried, looking over his shoulder. 'It's Granit!'

He turned – seeing the mercenary leader pounding towards them, gun in hand. 'Shit!'

Nina released him. 'We've got to get into the train.'

'No, wait. Look!'

A pale line cut arrow-straight across the grey and orange sands ahead. Another culvert, feeding water to a drilling rig somewhere deep in the empty wasteland. She immediately knew what he intended. 'You want us to *jump* into it? What if it's only six inches deep?'

'Then we only get wet up to our broken ankles! But it's either that or get shot.'

'Good point.'

Granit hurdled the gap onto the penultimate train car. The culvert swept towards him. Eddie gripped Nina's hand. 'Get ready,' he said. The water course was only seconds away. 'Try to land on your back.'

Granit raised his gun – but a sway of the train deterred him from shooting. Instead he continued towards them, striding with expectant triumph . . .

The train clattered over the little bridge spanning the culvert. Granit lifted his arms for balance as the carriage rocked beneath him – then caught the channel in his peripheral vision. Realisation struck. His gun snapped back—

Eddie moved. '*Jump!*'

He and Nina spun – and launched themselves off the carriage.

Water shimmered in the culvert below. It was deep enough to be flowing – but discoloured enough that they couldn't see *how* deep. Not that it mattered, as they would find out very soon—

Both brought up their legs to land on their backs. Nina let out an involuntary scream as she fell into the murky waterway – which was cut off as spray exploded around her. The concrete bed was not far beneath the surface. Her hips took the brunt of the landing, only a layer of sandy silt cushioning the impact. She cried out, spitting out dirty water.

Eddie's landing was harder – but he overcame his own pain to roll and grab his wife, pulling her towards the culvert's northern side. Little geysers burst from the water as bullets struck where they had just been. One final shot, then the train carried the seething Granit away out of range.

The Yorkshireman sat up with a wincing grunt, pain snaking up his spine. 'You okay?' he gasped.

'Considering that I just jumped off a train? *No!*' she gasped, putting both hands to her aching hips. 'I'm too old for this shit, Eddie!'

'*You're* too old for it? I'm five years older!' He tried to stand. 'Ow, buggeration and fuckery, that hurts.' He managed to bring himself upright, water streaming from his clothing. 'Can you move?'

'I'm not screaming in agony, so I guess so.' He helped her up. 'Okay, so where are we?'

Eddie surveyed their surroundings. The train was now a mere dot in the distance. Other than rocks and sand dunes, it was the only thing visible outside the culvert. 'Arse end of nowhere, by the look of it.'

'We're still an hour from Ruhnama,' Nina sighed. 'I don't re-member what else was along the route – if there even *was* anything.'

'There's a road,' Eddie remembered. 'Runs parallel to the railway.' He turned, looking eastwards. 'Can't see it, but it should be that way.'

'A nice walk in hundred-degree heat, great. At least we can dunk ourselves in this whenever we need to cool down. Not sure it's safe to drink, though.' She gave the grey water a distasteful look.

'If we can flag someone down on the road, hopefully we won't need to. Just need to get there before they send that helicopter to look for us.' He started to climb the culvert's northern bank – then changed his mind and splashed back across it to clamber up to the railway on the other side.

'Where are you going?' Nina asked.

'The bloke I punted off the train had a gun, and maybe other useful stuff too. Come on.' She crossed the waterway and joined him, heading southwards along the track.

It did not take long to reach Hellinger's broken body. Eddie searched him. He had more belongings than Granit's brother; the Englishman knew from his own experience that mercenary operations in some countries might entail frequent checks by the security forces – and also shakedowns. As well as identity papers, the American had over a thousand US dollars, along with a thick wad of local currency. He took the lot. The man's phone was as broken as his neck, so it was discarded. Hellinger also had two magazines for his pistol, but there was no sign of the weapon itself. 'Where's his gun?'

'Here,' said Nina, retrieving it from between sleepers a few metres away.

He inspected it. It didn't appear damaged. 'Don't need that,' he said, unscrewing and dropping the tubular suppressor. 'Makes it a bit hard to fit in a pocket.' He did exactly that with his new handgun – then at a sudden thought crouched again to feel the cuffs of the dead man's clothing. 'Ah-ha!' he said, extracting something from Hellinger's left sleeve.

'What's that?' Nina asked.

'Handcuff keys; skeletons,' he replied, showing them to her. 'Old merc trick, in case you ever get nicked.' He tried the little keys on the bracelet around his left wrist, which sprang open on the third attempt. 'Thank fuck for that,' he said, rubbing his bruised and bloodied skin.

Nina gazed off to the east. The horizon rippled with intense heat-haze, smears of oceanic blue appearing along it – but she also spotted something that was definitely not a mirage. 'I can see something moving,' she said excitedly, pointing. A boxy white shape rolled in and out of view through the distortions, heading northwards.

'The road can't be far,' was Eddie's assessment. 'Half a mile, maybe.'

'Let's see if we can hitch a ride.' They set out across the arid sands.

38

Granit was still livid by the time he reunited with his surviving men inside the train. Wilde and Chase had been at his mercy – only to escape!

The train slowed. The next stop was Ichoguz, practically the centre of the Karakum. The helicopter would be waiting for them. So far, no alarms had been raised. His threat had kept the civilians in their compartment, nobody had yet discovered the dead attendant, and the sound of the gun battle had been obscured both by the train's rumble and by the doors between it and the adjoining carriages. Granit suspected that even if any of the other passengers had heard it, they would not have been eager to involve themselves in the activities of the government agents.

He waited with Ort and Qabbani for the train to stop. The door opened and they jumped down. Nobody else disembarked. A small concrete building with a cellular mast on its roof stood at the platform's rear, a few other structures a few hundred metres beyond. The helicopter had landed on open ground, beside a road linking the station to the highway. Apart from that, there was nothing else in sight. The village of Darvaza once nearby had offended the eye of a past dictator when he passed through the area, and on his order been utterly demolished.

One of Granit's men, an Australian named Braddock, met them, noticing the absence of the expected prisoners – and also of some of his comrades. 'What happened?'

'They got away,' was Granit's curt reply. He took out his phone and made a call as the train set off again.

'Well?' demanded Rafael Loost. 'Do you have Wilde and Chase?'

'No,' Granit growled. 'They jumped off the train. I'm going to use the helicopter to search for them.'

Loost didn't respond at once. The Hungarian guessed he was checking something on a computer. 'Don't bother,' he said at last.

Granit was both surprised and irate. 'They might be wounded. We can finish them off.'

'If they're wounded in a desert under forty-five-degree heat without shade, they won't last long. If they're not wounded, they'll easily be able to reach the highway and flag down a ride. But we know where they're going. Wilde has arranged transport at Ruhnama. Catch them there.'

Granit frowned, displeased. But Loost was paying him a *lot* of money, so . . . 'Yes, sir,' he said. 'By the way, we took casualties. Chase killed two of my men.' He decided not to mention the shootout with the local security forces. If it appeared that he had lost control of the situation, Loost might reconsider his employment – and he was unwilling to give up the chance for revenge.

'That's . . . unfortunate.' Loost sounded unsure as to whether he should express sympathy. 'Did you clean everything up?'

'Yes. There's nothing that can link to you.' That was not certain, but again, he kept it to himself.

'Good. Okay. Get to Ruhnama and wait for Wilde and her husband. If she comes within range of a cell tower, her phone will automatically connect to Uzz and I'll know where she is. I'll keep you informed.'

'Okay,' said Granit, ending the call. He turned to his men. 'We'll intercept them at Ruhnama.' He signalled for the pilot to start the engine, then the men headed for the helicopter.

'Bloody hell,' said Eddie as he and Nina trudged across the sands. 'Bit warm today, innit?' Despite having been soaked in the culvert, their clothes were now almost dry.

She smiled. 'And there you are in a black leather jacket.'

'It's my good luck charm. Every bad situation I've got into while I've been wearing it, I've got out of.'

'Or another way of looking at it is that you keep *getting* into bad situations while you're wearing it.'

'All right, all right. I wear it 'cause I think it makes me look cool. Happy now?'

'I always think you look cool, Eddie,' she said, squeezing his hand. He smiled.

They kept walking. The shimmering mirages made it hard to judge how far they were from the highway, but they had already seen more vehicles travelling along it, in both directions. It seemed unlikely they would have to wait long for assistance.

Something closer came into view ahead. 'Ay up,' said Eddie. 'Glad we saw that before we fell into it.'

It was a sinkhole, a near-circular pit some forty feet across. Nina changed direction to give it a wide berth, but Eddie approached the edge. 'Eddie, don't,' she warned. 'It might not be safe.'

'Just want to see how deep it is,' he replied.

'Famous last words, often followed by "Aaaaargh!"'

He grinned, then peered into the hole – to her relief, from a few steps short of the edge. 'Must go down over a hundred feet. Wonder if there's anything at the bottom?'

'Like what?'

'A few million quid's-worth of gas would be nice. Or maybe this Iron Palace. That'd save us some time.' He caught up with Nina. 'The road can't be far now . . . you okay?'

She was gazing at the sinkhole, distracted. 'Yeah. Just thinking about the way the Brotherhood phrased something – oh, dammit!' She halted, looking back in dismay towards the railroad line. 'All my notes are on the train! I can't check the exact wording.'

'Do you remember enough to find the place?'

'When we get there, yeah. But . . . ugh!' She let out a growl of exasperation.

'Let's keep going,' Eddie said with sympathy.

Five more minutes, and the road finally took on clear form, a dark grey line bisecting the desert. 'At last,' said Nina with relief, wishing she had kept the headscarf. She had done what she could to shield herself, but her skin was prickling with sunburn. 'And there's something coming.' She pointed south. A vehicle was visible in the distance.

They increased pace, soon reaching the highway. By then, the approaching vehicle was revealed as a white SUV. Eddie stepped out into its lane and waved for it to halt. 'Maybe they'll be more likely to stop for you,' he said, seeing that it wasn't slowing. 'Go on, flash 'em.'

'Eddie,' Nina chided as she joined him. But the oncoming SUV did now reduce speed and pull over to meet them.

Its occupants, a man and a woman with a girl of about ten, were surprised to have encountered anyone on foot, immediately offering them water and a lift. Nina was equally surprised, once communication was established in pidgin English, to learn that they were tourists, driving from the capital to visit one of Turkmenistan's more unusual attractions. About twenty-five minutes later, after turning north-east off the highway onto a dirt track, they reached it, parking near a handful of other vehicles. It was another sinkhole – far larger than the one earlier, over two hundred feet across. But it was not its size alone that drew visitors.

The couple thanked their rescuers for the ride, Eddie insisting on giving them some money, then headed for the fence surrounding the crater. 'Well,' said the Yorkshireman as they reached it, 'that's not something you see every day.'

'Maybe if you live by a New Jersey garbage dump,' Nina quipped, but she was startled – and awed – by what lay before them. The Gates of Hell, as the feature was known, was ablaze, flames swirling ceaselessly inside the pit. Even behind the fence, the heat was almost unbearable.

The young girl had given them a creased tourist brochure in several languages, including English, that provided background information. Over sixty years before, Soviet geologists had started drilling into a pocket of natural gas beneath the desert; unfortunately for them, the ground was unstable and the rig was swallowed by a sinkhole. To prevent pollution, the escaping methane was set alight, the expectation being that it would burn itself out in a few months. But despite several attempts by the Turkmenistani government to cap the leak, it was still burning six decades later.

The sight brought other things to Nina's mind than the hubris of authoritarian states. 'This *must* be how the Iron Palace was lit,' she realised, gazing down into the fiery abyss. 'Afrasiab channelled gas from underground and ignited it – although he controlled it a lot better than this. Which means . . .' She chewed her bottom lip, deep in thought. 'Which means, I might have been wrong about its location. I thought it had to be in the canyon north-west of Ruhnama. But I don't think the Brotherhood ever actually said the cave went into the ground horizontally. They just said it was deep. What if it was a *sinkhole*?'

'Maybe,' said Eddie, nodding. 'But that doesn't help us find it. The whole desert might be full of them.'

'But we know we're in the right area, where the Atlantean and Brotherhood's journeys intersect. A geological map will show any possible candidates.'

'I don't think you'll get Wi-Fi out here.' Despite its being a tourist attraction, the fence and a short stretch of paved walkway were the only man-made structures at the crater.

'No, but . . .' She looked back towards the parked vehicles. Most were 4x4s, and three of them, all in a row, were kitted out for desert trekking, roof-racks laden with camping gear. Her gaze scanned the sinkhole's rim. Off to one side was a group of six people in their twenties. Some were taking selfies with the flaming pit behind them, while one man flew a drone out over it. 'I'm willing to bet at least one of those guys has a satellite phone.'

'You think they'll let you use it?'

'How many dollars did you take off that dead guy?'

'They'll let you use it.'

'Uh-huh. Let's go talk to them.'

They walked around the crater towards the group. It became clear long before they reached them that they were American, boisterous voices calling to each other in English. 'Hi,' said Nina when a young man looked around at their approach. 'I didn't expect to meet any other Americans out here.'

The tall and lean man gestured towards his friends. 'We're doing some trouble tourism!' he crowed.

'Trouble tourism?'

'Yeah! We're touring all these countries that nobody normally goes to 'cause they're run by dictators or whatever. Our Uzz channel's got over five million followers!'

'Bit risky, isn't it?' said Eddie. 'Dictators don't generally like people slagging off their country.'

'We don't do any politics, dude,' said another man in thick-framed glasses. 'Just natural beauty, cool buildings, that kind of thing. We're gonna keep the serious stuff for when we get a book deal – after we're long out of here, obviously!' The pair laughed.

Another of their number came over, regarding Nina first with curiosity – then recognition. 'Hey, aren't you – you are! You're Nina Wilde!'

'I am, yeah,' she admitted. 'But keep it quiet, or everybody'll want to talk to me.'

'Ah, working like us, hush-hush. Gotcha.' He tapped the side of his nose. 'So what are you doing here? This ain't Atlantis. This ain't much of anything!'

'I'm . . . doing research for a TV show,' she said. The lie was accepted; she had made archaeological documentaries in the past. 'But our car broke down in the desert, and we had to hitch a ride. I was hoping one of you has a satellite phone? I need access to data so I can check some maps.'

'I do,' said the drone operator, coming to them with his aircraft cradled in one arm like a puppy. 'I can set up my phone as a Wi-Fi hotspot so you can link to it. It's kind of expensive to use data through the satellite, though.'

Eddie took out Hellinger's wad of dollars. 'We'll pay for it.'

The man nodded enthusiastically. 'Yeah, yeah, that should cover it!'

'Thank you,' said Nina, taking out her own phone. 'Shall we get started?'

Connecting to the internet via the drone operator's phone proved relatively painless. Within minutes, Nina had access to the highly detailed maps she needed from the IHA's database. She sat cross-legged on the ground, Eddie standing over her to provide shade for her screen. He took the opportunity to connect his own phone to the hotspot to check his email. 'Jared finally got back to me,' he said. 'Says he'll do what he can to help out – once he knows what he's helping *with*.'

'We still don't know where Macy is,' said Nina. 'If he can do anything to find her . . .'

'Yeah, already telling him.' He tapped at his screen as she continued working.

The IHA had high-resolution satellite surveys of the majority of the planet's surface, both photographic and radar. The latter was more useful to Nina; by adjusting various settings, she could highlight sharp changes in elevation. She tested it on the crater beside them. It appeared on the map as a glaring red circle, standing out as brightly as the flames within its real-life counterpart.

'Okay,' she said, zooming out, 'let's see what we can see . . .'

More sinkholes were revealed. Another large one was not far south of the Gates of Hell, though its proximity to the road ruled it out as a potential target: someone would surely have explored it already. A smaller dot between the highway and railroad marked the hole they had come across after jumping from the train.

She scrolled the map, performing a methodical grid search. Toggling one setting on and off changed the topographic colours, causing anything that matched her criteria to flash very visibly. She zoomed in upon these for a closer inspection. The desert's general flatness meant there were few false alarms; most of what she found were indeed sinkholes. She copied each one's co-ordinates to a note on the phone, then checked them on a satellite view. The Brotherhood's records may not have been definitive about whether the entrance to the Iron Palace was a horizontal or vertical cave, but it had been clear on one thing: its size. She gave particular attention to her largest discoveries.

Refusing to feel pressured by the drone operator's occasional impatient glances, she kept working. Finally, she had noted every possibility in a search zone of over two hundred square miles. One in particular stood out. 'Eddie, look,' she said, showing him. 'It's a big sinkhole, at least a hundred feet across, and it's *deep* – much deeper than this one or the one we passed near the railroad. And . . .' She showed more of the surrounding desert. Several pale lines weaved across the sands, intersecting close to her target. 'They're dry now, but these are former rivers. Four of them. And according to Zoroastrian mythology, four rivers flowed into the Iron Palace. Look at this, too.' Another zoom, onto an almost reflective patch of greenish ground east of the sinkhole. 'I can't be sure without seeing it in person, but that could be sand that's been fused into glass. The Brotherhood said Afrasiab demonstrated the staff's power by calling down a lightning strike nearby.'

'That'd do the job.' Eddie regarded the screen thoughtfully. 'Where is it?'

'Roughly west of here, maybe twelve miles away.'

He frowned. 'Nowhere near where we were planning to go.' The canyon was almost due north of the fiery crater.

'I know. But I'm now thinking my assumptions about that being the only place to look were wrong. I'll have to see for myself to be sure, though.'

'See for ourselves, you mean,' he corrected. She gave him a grin of acknowledgement. 'Bit far to walk, mind. Especially in this heat.' The trouble tourists had given them some bottles of water, but it was still almost unbearably hot.

'I've had an idea about that.' She stood, signalling to the drone operator and his friends. They came over. 'Thank you so much for that,' she said, returning the young man's phone. 'Although, I was wondering if you could lend us something else . . .'

Eddie guided a battered Land Rover across the desert sands. 'Can't believe you persuaded them to sell you one of their four-by-fours,' he said with a chuckle.

Nina was less amused. 'I can't believe how much I had to pay for it!' The remainder of their dollars had been nowhere near the group's asking price, forcing her to use the satellite hotspot to transfer the remainder electronically to the owner's account. 'And technically, I didn't buy it. I'm renting it . . . with an exceptionally large security deposit.'

'You can always borrow it back from Macy.'

'If I see her again.'

Her dark comment took away Eddie's smile. 'We will,' he assured her. 'If she's used her cards or her passport, or if she's been on any of her social media, Jared'll be able to tell us. Might take a while, but he'll let me know what he finds.'

'*If* he finds anything,' Nina said. She gazed glumly out at the sandy vista ahead. This part of the Karakum was almost depressingly featureless, an endless slog of gently humped dunes providing a vaguely nauseating slow-motion roller coaster sensation. The railroad was the last evidence of human encroachment into the wilderness, already a mile behind them. 'How far away are we?'

A rugged satnav unit was mounted beside the steering wheel. 'About nine miles,' Eddie said. 'Should take under an hour, if we're lucky.'

'Some luck would be good right now,' she sighed, settling back in the passenger seat to endure the journey.

39

Eddie squinted at the desert ahead as the Land Rover crested a dune. The sun's arc towards the westward horizon meant he was now driving into its glare – and something on the ground half a mile distant had just intensified the light still further. 'You see that?'

'I see it,' said Nina, her boredom and discomfort evaporating. The mystery object acted like a mirror, as blinding as looking directly at the sun itself. She leaned across to check the satnav. 'We're less than a mile from the sinkhole. That could be what I saw on the satellite imagery – the spot where the lightning struck.'

'Or a really lost lighthouse,' Eddie offered, but he still adjusted course to head for the source of the light.

It did not take long to reach. The Land Rover stopped near a rocky outcrop, wind-scoured stone poking through the sand. 'Look at that,' said Nina, amazed, as they walked to it. 'That's *got* to be where the lightning hit.'

A twisted column of what looked almost like jade rose from the ground to over waist height. It was fulgurite, she knew: petrified lightning, the heat and power of a strike fusing sand into glass. She had seen an example in a museum as a child. That, though, had resembled a mere branch compared to the glistening tree-trunk before her. The pillar was more than two feet thick, stubby limbs projecting outwards where the bolt's intense force had arced through the sand.

It was not the only one, either. Other greenish crystals nearby caught the sunlight. If Afrasiab had indeed demonstrated his power on this spot, he had done so in a way calculated for maximum impact. She went to the fulgurite column and touched it almost gingerly, as if some fraction of the force that created it might still be present. 'The Brotherhood said Afrasiab called down lightning all around them,' she said. 'Can you imagine standing right here while it happened? With him laughing because he knows he's safe?'

'I'd be yelling, "You utter wanker!" over all the thunderbolts,' said Eddie. He looked off to the west. 'Ay up. I can see the sinkhole.'

Nina followed his gaze. A dark circle stood out from the sands, several hundred metres distant. 'Let's see if the rest of what the Brotherhood wrote was true.' They returned to the Land Rover and drove the short remainder of their journey.

There was no safety fence around this hole in the ground. They approached cautiously, Eddie holding on to Nina as she peered over the rim. 'What can you see?' he asked.

'Not much,' she replied. 'It's deep, over a hundred feet – and the bottom's in shadow. Although . . .' She spotted something on the shaft's side and moved for a clearer view. 'Those look like rungs. Somebody's carved a ladder into the rock! This *has* to be the right place.'

'Wouldn't want to risk climbing it, though.' Centuries of erosion had taken their toll, many of the steps missing chunks. 'We'll need to use ropes.' A beat. 'You did check there were some in the Land Rover when you bought it, right?'

'*Yes*, I did,' said Nina, with an exasperated laugh. 'Let's take a look.'

They drank more water, then while Nina put flashlights and other gear and supplies in a shoulder bag, Eddie took a coil of rope from the 4x4's rear. 'It's sixty metres, so should be long enough,' he said. 'There aren't any climbing harnesses, though. I'll lower you down with the winch, then climb down after you.'

It did not take long for the former SAS man to secure a makeshift harness around her body. He attached the winch hook to a loop, knotted where the rope crossed her chest. 'Right,' he said. 'Walk yourself down backwards, nice and slowly. I'll lower you.'

'Okay.' She had made similar descents before. Gripping the rope tightly, she carefully backed to the edge of the hole.

Her husband wrapped the line around one arm, then moved his other hand to the winch controls. 'You ready?'

She took a deep breath, then nodded. 'Yeah.'

'See you down there.' He flicked a switch, and the winch slowly unreeled its steel cable.

Nina began her descent. The rope pulled tightly around her as it took her weight, but Eddie's knots held firm, spreading the pressure evenly. Step by step, she was lowered into the sinkhole. Grit and sand crumbled away under her feet, but the underlying rock felt solid.

It took a few minutes to reach the bottom, a hundred and fifty feet below. 'Okay, almost there!' she shouted, her voice echoing back up the shaft. The winch cable halted with a jolt. She tipped herself vertically, holding on to the rock face. Her boots were less than a metre off the floor. 'Another couple of feet!' The cable obligingly lowered. With relief, she planted her soles on the sand and scree covering the sinkhole's foot, then detached the hook. 'All right,' she called to Eddie. 'I'll unfasten myself, then you can come down.'

She unhooked the cable, then worked loose the knots and moved clear. The rope shuddered as Eddie rappelled quickly down it. 'Ay up, love,' he said as he dropped the last few feet to the ground. 'You okay?'

'Yeah,' she said. 'It was straightforward enough. Getting back up will be harder, though.'

'I'll climb up, then use the winch to get you out. What've we got down here, then?'

They both turned to investigate the bottom of the shaft. The floor sloped; they had landed on its higher side. At the very bottom, cloaked in shadow, was a Z-shaped fissure, far too narrow for anyone to enter. What drew Nina's eye, though, was set back into the sinkhole's wall beneath an overhang.

A cave.

Sand had built up at the bottom of the opening, but it was still large, a ragged archway leading into blackness beyond. Eddie had brought the bag; he took out the flashlights. They shone them into the cave, revealing that the floor sloped downwards for a short way before angling back up. Even with the accumulation of debris, it was still high enough to stand in. 'You think that's it?' Eddie asked.

'It fits what the Brotherhood described,' Nina replied. 'Shall we look inside?'

'We've come all this way – be a bit of a waste not to.' They advanced cautiously into the cave's mouth.

Signs that it was more than a natural tunnel soon became apparent. 'That's been carved by someone,' said Nina, shining her light at a section of the ceiling. Smooth stone contrasted with its rougher surroundings where an obstruction had been chipped away. 'Afrasiab and his people?'

'We'll know if someone starts blasting lightning bolts at us,' said Eddie.

They continued, soon reaching the upward incline. Their torches revealed that the passage ascended at a moderate angle for perhaps sixty feet before levelling out. 'Looks like a cave at the top.'

'Let's see.'

They tramped upwards. The amount of blown sand that had penetrated the tunnel gradually diminished until only bare rock was underfoot. Nina found herself breathing heavily by the time they neared the summit. She was slightly surprised that Eddie was doing the same; he had maintained his fitness regime even decades after leaving military service. 'You okay?'

'Yeah. Must be dehydrated.' He paused to take out a bottle of water and drank from it, then offered it to her. She accepted gratefully. Thirst quenched for the moment, they pressed on.

They reached the top of the slope. The chamber beyond was close to thirty feet high, a path along its floor worn smooth by the passage of feet over countless years. 'This *has* to be the way into the Iron Palace,' said Nina, feeling an almost giddy surge of excitement. 'We found it!'

'Found something else, an' all.' Eddie aimed his torch at something off the path ahead.

A body.

It had been there a long time, what remained of its flesh almost mummified from desiccation in the dry desert air. Empty eye sockets gazed pitifully at them as they approached. 'What happened to them?' said Nina.

'Dunno. Ran out of water, maybe?' The Yorkshireman regarded the shrivelled corpse, then swept his light around the cave. 'Another one there.' A second figure was hunched against the wall.

Nina stared at it. There was something *wrong* about the body, but it took her several seconds to realise what. 'Those clothes are . . . sort of modern. I mean, they're not robes, the kinda thing people would have worn thousands of years ago.' She went closer, fixing her flashlight's beam upon its feet. 'Those are boots, desert boots. Like you would have worn in the army.'

Her husband joined her. 'No, there's no laces. These are more like jackboots.'

She reacted with surprise. 'He's a Nazi?'

'Probably Russian, Soviet. They wore 'em too. Did you know they hadn't invented socks? Wrapped their feet in bits of cloth.

I tried that once in survival training. Fucking hurts if you don't get it exactly right.'

'I bet. But this guy didn't die from foot blisters.' She giggled at the idea. 'So what *did* kill him?' She thought hard – then looked around in alarm. 'Shit, Eddie! We didn't check for booby traps!' Her light skittered frantically over the surrounding cave, but found nothing.

Eddie did the same, also with no result. 'Nothing that I can see. But – why *didn't* we check? Not like we haven't done this before.'

'I don't know. Something's wrong.' She took a deep breath – then another, worried. 'It's like I'm breathing okay, but I'm not getting enough air. I feel dizzy.'

'Me too.' He shone his torch deeper into the cave. Other corpses were revealed. 'More stiffs up there. Can't think straight. Don't like this.'

'I think we need to get out . . .' Realisation finally pushed through the sludge clogging her mind. 'Oh, shit! It's gas, it's the gas!' Eddie looked blankly at her. 'From the Iron Palace, the flames that light it up! They must have gone out, they're not burning any more – but the gas is still coming up out of the ground. It's lighter than air, so it's built up in here!'

His eyes widened. 'Fuckerbuggation and, er – you know,' he mumbled. 'Better go.'

They hurried back towards the tunnel. But the lack of oxygen was already affecting them, their movements drunken and sluggish. 'Oh, God,' Nina gasped, clutching at Eddie for support. 'We're not gonna make it!'

'We are,' he told her, voice brusque and professional as survival training kicked in despite his wooziness. 'Don't talk. Hold your breath.' He took hold of her arm, urging her down the slope. The daylight seeping in at the bottom seemed to retreat as he watched. He moved faster, hauling Nina with him.

They reached the halfway point – then Nina stumbled. Without Eddie's grip on her, she would have fallen. She gasped in bleary fright. 'Don't breathe!' Eddie rasped, staggering as he hauled her upright. 'Keep going!'

'I – I can't,' she said, her voice a weak croak. 'Legs are all, all wobbly. I can't, I—'

A last desperate pant, drawing in only gas-filled air – then she crumpled. Eddie almost fell as her weight unbalanced him. He braced himself, his own legs feeling rubbery, and continued his weaving, flat-footed descent.

The light grew brighter, but started to swim and waver in his vision, a terrible pressure building inside his chest. He had to breathe, but he couldn't. How many more steps?

He couldn't judge the distance. The sand and stones below blurred. Had to breathe. But couldn't. Keep going. Not far.

A deep sound grew ever-louder in his ears, like a boulder rolling towards him, rumbling, rumbling. His lungs were about to burst. He had to breathe or he would collapse. But if all he took in was gas—

His body made the decision for him.

He exhaled, coughing and retching – then drew in a desperate, choking breath, filling his lungs with . . .

Air.

His vision cleared. He was at the bottom of the slope, even the shadowed daylight in the sinkhole now dazzling. Another painful breath, then he half-carried, half-dragged the limp Nina into the open. She was still breathing – but after losing consciousness, all she would have taken in was the toxic gas. How badly had it affected her? He brought her almost to the hanging rope, then carefully set her down. 'Nina?' he said, cradling her head in his hands. 'Nina! Can you hear me? Are you okay?'

No reaction. His fear grew – then suddenly she convulsed, expelling the contents of her lungs with a hacking cough before gasping in clean air. It took several more deep breaths before she could speak. 'Oh, God! Eddie!' she wheezed, clutching at him. 'Are you okay?'

'I'm fine,' he said, smiling in relief. 'It's you I was worried about. How do you feel?'

'Like I hooked my lungs to a taxicab's tailpipe.' Her frenetic breathing finally slowed. 'Did I pass out?' He nodded. 'Jeez. How did you manage to keep going?'

'Remembered my forces training. They used to chuck us in a room full of tear gas without a mask. I got pretty good at holding my breath.'

'I should have kept running with Macy.' She had started doing so a few years before, but eventually lapsed as Macy spent more time with her friends. 'So now what? We've found the entrance to the Iron Palace, but we can't get in! I'm pretty sure there weren't any gas masks in the truck.'

'No, but this might help.' Eddie unslung the bag and rooted through its contents, taking out a distress flare.

Nina eyed it. 'Ah, you're going to signal the gas company to come fix the leak.'

'Had something quicker in mind.' He indicated a boulder half-buried in the sand nearby. 'Get behind that and take cover.'

The instruction filled her with alarm. 'What are you doing?'

'What I do best – blowing shit up.' He helped her up and they went to the rock. Nina lay flat behind it as he crouched, removing the flare's plastic caps and aiming it towards the cave entrance. 'If I shoot it in there, the gas'll ignite and burn off, and once it clears we'll be able to get through.'

'You sure that'll work?' she said, shielding her head.

'Nope. Fire in the hole, literally!'

He pulled the firing cord – and the distress rocket burst from its tube.

It arced across the sinkhole, dropping down into the cave –

where it bounced off the bottom of the slope and deflected upwards into the tunnel. For a moment, all Eddie could see was the flare's sizzling red glow, fading as the rocket skittered up the passage . . .

Then a bright flash overpowered it.

He hurriedly dropped flat behind the rock, shielding Nina. A thunderous roar came from the cave, growing louder – then the ground shook and a pounding wave of dust surged past them as a fiery explosion burst from the entrance. Nina shrieked as oven-hot air hit the couple, but the actual flames from the burning gas roiled up the sinkhole's side in a seething tornado. A secondary eruption came from the Z-shaped fissure, blasting out the sand clogging it. The fury continued for several seconds, then faded.

Eddie raised his head. Everything was shrouded in haze, burning debris scattered across the sinkhole, but the fireball itself had dissipated. 'Think that did the trick.'

'Let's hope we didn't just obliterate the entire Iron Palace,' said Nina. She looked up. The circle of blue sky above was partially obscured by a drifting column of smoke and particulates.

'I dunno; if this staff's as dangerous as it sounds, it might have been for the best.' He peered through the wafting dust at the cave mouth. 'If we give it five minutes, this should clear.'

'Okay.' Nina took water from the bag and washed out her gritty mouth. 'Then we'll see what's down there.'

40

A helicopter thundered northwards across the Karakum. Macy looked out of a cabin window at the endless wastes rolling by below. It seemed almost impossible that the Staff of Afrasiab could be hidden out here – that *anything* could be hidden out here. But everything she and the other Knights had learned suggested that the rebel king's desert stronghold was somewhere in the dusty desolation; somewhere within a relatively limited area, at that.

All they had to do was find it. Before the Brotherhood of Selasphoros.

Events had moved at an almost bewildering rush. Macy knew from accompanying her parents on their world-saving adventures that it was possible to arrange international travel at very short notice when necessary. But what oiled the gears of the system was power, and more importantly, money. The IHA was able to marshal both, but the speed at which the journey to Turkmenistan had been organised took even her by surprise. The Order of Behdet must indeed have considerable finances – and political influence. They were greeted as VIPs on their arrival by private jet in Ashgabat, met by smiling senior officials of the government and border service, and whisked through customs with barely more than a glance at passports and paperwork to a waiting helicopter, its cargo compartments already loaded with supplies and equipment for a desert sojourn.

Now, the final stage of the dizzying trip was upon them. She regarded her companions. The helicopter had twelve seats in the rear cabin, three rows of four divided by a very narrow aisle.

MacDuff and Meller were in the rearmost row, the Scot still perusing the analysis provided by Rafael Loost's quantum computers on a laptop. Leni, Idris and Rain were in the middle row; Macy had been sitting beside her friend in the aisle seat, but when Rain fell asleep, exhausted more mentally than physically, she moved forward to get a view of the landscape below.

Emilian had taken the co-pilot's seat in the cockpit. Naima Halko was the only other person in the front row with her. Macy knew the Finn had to be in as much emotional pain as Rain, but for the most part she had not shown it. Now, though, staring fixedly at the blank back of the pilot's seat, her façade was starting to crack. The redhead slid across the seats to be closer to her. 'Naima? Are you okay?'

Naima took a moment to react. The helicopter's passengers wore headphones to muffle the constant whine of the engines and rotor, which even with the cabin's soundproofing was still intrusive. Macy had left her headphones on her seat when she moved; Naima slid off her own. 'I don't know,' she said, voice flat. 'I don't even know why I'm here.'

'To stop the Brotherhood from getting the staff,' Macy reminded her.

She shook her head. 'That's not it. Not for me.' A long pause, emotions at odds just beneath the surface. 'For me, it's . . . to avenge Jari, perhaps,' she reluctantly admitted. 'But I hope it is not. He wouldn't want that. He wouldn't want me to risk my life for revenge.'

Macy didn't know how to take that. 'Hopefully you won't have to risk your life, for anything. Hopefully none of us will.'

Another look, this time with an unsettling air of resignation. 'I suppose we will see, won't we?' She sat up, unbuckling her lap belt. 'I'm thirsty. I need some water.'

'There's some in the back. I'll get you a bottle,' Macy offered.

'Thanks, but that's okay. I need to stretch my legs. Too long on a plane, too long in a helicopter . . . too long in my own mind.' She stood and squeezed down the aisle, heading aft.

Macy unhappily watched her go, not knowing if she had helped or made things worse. She considered going back to Rain, but a glance told her she was still asleep. Instead she peered through the gap between the pilots' seats. 'Hey, Emilian.' He didn't react at first, his own headphones still in place. She tapped his shoulder. 'Hey.'

He flinched at her touch, looking sharply around before realising who it was. 'Macy! Hi.'

'Hi,' she said. 'Are you all right? I didn't mean to startle you.'

He removed his headphones. 'It's okay. Sorry. I was just . . . thinking.'

'About what happened at the villa?'

'Yes. I'm . . .' He clenched his jaw. 'I'm still *angry* about it, as well as everything else that I'm feeling. It shouldn't have happened! Fernando, and Jari, and the others . . . they shouldn't have died. They *shouldn't*.'

'No,' Macy agreed. 'And . . . I can't help feeling responsible. The Brotherhood came after *me* in France, they were hunting for me personally – and somehow they followed me to Portugal. None of this would have happened if I hadn't been—'

'No,' he cut in firmly. 'It wasn't your fault. We were there to protect you. I don't know how the Brotherhood tracked us to the estate, but again, you weren't to blame.' His face tightened. 'It's our own fault for not doing enough to protect ourselves. I *told* the elders, we have to be prepared to take direct action, to be ready to defend ourselves. This wouldn't have happened if they had done what I wanted!'

She put a reassuring hand on his arm. 'Now *you're* blaming yourself. You can't do that. If none of this was my fault, then it definitely wasn't yours.'

Emilian said nothing for several seconds, staring off into the distance. 'They should have done what I said from the start,' he finally murmured. Another moment of silence, then he shook his head. 'But I can't change what's happened. All I can do is stop the Brotherhood from getting the Staff of Afrasiab. And I will do that. I'm the leader of the Knights now; I *will* do it.'

'I know you will.' Macy squeezed his arm again. He gave her a small smile.

The pilot, a Turkmenistani called Nuryev, gestured for Emilian to put his headphones back on. He did so, the two men having a rapid discussion via their headsets. 'We're nearing the search area,' the Dutchman told her. 'Get to a window – we need as many eyes on the desert as we can.'

She nodded. 'I'll go wake Rain.'

Her friend jolted awake when Macy returned to her seat. 'What is it?'

'We're almost at the search area,' said the redhead. 'We need to start looking.' She retrieved her headphones, hearing Emilian passing on the news to the others.

MacDuff stopped his work and brought up a map of the desert on his laptop. The helicopter had its own wireless node, letting him overlay the aircraft's position. 'Okay,' he said into his microphone. 'We're starting at the south-west corner of the search grid, am I right?'

'Yes,' Emilian replied. 'You track where we are on the map, Euripides. Everyone else, look for *anything* on the ground that might be what we're after.'

The other passengers spread through the cabin, the windows on both sides of all three rows covered. Meller and Idris took the rear, Macy and Rain the middle, Leni and Naima the front row. Macy didn't know how high the helicopter was, but guessed a few thousand feet, the desert horizon blurred by distance. Far away, she could just barely make out the thin line of the lone highway crossing the wilderness, but the search area they had determined was some way to its west. The thought occurred that if anything went wrong, they were an awful long way from rescue, but she suppressed it.

The first leg of the search brought them into sight of something that had already been marked as a potential target: a sinkhole. But a descent to circle it for a closer examination revealed it was little more than a crater, barren and sand-filled. If it had any secrets, they were deeply buried. 'I'll mark it anyway,' said MacDuff. 'I suppose it was too much to hope we'd find it on the very first try.'

The helicopter returned to its original course. Nothing of note was spotted. Nuryev came around in a wide semicircle to start the next leg, heading southwards a few miles east of their original track. Macy checked there were no potential targets on the ground as they made the turn, then crossed the cabin to Rain. 'Hey. Are you okay?'

'Yes, yes,' Rain replied. 'I'm good, I'm fine. As much as I can be. This is helping. Having something to do, I mean. Looking for the Iron Palace.'

Macy realised from her clipped speech that she was far from okay, emotion pent up tightly inside her. But now, she reluctantly decided, was not the time to draw out her true feelings. 'We'll find it,' she assured her instead. 'We'll get the staff, and stop the Brotherhood.'

'I hope they're there.'

Macy was shocked by her quiet but cold statement. 'Why?'

'So I can make them pay for what they did. To my parents, to Fernando . . . to everybody.'

'Rain, we're not out here to look for a fight.' She touched her friend's wrist. 'If they are there . . . promise me you won't rush in and do something crazy. I'll have your back,' she assured her. 'But I don't want to lose you.'

Different feelings – including anger – flicked across the French woman's face. But then a small smile, genuine despite the sadness behind it, appeared. 'Thank you. And I will have your back too.' Macy returned the smile, then went back to her seat as the helicopter began the next leg of the search.

Nobody spotted anything on the ground on the southward sweep – but as the chopper turned again to head back north, Macy saw something in the distance. A thin column of dust or smoke rose lazily into the sky several miles to the east. 'Hey, there's something there.'

'I see it too,' Meller confirmed. 'It could be a gas rig.'

MacDuff checked his map. 'No rigs around here. The closest one's near Ruhnama, quite a way north – and on the far side of the road.'

'We should check it,' said Macy, staring at the dark line. Could the Brotherhood have found the Iron Palace, and blasted their way in?

Emilian had reached the same conclusion. 'It might be the Brotherhood. Nuryev, take us over there – we need to check it out.' He turned to look back into the passenger compartment. 'Everybody get ready.'

Each of the Knights had their armour and weapons with them. Macy slipped the metal bands onto her body, watching the distant smoke trail with foreboding as the helicopter turned towards it.

Ruhnama barely qualified as a village, thought Granit as he surveyed his surroundings. The station was practically identical to the one at Ichoguz, no doubt built to a standardised design. The settlement that had grown around it appeared new and haphazardly developed, probably catering to the crews of a gas extraction facility somewhere in the region. His helicopter's arrival had drawn considerable interest from the locals, though it quickly tempered as they realised he and his men had no intention of buying anything from them.

It also drew attention from a man who in turn had caught

Granit's eye. The mercenary leader had noticed a relatively new Toyota Land Cruiser parked at the station even as he came in to land, the vehicle contrasting with the older, smaller vehicles nearby. The apparent owner observed the new arrivals warily. Wilde's contact? It seemed likely. He ordered his men to spread out and keep watch.

But Wilde and her husband did not appear. The train they had been on caught up, then departed; a while later, a clanking freight train of gas tankers rolled through in the other direction. A couple of cars came along the access road to the main highway, but only locals got out. Even in a building's shade, the heat was becoming intolerable, raising Granit's temper as well as his temperature. How long was he expected to wait here? The rest of the day? Into tomorrow? Longer?

The trill of his phone interrupted his irritable thoughts. Loost. 'Yes?'

His employer didn't pick up on his curtness. 'Good news, Anton. You can go home. I'll complete your payment.'

Granit was surprised. 'What do you mean? Wilde and Chase haven't arrived yet.'

'I've already located them. Wilde connected to somebody's satellite phone at a place called the Gates of Hell. That gave me access to her phone via Uzz. I listened in. She's now going to a sinkhole to the west.'

'Why?'

The pause at the other end of the line was longer than a mere satellite delay. 'That . . . doesn't matter,' Loost said. 'Another group will take over from here.'

'What!' Granit snapped in sudden anger. 'What about Wilde and Chase? You told me to deal with them!'

'That's no longer necessary. You've done everything you need to do.'

'They killed my brother.' The words were low, dangerous.

'I'm very sorry about that, but your job is now finished. I'll transfer the rest of your money right now. Thank you for your service; I hope we can do business again.' The call terminated.

Granit glared at his phone. After all that had happened, now Loost was just *dismissing* him and handing the job to somebody else? His men – his own brother – had died for *nothing*? His fury at the injustice rising, he thought for a moment – then remembered what the trillionaire had said. Or rather, let slip.

Like Ichoguz, Ruhnama's station had a cell tower, giving him a data connection. He opened his phone's browser and made a search. The results gave him the location of the 'Gates of Hell', back to the south. He checked the map west of the crater. Nothing except empty desert – but a sinkhole would stand out clearly from the air. As would anybody heading for it . . .

'We're moving!' he shouted to his men. 'Everybody into the helicopter!' He took his place in the co-pilot's seat as the other mercenaries boarded. His fists clenched. *This* time, Wilde and Chase would not escape.

41

The air inside the tunnel was still hazy with disturbed dust, Nina and Eddie found – but it *was* air. The fire and explosion had consumed the build-up of methane. 'I hardly smell any smoke,' Eddie noted as they reached the chamber at the top. 'Can't have been much flammable stuff in here.'

'Only the people,' Nina noted ruefully. All the human remains they had seen had been consumed. She hoped the same was not true of whatever lay beyond.

The cavern narrowed, sloping downwards again. Gas rising from below had become trapped at its top, forming a poisonous pocket. That danger was gone, for the moment, but the couple still moved cautiously. The weaving passage descended for some distance – then Nina stopped as her light caught something ahead. 'Eddie, hold it. Look at that.'

Eddie added his torch's beam to hers. 'It's metal.' The tunnel's wall was covered by a dark grey panel.

She brought her flashlight up and around. 'It's on the ceiling too – and the other wall. I think it's *iron*.'

'As in, the Iron Palace?'

Despite her wariness, she couldn't help but feel a rush of excitement. 'We've found Afrasiab's fortress.'

Eddie was less enthused. 'Shouldn't a fortress have a door?'

'There might still be one. Hopefully it's not bolted from the inside.'

'If it was, that explosion'll have taken care of it.'

That, they soon discovered, was the case. They entered the

metal-walled section of tunnel, before long reaching a defensive barrier. Any intruders would have been channelled into the field of fire of multiple arrow slits alongside hefty metal double doors. Whether said doors had been locked or not Nina didn't know, but the explosion had blown one almost off its hinges, the other buckled inwards. 'You were right,' she told Eddie, before turning her attention to the surrounding iron panels. 'Weird design.' Rather than being solid slabs, they were perforated, hundreds of inch-wide holes forming a dotted pattern in their surfaces. 'Wonder why they did that?'

'To save weight, maybe?' Eddie suggested. 'These things'd be a bugger to cart about. And they'd work just as well as barriers.'

'Maybe. It could be for ventilation as well. If you shut the doors for defence, you don't want to suffocate down here.'

He aimed his torch at an arrow slit – then looked back sharply at the doors as he caught something in his peripheral vision. 'There's light through there!' He drew the gun.

'I doubt anyone's down here,' said Nina.

'Let's not take chances, eh?' Eddie cautiously advanced through the gateway. Nina followed, sweeping her flashlight over the walls, floor and ceiling to search for traps.

There were none. The passage soon opened out into a large chamber. A *very* large chamber, Nina saw. The reason she could see the entire cavernous space . . . was that it was lit by the stars.

Not real stars. They were instead six-pointed holes cut into the metal panels covering the walls, hundreds upon hundreds of them forming constellations in the iron sky. Gas flames burned in each, their combined glow enough to illuminate the whole cave in a flickering twilight. Large fires crackled within bigger cut-outs representing the sun and the moon, on opposite sides of the great cave.

'The Iron Palace,' Nina whispered, awed. 'Just like it was described in the *Avesta*.' They stopped at the edge of a metal-floored ledge and looked down. The view was vertiginous. The cavern was roughly cylindrical, at its widest halfway down, like a barrel. Columns of iron resembling ribs rose up the walls, providing support for the metal panels between them. Their convergence drew her eye irresistibly to what lay at the bottom of the towering chamber, perhaps five hundred feet below. Buildings lurked in the half-light: the hidden redoubt of King Afrasiab.

'Bloody hell,' said Eddie, impressed. 'Must have taken a fair bit of work to build this.'

'I guess when you're a king who can control the weather, people are more likely to obey your whims.' She looked up. The walls narrowed to form a ceiling about a hundred feet above. There was a rift at the highest point; she realised it was the other end of the crack at the bottom of the sinkhole, forming a natural chimney that allowed the fumes from the burning fires to escape. It had become blocked over time, forcing the rising gas to find another route to the surface. 'I think all these flames went out after the place was abandoned, which is why the gas built up. We just re-lit them.' Small flickers around the walls where detritus had been set alight seemed to confirm her theory.

Eddie nodded, but his attention had been drawn by something higher up. 'There's a chain or something hanging down from there.'

Nina looked. The ledge they were on was a spiral, circling around the chamber both up and down. Its ascending path eventually met the chain, where some apparatus hung from the metal roof. She followed the dangling line downwards. It reached the bottom of the cavern behind the grandest of the structures below. Afrasiab's royal quarters?

She would find out when she got down there. As far as she could tell, the spiralling path was intact. Another look at the entirety of the Iron Palace. It was around six hundred feet tall – the height of a hundred men. Not a thousand, as the Persians had claimed, but it was not the first time in her archaeological career that mythology had exaggerated reality by a power of ten. Atlantis itself had been another example.

'So, we've found it,' she said. 'The question is: is the staff still here?' She surveyed the structures below. Another building near the royal quarters stood out: It was considerably smaller, but its position gave it prominence. It seemed to be on an island in an iron lake, a floor of metal panels surrounding it. A narrow bridge led to it from the cave's rocky floor. 'That could be a temple,' she said. 'The staff might be inside.'

'So we're going down there?' Eddie asked, before she could reply, then answering his own question with: 'Of course we bloody are.'

'You've known me for twenty-five years,' Nina said, grinning. 'Why even ask?'

They started down the spiral. The journey soon became nerve-racking: the iron path was not wide, and there was nothing between the explorers and the sheer drop to one side. They pressed against the metal wall for support. Some sections had also been damaged over the centuries, cracks and holes forcing Nina and Eddie to move very carefully. Luckily, the holes perforating the wall panels provided convenient finger-holds as they navigated the trickier areas.

Once they passed the halfway point, the trip became less tense, as the cave's inward slope meant that lower sweeps of the spiral rather than empty air were now below them. As they neared the bottom, new features appeared. The path widened, small dome-like structures – of stone and clay rather than metal – built against the wall. 'I think these were houses,' Nina said, pausing to investigate one.

Eddie peered over her shoulder. The interior was low-ceilinged, a hole connecting it to the next like a warren. 'Bit cramped. I'd want a discount on the rent.'

'I don't know, three thousand dollars a month for one of these would be a bargain in Manhattan. It's maybe more a shelter than a home. This isn't somewhere you'd live – but you *would* come here for protection. Afrasiab's people came down here with him when they were threatened.'

He glanced across at the largest building. 'Going to guess he lived in there, away from the plebs.'

'Again, if your king can summon lightning bolts, you let him have the nice house.' She continued downwards, Eddie behind her.

Nina got a clearer view of the isolated building as they came around behind it. Her suspicion that it was a temple seemed correct: it was ornate in design, decorated with elaborate carvings and precious metals. If the staff of Afrasiab was real, that was its most likely location.

But something tempered her anticipation of discovery. 'Eddie,' she eventually said, 'do you think this place feels . . . weird?'

'We're in a cave with metal walls lit by gas fires made to look like stars, where we might find a magic staff that can control the weather,' was her husband's prompt reply. 'Yes, it feels weird!'

She laughed, but her unsettled feeling didn't go away. 'That's not what I meant. I've found lost places underground before – like the Atlantean city in the Himalayas. But none of them *felt* like this. It's . . . *dead*, as if it's somehow been cut off from the rest of the world. Like something's missing. Don't you feel it?'

He shrugged. 'Can't say that I do.'

'Huh. Maybe it's just me, then.' The disturbing sensation of *absence* remained, though.

They reached the last section of the path, which angled to become a ramp down to the cavern's floor. She looked up. The view above was spectacular, if bizarre, the fires within the iron walls forming a distorted skyscape as if the firmament had been stretched into a tube. The light at ground level was low, but enough to see by. She was still grateful for her flashlight, however. She shone it around. Closely packed stone buildings stood to one side. Their blunt functionality made her think of military barracks. Something else caught her eye: a stream. The thin line of water trickled sluggishly through a deeper channel cut into the rock. It had clearly flowed more strongly in the past.

Eddie aimed his light at it. 'Wouldn't want to drink that,' he said. The stream was discoloured, with the reddish tinge of contamination by iron oxide – rust.

'Not this one, but I noticed another three channels on the way down,' said Nina. 'Exactly as described in the Persian texts. According to legend, four rivers flowed into Hankana; one was water, and the others were wine, milk and beaten sour milk. I bet this,' she pointed at the red trickle, 'is the wine.'

'Beaten sour milk?' Eddie said, with distaste. 'Wouldn't that be like yogurt that's been left out for a week?'

'I wouldn't want to drink it either! But it all matches Zoroastrian mythology.'

She looked ahead. Some of the buildings had suffered damage. From earthquakes? It was entirely possible; Central Asia as a whole was prone to them. Which made the Iron Palace all the more remarkable – its metal walls had withstood the assault of time almost undamaged. A few panels, she'd noticed on the way down, had broken loose and fallen, but the vast majority were intact. The place had been built to last.

She and Eddie advanced. The temple was off to the side across its bridge, but ahead stood the building she assumed to be Afrasiab's quarters, a palace within a palace. Though she imagined she was most likely to find the staff in the temple, she decided to investigate the grander structure first purely from archaeological curiosity. 'Let's see how a rebel king lived,' she said, starting towards it.

The path to the building crossed a small bridge, beneath which

ANDY MCDERMOTT

flowed another of the four rivers – though this too had been reduced to a feeble stream. Like the first, it was discoloured, but in this case a milky white rather than red. Eddie dipped an experimental finger into the flow and sniffed it. 'Smells clean,' he remarked, before holding his torch just above the water. 'It's fizzy! It looks white because it's full of bubbles. They had a natural Perrier supply.'

'Hopefully they're carbon dioxide rather than methane,' said Nina.

'Ugh, I'm drinking farts.' With an expression of distaste, Eddie hopped back out of the channel to follow her to the palace.

Two large statues of bearded warriors with raised swords stood before the building. There were no doors at the entrance. Recesses beside it told Nina guards would have been stationed there. She cautiously entered, sweeping her flashlight beam to check for booby-traps. None were apparent. She and Eddie proceeded inside, checking the first rooms they reached. 'This one's empty,' the Yorkshireman reported.

'So's this,' Nina replied. The chamber was devoid of anything but dust and scraps of debris. 'I think the place was cleaned out before the cavern was abandoned. They took everything with them.'

'Not quite everything.' Eddie had already continued on, his torch beam finding the hall's far end – and what stood there.

Nina hurried to it. 'Oh, my God,' she exclaimed. It was a suit of armour upon a stand, a vest of black chainmail accessorised with iron gauntlets and a black helmet inlaid with intricate patterns of gold. There had once been garments of cloth or animal skin underneath, but they had long since decayed, even in the dry air. 'This is Afrasiab's armour. It matches the descriptions from the ancient texts. And this . . .' Her light went to the wall behind, which was decorated with painted scenes. 'This must be Afrasiab himself,' she said of one particular figure on horseback, overseeing a pitched battle between two large armies. 'The armour's the same. This is interesting, though. The other paintings I've seen of him always portray him as bearded.'

Eddie regarded the clean-shaven person in her light. 'Must have whipped out the Gillette just before he was painted.'

'I don't know.' She pursed her lips, making a more detailed examination. 'The features, the way they're portrayed, look almost feminine. But Afrasiab was definitely male; he fathered several children.' A thoughtful frown. 'Intersex, maybe?'

Her husband smirked. 'Yeah, I'm into sex too.'

'In*ter*sex, Eddie. Both male and female characteristics. Maybe later pictures by his enemies portrayed him as undeniably masculine because they didn't like that someone so dangerous and powerful appeared feminine. And if Afrasiab *was* intersex, that could explain how a man had such fine control over an Atlantean artefact that would normally be used by a priestess . . .' She considered the question for a long moment – then stepped back. 'But that's what we need to find – the artefact, the staff. It's not here with the armour, so it's probably in the temple.'

'Then we need to get it out of here before Granit and his arseholes find us,' Eddie reminded her.

She had forgotten all about the mercenaries in the rush of discovery, and the reminder abruptly chilled her enthusiasm. 'You're right, we do,' she said.

Side passages led on from the armour, but they ignored them, quickly heading back out into the cavern. Nina's uneasy feeling that the place was somehow cut off in a way beyond mere inaccessibility had not left her; even the echoes of their footsteps sounded oddly muted and flat. There was something *wrong* about the Iron Palace, affecting her on an inner level. But what, she still had no idea.

She put such thoughts aside as they reached the stone bridge to the temple. The 'lake' surrounding it was more of the perforated metal panels, this time laid flat. Now, though, she could see they were not merely covering the ground. Several were missing, perhaps where other panels had fallen from above. She shone her flashlight into the nearest gap. The cavern's rocky floor dropped steeply away into a chasm, the bottom of which was beyond the range of her beam. The building stood at the very top of a feature resembling a giant stalagmite, the stone glinting with reflected light. The faint sound of running water rose from below. A spring, maybe, the source of one or more of the four streams? The rock was scattered with a greenish sand. She recognised it as olivine – a mineral that absorbed carbon dioxide. Could that have helped Afrasiab and his followers avoid suffocation in the deep while gas flames burned endlessly above them?

It was possible, but again, finding out was not her priority. She brought her light to the bridge. It seemed intact. All the same, her first couple of steps were tinged with trepidation. But the walkway was solid. 'Think I should go first,' said Eddie all the same. 'Make sure it's safe.'

'I'm lighter,' she pointed out. She carefully continued, passing the point where the floor dropped away into the chasm below. If the bridge collapsed now, she would die . . .

But she completed her wary passage without incident. Eddie let out a relieved breath, then followed. 'So what's in here?' he said as he reached her.

Nina had anxiously watched his crossing; she turned to investigate the temple's interior. The room within was not large, and in contrast to the carved and decorated outer walls, almost austere. But that absence of distraction made what stood at its centre all the more imposing. 'I'm gonna guess,' she said, illuminating the object before them, 'the Staff of Afrasiab.'

42

The helicopter slowed as it approached its destination. The column of smoke had thinned since Macy first spotted it, but was still visible from miles away. It rose from what turned out to be another sinkhole. This was larger and deeper than any the aircraft's occupants had already seen, that alone making it a prime candidate for investigation, but something close to it immediately made her suspect they had found what they were looking for. 'Look, there's a Land Rover,' she said, seeing a dusty 4x4 facing the circular pit. 'Someone's already here.'

'It must be the Brotherhood,' Emilian said at once. 'Damn it! They got here first.'

'How could they figure out where to look so quickly?' she asked. 'I mean, we used the world's fastest quantum computers, and it still took us this long to get here.'

'They must have had something in their archives that gave them a head start.'

'I would have thought they'd come in force, though, just like in Portugal. They only brought one truck? There can't be many of them.'

'But that is good,' said Meller. 'They think they have beaten us. They did not expect us to find them.'

'Their mistake,' said Emilian. Before Macy could say more, he began issuing orders. 'Nuryev, land near the truck. Oleksiy, cover it, in case they left a guard.' Meller nodded and raised a sub-machine gun, clicking off the safety. 'When we land, we'll transform and secure the area. Once it's safe, we'll go down into the hole – and find the Iron Palace. If the Brotherhood are there . . .' His gaze flicked back to Rain and Naima. 'We'll make them pay for what they took from us.'

'Wait – we shouldn't rush into this,' Macy said, but her voice was lost as the others prepared for a landing. Nuryev brought the helicopter towards the sinkhole, swinging it around so its right flank faced the Land Rover. Meller opened the rear hatch, training his gun on the 4x4 as the rotor wash whipped up a swirling sandstorm around it.

Nobody reacted to the aircraft's arrival. The Land Rover was empty. The helicopter touched down, Meller jumping out and scurrying to check the vehicle. After a few seconds he waved, signalling that it was safe.

'Come on,' said Emilian, donning his biker jacket and opening his own door. Macy climbed out from the other side of the cabin, shielding her face from the billowing dust. Rain emerged behind her. The redhead led her clear as the other passengers left the chopper, Naima bearing a backpack containing exploration gear.

Meller returned to the group, shouldering his weapon. 'They climbed down into the hole. But nobody is there.'

'Then this *is* the place,' Emilian said triumphantly. 'There must be an entrance to the Iron Palace at the bottom.' He collected a rugged plastic case from the chopper's cargo bay, taking it to a large boulder standing proud of the sands.

From the case, he took out what Macy at first thought was a folded umbrella; when fully opened, it was revealed as a dish-shaped antenna. MacDuff regarded it curiously, but she beat him to the question: 'What's that?'

'A satellite link,' Emilian replied, using straps to secure it to the rock before aiming it up into the sky. 'So we have communications if we need them.' A small screen in its base unit told him when he had clear reception.

'With who?'

'Anyone we need to,' he replied with veiled impatience. He took a smaller piece of gear from the case and summoned Meller. 'This is a repeater unit,' he said, giving it to the Ukrainian. 'Fibre-optic link. We'll be able to use comms even underground.' Meller nodded and unspooled a length of hair-like optical cable, plugging it into the base unit. Emilian, meanwhile, readied his whip, then addressed his companions. 'Okay, Knights. Let's get ready.'

One by one, the surviving Knights of Atlantis transformed into their armoured angelic forms: Emilian; Leni; Idris. Rain, however, hesitated. Macy was about to ask if she wanted to go through with it, but Emilian spoke first. 'You can do it, Rain,' he said. '*We* can do this, together.' Though reluctant, the young French woman finally nodded – and her features vanished behind the obscuring halo.

All faces turned to Macy. She too was reluctant to transform, but for different reasons. Something did not feel right. Despite Emilian's words, she still didn't see how the Brotherhood could possibly have beaten them here. They had also sent a small hi-tech army to attack in Portugal – so why go the final mile in a single battered old Land Rover?

But Rain spoke before she could express her doubts. 'Macy,' she said, her voice made hollow by the halo. 'Please, come with me. I can't do this without you.'

The quiet plea was enough to nudge Macy into motion, despite her concerns. 'Okay,' she said. 'I'll help you. You know I will.'

'And I'll always help you,' came the reply. Macy managed a smile, then focused her willpower. The cold, strange chitter of metal sliding over her, and she too became an angel.

'All right,' said Emilian. 'We'll fly down into the hole.'

Meller had already donned the backpack and gone to the rope attached to the Land Rover. 'I will climb down here. See you at the bottom.'

MacDuff watched unhappily as the Ukrainian disappeared

from sight, the optical cable reeling out in his wake. 'Just so you know, it's been a few years since I last climbed a rope. Like, since-I-was-at-school years.'

'We'll carry you,' Idris told him. The Scot did not seem thrilled at the prospect.

'What about you, Naima?' asked Rain.

'I can climb down too,' replied the Finn. 'Jari and I go climbing sometimes . . .' She trailed off, raw grief resurfacing.

'I'm sorry,' said Macy. 'Are you sure you want to climb? We can take you.'

Naima shook her head firmly. 'No.' She wore a belt holster; she drew an automatic and tugged back its slide to chamber the first round, then slid it back into its nest, ready for action. 'I can do it.'

'Okay,' said Emilian, turning away and marching to the sinkhole's edge. His wings extended with a sharp metallic *schnack*, filaments glowing brightly even in daylight. 'Then let's go.'

He stepped over the lip, gliding into the void below. Leni followed, leaping from the edge with a whoop – wings still retracted. Even knowing his predilection for thrill-seeking, Macy winced; if something went wrong, the fall would be fatal. But a second, longer cry of exhilaration told her he had successfully taken flight.

MacDuff gave the three remaining Knights an uncertain look. 'So, who's going to carry me?'

Idris stepped towards him, extending his arms. 'I will.'

'Oh, no, what?' MacDuff waved his hands in protest. 'You're gonnae sweep me off my feet like a blushing bride? No offence meant, but I'd feel safer being supported by two of you. I don't know how much spare lifting power those wee wings have.'

'I'll help,' said Macy. She didn't know either, but based on how *easy* her flight had felt over the Portuguese countryside, she guessed the armour could carry considerably more than her

371

bodyweight. MacDuff raised his arms so they could support him. She glanced back at Rain. 'Are you okay?'

'Yes,' came the muted reply. 'I'll follow you down.'

'Okay,' said Idris, nodding to Macy. 'Let's go.'

'Are you not going to practise first?' asked MacDuff, with considerable trepidation.

The Algerian sighed, then extended his wings and rose a few inches from the ground, hauling his passenger up with him. Macy followed suit. She immediately felt MacDuff's weight – but her armour seemed able to cope.

They slowly glided forward, the stone shaft a dizzying drop into shadow below. MacDuff tensed. 'I'll just, ah, shut my eyes, then,' he said in a strained voice. Idris chuckled, then he and Macy descended at a modest rate. Rain came down after them.

The drop to the bottom of the sinkhole took twenty seconds, though Macy imagined that to MacDuff it felt like a lifetime. The Scot exhaled in relief, then checked the numerous pockets of his khaki gilet to make sure he hadn't lost any of their contents in transit. Looking around, the redhead saw that Emilian and Meller had gone to a cave entrance hidden beneath an overhang. 'This is it!' cried the Dutchman. 'The Iron Palace. The Staff of Afrasiab is in here!'

'And so are the Brotherhood,' warned Meller, readying his weapon. 'Be careful.'

Idris detransformed and peered into the opening. 'It won't be safe to fly through there. It's too dark, and too low.'

'I'm willing to try it,' proclaimed Leni, striding to the entrance.

'Okay, but if you crash head-first into a rock, remember that I warned you.'

Emilian also detransformed. 'Idris is right. It will be dangerous enough without making things harder on purpose. We go in on foot. Oleksiy, you have the gun. Take the lead.'

Meller distributed flashlights from his pack. His gun had a

tactical light mounted under the barrel; he switched it on and advanced into the tunnel. Emilian went with him.

The other Knights detransformed and followed. Macy and Rain were the last to move, the French woman hesitating. 'Are you sure you're okay?' Macy asked.

'I . . . I think so,' she replied. 'I can do this.'

'Of course you can do this,' Emilian called back to her. 'You're a Knight, just like your father. You're strong. Do this for him – and for your mother too. We'll deal with the Brotherhood together.'

Rain's face hardened. 'Yes. We will.' She overtook Macy and entered the cave. 'Come on,' she said to her friend. 'Let's do this.'

It was now Macy's turn to feel trepidation. More than ever, the situation felt *wrong* – as if there was another layer to it that she couldn't see. But she had no time to think about it, as her companions disappeared into the darkness. She reluctantly followed, trikan heavy in her hand.

The entrance led to a passage, which first sloped upwards into a cave before beginning a lengthy descent. The floor had been worn smooth by countless feet. Despite her nervousness, Macy felt a tingle of anticipation – of discovery. This *had* to be the way to the Iron Palace of Afrasiab. Lost for centuries . . . now unearthed.

But she was not the first to find it. Someone – the Brotherhood? Uncertainty still gnawed at her – was already here. Conflict seemed inevitable. Was she ready for it? Were any of them? The realisation that even in their armour, the Knights were not invulnerable had hit the group hard . . .

A voice broke through her concerned thoughts. 'There is something here,' Meller warned. Everyone slowed. Lights locked onto plates of dark iron covering the tunnel walls ahead. 'A gate.'

Emilian's own beam danced across the broken doors. 'Looks like it's been blasted open.'

Meller advanced on the entrance, taking up position beside the wrecked gates. A pause to listen for movement, then he whipped through the barrier, weapon snapping to any potential hiding places. 'Nobody here,' he said, relaxing slightly. 'But there's a large cave ahead. They must have gone down into it.'

The group cautiously filed through the gateway, Meller still leading. Macy was the last to pass through the threshold. She shivered, a disturbing feeling of *emptiness* rising as the metal walls surrounded her. Why, she had no idea. But something had been taken from her, something vital . . .

The group spread out as they arrived at a ledge – overlooking a vast vertical chamber, lined with iron and lit by hundreds of flickering fires inside star-shaped holes in the metal walls. 'Oh my God,' said Macy as she took in the astonishing view. The enormous space dropped dizzyingly away towards buildings on its floor hundreds of feet below. 'This is incredible!'

'No time for archaeology,' said Emilian. He pointed down at brighter lights in the low firelight glow permeating the chamber: flashlight beams. 'The Brotherhood are there.'

Leni raised his moon blade. 'They don't know we're here. We can fly down and catch them by surprise – take them all out.'

'Are you sure that's a good idea?' Macy asked, alarmed – both by his suggestion, and that most of his fellow Knights agreed with it. 'We don't know what's down there, how many of them there are—'

'No, he's right,' Emilian cut in. 'They may already have found the staff. We have to hit hard, hit fast – and make sure they don't escape with it. These bastards killed people we care about, all so they could find this place. We have to stop them. Otherwise Jari, and Fernando, Rain's parents, all the others will have died for *nothing*.' That last word was practically a snarl.

Naima drew her gun. 'Do it. If any of them make it back here, I'll be waiting.' Meller set down and activated the repeater, then moved alongside her, nodding in agreement.

Emilian turned to the Knights, about to issue an order, but Leni was already moving. 'See you down there!' he said, raising his moon blade and rushing to make a flying leap.

'No, wait!' cried Macy, a reason for her disturbing feeling of loss and isolation suddenly coming to her – but too late.

Leni threw himself into the void, arms outspread, the scales of his armour starting to skitter across his body . . .

They stopped.

The Croatian plunged wingless towards the ground far below, his scream of terror echoing behind him.

43

Nina and Eddie entered the temple. The staff within was roughly six feet long, made of a dark metal that glinted with flecks of purple and gold. Plain and simple, unadorned except for a clear gemstone mounted in gold at its top, it did not seem especially remarkable.

But the dedication of an entire building to its storage told Nina it was an item of great power. Whether that power was merely symbolic or genuine, she didn't yet know. But as her light moved down to the dais on which it stood, slotted into a small hole, she felt a chilling certainty that it was the latter.

Eddie saw it too. 'Wait, that looks like the same kind of stuff as . . .'

'As Earthbreaker,' Nina finished for him. The ancient Atlantean weapon had been cut from a colossal mountain of strange jade-like stone spreading deep into the earth beneath South America. Through some process she couldn't fully explain, touching the stone dagger to a map carved into the pinnacle of the vast rock caused sympathetic vibrations that grew and grew in force until they were released as an earthquake on the corresponding location in the world above. In the wrong hands, Earthbreaker possessed enormous destructive power.

The same kind of stone was here.

The dais was also green, carved smooth and polished to a reflective sheen. Nina realised that, like the map in the Temple of Skulls in Guatemala, it was the very tip of a much larger stone: the stalagmite she had glimpsed beneath the iron 'lake'. The power of earth energy coursed through it – dangerous, deadly.

At least . . . she thought it did. There was only one way to be sure.

'You sure that's a good idea?' Eddie cautioned as she reached out a hand.

'No, but if it's a bad one, at least down here we won't be struck by lightning,' she replied.

'With our luck, I'm sure we'll find a way.' He took a heavy breath. 'Go on, then.'

Nina drew in a nervous inhalation of her own . . . then gripped the staff.

A surge of power ran through her body, every muscle tensing – then she relaxed, her senses expanding beyond the little temple to take in what was beyond.

It was a sensation she had felt before. When attuned to the earth's natural energy flow, she became aware of what was happening far beyond her physical location. Yet each time she had previously done so, it had been subtly different depending on the artefact she was using to tap into the power, and this was no exception. She was not so much feeling the earth as its influence over the sky above it, the vast patterns of weather swirling and churning over the desert, the region, the continent – the whole planet. It was almost overwhelming, a vastness nearly beyond comprehension, threatening to crush her mind . . .

But her past experiences saved her from panic. She calmed, concentrating on one specific place – the Karakum, its heart, the miles of wilderness surrounding the sinkhole. The experience was bizarre. Even though the sky was clear, the sun-baked sands hot and dry, she could *feel* how much moisture was hanging in the air, waiting to be tapped. She sensed the highs and lows of pressure, and the flow of the winds between them. Even the disruptive churn of aircraft reached her, metallic interlopers forcing their way through the firmament. She was sure that if she focused, she would sense the movements of individual birds.

That was not foremost on her mind, though. A knowledge also came to her, a powerful *certainty*. She could not merely sense the weather. She could affect it – *control* it. Somehow, she felt the presence of the staff's last user. Afrasiab's influence was still there, a residual echo of the renegade king. She knew how he had used the staff, how he had held back the rain from his enemies to the south and redirected it to benefit his own people here.

And she also knew . . . her power was greater than his.

The revelation burrowed into her thoughts, tempting, seductive. Control was hers, to use as and when she wished. Why *not* use it? Try it, just to see what happened, to know how it felt to have the power of a god . . .

Eddie said something. Even though he was right beside her, his words were distant, indistinct. He could wait. She *had* to show him what the staff could do – what *she* could do. A demonstration. Something that would reach even this far underground. A thunderstrike, shaking the ground, making a noise loud enough to echo through the tunnels. Perfect. Even as she thought it, she felt the staff reacting to her will, energy streams rising in the sky to reshape and corral the weather, focusing it on one specific spot. Right above them. *Here*. She gripped the staff more tightly, lifting it almost in triumph from its slot—

The power vanished.

Nina gasped as she snapped back to reality, almost startled to find herself in the subterranean temple. 'What – what happened?' she said, momentarily bewildered.

Eddie regarded her with concern. 'That crystal started glowing, then you went a bit weird. I asked if you were okay, but you didn't hear me. I was about to get your hand off the staff when you took it out – and came back to normal. As normal as you get, anyway,' he added with a lopsided smile.

Nina didn't share his amusement. 'Oh my God, Eddie,' she

said, staring at the staff. The crystal was now inert. 'This thing, it's . . . it's powerful, but not like any of the other earth-energy artefacts I've seen before. It's almost as if it *wants* me to use the power.'

'What, so it really can control the weather?'

'Yes. And I was just about to give you a demonstration – even though that wouldn't have been a great idea. But when I lifted it from the stone, I was – cut off. And I don't know why.' She gripped the metal rod with both hands, trying to recapture the feeling of connection. All she found was the very faintest whisper of the wider world, a tickle at the fringes of her consciousness . . .

The answer struck her. 'Of course!' she cried, hurrying back outside the temple to stand on the bridge. Eddie followed her. 'The dais in there, where the staff's kept – it's the tip of a stone going into the ground.'

'Like in Guatemala?'

'Yes, except this one's a lot smaller. When the staff's touching it, it's directly connected to the flow of earth energy. But this cave, the Iron Palace,' she turned in place, arms out to encompass the metal-walled cavern, 'it's *cut off* from that flow. That's why it felt dead to me, but you didn't notice anything wrong. I can feel earth energy, subconsciously, because I'm descended from the Atlanteans. This place, though . . . it's blocking it. The metal's preventing it from getting through – except when the staff's in direct contact with the only part of the stone inside it.'

Eddie regarded the iron walls. 'So it's like one of those wallets that stop people from hacking your cards wirelessly?'

'Yeah. A Faraday cage – except this blocks earth energy rather than radio waves. I don't know whether Afrasiab knew about it, or it happened by chance. But that explains how he defeated the Knights of Atlantis,' she went on, excited again. 'They came here thinking they could use their powers to kill him. But once they were inside the walls . . .'

'Their weapons wouldn't work,' he concluded.

'And nor would their armour. They'd be as vulnerable as anyone else. And if they couldn't fly either, they'd be sitting ducks once they were in here. They probably took casualties.'

'Except now, they want to come back to finish the job.' He nodded towards the staff. 'They want that.'

'And so does Loost. They can't get it, Eddie,' she insisted. '*Nobody* should have this power.'

'Not even to do good with it? Like ending a drought or something?'

'Could you trust someone like Loost to do that without demanding something in return? Who *could* you trust to do that? This thing, it's . . . *insidious*,' was the only way she could describe it. 'How long was I holding it? Ten seconds, twenty? And I was ready to start blasting down lightning bolts. It's worse than the Chinese qi weapon. That was technological – a tool, even if it was one created for war. But the staff . . .' She clanked its end against the floor, contemplating the gem at its top. 'It's like a weapon that *wants* to be used. You have to be strong to resist. And I'm not sure I'm strong enough. Would anyone else be?'

'Seems like the best thing we could do with it is chuck it down that hole,' said Eddie, gesturing towards the broken section of iron floor.

'Someone would find it, eventually. And I'm not sure I want to hand it over to the IHA – not with Hoffman in charge. I don't want it to end up as an American weather-control weapon any more than I would a Chinese or a Russian one.'

'Then we need to destroy it, right? An oxy torch should do the job. Chop it into bits and melt 'em down, sorted.'

'I was thinking more drop it into a few thousand feet of water, but your way works too. We need to get out of here first, though.' She looked up towards the top of the fire-lit cavern. 'I can tell the IHA that we found the Iron Palace, then they can pass that on to the Turkmenistanis to decide what they want to do – after we've got rid of the staff. So we'd better—'

A terrible scream echoed through the chamber from above – rapidly growing louder.

'What the *fuck*?' Eddie yelped. He pulled Nina sharply back into the temple. Something flicked past the burning stars above, a figure plunging towards them—

The shriek of terror reached a piercing crescendo – then ended abruptly with a wet bang as the falling man hit the flat expanse of iron. Nina gasped, shrinking back in horror. Eddie winced, but training compelled him to check the gory impact site. Had Granit and his men found them?

The luckless faller had been mashed almost flat, blood splattered in all directions from the mangled body. Eddie couldn't tell if he was one of the mercenaries from the train, the corpse's head a crushed mess – but he wasn't wearing the military-style clothing of Granit's team. Nor was he armed, at least not with standard firearms. Something had landed near the body, a long metal rod. It had a spearhead at one end, a metal ball the other, but the hard landing had bent the weapon almost in half. The panels around the dead man had also been damaged by the impact, one bent downwards to expose the void below and a neighbouring one jolted loose from its supports.

Something else caught his eye. 'I don't think it's one of Granit's lot,' he said. 'But . . . there's something weird about him. I think you should look.'

'Oh, Jesus. Do I have to?' Nina moaned. But she dropped the staff back into its slot, then overcame her appalled reluctance and peered out. 'Shit,' she gasped. 'That's something I could have gone the rest of my life without seeing.'

'I don't mean him. I mean what he's wearing.'

She tried to fix her eyes on the dead man's clothing rather than his remains. A glint of gold helped her concentrate. 'It's like –

381

armour?' she said, uncertain. It resembled a metal fabric, forming sleeves and leggings extending from thick golden bands around his wrists and ankles, and a kind of doublet descending from a matching torc or collar. But the sleeves did not reach as far as his elbows, the leg coverings halting unevenly part-way up his calves. The top section only just reached his shoulders. 'Wait a minute. Golden armour—'

Eddie nodded. 'Sound familiar?'

'Yeah.' She looked up sharply. 'Shit. The Knights are here! They've come for the staff!'

Her husband drew his gun. 'Like you said, we can't let 'em get it.' He stared into the heights of the fire-lit chamber, hunting for movement. 'I can't see anyone.'

'They can't fly – not in here,' she realised. 'They can't do *anything*! The Iron Palace is still blocking their powers, just like when their ancestors tried to attack Afrasiab. And they didn't know about it. That guy probably jumped off the ledge, expecting his armour to catch him. It didn't.'

'So they've got to come down the same way we did.' Eddie turned his gaze to the nearby buildings. 'We need to find cover – somewhere I can take them out before they reach ground level.'

'What if they don't come down here, though? What if they try to wait us out?'

He rapped the staff with a knuckle. 'They want this – and they'll be worried we've got it already. They'll come down to stop us from destroying it.'

'Too bad I forgot my smelter.'

He managed a half-smile. 'Come on. Let's find somewhere safe.'

They hurried back across the bridge. They were halfway over when both flinched at a sudden shrill of metal nearby. For a moment Nina feared the bridge was collapsing – but then saw one of the damaged panels drop away, the smashed body going with it.

Silence for a few seconds, then a distant splash reached them.

Eddie reached solid ground and looked back at the new hole. 'You sure we shouldn't just chuck the thing down there?'

'If they kill us, they can take all the time they need to find it. Maybe we can use it as leverage.'

'What, to stop them killing us? So we give it to them and then they kill us anyway?'

'Okay, I hadn't thought that far ahead.' They hurried towards the crumbling ancient buildings.

Nuryev wiped away sweat as he waited in the helicopter's front seat. Even with the doors open to allow airflow, the cabin was oppressively hot, the sun streaming in through the expansive windows. Without the engine running, there was no way to power the air conditioning. He was tempted to start up to cool the aircraft's interior, but wasting fuel purely for personal comfort was a risk this deep in the desert . . .

A sound intruded on his discomfort. Distant, but instantly familiar – and growing louder.

Another helicopter.

It was approaching fast from the north-east, almost directly behind. His own chopper's fuselage blocked any view. His eyes flicked to the satellite dish. His client had said it was a relay. Meller surely had a walkie-talkie. He turned the radio's channel selector to an appropriate frequency. 'Mr Meller, can you hear me? Mr Meller, come in. Come in.'

No answer. Was the relay digital rather than analogue? He took out his phone, wondering if he could get a signal. To his surprise, he could – only weak, but the connection icon was there. He had spoken to Meller while arranging the mission; he scrolled through his recent calls to find the Ukrainian's number—

The other helicopter's rumble rose to a roar, gritty dust blasting into the cockpit. Nuryev shielded his face and squinted into the whirling sand. A red and white Airbus H175 made a wide, low-altitude circle around his aircraft. The co-pilot's door opened. He watched in puzzlement as someone leaned out . . .

Confusion became fear as the man in the doorway raised a rifle.

Nuryev started to scramble from his seat—

A burst of bullets punched through the cockpit window, ripping into his torso.

Granit knew from the blood spatter inside the cockpit canopy that he had hit his target. Another couple of seconds of orbiting confirmed the kill, the man flopping limply out of the open door. No other movement in the stationary aircraft: it was empty.

'Bring us around,' he ordered his pilot, a Lithuanian named Zdanys. 'Give me an angle on that jeep.'

Zdanys obeyed. Granit took aim again and fired. The Land Rover's dusty windscreen shattered. The front seats were empty. As expected, but he wanted to be sure. His aim shifted to the 4x4's front. A rapid burst riddled its radiator grille, discoloured water gushing out. Another short barrage blew out one of the front tyres. The Land Rover would not be going anywhere.

Not that he intended to let its occupants ever return to it. Wilde and Chase must have bartered for the vehicle after escaping the train. The identity of the helicopter's passengers was unknown – but he knew they were working for Loost. The trillionaire had tried to pay him off so some other group could take over. That thought rankled. GCM's entire purpose was to provide specialist force projection to wealthy clients, and there were none wealthier than Loost himself – but it was now clear his paymaster regarded him and his men as disposable, even sacrificial.

Whatever Loost was after in this hellhole, he was willing to spend a great deal of money to get it. Granit decided to find out exactly how much. Neither his personal targets nor his unknown competition knew he was here. It should be easy enough to ambush and eliminate them – and take whatever they had found. Then Rafael Loost would have to pay whatever price he demanded for it. Fair compensation for the deaths of so many of his men . . .

'Land us there,' he said, pointing at a patch of flat ground. Zdanys complied, bringing the helicopter down in a storm of dust. Granit turned to address his men. 'Whoever is here, they've gone down into that hole. We'll go down after them, find them . . . and kill them.'

44

Eddie peered out from a building near the foot of the spiral path. His position would give him good cover, while also providing a decent arc of fire on anyone descending.

That was, if they couldn't just fly down. But their companion's fate would probably deter them from trying . . .

Nina was watching the Iron Palace's inner walls through a hole in the ceiling. 'I can see them,' she warned.

'How high up?' he asked.

'Ah . . . about a hundred feet. Three levels up.'

Eddie drew back into the darkened building to see for himself. Shadowy shapes moved carefully down the iron pathway, backlit by the burning sun above. The intruders – the Knights of Atlantis – had reached the first of the little shelters. 'Won't be long before they get to the bottom. Maybe I should warn 'em off.'

'That'll give away our position.'

'Have to do it sooner or later. Better when they're a hundred feet up than ten.' He raised his gun. Nina drew back, covering her ears. He locked onto the leader – and fired.

The gunshot was almost painful in the enclosed space. But he scored a hit, his target lurching sideways. Those behind reacted in alarm. Someone shouted, 'Down, get down!' Most of the shadowy shapes dropped. A couple were slower to react. The Yorkshireman found another target near the rear. Smaller and slighter than his first – a woman? The thought caused him a split-second of hesitation, before it was overcome by the knowledge that the intruders wanted him and Nina dead. He pulled the trigger again—

Another woman yanked his target down. The round clanked off the metal wall above her. Eddie muttered a curse. But the shots had done their job. One person was at the very least wounded, and the others now knew that descending would bring them under fire. 'Come down any further and you're dead!' he shouted.

There was no response for a moment . . .

Then a very familiar voice called back: '*Dad?*'

Macy gazed at the buildings below. Even her horror at Leni's appalling death couldn't overcome her amazement. The largest building had to be Afrasiab's royal quarters, a stone palace within the much larger iron one. Before it were what were probably barracks for the king's soldiers—

A flash from one of the tumbledown buildings – and Meller, leading, suddenly lurched as a bullet clipped his shoulder. He cried out, falling against the wall.

Macy instinctively ducked. 'Down, get down!' yelled Naima, dropping to the metal walkway. The rest of the group were slower to react, shocked by the unexpected attack. Emilian threw himself flat behind Meller, the others hunching down one by one—

Except Rain, paralysed by confusion or panic. Macy sprang back up and dragged her to the ledge – as another round impacted above her with a shrill clang. 'Jesus!' she gasped. 'Rain, are you okay?'

She felt the French woman shiver as she realised how close she had come to death. 'Yes, yes,' was Rain's breathless reply.

'What about everyone else?'

'I'm hit,' groaned Meller. 'It hurts, but – I don't think it's too bad.'

'It's the Brotherhood,' Emilian snapped. 'They'll try to kill us to stop us from taking the staff. We have to—'

A shout reached them from below. 'Come down any further and you're dead!'

Macy's shock as she recognised the voice was greater than when they came under fire. '*Dad?*'

Nina stared wide-eyed through the hole in the ceiling. '*Macy?*'

'*Mom?*' came the reply. 'Oh my God! What are you doing here?'

'I could ask you the same thing!'

'They've fucking taken her hostage,' Eddie growled, his worst fears confirmed. He raised the gun again. 'Macy! Come down to us! If any of them try to stop you, I'll kill 'em!'

Macy nervously peered over the pathway's edge. The building the muzzle flash had come from was dark. No sign of her parents – or anyone else who might be with them. 'What? No, Dad, you don't understand!'

'I told you,' said Emilian coldly. 'They're working with the Brotherhood. They tried to kill us all in Portugal – and now they want to finish us off. Your parents are helping them!'

'They wouldn't do that!' Macy protested. 'They'd never do anything to hurt me!'

'Which is why they want you down there with them – so they can kill the rest of us!'

'No, I don't . . .' She trailed off, torn. Her parents surely hadn't been involved with the attack on the villa – but they *had* gone to Rome to work with the Brotherhood, her mother openly stating the fact . . . 'How can you help the Brotherhood of Selasphoros?' she shouted. 'They tried to kill you!'

'We're not!' Nina replied. 'Macy, whatever's going on, the people you're with have lied to you – manipulated you! They're murderers. They attacked the IHA – and they tried to have me assassinated in Rome!'

Macy glanced at Emilian in shock. 'That's ridiculous,' he told her. 'You *know* we didn't try to kill her. You were with us! She's lying, she's trying to turn you against us.'

'They – they wouldn't—'

'They just shot Oleksiy!' He gestured angrily at the wounded Ukrainian. 'If you hadn't pulled her down, they would have *killed* Rain!'

'It's dark, Dad couldn't have seen who she was . . .' But she couldn't deny that her friend had escaped death by inches. 'I don't . . .'

Before she could overcome her confusion, her mother called out again. 'Macy! We have to tell you something. Rafael Loost is behind this whole thing!'

'I already know about Rafael,' Macy shot back. 'He's helping us!'

'That kinda proves my point! He's not who you think he is, Macy. He's not your friend, even if that's what he said on Uzz. All of this is because he wants to get his hands on the Staff of Afrasiab!'

'Do you have it?' shouted Emilian before Macy could reply.

Her father responded. 'Yeah! And we'll destroy it if we have to!'

Emilian tensed at the warning, but Macy had already come to a realisation. 'Wait – why don't we let them?' she suggested to her companions. 'We're trying to stop anyone from using the staff for evil, so if it's destroyed . . . nobody can!'

That produced hurried discussion amongst the group. 'The lass makes a good point,' said MacDuff, 'Do that, and it'll never trouble anyone again.'

'No,' snapped Emilian. 'It must be a trick. But that doesn't matter!' Anger entered his voice – at the situation, Macy wondered, or at being challenged? He took out his phone.

'What are you doing?' Macy asked.

'Contacting Rafael. Maybe he can convince your parents to give up the staff.'

'Why would he be able to when I can't?' But the Dutchman was already making the call.

'Why've they gone quiet?' Nina wondered.

Eddie shifted position, trying to spot any movement. 'Probably deciding if we're serious about destroying the staff. Or someone's crawling down the path so I can't get an angle on them.'

'Or both.' But if anyone was moving, they were completely hidden from those below. He returned to the doorway. 'Can you see anyone from there?'

'No, but I will if they—'

Nina's phone rang.

The sound was so unexpected, it took them both a moment to realise what it was. 'The *hell*?' Nina exclaimed, digging it from a pocket.

'Who's calling you here?' Eddie asked, followed by the more pertinent question: '*How's* someone calling you here? We're a quarter of a mile underground in the middle of a desert!'

'Inside a Faraday cage, at that.' She checked the screen, seeing that somehow, she did indeed have a signal. It also revealed the caller's name. 'It's Loost!'

'You going to answer?'

'I suspect he's gone to an awful lot of trouble to make this call, so . . .' She tapped the screen.

Loost appeared. The picture quality was low, bandwidth apparently limited, but she could see him clearly enough. The earth was a brilliant arc of blue and green behind him. 'Professor Wilde,' he said. His tone was businesslike, devoid of warmth. 'So you found the Iron Palace of Afrasiab. Congratulations.'

'Why, thank you,' was her sarcastic reply. 'We found his staff too. And no, you can't have it.'

'Before you do anything rash, would you at least hear me out?'

'This should be good,' Eddie muttered.

Nina glanced up through the hole. Was Loost stalling for time to let the Knights sneak downwards? 'Macy?' she called. 'Are you still there?'

Macy looked over the path's side – in the same place she had been previously. 'Yes! Mom, what's going on? What are you doing?'

'Just wait there, honey. Let's see if we can sort this out.' Her gaze turned cold, returning to Loost. 'Go on, then. Justify yourself.'

'I don't need to justify anything, Professor Wilde,' he said. 'Merely explain. For a start, you were probably wondering how I would even *know* about Afrasiab, never mind what he could do.'

'It had crossed my mind. He's hardly a well-known figure, especially in the West.'

'That depends on your upbringing. My parents, who were Iranian by ancestry and Canadian by choice, were Zoroastrians. Not a common religion outside its region of origin, and also not one I share.'

'Yeah, I can imagine,' said Nina. 'The only religion that would appeal to you is Mammonism.'

A small smile, empty of humour. 'But growing up with a religion,' he continued, 'you take in its mythology by osmosis. I learned about Afrasiab when I was young. First from the *Avesta*, where he's presented purely as an evil and deceitful villain, and then more about him from texts like the *Shahnameh*. He was . . . fascinating. Far more so than the supposed great heroes set against him.'

'Interesting that you sided with the bad guy.'

'You of all people should know that history is written by the victors. It suited Zoroaster to vilify Afrasiab to make the actions of Rostam and the others more impressive. But even then, Afrasiab's deeds are clearly the ones most worthy of attention. He lived in a vast underground palace made of metal. He used drought as a weapon against his enemies, while providing for his own people in the middle of a desert. He could control the weather!' He moved closer to the camera again, expression intensifying. 'The stuff of legend . . . but once again, you've proven it true. In fact, it was your discoveries that first made me wonder if the Iron Palace really existed. Atlantis, El Dorado, the Pyramid of Osiris – if they were real, then why not that too?'

'And more importantly,' said Nina, 'if it was real, maybe so was whatever allowed him to control the weather. And if you had the power to do that, it would be worth infinitely more than any amount of funny cat videos on social media.'

His eyes narrowed with an impatience she had seen from Macy many a time: *you just don't get it*. 'I created Uzz to do good for humanity. The world *can* be a better place. Which is why I want the Staff of Afrasiab. If we use it to alter the weather, we can counter the effects of climate change. We can save lives. Isn't that a cause you want to be on the right side of?'

'I would,' said Nina, 'if I believed your motives.'

'Trying to murder Nina isn't exactly saving lives,' Eddie added.

Loost sighed. 'Repeating the same actionable slander as your wife, Mr Chase? I should remind you that my lawyers can review all of my conversations.'

Nina dropped her bombshell. 'Anton Granit admitted to us that you hired him to kill me in Rome.'

'I terminated his company's employment some days ago, following an unrelated incident,' came the controlled and careful reply. 'Anything he may have said to you has nothing to do with me.'

'He tried to kill us on a train this morning! The only way he could have found us is if *you* sent him.'

The trillionaire's face briefly froze, as if the connection was unexpectedly buffering. Then Loost reached out to touch something offscreen, before kneading the bridge of his nose between thumb and forefinger. 'Well, you got me there,' he said wearily. 'I just took my lawyers out of the loop. So now we can all talk freely and honestly.'

'*We* haven't been doing anything else, you fucking bell-end,' said Eddie.

Nina couldn't help but smile. 'But maybe you can be honest about why you want the staff,' she told the aggrieved Loost. 'You don't care about saving the world, do you? It's just a side-effect of what you really want. You already have money; now you want power as well. And being able to control the weather, being able to control whose crops get water, whose land is turned into a desert . . . now *that's* power.'

When Loost finally spoke again, his voice was uncharacteristically threatening. 'You wondered why I sympathised with Afrasiab, Professor Wilde. It's because . . . he *inspired* me. He forced others to respect him, to *fear* him. Everything I've achieved in my life is to get that same respect. My own parents thought I was weak – because of a genetic disorder *they* gave me. They favoured my brother and my sisters. Everyone thought I would be dead by twenty-five. Why waste their time and effort and money on me? But I used the one strong thing I had, my *mind*, to keep myself alive. I worked my ass off to pay for my own treatments. I built one business, then another, and another. And still, people like *you*,' a sudden burst of anger, 'think I'm a joke! How *dare* you! I've created something worth trillions of dollars, something with the potential to change the world. What have *you* done? Dug in the dirt to find the remains of civilisations that died thousands of years ago! And for all your so-called achievements, you've done nothing in twenty-five years my AI couldn't have done in twenty-five *minutes*, like deducing that "angels" were really the Knights of Atlantis. You've made nothing, you've done nothing – you've just profited from looting ancient trash!'

The New Yorker gave him a look of disgust. 'Fuck. You,' she said firmly. 'I *have* the ancient trash you're so desperate to get your hands on. I can tell you now: that ain't gonna happen.'

'I'll fire up the angle grinder,' said Eddie.

The corners of Loost's mouth twitched with barely contained fury. 'The Knights will take the staff, Professor Wilde.'

'They'll have to come and get it. And down here, they're no angels. That armour of theirs is useless inside the Iron Palace.'

'Anyone tries to come down here, I'll blow their head off,' Eddie added.

'And how long do you think you can hold out? How many bullets do you have?' A sudden shift in his attitude as something occurred to him. Nina suspected it was not to her benefit, and her worries were quickly confirmed. 'Are you willing to shoot your own daughter?'

'You leave her alone, you son of a bitch,' she growled.

'I'm not going to do anything to hurt her. The question is: are you?' The call abruptly ended.

'Shit,' Nina said, free hand clenching into a fist. She looked up. 'Macy! Whatever Loost says to you, don't believe him!'

'Answer it,' said Emilian on Macy's startlement as her phone rang. 'It's Rafael.'

Someone was calling her through Uzz: it was indeed Loost. She looked helplessly between the screen and the building her mother had just called out from, then answered. 'Hello?'

Loost appeared. 'Macy. Hi. I know you're in a difficult situation,

394

and it must be very confusing – you don't know who you can trust. But your parents have been listening to the wrong people. They think your friends are their enemies. You're the only person they'll listen to – the only person who can make them see reason.'

'Oh, God,' she said, scared. The Brotherhood had convinced her mother and father that she had joined the bad guys? 'What – what do I have to do?'

'Go down and talk to them. Convince them that the Knights of Atlantis are not a threat – to them, or to the world. It's all up to you, Macy. You have to change their minds. Make them see that you're doing the right thing . . . and stop them from handing the Staff of Afrasiab to people who will use it for bad purposes.'

'Macy!' Nina shouted again. 'Don't listen to Loost! He set all of this up. He wants the staff for himself!'

'I assure you, that's not true,' Loost told the bewildered Macy. 'How could I even use the staff? Only people of very specific Atlantean ancestry can do that, as I understand it – and I'm not one of them. It's a conspiracy theory. Don't believe it.'

'I don't,' she said – but with uncertainty.

'I'll come with you,' said Rain. 'They know me.'

'I'll come too,' Emilian insisted. 'If they see I'm with you, it should convince them that I can be trusted.'

Macy hesitated, but then nodded. 'Okay.' She put away her phone, then stood. 'Mom! Dad! I'm coming down – with Rain, and another one of my friends.'

Her father replied. 'No! Just you, Macy.'

'Dad, you can trust them! *I* trust them. You trust me, don't you?' She took the lack of a reply as a positive . . . she hoped. 'Come on,' she said to Rain and Emilian. 'Just . . . stay behind me and keep your heads down.'

She and Rain picked their way past the others to reach Emilian. 'Once we get to the bottom, everyone else stay low and follow us down,' said the Dutchman.

MacDuff indicated the bullet dent on the iron wall. 'You think that's a good idea? No offence, Macy, but your dad seems a wee bit quick with his trigger finger.'

'I'll talk to him,' Macy replied, before calling down again: 'Dad! Please don't shoot my friends, okay?' She squeezed past Emilian to take the lead, then resumed her spiralling descent.

45

The journey took several minutes, but eventually Macy, Rain and Emilian neared the ramp to the cavern's floor. The buildings there spread out before them, shadow-draped and ominous in the firelight.

Rain let out a nervous sound as a figure emerged from a darkened doorway. 'It's okay,' said Macy. 'It's my mom.' She glanced around. 'Where's Dad?'

'I'm here, love,' said Eddie, voice echoing. Macy looked towards the source of his voice, but couldn't see him; he was somewhere inside the structure. 'Just making sure your friends don't do anything stupid.'

'I told you, you can trust them!'

Nina switched on her flashlight, shining it over each of the trio in turn. 'That's far enough,' she warned. 'Rain and whoever you are, stop there. Macy, come to me.'

Emilian and Rain halted. Squinting at the bright light, Macy advanced. 'Mom, I don't know what the Brotherhood told you, but the Knights of Atlantis aren't the bad guys. They do the same thing as the IHA – they recover and safeguard Atlantean artefacts. They've even found Earthbreaker.' That produced visible shock from Nina. 'The difference is, they've been doing it for centuries.'

'The difference is, the IHA have legal authority and account-ability,' Nina replied.

Macy halted. 'Oh, come on, Mom. You've said yourself that you don't approve of the way the IHA is run now. They want to exploit what they find. The whole purpose of the Knights is to make sure *nobody* uses these artefacts!' No sooner had she said the words than she shot an uncertain glance back at Emilian. He had pushed for a more activist stance . . .

The Dutchman picked up on her hesitancy and took over her explanation. 'The Knights turned their backs on conquest and war centuries ago, Professor Wilde. We're now protectors, making sure the secrets of Atlantis don't fall into the wrong hands. We act for the good of humanity.'

A sarcastic sound from the darkened building. 'Are you and Loost working from the same script?' said Eddie.

'Whose definition of good?' Nina demanded. 'Yours? Loost's? The trillionaire tax-dodger who considers himself literally above everybody else?'

'Every bugger thinks they're in the right,' her husband added. 'Hitler didn't wake up each morning cackling like Ming the Merciless and going, "How evil can I be today?"'

Macy let out an exasperated tut. 'Straight to the Hitler comparison, of course. My dad, who thinks *Where Eagles Dare* was a documentary.'

'Okay, ask your new mate there what his idea of doing good for the world is. How's he going to use something like Earthbreaker for good? Cause a good earthquake?'

'Or rather, ask how he'll use *you* to use Earthbreaker,' Nina added. 'Or any other Atlantean artefact. Because that's why they were so keen to recruit you. Women have been the ones best able to channel earth energy through these artefacts, all the way back to the Atlantean priestesses. This guy needs you. *Loost* needs you. That's why he befriended you on Uzz in the first place. He set all of this up so you could find the Staff of Afrasiab – for his purposes.'

'Why would he do that?' Macy objected. 'He's the richest man in the world! Why would he need the staff?'

'Money isn't enough for him any more. He wants power – he wants *control*. That's all these hyper-rich people want: control.'

'Over what?'

'Over everybody! If he can control the weather, control who gets water and who dies of thirst, whose crops get to grow . . . he wouldn't just be the richest person in history. He would also be the most *powerful*. More than any king, any pharaoh or emperor or president. If you don't pay him tribute, you die.'

Macy threw up her hands in disbelief. 'This is insane! He wouldn't do that. You don't know him – but I do. Rafael gave ten million dollars to a charity just because I suggested it, for God's sake!'

Eddie finally appeared behind a crack in the wall, lit by the fiery glow. His gun was pointedly aimed at Emilian. 'How do you know he's actually done it?' he said. 'He show you the receipt? You've never met the bloke – well, how can you have? He lives in a bloody space station!'

'It's better that the Knights have control of the staff than your new friends, the Brotherhood,' Macy said angrily. 'They tried to kill all of the Knights – including me. They killed Rain's mom and dad!' Shock from both her parents; they knew the Belcourts. 'Just like they killed *your* parents, Mom! I can't believe you would have anything to do with them!'

Nina overcame a stab to her heart to reply. 'I know what they did. But they didn't do it this time. The Brotherhood were framed, Macy – their leader was killed in Rome by someone trying to assassinate me. A mercenary. And we were attacked just a few hours ago by more mercenaries, led by a man called Anton Granit.'

'And Granit works for Loost,' said Eddie as he clambered out through the hole.

'Bullshit!' Macy protested.

Eddie frowned. 'I can show you his company's client list if you want proof.'

'He's tricked you, Macy,' Nina told her daughter, almost pleading. 'The whole thing is a set-up. He befriended you, and he offered me a job so I'd stop investigating the raid on the IHA – then when I turned him down, he hired Granit to kill me. Loost's been manipulating everything, right from the start.'

'It's true, love,' Eddie added as he joined his wife. His gun was still fixed upon the Dutchman. 'And this lot you're with killed someone at the IHA so they could steal Atlantean and Nephilim stuff.'

'We didn't *do* that,' insisted Rain.

'Rain, we saw the video,' Nina told her softly. 'It was someone in armour with glowing wings like an angel's, who could fly. Maybe you personally didn't know about it, and maybe the rest of you claim not to as well – but someone's lying.'

'They're not,' Macy said – but with less confidence than before. 'Look, these people are my friends – they saved my life! The Brotherhood tried to kidnap me, in France.'

'Yeah, we saw your holiday house, or what was left of it,' said Eddie.

'But that's what we keep trying to tell you,' Nina said. 'They *weren't* the Brotherhood. Loost sent them. This whole thing has been set up from the beginning. He's played *both* of us – and your friends too. Loost has tried to drive a wedge between us, and killed some of these Knights, so that you'd be alone. So that you'd *have* to turn to him for support – and then he could persuade you to do what he wants with the staff!'

'Where *is* the staff?' asked Emilian.

'Never you bloody mind,' Eddie growled. The Dutchman's gaze flicked calculatingly towards the temple, but he said no more.

'I don't believe that,' Macy told her mother. 'I *can't* believe that. I know Rafael, I've spoken to him, I follow what he does. Someone like him wouldn't do what you're saying!'

'Honey,' Nina replied, 'he's the richest man in the world – the richest person who's ever lived. Nobody gets even a *thousandth* of his wealth without being a ruthless asshole who thinks the rules don't apply to them, and probably finds that they don't. There are no good billionaires – never mind trillionaires.'

'Trust us on this, love,' added Eddie. 'We've got plenty of prior experience with these dickheads.'

'You've been manipulated into finding this place,' Nina went on. 'You find the staff, and – then what? Lock it up alongside Earthbreaker and everything else, never to be seen again?'

'That's the plan,' said Macy – though again, with uncertainty. She glanced back at Emilian, hoping for reassurance, but now couldn't help thinking about some of his past actions . . . 'Emilian? That transmitter you set up on the surface – was it part of the Knights' gear . . . or did Loost supply it?'

Emilian didn't reply, fixing her with an increasingly unsettling stare. Had he been caught out, or—

'Drop the gun!'

A man's shout, from not far above. Everyone looked up to find that Meller had crawled down the spiral path as far as he could without being seen – and popped up to aim his sub-machine gun at Eddie. Farther back, Naima also appeared with her own weapon, covering the Yorkshireman from two different angles. There was no way he could target both at the same time.

He didn't try. Instead he kept his gun firmly locked onto Emilian. 'Try anything, and I shoot this clag-nut,' Eddie snapped back. 'Seems like he's in charge, so you'd probably prefer he doesn't get a hole in his head?'

'*Dad!*' Macy cried, horrified. She looked up at Meller and Naima. 'For God's sake! Nobody shoot anyone, put your damn guns down!'

None of the weapons were lowered. Meller rose and warily continued down the path, the other members of his group descending behind the Finnish woman. Eddie also changed position, sidestepping towards the bridge to keep them both in view while holding his sights upon Emilian. Nina followed him.

'Macy,' said Emilian, his gaze tracking Eddie's gun. 'Rafael was right. Your parents are working with the Brotherhood. You can't trust them any more. But you *can* trust me. You know that.'

Eddie's already hostile expression became one of open, personal dislike. 'And why would that be? Got your eye on her, have you? Been a bad boy in your biker jacket? You put even a *finger* on my little girl, and I'll—'

'Dad!' Macy's cry was this time one of embarrassed exasperation. 'It's nothing like that.' Meller came down the ramp, Naima behind him, both still covering Eddie. 'But please, can everyone stop pointing guns at each other so we can fricking sort this out by *talking*, okay?'

'I'm afraid that will not be possible,' called an echoing voice from on high. 'Nobody move!'

Nina looked up, shocked – and saw men with rifles on a higher loop of the spiral path, aiming their weapons at those below. Even in the half-light, she knew the speaker instantly. Macy also gasped at the sight of the man who had tried to kidnap her in France.

Anton Granit.

46

G ranit and his men had secured ropes to the ledge above the towering cavern's entrance, then silently descended. The Iron Palace's convex walls meant they touched down some eighty feet above the chamber's floor. After attaching powered ascender units to their lines so they could make a rapid exit when their task was completed, they crept downwards to catch their prey unawares.

The Hungarian had no time to be astonished by the subterranean wonder. His attention was fixed upon the targets below; two in particular. 'Professor Wilde, Mr Chase!' he called, his weapon aimed at the couple. 'Did you think I had given up? You killed my brother. I was not going to let you get away. No matter what my *former* employer ordered.'

'Oh, Loost fired you, did he?' Eddie shouted back – while quickly assessing his tactical position. It was not good. He counted ten mercenaries, plus Granit himself. Even had everyone on the chamber's floor been armed and on the same side, they would still be outgunned. 'Not surprised, considering how often you fucked up.'

'Why are you pissing off the guy pointing a gun at us?' Nina hissed.

'If he's talking, he's not shooting.'

The statement was made more in hope than certainty, but it was proven as Granit roared a reply. 'Fuck you, Chase! You think you're going to get out of here? The only reason I didn't shoot you already is because I wanted you to *know* who is going to kill you!'

'Always thought that'd be a bad cheeseburger!' Eddie retorted – while twitching his free hand's fingers to give Macy a wordless signal. She saw it, eyes widening, then nodded. 'Get ready to run to the temple,' he warned Nina, before raising his voice again. 'You know what the last thing your brother said was?' As he spoke, Macy surreptitiously alerted her own companions. '"I'm feeling a bit run-down—"'

Lightning-fast, he whipped up his gun – and fired a snapshot at the nearest mercenary.

Even with his years of combat experience, Eddie knew the odds of scoring a hit without aiming were minuscule. The action was meant to startle his opponents and give their targets a chance to break for cover. So he was almost as surprised as the man called Prestmark when the bullet punched messily into the merc's throat.

But he overcame it faster than the shocked gunmen. 'Go!' he snapped, running with Nina for the temple. Macy similarly burst into motion, racing towards the royal quarters with Emilian and Rain. The other Knights all scattered to find their own hiding places.

Prestmark slumped against the metal wall, clutching helplessly at his ruptured neck. The attack had indeed caught Granit and his men off-guard; it took almost a second for the mercenary leader to shoot back. Bullets cracked against the bridge behind Eddie and Nina. The other mercs also opened fire, hurriedly retargeting the fleeing Knights.

Meller dropped back from the others as he brought up his gun. 'Get into cover!' he yelled, sweeping bursts of fire up at the ledge. Granit's men hurriedly ducked as rounds clanged against the iron panels around them.

Nina reached the temple, Eddie diving in behind her – and hurriedly rolling as one of Granit's bullets blasted a jade chunk from the dais. She peeked out of the entrance. 'Macy, *run!*' she cried.

Macy was doing just that. She had been a keen runner since her early teens, now putting every last ounce of energy into breaking her sprint record. Gunshots echoed across the metal-walled cavern, bullets striking stone behind her—

Rain cried out as shrapnel nicked her leg. Macy glanced back, seeing her friend stumble. Emilian overtook as she hurriedly reversed direction. 'Macy, keep running!' he shouted.

She ignored him, catching Rain. There was no time to see how badly she was hurt. Instead she pulled the French woman with her after Emilian. He reached Afrasiab's quarters and disappeared into the shadows within. Macy followed, cover just twenty feet away, fifteen—

A sharp *whip* as a bullet passed behind her. Then a second, even closer. The third would find its target—

Meller fired again. The mercenary tracking Macy jerked back as rounds impacted beside him. She ran on, practically dragging Rain through the threshold.

Meller saw that they had reached safety, then dashed for one of the smaller structures to find cover for himself—

He didn't make it.

Having lost sight of his primary targets, Granit switched to the greatest threat. He locked his sights onto the running Ukrainian – and pulled the trigger. A bloody exit wound burst open in Meller's back.

Eddie saw him collapse. He swore. Not because Macy had convinced him the man was no threat – the jury was still out on the Knights – but because his gun had landed in the open, impossible to reach without being exposed to the mercenaries above. That meant only he and the dark-haired woman were armed, against ten men—

One of the mercs from the train came into view on the ledge, trying for a better angle on somebody behind a building. Even with a handgun, the aimed shot was straightforward for the former

405

SAS soldier. Qabbani toppled from the walkway with a choked scream. *Nine* men.

The other mercenaries instantly rounded on the new danger. Eddie jerked back as bullets hammered around the entrance. He waited for the assault to stop, then rounded the little building's interior to use the dais as a shield. From here he could cover the bridge, hidden by the shadows inside the temple. The other Knights of Atlantis had all now found cover, but he was only interested in the fate of one person. 'I can't see Macy,' he said. 'But I think she got into the big building.'

'God, I hope so,' Nina replied, fearful. 'Okay, we're trapped in here – what are we going to do?'

Eddie glanced at the staff. 'Can't you do something with that?'

'Like what? Make it snow so they all slip off the ledge?' But despite her sarcasm, she suddenly realised something. Her feeling of isolation, of being cut off, was less oppressive than before . . .

She looked back outside, at where the fallen man had damaged the metal panels covering the chasm below. Was that allowing earth energy to leak through, breaching the dead zone of the Iron Palace?

If it was, it didn't help her. The staff's power only affected what was above the ground, not below.

And now she heard Granit shout new orders to his men. They were coming down the spiral path to find her.

Panting, Macy released Rain's hand. Her friend slumped against a wall. 'Are you okay?' Macy asked. She shone her light at Rain's leg. There was a ragged cut in her trousers, but the shrapnel wound appeared only superficial.

'I think so,' Rain replied, breathless. 'It doesn't hurt too bad.' She shifted her weight, lips pursing tightly. 'It stings, but – I can run.'

'Run to where?' demanded Emilian. 'We can't fly, so we're trapped down here. There's only one way out – and those bastards are coming down it! We can't even use our weapons.' He glared at the metal whip coiled over his shoulder, as if it had failed him personally.

Macy gave her trikan a look more of despair – which changed to surprise as she sensed that something had changed. 'Wait – I can feel something,' she said. Where before there had been nothing, there was now a hint of tingling energy within the weapon, as if the crystal at its heart had finally made contact with the currents of power flowing outside the Iron Palace . . .

She focused, trying to activate her armour. She briefly felt the thousands of thin leaves of metal try to shift into their protective form . . .

But nothing happened. Even if earth energy was seeping into the chamber, it wasn't enough to power her armour.

She raised her weapon. What if—

'Rain, stand back,' she warned, making an experimental throw. The trikan shot from its holder, spinning towards the entrance. An effort of will—

Its blades extended with a sharp *clack*.

Macy gasped in excitement and relief. Another guiding thought – and the trikan tipped vertically before righting itself at her command. She jerked her hand back, and the ancient weapon whirled to her on its retracting wire. The blades vanished into the orichalcum shell a split-second before it clanked into its home. 'It works!' she cried. 'There isn't enough earth energy to transform the armour – but there's enough for this.'

Rain put a hand on her sword's hilt, giving Macy a startled look as she too felt it. Emilian went further, hurriedly snapping his whip at one wall. The tip glowed faintly, cutting a shallow gash into the stonework. 'Then we can still fight,' he said, before going to the entrance. 'Knights, listen!' he shouted. 'We can still use our weapons! They're coming for us – be ready for them!'

'Stay in cover until you're sure you can hit your target,' Naima warned. 'They can shoot you from a lot further away than your weapons can reach.'

Macy regarded Rain's sword. 'You'd better stay back,' she told her friend.

Rain readied her weapon. 'I know what to do, Macy. I've trained for it. But thank you.'

'Training's nothing like reality,' Macy cautioned her. 'I'll make sure nobody gets that far.'

Emilian indicated the entrances to the first rooms off the passage. 'Go in there. We can stop anybody from coming inside.'

Macy felt far from confident about that, but she went to the left-hand opening as he took up position on the right. Through the entrance, she could see the ramp to the spiral – and the temple where her parents were hiding. She was about to call out to them when Idris Benichou shouted first.

The Algerian spoke in Portuguese, Macy getting the gist of his plan. None of the mercenaries appeared to be from the Iberian peninsula; hopefully they would not understand what they were overhearing. He intended to sprint up the ramp to the ledge, using the interconnected little shelters for cover until he could attack the descending men with his gauntlets. 'That's, uh, not a good idea,' said Macy. 'He'll get shot before he gets up there, however fast he runs.'

'Naima can give him cover,' said Emilian.

'It won't be enough. Unless—' She looked out at the temple again. 'Mom! Dad!' she called. 'We have to work together!'

'No arguments there!' Nina replied.

'One of us will need—' She halted mid-sentence. How to tell them without alerting their attackers?

The answer came quickly. She took out her phone and hurriedly found her mother's number. Blocking incoming calls from it did not limit outgoing ones. A reply soon came. 'Macy?' said Nina, surprised.

'Mom, listen,' she said. 'One of us is going to run up the ramp. I need Dad to give them covering fire. Can he do that?'

Macy heard her ask Eddie how much ammunition he had left. She couldn't make out his words, but his tone sounded at least positive-adjacent. 'Yeah,' Nina told her. 'But he doesn't think it's a good idea.'

'Nor do I! But our weapons have got some power – I can use my trikan now.'

'I think it's because the metal panels around this temple are broken,' said Nina. 'The whole place is like a Faraday cage, the—'

'Can he do it?' Emilian demanded impatiently.

'Yes, he can,' said Macy. 'Mom, I've gotta go. Stay safe. I love you.'

'I love you too,' her mother replied.

She ended the call, readying the trikan. 'Any second . . .' said Emilian, fingers twitching with adrenalin around his whip's handle . . .

Idris burst from hiding and sprinted for the ramp.

Eddie returned to the temple's entrance to give himself a wider firing angle. He saw the young man start to race across the open ground – but his attention was on the ledge circling above. Granit and his men were nearing its bottom, spread out in a long chain to cover the area below – and also to make themselves harder targets.

A mercenary shouted as he spotted the running figure. Rifles whipped around to track him – but Eddie had already found a target of his own. Granit was almost diametrically opposite him across the cavern, at the limit of his pistol's effective range. He took the shot anyway—

It missed. Not by much, Granit flinching as the round struck iron behind him, but in combat a miss was a failure however close. He dropped, aiming his rifle back at the temple. 'It's Chase!' he bellowed. 'Kill him!'

Most of his men followed the order, switching targets and opening fire. Eddie hurriedly retreated as more rounds pitted the ancient stones. But a few were still tracking Idris—

Naima swept from her cover amongst the buildings and fired. One man yelled as a bullet clipped his hip. The other mercs hastily swung around to find the new danger. Eddie used their moment of confusion to target the man who had just been wounded. A bullet slammed into the mercenary's skull.

Taking fire from two angles, the remaining mercs dropped flat. Idris used the brief respite to charge onto the ramp. By the time the gunmen recovered, he was over halfway up it. The man leading the way down, a Russian called Annenkov, was barely twenty metres away. He hurriedly swung his rifle after him, sending a blazing storm of bullets in the Algerian's wake. Idris threw himself headlong into one of the little shelters as rounds shattered stones behind him.

The rest of Granit's men fired back at Eddie and Naima, forcing them to retreat. 'Annenkov, get him!' Granit shouted as he scuttled in a half-crouch down the path. 'Use a grenade!'

'He's trapped, I can shoot him!' the Russian replied. He hurried to the top of the ramp, keeping his rifle trained on the shelter's bullet-pocked entrance. No movement in his tactical light's beam. He reached the opening and thrust his gun inside—

Nobody was there.

Annenkov was startled. Where had he gone? He peered in – and saw the dwelling was connected to its neighbours by tunnels, just big enough for a man to crawl through. Which way had he gone? Only a few more of the bulbous structures stood on the ledge beyond the ramp. He would have gone up, to give himself more hiding places. The mercenary side-stepped back, thrusting his rifle into each entrance to illuminate the interior with his tac-light. The first was empty apart from dusty scraps and trash. So was the second. He looked into the third—

Idris's gauntlet, aglow with earth energy, hit his face with the force of a hammer.

The effect on Annenkov's head was far greater than a mere hammer-blow. The spiked knuckles pulsed, releasing their power – and the Russian's skull exploded as if a grenade had detonated in his mouth.

Granit saw another of his men fall. 'There, *there*!' he yelled, murderous fury rising. He opened fire on the shelter. 'Shoot him!'

The other mercenaries also targeted the spot where their comrade had died. Bullets shattered stone in a terrifying, pounding onslaught. The shelter's ceiling collapsed, pinning Idris as he tried to pull himself into the next hut. He cried out.

Granit heard him even over the thunder of gunfire. He ran along the ledge, the shots stopping as he reached Annenkov's corpse. The shelter's fallen roof resembled a cracked eggshell. A man inside struggled to kick stones and debris off his legs. The Hungarian fired a burst at point-blank range into his back. The trapped man spasmed, then was still.

The mercenary leader glared down at the temple. Enough of this. He had wanted to look his brother's murderers in the eyes as he killed them, but the situation had escalated out of control. Time to end it.

Two hand grenades were clipped to the equipment webbing across his chest alongside his flashlight. He detached one and pulled out the pin. 'Fire in the hole!'

The warning to Granit's men also reached his targets. 'Oh, shit,' said Nina. 'Is that aimed at us, or—'

A hand grenade bounced through the temple's entrance.

'*Yes!*' Eddie yelped. They rushed outside and vaulted from the bridge to land on the metal panels beyond, scrambling clear—

The grenade exploded.

The blast erupted from the opening in a cloud of dust and

shrapnel. But the force of the detonation also damaged the structure itself. A section of one wall pitched outwards, carved blocks smashing down on the surrounding metal—

A panel ripped from its supports, one side tilting sharply downwards.

Nina and Eddie stumbled as the floor lurched beneath them. Nina landed on the next panel – but her husband slipped sideways, following the fallen stones towards the abyss below—

He clawed at the metal – and hooked two fingers into the holes perforating it, jerking to a halt. His feet hung over the dark void below. 'Eddie!' Nina gasped, grabbing his arm. 'Climb up, come on!' The iron panel shook as its remaining supports weakened.

Eddie twisted, swinging up his free hand to grab the neighbouring sheet of metal. Nina hauled at his arm, raising him higher. He managed to get both elbows over the edge of the next panel – just as the damaged one fell away. It tumbled towards the water below.

Panting, he pulled himself up, Nina helping – but the couple were far from safe. By fluke rather than conscious decision they had been shielded behind the temple from the descending mercenaries, but now Granit's men had come around the spiral far enough to see them. A bullet shrilled off the floor inches away. They jumped up and ran – as more rounds followed.

Naima shot at the gunmen again. Several switched targets to the greater threat. But Granit's attention was fixed on the two figures running across the metal expanse. 'This is for my brother,' he snarled – as he threw a second grenade.

It hit the panels ahead of Eddie and Nina with a ringing bang. They hurriedly reversed direction as it rattled towards them. '*Dive!*' the Yorkshireman cried. Some of the stone blocks dislodged from the temple were scattered around its base. The couple threw themselves over them, flattening themselves on the metal beyond—

Another explosion shook the cavern. The fallen blocks were just large enough to shield Nina and Eddie from the flying razor-sharp shrapnel. But they didn't have time to be thankful for their survival.

The blast tore more panels from their supports. They dropped into the chasm, pulling others after them in a widening circle of destruction—

The floor fell away beneath Nina and Eddie, pitching them into the void below.

47

Macy couldn't see her parents, her view blocked by the temple. But the grenade explosion behind the building filled her with sudden fear for their lives – which became full-blown terror as the iron floor collapsed. *'Mom!'* she screamed. *'Dad!'*

No reply, only a fading scream and the resounding clamour of metal plates tumbling into the chasm. She froze for a moment – then readied her trikan, about to run out to help them—

Emilian pulled her back. 'If you go out there without armour, they'll shoot you!'

'Let go of me! Let go!' She tried to break free, but his hold was painfully strong. 'Get your fucking hand off—'

He yanked her forcefully back. She angrily whipped up her trikan, setting the weapon spinning inside its holder. The crystal at the disc's centre glowed with sudden intensity. Fury in his eyes at being threatened . . .

Then both realised the significance of the shimmering light. 'We have more power!' Emilian cried.

He released her, concentrating – and the bands around his limbs and neck transformed.

But the earth energy now penetrating the cavern was still only a fraction of that outside. The metal scales crawled sluggishly over his body, taking several seconds to combine into the golden covering of armour. Even the halo, when it finally appeared, was feeble. 'Something's wrong,' he said.

Macy reached out her left hand to his halo. The strange

pulsating sensation that previously would have blocked contact was there, but offered only limited resistance. Rain hurried to them. 'It's not working!'

'It is – but not enough,' Emilian said, dismayed. 'It won't stop a bullet.'

Macy looked back towards the temple. The cacophony of falling iron had ceased, a gaping hole now visible in the metal plain. What had her mother said, just before the end of the phone call? Something about a Faraday cage—

More gunshots came from close by.

Naima found new cover behind another damaged building as the mercenaries descended the spiral. To her alarm, she found MacDuff hunched in a doorway blocked by rubble. 'You've got to move!' she told him. 'They're coming.'

'I'd love to,' the Scot replied fearfully, 'but there's nowhere to go! They got Oleksiy. If I run, they'll get me too!'

'I'll draw their fire,' said the Finn. 'When I shoot, you run for that big building. I think Emilian's in there. Are you ready?'

MacDuff nervously rose. 'Suppose I'll have to be, won't I? Good luck.'

She nodded, then cautiously moved to get line of sight on the mercenaries—

A shout from above – but Naima had already spotted one of Granit's men and fired. The bullet clanged against the wall beside him. She sprinted towards another building. The movement drew fire from the other mercenaries. MacDuff burst from his hiding place and ran. Naima kept shooting as she raced in the other direction. The wild snapshots had almost no chance of hitting a target, but would keep the attackers' attention on her rather than the fleeing civilian—

Another shot – and her pistol's slide locked back. The magazine was empty. Shit! She had miscounted her rounds. She ducked behind a small building. The gunfire from above stopped. Had MacDuff reached safety?

She fumbled for a replacement magazine—

Movement on the spiral, a merc reaching a position where he could see her – and a bullet wound exploded in her chest.

MacDuff rushed into the palace, the Knights moving to let him past. 'Where's Naima?' asked Rain.

MacDuff staggered to a stop. 'Back there, giving me cover,' he panted. 'She's going to—'

A single gunshot echoed from the chasm's iron walls with a chilling finality. That no pistol fire came in response confirmed everyone's fears. 'Oh, God,' the Scot muttered. 'They got her.'

Rain put a hand to her mouth in horror. 'We're trapped!'

'No,' Macy said firmly. 'We're not.' An exertion of will, and she transformed her armour. The slowness with which the metal bands broke into their constituent parts and linked together was almost physically uncomfortable. She could *sense* how weak the energy field was compared to normal. But it was there – and if her mother was right, the closer she got to the breach in the iron cage, the stronger it would get.

If her mother was right. But there was only one way to find out . . .

Before anyone could stop her, she ran out into the open.

Emilian and Rain both shouted for her to come back. She ignored them, focused on finding a clear path through the ruins. Shock as she spotted Meller's body, her horror rising as she rounded a building to see Naima slumped nearby. But there was nothing she could do for them; all that mattered was finding her mother and father . . .

Macy emerged into the open near the bridge. The ramp to the spiral lay beyond it – and men were descending towards her.

Someone shouted. She'd been seen.

She ran onto the bridge. The hole in the damaged iron plain was some fifty feet across, more panels around its edge hanging precariously from their supporting framework. 'Mom! Dad!' she shouted. No sign of them—

Something hit her so hard in the back that she fell.

The crack of a rifle echoed from the walls. She gasped in pain. She'd been shot!

But . . . she wasn't dead.

The bullet hadn't pierced her armour, its impact absorbed, spread. Earth energy *was* getting through the cavern's iron lining—

Another gunshot – and a round hit the bridge's wall beside her. She ducked and scrambled forward. The leading mercs were hurrying down the ramp. When they reached the bridge they would have a clear line of fire. Shield or no shield, enough bullets would kill her.

Despite the pain, she ran again. The temple's entrance was a dark mouth ahead. More shots snapped past, striking stonework. She saw something inside the damaged structure, a tall, thin object mounted upon a dais. Was it the Staff of Afrasiab—

A bullet hit her left shoulder.

The impact sent her spinning. She stumbled through the temple's entrance, falling hard against the dais. Her armour had again saved her. She dragged herself clear of the archway as more rounds impacted outside.

Her parents weren't in the small building. But maybe they had found cover behind the temple . . .

One wall had been damaged by the grenade explosion and toppled outwards, leaving a ragged hole. She crawled to it. The broken black void came into view. Only darkness was visible below. 'Mom! Dad!'

The words came back to her as mocking echoes. She called out again, more fearfully. 'Mom? Dad?'

Still nothing.

'Mom . . .' She was the only person who heard the whisper. She suddenly realised she was crying, startled when a tear touched her lips. 'Dad . . .'

They were gone.

This has happened before, she told herself. *I thought they were dead. They weren't.* The words became more insistent, more desperate. *They came back. They* always *come back . . .*

But nothing moved beyond the fallen wall.

Afraid, she backed away, bumping against the dais. She grabbed the staff to pull herself up—

A new reality hit her like a speeding truck.

The world outside the Iron Palace rushed in, overpowering, overwhelming. She pulled away in shock – and snapped back to the dimly lit temple as she lost her hold on the staff. Panting in fright, she stumbled back. What the hell had just happened?

But she already knew. It *was* the Staff of Afrasiab, the Atlantean artefact that had been the source of the renegade king's power.

A power that was now hers.

A power almost *demanding* to be used . . . however she wanted.

Shouts from outside the temple – and in that moment, she knew *how* she wanted to use it.

Grief and denial were swept away by fury. She dropped her trikan and seized the staff again, this time with both hands. The world inverted, what was outside now encompassed by her will. She could feel . . . *everything*.

Her focus narrowed, finding the sky over the Karakum, over the sinkhole. The day was clear and hot, the desert sands arid. But there was still water there, oceans of it suspended in the air, rendered inaccessible by the conditions.

She could *change* those conditions.

She did.

Like controlling her trikan or armour, it required only an effort of will. The staff magnified it, passing it through the great green stone she sensed beneath the cavern. It was only a fraction the size of the one that gave Earthbreaker its power, perhaps a mile deep, a splinter compared to a mountain. But it could affect the swirling flow of earth energy around it just as strongly.

And that power was now hers to control.

'Bring the storm,' she growled, clenching the staff more tightly as her vengeance took on physical form.

'Cease fire!' Granit ordered as he reached the bottom of the ramp. The armoured figure had made it into the building despite being shot twice. Whatever her protection was made of, it was a match for the very best on the market.

But it wasn't indestructible. His men had killed two of the defenders in Portugal despite their protection. As with most problems in life, enough bullets would end them.

'Split up,' he ordered. 'There are more of them in the big building over there.' He gestured towards the royal quarters. 'Maziq, Yeston, with me. We'll get the girl.'

'Are we going to kill her?' asked Maziq.

A humourless smile. 'If it's not Wilde's daughter, then yes. If it is, that depends on how much Rafael Loost is willing to pay to keep her alive. Okay, let's—'

A deep, rumbling boom rolled through the cavern – from above.

Zdanys, Granit's pilot, watched in alarm as the sun was suddenly obscured by clouds. No ordinary clouds, either. In his years of flying he thought he had seen every weather condition imaginable – but this was new, almost unbelievable. They were forming from nothing, dense and dark thunderheads swelling in a clear sky. How was that possible?

A rumble shook the cockpit. Then another, accompanied by a flash within the deepening mass overhead. The lightning was right on top of him. More booms, louder and louder as the desert darkened. The black clouds lowered like a giant boot about to crush him. But he could see a line of blue sky along the horizon. The storm was centred precisely on the sinkhole!

Whatever was happening, it wasn't natural. He hurriedly started the helicopter's take-off sequence—

Torrential rainfall hit the cockpit canopy, the noise of the fat raindrops bursting against the fuselage like the roar of a football crowd. The desert sand instantly turned to mud. But the downpour was so intense there was no way the parched ground could soak it up. In moments, rivulets turned to streams, then rivers, churning torrents of brown water rushing towards the sinkhole.

The helicopter lurched as the flow hit its landing gear. Zdanys grabbed the controls in sudden fear. Flying in these conditions would be extremely dangerous, but if he didn't take off his aircraft would be swept into the pit—

He jerked back in his seat, almost blinded, as lightning bolts pounded explosively around the crater.

The walls of Afrasiab's quarters shuddered, shaking loose dust. 'What was that?' said Rain, alarmed.

MacDuff peered nervously through the entrance. 'Are they using explosives?'

Emilian shook his head. 'It sounded like thunder—' He regarded his companions in shock. 'Macy has the staff!'

'What's she doing?' asked MacDuff. 'Being able to control the weather's no use when you're six hundred feet underground!'

'I don't know, but it won't help us.' Rain pointed towards the ramp – where figures were now advancing between the buildings. 'They're coming!'

'We'll have to fight them,' was the Dutchman's grim conclusion. 'Rain, transform. Any armour is better than none.' She did so, the glinting scales sluggishly slithering into position. 'Euripides,

find somewhere to hide. We'll try to keep them away from you.'
Using his phone for light, MacDuff retreated into the building as
he readied his whip and Rain raised her sword. Both weapons
glowed as earth energy ran through them, but the light was only
pallid.

They took up defensive positions as the mercenaries advanced.

The helicopter's main rotor reached minimum take-off revolu-
tions. Zdanys hauled at the collective control, lifting his aircraft
from the ground. Just in time: a new surge of flood water rolled
past beneath him, the blades' downwash kicking up a blinding
cloud of spray.

He switched on the wipers. They were little help against the
tumultuous downpour. But if he kept the chopper a hundred
metres above the desert, he could fly clear of the impossible storm,
then return for Granit and the others when it had passed—

A flash outside, almost blinding – and the helicopter lurched as
if hit by a giant's club. Alarms honked and squalled, warning lights
flashing urgently on the instrument panel. The engine was on fire!

It had been struck by lightning. But this was no ordinary bolt.
Zdanys had flown through dozens of hits in the past; helicopters
could even trigger strikes. But they were engineered to withstand
them. This one, though, had somehow burned into the engine
compartment . . .

The altimeter needle dropped. Zdanys looked desperately
through the footwell window to see what lay ahead, but his view
was obliterated by the pounding rain. All he knew was that he was
falling. He pulled back on the cyclic control stick, trying to keep
his aircraft level—

Something rushed at the lower windows. He realised it was a
boulder a split-second before it ripped through the fuselage,
crushing his legs.

The helicopter pitched forward, nose slamming into the ground

– and the entire aircraft flipped over and blew apart in a seething fireball.

Rain looked back as MacDuff hurriedly returned from the interior of the royal quarters. 'There's no other way out back there,' he told her and Emilian.

The Dutchman looked out of the entrance. Beyond the statues, the mercenaries were drawing closer. 'We'll decoy them away from you. Rain, you run for that building over there.' He indicated a nearby structure. 'I'll go the other way.'

'If they see us, they'll shoot us!' Rain warned. 'What if our armour doesn't work?'

'We'll have to risk it. Get ready.' He moved to the threshold, signalling for her to follow. Reluctantly, she did so. 'Okay – go!'

He rushed from the shadowed entrance, angling to one side. A shout as an approaching man spotted him – but he had already lashed out with his whip. Even with only a low charge of earth energy, it still sliced through one of the statues as he passed behind it. The stone figure broke apart, its upper half toppling to the ground and smashing into pieces. The startled mercs jumped back from the scattering debris as Emilian ran clear.

Rain followed him from cover, heading the other way. Another shout came almost immediately. But her own weapon gave her no way to defend, or even distract. All she could do was run—

It wasn't enough. One man tracked her with his rifle – and fired.

The bullet hit her side. Her armour was just strong enough to stop it from penetrating the metal sheath, but the impact was like a blow from a baseball bat, sending her spinning as her ribs took the painful strike. Her sword flew from her hand and clanged back into the royal quarters. Another shot whipped just over her head as she stumbled. Gasping, she forced herself upright and ran again. 'Emilian!' she cried, breathless. 'Help!'

Emilian reached the building. He glanced back, seeing Rain in the open . . . then continued into cover.

Another bullet cracked past Rain, hitting the wall of Afrasiab's quarters behind her. She made a sound of fright – but reached the other statue and flattened herself behind it. Another mercenary fired, his round chipping the ancient stone figure. She hunched down, petrified, as Granit's men closed in.

Granit reached the end of the bridge, checking for possible threats. He found none. The only person nearby was the girl who had gone into the little temple.

He raised his HK437 rifle and looked down its sights along the bridge's length. His target was visible inside the building, the bizarre glow of her armour illuminating the interior. Was it Wilde and Chase's daughter? He couldn't tell, her face hidden by light. She was holding a spear or staff mounted on an altar.

What she was doing, he had no idea. It didn't matter. She was in his sights – and he knew from Portugal that her armour was not impenetrable. At this range, it would only take a couple of bullets to punch through. He would shoot to wound: her legs, or stomach. If it was the daughter, she could be patched up enough to ransom to Loost.

If not . . . one more bullet to the head would finish the job.

He refined his aim, fixing upon the centreline of her torso—

Granit suddenly realised his gun was trembling.

A low rumble had grown louder while he found his target, reverberating through the iron-walled cavern. Rock and metal shuddered and moaned, the sound echoing with increasing fury . . .

Then water erupted through the cavern's ceiling, tearing away panels as the deluge plunged towards those below.

48

Nina screamed as she plummeted helplessly into the black chasm beneath the Iron Palace—

Water exploded around her.

She had fallen feet-first into the underground lake, but the impact still caught her jaw like an uppercut. Dazed, she instinctively gasped, only for the water to rush into her nose and mouth. She kicked and thrashed in panic as she struggled to breach the surface. 'Oh, God! Eddie!' she spluttered. 'Eddie, are you there? Eddie!'

Splashing close by, then a loud whoop as her husband drew in air. 'Yeah, I'm here, I'm okay,' he wheezed. 'Are you—'

One of the iron plates smashed down beside them.

The wave it made rolled over their heads. Choking again, Nina looked up. The firelit cavern was visible through the ragged hole above—

And more panels were falling towards them.

'Hold your breath!' Eddie yelled – before pulling her under the surface and swimming deeper.

Iron slabs pounded into the lake, shockwaves and frothing bubbles hitting them. Eddie rolled to position himself above her. If they were struck, he would take the lethal blow . . .

But the onslaught stopped.

Slowed by the water, the panels fell away towards the cistern's unseen bottom. The couple kicked upright, returning to the surface. Nina fought for breath. 'We've got to get out from under that hole,' she panted. 'If the rest of those panels fall, we'll get squashed!'

Eddie fumbled in his sodden leather jacket for his phone. The screen lit up; it was waterproof, to a point. He turned on the torch and shone the beam around. The cavern was large, the farthest wall beyond the light's range. 'Over there,' he said, finding a sloping slab of rock rising from the lake.

They swam towards it. Smaller splashes echoed behind them as loose debris fell, but the other panels above stayed – for now – in place. Nina sighed in relief when she felt solid stone beneath her. 'Thank God,' she said. Water streamed from her clothing as she dragged herself up the slope.

Eddie helped her stand, sweeping his torch from side to side. 'We're not that much better off. Must have fallen a hundred feet, and I doubt there's a flight of stairs leading back up.'

'I'm not so sure about that.' Nina took hold of his hand, bringing the light back to something she had glimpsed. It revealed markings on the rock wall – with characters she instantly recognised as Atlantean. 'This must have been the Iron Palace's reservoir – those show the water level.' The highest of the painted lines was well above her head, so the cistern could clearly store a huge amount of water. 'I doubt they lowered someone on a rope every time they wanted to check their supply, so . . .' She panned the torch across and up from the markings – and found an oval opening in the rock face, a tunnel beyond angling upwards. 'Ah-ha!'

'You think that goes all the way back up?' Eddie asked, dubious.

'Since it's close to the depth markers and also looks at least partly man-made, yes,' she replied, advancing for a closer look. 'But even if it doesn't, we still have to check it, because I didn't see any other ways out.'

He turned in a full circle. The probing beam found nothing but rock and water. 'Tchah. Not even a waterslide. Rubbish, two out of ten.'

She smiled. 'I've had more than enough thrills for one day.'

Humour vanished at the thought of what awaited above. 'Come on. We've got to find Macy and get out of here.'

Footholds had been cut into the rock. They climbed to the opening and started up the tunnel. In places it was steep enough that Afrasiab's people had needed to carve steps into the floor. But while sand and gravel had accumulated, the passage was easy to traverse. Nina realised why: it had been made wide enough to accommodate a person carrying water jars on a shoulder yoke. The Iron Palace might have had a plentiful supply of water, but the desert did not give it up easily.

They soon crossed a threshold where the walls became smoother, rough natural textures carved away. 'I think we're getting near the top,' said Nina.

'Better be careful,' Eddie warned. 'I've lost the gun, and Granit's arseholes are probably still—'

He broke off as a deep rumble rolled through the tunnel. Nina had a hand against the wall for support; she gasped as she felt it tremble. 'What the hell was that?' she said, unnerved. 'Thunder?'

'Might have been explosives. Shit, what if they're trying to seal us in?' They continued upwards more rapidly.

Something came into sight above. 'It's a trapdoor,' said Nina, seeing a metal plate covering a square opening in the ceiling. 'We're at the top!'

'Just hope they didn't leave a three-ton statue on it,' Eddie said. He gave the iron slab an experimental upwards push. It was heavy, but to his relief moved. 'Okay, hold this. I'll open it.'

Nina took his phone. The Yorkshireman braced himself and forced the trapdoor wider. It was hinged at one side, slowly swinging open. 'Bloody hell, this thing's heavy.'

'Eddie, hold on,' said Nina, suddenly wary.

'What do you mean, hold on? I'm trying to lift something the weight of a Mini!'

'No, really – I can hear something—'

Another low rumble grew louder – then a cacophonous roar came from above, overlaid with bangs and shrills of tearing metal. Eddie winced as a rising wind blew dust into his face. 'Jesus!' he said, squinting. 'Sounds like a fucking waterfall—'

It was.

The deluge that had broken through the cavern's roof smashed down, churning waves sweeping towards him.

Eddie yelped and dropped, the heavy trapdoor slamming shut. But the passage was far from watertight. Cracks burst open, frothing jets spraying from them. The ruptures widened, grit and stones and then entire chunks of rock ripping free. 'Get back!' he warned Nina. 'This isn't going to hold—'

One side of the opening crumbled – and the flood rushed in.

It knocked him off his feet, sending him sliding down the slope – crashing into Nina as he went. Water seethed around them as they were swept back the way they had come. Eddie clawed at the walls, but found no purchase on the smoothly carved surface.

Nina still clutched his phone, the beam skittering wildly as the torrent battered her – and she saw the threshold rushing towards them. Beyond it was rough, raw rock. The risk of injury was about to shoot up – but so was the hope of halting their plunge. 'Eddie!' she cried. 'Try to grab on!'

She twisted to bring up her feet as the water carried her through the threshold—

Her soles slammed painfully against a projecting rock. She bent her legs to absorb the impact, the current swinging her around – and threw out both hands to find the other wall. Ragged stone cut her skin, but she forced her limbs straight, locking her joints against the relentless force from behind—

Eddie collided with her again.

She yelled, but somehow held her position. Her husband kept

going, though, the flood sweeping him up over her legs. He grabbed desperately at her—

He caught her shirt. It yanked taut as he was carried onwards, buttons popping and seams ripping – then he jammed one heel against a crack in the floor, halting his slide.

Nina gasped as waves splashed over her head. 'God damn it!' she yelled. 'You *had* to wish for a waterslide!'

His position was too precarious for him to offer a retort. Instead he pushed himself slightly higher, trying to ease the strain on her overstressed clothing. 'I think it's stopping!' he eventually gasped.

The pressure of the water against Nina's back was indeed gradually falling. All the same, she didn't dare relax. She had managed to keep hold of Eddie's phone, grinding its screen against the rock, but the torch remained shining. She looked back up the tunnel. A sediment-heavy stream still gushed down it, but its force was much reduced. 'Can you let go of me?'

'Hold on.' Eddie found another foothold, then released Nina's shirt. He immediately slithered down the slope, but easily caught himself.

She gasped in relief as his weight was removed from her. 'Oh, my God. That was too damn close.' Muscles trembling, she hesitantly shifted one leg. The water didn't whisk her away. 'It's easing.'

'How could there be a fucking flash flood?' Eddie demanded. 'There wasn't a cloud in the sky when we came down the sinkhole!'

Nina wearily rolled into a sitting position. 'Someone used the Staff of Afrasiab.'

'Macy?'

'Yeah. Or one of the people with her. When Granit blew up the floor and dropped us into that hole, he also broke open the Faraday cage – and that might have given them back their powers.'

'Powers like flying, and making people explode?'

'We've got to find her before she does anything else crazy.' She rose, helping Eddie stand before they both slogged back up the muddy slope.

49

Macy forced herself to release the staff and opened her eyes. Devastation greeted her through the hole in the temple's wall.

The metal floor over the chasm had been almost completely torn away, only a few battered panels still clinging to the remnants of its supporting framework. The cause was clear: a waterfall hissing down from the ceiling of the Iron Palace. She had stopped the storm, but the deluge it unleashed was still finding its way into the earth through the crevice at the bottom of the sinkhole. Other, smaller flows jetted from the cavern's walls, in places strong enough to have ripped away the metal panels.

She turned to the temple's entrance. To her relief, the bridge was still intact. The largest waterfall was coming down on the other side of the little building. It must always have done so when rain struck the desert, she realised; the holes in the iron plates covering the abyss let it act as a drain.

Where were the mercenaries? She cautiously peered out. It was harder to see than before, some of the flames above extinguished. But there was enough light to make out two corpses near the bridge's far end. No, wait – one corpse, cut in two by a fallen panel. Her emotions were so overwhelmed, she barely even felt disgust at the sight.

Had anyone else survived? If her friends were still alive, she had to find them. But first, she had to take the Staff of Afrasiab. She turned back to the dais, the metal rod almost calling out to her. She took hold of it. The sensation of inversion swallowed her again, the world now in her hands. Hers to influence, to shape, to control . . .

No. *No*. She shook off the urge, pulling herself back to reality. She still felt the power running through the staff, but resisted its seductive draw. Instead, she lifted it from the dais, then scooped up her trikan and, after checking that none of the mercenaries were in sight, hurried out onto the bridge.

The stones were wet. She almost slipped, instinctively flinching back from the drop beyond the bridge's sides – and her armour's wings snapped out in response, glowing brightly.

She drew in a surprised breath – then propelled herself upwards. The jump turned into flight. Earth energy was indeed flowing freely through the cavern now that the Iron Palace's walls had been breached. She gained height, surveying what lay below. The great spire of jade rock on which the temple stood was now exposed, stabbing into the darkness of the chasm. Elsewhere, the flood had been so intense it had overflowed the 'drain' and further damaged the ruins, some of the smaller structures partially or fully collapsed.

But the royal quarters still looked intact. She dropped towards them. 'Rain! Emilian! Is anyone there?' she shouted. 'Rain!'

'Macy?' The light of Rain's halo revealed her friend peering out nervously from a building near the quarters. She was wet; the flood had reached her. '*Mon dieu!* You're okay!'

Macy descended to meet her. 'Yeah. What about you? Are you hurt?'

'I got shot, but – the armour stopped it.' The memory seemed almost as painful as the actual impact.

'What about Emilian, and Mr MacDuff?'

'I'm here.' Emilian dropped down from above, wings retracting as he landed. 'I don't know where Euripides is. I haven't seen him since the water came in.'

'What *was* that?' said Rain, before she registered what Macy was holding. 'Is that . . .'

'Yes, it's the Staff of Afrasiab,' Macy confirmed. 'I used it to take out the mercenaries.'

'You almost took out everything!'

'She did the right thing,' said Emilian firmly. 'But now that we have it, we need to—'

They looked up at an echoing shrill of metal high above. The water gushing through cracks in the chamber's side had dislodged another heavy panel – which plunged towards them.

'Move!' yelled Macy. She took flight, sweeping clear of the falling object. Emilian and Macy followed. The panel smashed down on the building Rain had been using for shelter, broken stonework exploding from it.

The trio hovered thirty feet above the plaza before Afrasiab's quarters. Macy looked up again. The outflows in the cavern's walls were growing in strength, tearing away more debris. As she watched, a higher section of the spiral path peeled away like the skin of an orange before breaking loose and smashing down on the level below. 'The whole place is collapsing. We've got to get out of here.'

'What about Rip?' asked Rain. 'And your mom and dad?'

'They're dead,' was somebody's blunt reply. Macy was startled when she realised she was the speaker. Another heavy piece of wreckage hit the ground nearby. 'We need to move.'

Rain turned back towards the royal quarters. 'Rip! Are you there? We have to go, now!' There was no reply. 'We have to find him!'

'No time,' said Emilian. 'Look!' Another section of the spiral sheared from the wall, gas flames erupting. 'If the tunnel to the surface gets blocked, we'll be trapped in here. Come on!'

His wings glowed more brightly, and he rocketed upwards. Rain hesitated, giving Afrasiab's quarters one last unhappy look, then followed. 'Macy!' she cried.

Macy's own eyes were not turned towards the quarters, but the temple where she had found the staff – where her parents had died. A surge of loss, and anger . . . then she clenched her jaw and flew after her friend, the echo of her name ringing behind her.

Nina and Eddie made their waterlogged way back to the top of the tunnel. This time, there was no barrier; one side of the opening had collapsed, the trapdoor hanging down.

The redhead emerged inside a small, low-walled enclosure. Large metal and pottery jars were scattered all around. They had doubtless been used to bring water up from the underground lake. She crawled clear of the hole, getting her bearings. They were near the cavern's side, not far from Afrasiab's quarters. 'Oh, jeez,' she muttered as she took in the damage the Iron Palace had suffered in the flood. 'How many goddamn times . . .'

'What are you complaining about?' Eddie grunted as he climbed out.

'I find *yet another* ancient wonder, untouched for thousands of years – and five minutes later, the entire place is trashed! Why does this keep happening to me? I really need to – holy crap.'

She broke off in astonishment, staring at three figures beyond the palace – three figures that were floating in the air, borne upon glowing wings. 'Bloody hell!' exclaimed Eddie. 'They're really real!'

Nina saw that one of the trio held the Staff of Afrasiab. 'And that must be – oh, my God. Macy!' She shouted the name as the angelic forms silently accelerated upwards. '*Macy!*' But her cry went unheard, echoing uselessly from the ruins.

Granit heard a voice, but couldn't tell whose it was, or where it had come from. He no longer cared; survival was now his sole objective. A colossal flood wave had almost swept him to his doom in the chasm. He had only stayed alive by clinging to the framework that had supported the metal panels beside the bridge as the torrent threatened to tear him away.

He strained to pull himself up onto the crossing, then shakily made his way to solid ground. 'Is anyone else still alive? Report!'

'Here, sir,' came a reply. Maziq, holding a flashlight, peered owlishly from a half-demolished building nearby. 'Are you okay?'

'Yes,' Granit replied. He surveyed his surroundings. No enemies in sight – but nor were any other of his men. Not alive, at least; the bisected remains of Ort lay not far away. 'Have you seen anyone else?'

Maziq shook his head. 'Liu and Braddock are definitely dead – they fell down there.' He indicated the gaping chasm. 'And Tarlev was taking cover behind that building when it collapsed on him.'

Granit followed his gaze, seeing only piled debris and rubble. 'So it's just us left,' he said, regarding his companion. He was not carrying his rifle. 'Are you armed?'

'Only my sidearm, sir.' Maziq turned to show his holstered automatic.

Granit had lost his own pistol in the flood; his HK437 was also gone. 'We need to evac,' he said. 'Fast.'

They ran for the ramp and hurried as quickly as they dared up the spiral path. Granit knew it had been destroyed higher up, but they didn't need to go the whole way – only far enough to reach the ropes his team had used to descend. The lines still had their powered ascenders attached. He found the first and hooked himself into its harness as Maziq continued to the next. A flick of a switch, and with a low whine the powerful device started to pull him upwards. Maziq clipped his light to his harness and followed, twenty metres lower.

Even with the ascender at its maximum speed, travelling at half a metre per second, the climb was still frustratingly slow. Granit was painfully aware that without a helmet, even a small falling stone could knock him out, or kill him. And if one of the big panels broke away directly above . . .

The ascent continued. The Hungarian grew steadily more tense as he rose through empty space. How much longer? It was hard to judge the distance, drips and spray from above forcing him to squint. But the cavern was narrowing again. It couldn't be far now—

Maziq's rope suddenly juddered, vibrating like a plucked guitar string. Before Granit could react, a screech of fracturing metal came from above – and the panel to which the Libyan's line had been hooked broke from the cavern wall. Maziq screamed as he fell, the sound abruptly terminated as he hit the ground over a hundred metres below – followed by the explosive clang of the iron plate also ending its fall.

Granit swore, but could do nothing except continue his power-assisted climb. He readied himself as the ascender finally reached the last few metres of rope. Closer, almost there – stop! He flicked the switch, halting the device centimetres below the path's edge. The rope continued over it, hooked to the metal wall. He reached up and grabbed the taut line, then swung his legs to catch the ledge with his heels and pulled himself up.

The cavern's entrance was not far away, slightly lower. His escape route was clear. He detached himself from the ascender, then carefully picked his way to the opening. The piece of equipment – a radio signal booster? – that had been there when he arrived was gone, washed away. It wasn't important. He lit his flashlight and hurried into the tunnel, heading back to the surface.

50

Macy led Emilian and Rain down the sloping tunnel to the sinkhole. Bright daylight was visible ahead; the clouds she had summoned had already evaporated. What they had brought down upon the desert remained, though. Water shimmered at the foot of the incline.

The trio reached the cave mouth. Rain made a sound of astonishment. Where before there had been only sand and stones at the pit's slanted bottom, there was now a great pool of dirty water, churning as it drained through the narrow crevice into the Iron Palace. Waterfalls gushed over the sinkhole's lip and from cracks in its sides to refill it. They had swept the Land Rover with them, the mangled 4x4 half-submerged in the pond.

Some of the ropes that the mercenaries had used to enter the pit still hung from above. 'Those don't look safe,' said Macy, regarding the wet lines. 'Glad we don't need to use them.' She and her companions had detransformed when they left the Iron Palace, unwilling to risk flying through the confined tunnel. A mental command, and her armour rapidly reappeared, wings extending. Rain and Emilian did the same. 'Let's get to the top.'

They took off, rising towards the surface. Macy looked up, changing direction to avoid one of the waterfalls. For some reason its flow had just shifted, as if something was redirecting it—

Something was.

She gasped as the overturned fuselage of the Knights' helicopter slithered over the edge – and plunged towards her.

She veered clear, the carbon-fibre spear of one of the battered aircraft's broken rotor blades barely missing her. Rain and Emilian hurriedly darted aside as the chopper hurtled past. It smashed down on the ground by the ropes, the impact crushing its fuselage like an eggshell.

'My God!' Rain cried, hovering to stare at the wreckage. 'What happened to the pilot?'

Macy had caught a split-second glimpse of bullet holes riddling the cockpit canopy. 'They killed him,' was her emotionless report. 'Be careful. They might have left someone on guard.'

But nobody was in sight when they rose from the sinkhole. Turning, Macy saw why. The smouldering remains of another helicopter were scattered across the muddy sands not far away. She landed and dispelled her armour. There was nothing in sight except sand and rock in every direction.

Rain detransformed beside her. 'Everything is gone,' she said quietly. 'Now what do we do?'

Macy didn't have an immediate answer, but Emilian went to the large rock where he had placed the satellite link. 'It's still here!' he said with relief. The device's straps had kept it in place. 'We can call for help.'

'Call who?' Macy asked.

'Rafael,' came the reply. 'He can arrange transport. Then,' he pointed at the staff Macy was holding, 'we'll take that back to Portugal.'

'I'm not sure we should take it anywhere,' said Rain, but he had already raised his phone. She turned to the redhead. 'Macy, what did you *do*?'

'What I had to,' Macy told her, voice flat. 'If I hadn't, we'd be dead.'

'But now . . .' She didn't finish, but Macy knew what she was thinking: *now everyone* else *is dead*. Rain was quiet for a moment, then held her friend's hand. 'I'm sorry. About your mom and dad.'

'Yeah,' was all Macy could say, a sudden, numbing exhaustion overcoming her. She clenched Rain's hand more tightly, the two young women bonded by loss.

'So,' said Eddie, as he and Nina picked their way across the debris-strewn cavern, 'our little angel's now a *literal* angel. Or a superhero. Not the life choice I'd expected her to take.'

'She's neither of those things,' Nina complained. 'She's fallen in with the wrong people – and now she's taken an artefact that can control the weather and is going to hand it to the absolute worst person who could have it.'

'I dunno, I can think of some dictators and religious nuts who'd be—'

He hurriedly broke off as they heard a noise. They were rounding Afrasiab's quarters – and someone within had coughed. 'Stay back,' Eddie whispered, ducking into one of the niches beside the entrance.

The unseen person neared the entrance, wet footsteps slapping on the stone floor. Eddie flexed his hands, readying himself for an ambush – then lunged.

He had expected to see one of the mercenaries. It was actually the dishevelled middle-aged man he had seen amongst Macy's companions. That tempered his assault – but only slightly, as the new arrival was still armed, even if only with an awkwardly held sword. A solid punch to his target's jaw instantly liquefied his legs. The sword clanged to the floor beside the new arrival. 'Ay up!' Eddie snarled. 'Found a *shite* of Atlantis!'

'Christ on a bike!' groaned the man, his accent strongly Scottish. 'What was *that* for?'

Nina joined her husband. 'Because you're one of the bad guys, and we don't have a gun to shoot you with?' She snatched up the slender sword, which shimmered with earth energy when her hand closed around its hilt.

'I'm not one of the bad guys!' the man protested. He tried to get up, but his legs were still uncooperative. 'Okay, maybe a wee bit of explanation is in order. Before you hit me again,' he added, seeing the Yorkshireman's fist balling for another strike. 'My name's Euripides MacDuff.'

'Euripides?' Nina echoed disbelievingly.

'What, as in, "Euripides trousers, you menda dese trousers?"' added Eddie.

Even through his fear, MacDuff couldn't contain his sarcasm. 'Oh, I've never heard *that* one before.'

'You want it to be the *last* thing you hear?'

'I'd prefer not.' Keeping a wary eye on the Yorkshireman, he got back to his feet, rubbing his aching jaw. 'I'm a genealogist, but I'm also part of . . . I suppose you know they're called the Knights of Atlantis.'

Nina nodded coldly. 'We do. The group that's taken our daughter.'

'We've never *taken* anybody,' MacDuff replied testily. 'What I do is find people who are suited to join us – people who have a direct line of descent from the Atlantean high priestesses. People like you, Professor Wilde, ironically enough. Aye, I know who you are. As I told Macy, I would have considered approaching you a long time ago – if your links to the IHA hadn't meant you'd be predisposed not to trust us.'

'If it helps,' she said, 'I don't especially trust the IHA's current leadership – but I still don't trust you either. Get to the point.'

'The point is, Macy was the strongest candidate I've ever seen to join the Knights. I suppose she has good genes, hmm?' He gave her parents a hopeful half-smile, but it was not returned. 'So I came to her in France, to offer an invitation. Unfortunately, some gentlemen with guns turned up too.'

'Granit and his mercenaries,' said Eddie, glancing across the cavern for any signs of activity. There were none, but he remained on guard.

'Hired by Rafael Loost,' Nina added. 'He set this whole thing up to manipulate Macy into retrieving the Staff of Afrasiab.'

MacDuff frowned. 'Aye. The more I thought about it, the more off everything seemed, but by that time, well . . .' He held up his hands in a helpless shrug. 'We were already down here.'

'And now we're *stuck* down here.' Nina looked up, seeing where a section of the spiral path had been torn away. 'It'll take us a long time to climb out of here – if we even can.'

'There might be another way,' said Eddie. He backed up, peering at the towering iron walls. 'Yeah,' he said, spotting something. 'Over here.'

He set off, Nina following. MacDuff hesitated, then started after them. Eddie shot him an unfriendly look. 'Where do you think you're going? You got yourself down here, you can find your own way out.'

'No, we should bring him,' said Nina. MacDuff was about to thank her, when she went on: 'We can use him as a hostage.'

'And I thought you were supposed to be the good guys,' MacDuff said sourly.

'If my daughter's in danger, then I'll do whatever it takes to save her,' she told him coldly.

'Then we're on the same side. Everything I've done is to try to protect her—'

A deep rumbling from above cut him off. 'Earthquake?' said Eddie, worried.

'I don't know,' replied Nina, 'but whatever way you think you've found out of here, we need to get to it, fast!'

Eddie leading, they ran around damaged buildings behind Afrasiab's quarters towards what he had seen: the long chain hanging from the chamber's high ceiling. 'Wait, you want us to climb up *that*?' asked Nina in disbelief. At no point other than its very top did it come close to the spiral, and she doubted she could manage a six-hundred-foot ascent.

'It's not for climbing,' said Eddie. 'I think it's Afrasiab's own personal lift!'

'What do you mean?' An answer came as they entered another enclosure. Inside was a small metal platform, handrails on two of its sides decorated with gold. It was attached to the heavy chain – itself revealed as a loop running around a hefty roller secured to the ground. The side of the loop carrying the platform was drawn taut, while the other had a small amount of slack on the links. Nina peered at the cavern roof far above. With many of the flames now extinguished, it was hard to pick out details, but there was something hanging from the chain's top. A counterweight?

Eddie went to the platform. 'Afrasiab was a king, right? And no king's going to haul his arse all the way up that path on foot if there's a quicker way up and down. I think this—'

Another low rumble rolled through the Iron Palace, louder and more ominous. Nina felt the ground tremble. The chain swayed, links rattling. She looked up – and saw that the waterfalls above were growing stronger. As she watched, several iron plates were blown loose by the swelling flow, exposing a widening crack two-thirds of the way up the cavern's far wall. The immense downpour that struck the desert had soaked into the sand until it reached an impermeable layer of rock, and it was now seeking out a new route to the cistern below. 'We're gonna get wet again!' she warned as the broken panels slammed noisily into the ruins. 'How does this thing work?'

Eddie crouched to see. One end of a thick U-shaped hook passed through the links, the other into a sturdy metal eye driven into the rock floor. 'This is holding it in place. Pull it out and we'll go up. Probably.'

MacDuff eyed it unhappily. 'Up nice and steadily, or up like a rocket?'

'Is my name Otis? How the fuck would I know? Nina, get on—'

The entire cavern shook – and a colossal surge of water erupted from the rift in the wall.

'Oh my God!' Nina cried, jumping onto the platform beside Eddie. MacDuff hastily squeezed in behind them. 'Get us out of here!'

Eddie tugged at the metal shank – but it refused to move. Even the weight of three people was not enough to balance out the sheer mass of the chain and its counterweight. 'It won't fucking budge!'

The wave hit the ground, sending a blast of wind through the cavern. The already damaged buildings were smashed into rubble by the water's relentless force. 'Come on, get it loose!' yelled MacDuff.

The Yorkshireman kept hauling at the bar, but to no avail. 'What do you fucking *think* I'm trying to do?'

Nina watched his fruitless efforts in horror – then suddenly remembered what she was holding. 'Eddie, move!' She raised the sword – which still shimmered with earth energy. 'If it's anything like Excalibur—'

'It is,' MacDuff hurriedly told her. Eddie changed position so she could reach the shackle. She hunched down, readying the sword—

The wave hit Afrasiab's quarters.

Walls that had withstood earthquakes and millennia were obliterated in an instant by the flood's raw power. Spray carried in the rush of displaced air hit Nina's face, the seething waters following right behind—

She swung the sword.

The first time she used Excalibur, years before, it demonstrated its power in the right hands when she accidentally sliced a chunk from the block of solid granite in which it had been stood. This weapon was smaller and lighter – but no less effective. The blade cut almost effortlessly through the shackle—

And the platform shot upwards.

Nina shrieked, falling against the rattling chain. She clutched at it, dropping the sword into the maelstrom sweeping beneath her. Eddie grabbed her with one hand as he clung to the railing with the other. MacDuff almost toppled backwards, barely keeping his own grip as the platform swayed. The floor of the Iron Palace, swallowed by the churning waters, rapidly fell away beneath them.

Eddie pulled Nina to him. 'Got you! Are you okay?'

'Yes,' she replied. 'But I lost the sword!'

'I've lost more than that,' said MacDuff quietly, watching the ruins disappear below. 'Those people – some of them I've . . . I've known since they were kids.'

Nina gave him a brief look of sympathy, but there was no time for anything more. They were already halfway up the cavern. She flinched as the counterweight, a solid metal cylinder as big as a man, shot past on its way down. Presumably Afrasiab's servants had had some way to control the speed of his ascent. She could now make out the elevator's final destination, another roller on the cavern roof at the top of the spiral path. 'This thing's not gonna slow down,' she realised. 'If we don't get off, we'll be bug-splats on the ceiling!'

'How?' demanded MacDuff. 'It's too far to jump!' The Iron Palace's barrel-like profile kept the chain well clear of the walls for almost the entire ascent.

'We'll have to aim for the level below where the path ends,' said Eddie. 'If we time it right and jump far enough, we'll land on it.'

'And if we mess up,' MacDuff said, incredulous, 'we'll go all the way back down to where we started!'

'Well, if you'd come to me instead of Macy, I'd be able to sprout wings and fly us out,' Nina snapped. The spiral's loops whipped past, getting closer as the great space narrowed again. 'Although, Eddie, I'm really not sure this will work.'

'Nor am I!' He stood. The platform was mere seconds from smashing into the ceiling. He gripped Nina's hand, then reluctantly took MacDuff's too. 'Ready, ready . . . *now*!'

The trio threw themselves into the void.

If they had only been jumping horizontally, they would have fallen short of the path. But the ascending platform was also propelling them vertically, flinging them into a tall arc – which met the next sweep of the spiral. They reached the highest point of their course just above it, dropping back down onto the iron walkway as if they had only fallen a couple of feet.

The momentum of their leap across the space, though, carried them all into the metal wall. Nina managed to hook her fingers into the holes in the panels. Eddie hit harder, dropping to his knees to stop himself falling backwards.

But MacDuff rebounded from the impact, arms windmilling as he teetered on the edge—

Eddie grabbed him by his gilet. The sudden strain on the garment made several items pop from its pockets and fall into the abyss. 'C'mere, you!'

'Watch out!' Nina yelled, shielding her head. The platform hit the roller above – and was smashed to pieces. Debris clanged against the walls around them, the redhead crying out as a chunk of handrail struck her back. Then the roller broke from the ceiling, dropping towards the flooded ruins with the chain clattering and shrilling as it fell.

Eddie hauled MacDuff back onto the ledge. 'Christ!' gasped the Scot. 'That was too bloody close for comfort!'

'Yeah, bit of a brown trousers moment,' Eddie agreed. He checked on Nina as MacDuff, taking him literally, tried to see if the dampness of his own clothing was something other than water. 'Are you all right?'

She straightened, grimacing at the new pain. 'I'll be okay – once we get out of here.'

They picked their way down the spiral, stepping carefully over the ropes the mercenaries had used for their descent. Eddie stopped at the last one, spotting something attached to it. 'This might be handy,' he said, crouching.

'What is it?' Nina asked.

'Powered ascender. Save us from having to climb up out of the sinkhole. Well, some of us.' He detached it from the line. 'Should be able to carry two people.'

'Ah . . . I'll tell you the same thing as I told your daughter,' MacDuff piped up nervously. 'I havenae climbed a rope since I was a schoolboy?'

Eddie grunted irritably. 'Guess I'm the one who'll be free-climbing a sixty-metre rope, then.' He hefted the ascender. 'Feels like I've been stuck in this bloody hole for months. Let's go.'

They reached the tunnel mouth. The Iron Palace rang with the sound of more panels plunging into the waters below, the great chamber falling into darkness as the fiery stars illuminating it were extinguished. Eddie and MacDuff started up the passage; Nina paused, taking one final look at the lost wonder she had discovered before it was destroyed for ever . . . then followed them towards the surface.

51

Emilian lowered his phone. 'Everything is arranged,' he said, coming to Macy and Rain. The two young women sat on a rock near the sinkhole's edge, silent yet sharing each other's pain. 'Mr Loost will send another helicopter to pick us up from a railway station fifteen kilometres south-east of here. We can transform and fly there without being seen – there won't be anyone else this far out in the desert.'

'Great,' said Macy, without enthusiasm. She stood, stretching her aching muscles. The Staff of Afrasiab was propped against the rock. She reached for it – but Emilian picked it up first. 'What are you doing?' she asked, suddenly defensive – or possessive? She wasn't sure.

'I just want to see what its power feels like.' He raised it, closing his eyes. A look of deep concentration formed on his face. Macy glanced in concern at the sky, but the empty azure dome remained devoid of clouds. His expression turned into a frustrated scowl. 'Nothing's happening! I can feel it, but . . . it won't do what I want.'

'I think it's one of those *women-only* incredibly powerful ancient Atlantean artefacts,' said Macy, impatiently gesturing for him to return it.

He didn't. 'It worked for Afrasiab.'

'Well, maybe he was more in touch with his feminine side than you.' Emilian appeared offended by the idea. 'Now, can I have it back?'

With clear reluctance, he handed it to her. She took it – briefly flinching as the electric thrill of its power ran through her, waiting – *wanting* – to be used. She forced it down before the feeling could overcome her. Emilian seemed to know what she was thinking, about to speak – but then Rain gasped. 'Look!'

One of the ropes secured to the rocks was shuddering. Somebody was climbing out of the sinkhole.

Rain hurried to it. 'Maybe it's one of us! Someone's still alive!'

Macy joined her and peered over the edge. A deep, dark anger rose as she saw the person below. 'It's not one of us,' she said. Her hands clenched more tightly around the staff and her trikan. 'And they won't be alive for long.'

Granit cursed as he climbed the rope, wishing he had brought the ascender unit. But at the time, his only thought had been to escape the iron hell.

Regrets were a waste of time, though. Besides, he had more pressing concerns. The helicopter's wreckage below showed how powerful the flood had been on the surface. What had happened to his own aircraft? His attempt to radio Zdanys had been met with silence. Had his pilot got clear – or was he now stranded in the desert?

He would soon see. The top of the sinkhole was just metres above. He hauled himself to the surface . . .

An angel loomed over him.

The winged figure, golden armour shimmering in the bright sunlight, bore a weapon in each hand, a whirling disc and a metal staff. Even though its face was hidden by a glowing halo, Granit somehow knew that it was filled with rage – a fury aimed directly at him.

He was facing a manifestation of death.

Despite that realisation, he still lunged, trying to pull himself from the sinkhole to give himself a chance to fight—

The disc-like weapon shot from the figure's right hand – and slammed into his, impossibly sharp blades hacking off his fingers.

He slipped back with a shriek, other hand barely catching the rope before he fell. His attacker stepped closer as he swayed from the precipice. The glowing armour vanished – to reveal the angel's true face, and the expression of lethal coldness upon it.

Macy Wilde Chase.

Macy detransformed and stared down at the man who had killed her parents. She could avenge them with a single movement: one kick to Granit's face would send him plunging back into the pit. But she held back – for the moment.

Granit took her hesitation as weakness. 'Well?' he snarled. 'What are you waiting for? If you're going to kill me, then do it. Do it!'

Rain moved up on her right, Emilian on the left. 'Are you going to kill him?' the French woman hesitantly asked.

'He deserves it,' Emilian said coldly. 'He killed a lot of us in Portugal. He murdered your parents. He has to pay for what he's done.'

'That won't bring them back,' Rain whispered. 'And Macy, it won't bring back your mom and dad either.'

'I know that,' Macy said, jaw set. 'But if anything had happened to me . . . my mom and dad would find the person who did it. So I'm going to do the same for them.'

Granit let out a mocking laugh. 'You don't need to find me. I'm here! Are you just going to murder me?' When she didn't reply, he continued: 'You aren't strong enough to do it. Go home, little girl.'

Emilian stepped angrily towards him. 'I'll do it,' he snapped.

'No,' said Macy, waving him back. 'You're right,' she told Granit. '*I'm* not going to kill you.' His lips curled into a cruel smirk of victory . . . which faded as he realised her own deadly expression had not changed. 'I'll let nature take its course.'

Her left hand closed more tightly around the staff, the crystal at its head glowing with an eerie light – and the sky directly above began to darken.

Granit watched in disbelief as vaporous clouds formed from seemingly nowhere, within moments thickening from white to grey to black. A rumble of thunder shook the desert. 'What the fuck is this?' he demanded.

Macy looked directly at him – but her gaze encompassed something far larger than one man. 'There's a storm coming. For *you*.'

Granit's eyes widened as he realised that he was about to die. He pulled himself higher, trying to scramble out of the pit—

A bolt of lightning lanced from the dark sky.

It weaved like a snake hunting its prey, homing in – and struck Granit in the face.

Three hundred million volts surged through his body, his eyeballs exploding as the liquid within was instantly superheated to become hotter than the surface of the sun. Wreathed in flames, he was flung back into the sinkhole, screaming as he plunged a hundred and fifty feet straight down – to be impaled on the wrecked helicopter's rotor blade, the ragged carbon fibre spike bursting through his torso like a spear. A final agonised gurgle escaped his lungs, then the hellish fire consumed him.

Rain and Emilian had jumped back in shock from the strike, its explosive boom almost deafening at such close range. Macy, though, stood firm, energy shimmering over the Staff of Afrasiab. She looked down into the pit. Granit's body was a cross of fire far below. A moment to contemplate what she had just done. There was no guilt, but no satisfaction either. She wasn't sure *what* she felt, a numbness in her soul. Then she retreated, walking past her stunned companions and in a blink transforming her armour and extending its wings. 'We're done here,' she said, voice affectless. 'Let's go.'

Emilian and Rain exchanged concerned looks, then powered up their own armour. The trio took off into the clearing sky and wheeled south-east across the empty desert, leaving behind the sinkhole and the secrets it contained.

Eddie emerged from the tunnel's mouth. The first thing he saw was the pool of water draining into the Iron Palace – and the second a helicopter's smashed remains, a burning figure transfixed upon the spike of a rotor blade. 'I think we missed something.'

Nina and MacDuff came into the open behind him. The redhead was momentarily shocked – then through the licking flames spotted that the corpse was wearing combat gear. 'That's Granit!'

'Serves the bastard right. But what happened to him?'

She looked up. A strange vortex of clouds swirled beyond the sinkhole's circular top. They dissipated as she watched, the sky returning to its previous deep blue. 'Macy had the staff,' she said. 'And she used it.'

Eddie gestured at Granit's body. 'Macy did *that* to him? That's my girl.'

'She did *all* of this. The flood, everything. Remember the fulgurite we found? Afrasiab could bring down lightning strikes wherever he willed it. Now Macy can too. She can't merely control the weather – she can *weaponise* it.'

'And now that arsehole Loost's going to get his hands on it.' Eddie rounded on MacDuff. 'So what's your part in this? How long have you been working for Loost?'

'Loost had nothing to do with us until two days ago – when Macy called him,' MacDuff insisted. 'She persuaded him to use his quantum computers to find this place, by analysing my genealogical database. Which . . .' He shot a look of realisation towards Granit's remains. 'Which that fella's soldiers made a copy of! Loost already had it. No wonder he did it so fast.'

'Granit was working for Loost,' Nina confirmed. 'All of this was a set-up, right from the start. Loost knew you were planning to contact Macy in France – so he sent the mercenaries to force you to show yourselves. Everything he's done was to make Macy trust him, and to bring her here – so she could find the staff for him.'

'Aye, I suppose that makes sense,' MacDuff admitted. 'But how did Loost know about us in the first place?'

'The same way he found out about the artefacts at the IHA, and that Eddie and I were in Turkmenistan. He spied on us, through Uzz. A third of the world's population have it on their phones, always listening – so he knows where they are, what they're doing, who they're with, their likes and dislikes and personal data . . . He told me his AIs analyse *everything* that goes through Uzz. His computers tracked you down. Do you use Uzz?'

MacDuff's unhappy expression told her the answer even before he spoke. 'Not the silly video stuff, but I've used the messaging and online ordering. It's . . . convenient. And I know the Knights use it to talk to each other.'

'So whatever they said, he knows. And if they're carrying their phones when they do their angel thing and fly, their movements'll be tracked. Maybe that's how he found out about the Knights in the first place. His AIs were essentially looking for people with superpowers – moving in ways that couldn't possibly be on foot or in any vehicle.'

'Oh, Christ,' MacDuff exclaimed in sudden realisation. 'Emilian, the lad with Macy and Rain – he liked to sneak off at night and go flying over the forest. If he had his phone with him . . .'

'That could be how he first found you. He suspected this Emilian was one of the Knights, so he finds out who he's close to, investigates them, and so on until he knows all about you. And when you decided to make contact with Macy, he made his move.

He engineered everything.' She looked towards the sky above the sinkhole. 'We have to catch up with Macy and warn her what's really going on.'

Eddie regarded the rocky walls. 'There are still some ropes in place. I'll rig the ascender for you two, then climb up and make sure it's safe at the top.'

Nina gave Granit's body another distasteful glance. 'Somehow, I don't think any of his men are still alive up there.'

Eddie's ascent was relatively straightforward. The recent deluge made the journey more difficult in places, water-laden sandstone crumbling under his boots. But he was an experienced climber, and before long neared the lip of the pit.

He held himself just below the edge, listening. The only sound was the flitting of insects. Cautiously, he raised himself higher. Nobody there. Nor were there any vehicles. One helicopter and the Land Rover were at the bottom of the hole. What was left of another aircraft was strewn across the sands.

He clambered up and looked around. The ropes were secured to boulders heavy enough not to have been swept away by the flood. One had what looked like a satellite link fixed to it. The gossamer strand of a broken fibre optic line caught the sunlight as it shifted in the breeze. It must have been connected to a signal booster brought into the Iron Palace, explaining how Loost had been able to call them underground.

That thought prompted another, and he took out his phone. It had cellular reception . . .

He went back to the sinkhole, seeing Nina and MacDuff below. He waved to signal that it was safe for them to come up, then, with another glance at the satellite dish, checked his contacts.

A few minutes later, the powered ascender had carried Nina and MacDuff to the surface. She surveyed the surrounding desolation.

'Well, I guess we've got a long walk back to the road.'

MacDuff squinted towards the horizon. 'How far away is it?'

'About twelve miles,' said Eddie.

'Twelve miles! In this heat, without water? We'll never make it!'

The Yorkshireman shrugged. 'Just wring out your clothes into your mouth, you'll be fine.'

MacDuff stared at him in dismay, but Nina could tell her husband was hiding a smile. 'Okay,' she said, 'what do you know that we don't?'

'I made some phone calls while you were coming up,' he replied, nodding towards the satellite dish. 'One was to Ozzy.'

'Why did you call Oswald?' she asked. 'Like he said, we're here under the radar. The UN and IHA can't help us.'

'They can't – but his mate who was supposed to meet us in Ruhnama *can*. I passed on our GPS coordinates via Ozzy; he's on his way. He'll take us back to Ashgabat.'

'I knew there was a reason why I married you,' said Nina, smiling.

He grinned. 'That, and my enormous wanger.'

She sighed; MacDuff pretended not to have heard. 'So who else did you call?' she asked.

His smile disappeared. 'Tried Macy, but couldn't get through. Although even if she hadn't blocked us, she still wouldn't get reception if she's doing her angel thing somewhere over the desert.'

Nina quickly turned to MacDuff. 'But you could leave her a message, couldn't you? Or Rain.'

'I could!' he said, going through his damp pockets. His excitement rapidly turned to disappointment. 'Or I could . . . if I had my phone. Shite! I must have lost it down there.' He glared back into the sinkhole.

'I don't suppose you memorised their numbers?'

'No, but who does? That's why we have all these apps – so we don't *have* to.' The Scot sighed. 'I suppose there's a wee morality tale there.'

'I memorise numbers,' said Eddie. 'Considering how often I've lost or broken my bloody phone, I have to. But I did get through to Jared Zane.'

'What did he say?' Nina asked.

'He told me that Macy's passport had been used to get her into Turkmenistan. Which was *really* fucking useful information.' He and his wife smiled. 'But I also asked him – well, the Mossad – for a big favour: can they get us out of this country, pronto? He said he can arrange it. He just needs to know where we want to go.'

'Portugal,' said MacDuff. The couple looked questioningly at him. 'That's where we're based. It's most likely where they're going – back home.'

'I hope you're right,' said Nina. 'Because if you're not . . . we might never see our daughter again.'

52

Portugal

Macy's journey from the desert to the old factory in Barreiro was a blur. Flying to the isolated railroad station, a helicopter back to Ashgabat airport, an overnight voyage in the private jet, crossing the great suspension bridge across the Tagus, a statue of Jesus with arms outstretched watching her from the far bank . . .

Then, once she reached the safehouse, time lost all meaning. Blank numbness alternated with waves of grief, the blackness of loss leaving her sobbing in her bed. Rain stayed with her, her own still-raw sorrow at times overpowering her too. It was not until early evening, hunger and thirst finally too strong to ignore, that they emerged from their shared room.

The building was eerily quiet. Macy went to the kitchen to find some bottled water. 'Emilian?' she called out. 'Are you here?'

No reply. 'He might be in the office,' suggested Rain, following. 'Or have gone to the villa.'

Macy opened the bottle and took a long swig. After spending time in the baking Karakum, it was no wonder she felt drained and desiccated. 'God, I'm hungry.'

'So am I.' Rain started to open cupboards. 'I can cook something for us.'

'You don't have to do that for me.'

'I want to. I don't mind.' She took out a packet of pasta. 'See if Emilian wants anything.'

'Okay. Thank you.' Macy smiled, then left the room.

Physical pains beyond mere hunger pangs prodded at her. Her back ached where the armour had stopped a bullet, and she had too many other bruises and cuts to count. She reached around to rub her spine, only registering as the bracelet caught on her clothing that she was still wearing the metal bands. The armour had become part of her, so natural a presence as to be forgotten.

But for now, it wasn't needed. More than that, it was an unpleasant reminder of what had happened in the Iron Palace. For all the powers given to her by the Atlantean artefact, it had failed when she needed it the most. And *she* had failed as a result. Her parents were dead because she had been left utterly helpless.

A rush of anger, and Macy yanked off the orichalcum bands. She went to discard them in the bedroom, then changed her mind, not wanting them anywhere near her. The same applied to her trikan, on the floor under her bed. She snatched it up. Rain's armour pieces were beside her own bed; she thought about taking them too but resisted. What to do with them was her friend's decision, not hers. She left the room again and headed to the stairwell.

An innocuous metal shelf unit stood against the wall at its top. She found the concealed release switch and pushed it. A low *clack* from the lock, and she swung out the shelves and the fake section of wall on which they were mounted to reveal the small room hidden behind. A light came on automatically, reflecting off the treasures within.

Macy regarded them unhappily as she discarded her armour and trikan. More Atlantean artefacts that had brought nothing but death and misery. Excalibur had almost gotten her parents killed, while Earthbreaker had ended thousands of lives—

456

She suddenly realised one artefact was conspicuous by its absence. The Staff of Afrasiab.

She had put it into the vault herself when they arrived. So where was it now?

Emilian must have taken it. Why, she had no idea, but it was the only explanation. If surviving members of Granit's mercenaries had somehow found the safehouse, they would surely not have limited themselves to just the one artefact when there were golden items potentially worth millions beside it.

Not knowing the staff's location, even if it was with someone she trusted, was unsettling. Emilian was most likely in the office. She closed the vault and descended the stairs, going through the door beside the roller shutter into the long factory floor.

The lights were off. Darkness had fallen outside, only a dim twilight creeping through the courtyard windows. The machines and stored items in the echoing space were reduced to creepy shadows. Feeling an odd twinge of nervousness, Macy turned on the lights. The room felt scarcely less disturbing even when lit.

Find the staff and make sure it's safe, she decided. That would reassure her. She started along the towering room towards the office wing at its far end.

Eddie checked his phone as he, Nina and MacDuff left the terminal at Humberto Delgado airport and headed into the short-term parking lot. 'Okay, Jared's people left us a car,' he said, reading the text he had received. 'Silver SEAT, number plate ends in TF.'

'I don't know a SEAT from a Fiat,' Nina admitted. Many of the mostly European-made vehicles in the lot were unfamiliar to the American.

'I'll look out for it,' said MacDuff, checking plates as they walked along.

'How long will it take to get to this safehouse?' she asked.

'This time of night, traffic should be light, so . . . half an hour, maybe. Once we find this car.'

'Ay up,' Eddie called, angling towards a large SUV. Its licence plate did indeed end in TF. 'Found it. Should be unlocked.' He tried the hatchback, which to his relief opened, and saw a key fob in a corner of the cargo space.

Also present was a bulky black polycarbonate case. 'What's that?' Nina asked.

'Present from Jared. Hopefully we won't need it, but with our luck . . .' He took the keys and closed the hatch. 'So you reckon it'll take us half an hour to get there?' he asked MacDuff – before giving him and Nina an alarming smile. 'Bet I can do it in less.'

Macy ascended the stairs to the factory's offices. Halfway up, she heard voices. A moment of alarm – who else other than Emilian was here? – but it subsided when she realised that one was coming through loudspeakers. He was talking to someone on the AR screen.

She was about to call out to him, but decided not to interrupt. Instead she reached the top landing and headed down the hallway. The door ahead was ajar, lights on beyond. She now recognised the other voice. It was Rafael Loost . . .

And he was arguing with Emilian.

She slowed, unable to resist the urge to eavesdrop. What was going on? Emilian was definitely angry – and frustrated. Loost, meanwhile, had adopted a slower, more forceful tone, one she immediately associated with authority figures imposing their will on others. That didn't sound like the man she knew.

Thought she knew. As her father had pointed out, she'd never met him in person . . .

'I don't think you fully appreciate the situation, Emilian,' said the Canadian. 'Did you really think I wanted to use the staff to create some kind of simplistic might-makes-right utopia?' He put on a higher-pitched, mocking voice. '"Do as I say, or I'll drown you!" How many days, or more like hours, do you think it would be before the secret services of the countries you were trying to control assassinated you?'

'But we had a deal!' Emilian snapped back.

'To quote one of my favourite movies, "I am altering the deal." The best way to get people to obey you isn't to threaten them. It's to make them *dependent* on you. How many people would tell you they now couldn't manage without Uzz? Answer: billions. They *need* it, and what they see on it sways their actions. And people – countries – will *need* the Staff of Afrasiab. They just won't realise it.'

Increasingly unsettled, Macy tiptoed closer to the doorway. 'I . . . don't understand,' said Emilian.

'Of course you don't,' Loost replied patronisingly. 'But I've already founded a geo-engineering company dedicated to fighting climate change through weather control. Guess what? Suddenly, its technology will work – or at least seem to. Deserts get rain, flood zones don't, ski resorts get extra snow to top up their glaciers. All apparently thanks to my tech. It doesn't matter that it's just used pinball-machine parts in a fancy box. If they want to keep things nice, they keep paying me. If they don't, well, that's when they see the flipside of what the staff can do.'

'You mean what *Macy* can do.' The mention of her name startled the redhead – did they know she was there? But there was bitterness behind Emilian's words. 'You need her more than me.'

'I need you to persuade her to do what I want her to. You've done a good job so far. Now that her parents are dead, that will make it easier. She'll need someone there for her, someone she can depend on. And like I said, when someone depends on you, they do what you tell them.'

A cold sickness welled in Macy's stomach. It was not solely

from the casual, callous dismissal of her loss. Had Emilian been working with Loost from the beginning? If the trillionaire already knew about her even before befriending her on Uzz, that meant—

Emilian spoke again before she could finish the thought. 'Why should I help you now? You just said everything I thought we were going to do will never happen. What's in it for me?'

A faint laugh. 'You'll get to fuck Macy if you play things right.' Macy drew in a sharp, appalled breath. Loost's stern, controlling tone returned. 'But what's in it for you is that you stay out of prison for murder. You had your phone with you when you raided the IHA with Gael, remember? Uzz tracked you. I can prove to the cops that you killed that security guard – and also that you were at the exact spot where Gael's buried.'

Emilian also took in a deep breath – though his quavered with fear. 'You wouldn't. You'd be incriminating yourself.'

'I wasn't there. I was in space. And I'm kind of beyond the jurisdiction of the Portuguese police. To reiterate: I'm in space! But if you think I'm bluffing, let me show you the tracking logs.'

Macy peered nervously through the crack in the door. Emilian faced the large screen, back to her. He partially obscured her view of it, but enough was visible to reveal Loost looking down from the camera as he worked. Then a new window popped up – a map, showing what she assumed was Lisbon and its surroundings. A glowing line was overlaid upon it. Emilian's flinch told her it was exactly what Loost had threatened.

'You see?' Loost went on, looking back at the camera. 'I can track—' His eyes widened, snapping to something on his own screen. Then his gaze rose again. 'I can track the movements of anyone who has Uzz on their phone, either in the past – or in real-time,' he intoned, more deliberately. 'And that includes you . . . *Macy*.'

Macy gasped, caught. Emilian whirled at the sound.

'She's outside the door,' Loost went on. 'She's been there

for . . . huh, almost three minutes. Come on in, Macy. You're part of the conversation; you may as well contribute.'

She pushed the door fully open. 'How much did you hear?' Emilian asked hesitantly.

'Enough to decide that you're never going to fuck me,' she snarled. 'You were both working together the whole time?'

'For the good of humanity,' Loost said smoothly.

'Bull*shit* for the good of humanity,' she shot back. 'For the good of your pocketbook!' She saw the Staff of Afrasiab propped against a wall. 'Everything that's happened was just your plan to get hold of the staff? What happened to what you said to me about keeping your idealism?'

The trillionaire shrugged. 'Success tip: at a certain point, you have to choose between being idealistic or being rich.' He held up both hands, as if weighing invisible objects. 'It's an easy choice.'

'My mom and dad are *dead* because you chose money!'

'At least your mom and dad didn't write you off as a lost cause. If we're comparing pain, I think mine wins.'

Macy stared at him in outraged disbelief. 'Fuck. *You!*'

Loost shook his head in distaste. 'Just like your mother. No class.'

'Don't you fucking *dare* talk about my mother.' She started towards the staff. 'I'm taking the staff, and I'm taking Rain, and we're outta here.'

'Emilian,' said Loost sharply. The Dutchman moved to block her. She halted, realising he was still wearing the bands of his armour. 'You're as important as the staff, Macy. I need you, and it, together. So you're not going anywhere. If you don't do what I say willingly . . . Emilian and I will have to force the issue.'

She fixed her eyes angrily upon Emilian's. 'You're going to stop me? After this asshole just betrayed and threatened you?'

'The correct term is "blackmailed",' said Loost. 'Which means that yes, he is going to stop you. Aren't you, Emilian?'

Conflict roiled on Emilian's face . . . then, as if a switch had been flicked, it became an emotionless mask. 'I'm sorry,' he said flatly. 'But I have to.'

He lunged to grab her —

Macy gripped his right wrist with both hands – then spun, twisting his limb as she swept out a leg to scythe his feet from under him. Emilian fell heavily to the floor. She dropped, wrenching his arm up behind his back and jamming a knee hard against his neck. It was one of the moves her father had taught her, but the first time she had used it for real. 'You think so, huh? Stay down! I'm calling the cops.' She fumbled for her phone with her free hand.

Emilian struggled beneath her. She shifted, forcing her knee down harder. He rasped in breathless pain – but kept twisting his upper body to try to buck her off. Macy realised with horror that she wouldn't keep him pinned for long. He was bigger than her, considerably stronger. Another furious wrench, and her knee slipped—

Her phone was out of her pocket. She cracked its corner as hard as she could against the back of his head. He cried out. She hit him again, then leapt up and ran to grab the staff.

Despite her attacks, Emilian was already rising. He turned with a raw snarl of rage—

She swung the staff. Its jewelled headpiece hit the side of his skull with a ringing thud. He staggered – then fell again as Macy struck him a second time. He moaned, clutching his head. Macy glanced back at the screen, where the startled Loost was still watching. She jabbed the staff towards him. The 3D effect was realistic enough to make him twitch back. 'You're going *down*, asshole,' she said, before hurrying from the room.

Loost reacted with alarm, then anger. 'Emilian! Get up! Get *up*!' he ordered. 'Go after her!'

The Dutchman painfully clambered upright. His whip was on

a desk in a corner. He grabbed it – then crouched to open a cardboard box beneath the table.

Inside were some of the artefacts he and Gael Adriano had stolen from the IHA.

The orichalcum gauntlet went on his left forearm, the bird clacking into position in the raised slot. A shimmer of earth energy, and it held in place as if magnetised. The bird's crystalline eyes glowed. Then he transformed his armour, golden leaves flowing over him and the halo flaring around his head with a seething brilliance. The scales on his left arm linked with the vambrace as if they were made for each other.

It was the first time Loost had witnessed the transformation, but any wonderment was lost behind impatience. 'Go on! She's getting away!'

'Not for long,' Emilian growled. He started after Macy.

'And remember,' the trillionaire said sharply, 'we need her alive.'

Emilian paused at the doorway. 'She'll be alive,' he promised, raising his whip. Eerie energy crawled along the metal lash. 'She just might not be in one piece.'

53

Macy raced down the stairs two at a time, running out into the main factory hall. 'Rain!' she yelled, voice echoing from the brickwork. 'Rain, help! Help me!'

No answer. Her friend was too far away. She turned to sprint along the huge room's length—

A loud *whump* from the stairwell. Emilian hadn't run down the stairs after her. Instead he had simply dropped from the top landing, using his armour's wings to catch himself before hitting the ground. He was right behind her.

Fear struck her like a chill wind. She looked for a hiding place – also spying a nearby bank of light switches. She flicked them all off, plunging the chamber into darkness. The only illumination leaked from the stairwell entrances at each end. Macy ducked into the shadows behind a tarpaulin-covered boat.

Emilian entered the factory.

Even if he didn't turn the lights back on, the silence would tell him that she wasn't running for the far end. He would know she was close by—

The low light from the stairwell revealed a shape near her feet. She picked it up. Broken wood with a metal bracket at one end, some piece of detritus not cleaned up when the Order of Behdet took over the building. She looked down the factory's length – and lobbed it as hard as she could.

Emilian was already moving towards her. His halo's glow grew brighter, the shadow cast by the boat's bow shifting and sharpening as he approached—

A dull clatter as the wood landed amongst the stacked boxes. Emilian spun towards the noise. Macy held her breath. It sounded like such an obvious distraction; surely he wouldn't investigate . . .

But she knew the cause. He didn't, striding away. She hurriedly scuttled towards the factory's towering end wall. Ironwork steps led up to the catwalks running along the room. If she reached the top undetected, she could sneak along and enter the accommodation wing's upper floor.

The staff hindered her as she crept upwards. One accidental knock of metal against metal would tell Emilian where she was. But she could see him now as she ascended, his halo a bright ring in the near-darkness as he searched. She reached the first catwalk level, but continued upwards, wanting to be as far away from him as possible—

'Macy.'

She froze. Had he seen her? But he was facing away from her, stationary. 'Macy,' he called out again, voice now a creepy facsimile of friendly. 'We don't need to fight. We both want the same thing. We can use the staff together, to make the world a better place. Forget about Loost. You're more powerful than he knows. If we join together, he won't be able to stop us.'

You gaslighting fuck, Macy thought, resuming her climb. Emilian kept talking, but she ignored him. She reached the top catwalk and carefully moved along it. The Dutchman was investigating the items stored on the factory floor, lifting tarpaulins and looking behind crates. She passed his position and kept going. Almost halfway along the room. The faint spill from the stairwell at the far end lit her way . . .

The way abruptly ended.

Macy held in a gasp as her fingertips, brushing along the guardrail, suddenly reached its terminus. She cautiously probed with a foot – finding only empty space. There was a gap in the catwalk!

She hunched down, trying to see how wide. The silhouette of the grillework floor resumed about eight feet away. She could jump it even in the dark – but the noise when she landed would alert Emilian . . .

Warn Rain. She took out her phone. The screen lit up as it recognised her face. She cringed: too bright! A flick at the screen brought up the controls, and she hurriedly lowered the brightness. Even then, its glow felt alarmingly visible.

There was nothing she could do about that. Rather than use Uzz, she brought up the phone's rarely used messaging app and hurriedly entered Rain as the recipient. She tapped in a message: *HELP! Emilian is traitor, wants to kill me. In big factory room. Use your armor. PLEASE HURRY!*

She hit the send button. The message swept into a coloured bubble—

And her phone made a whooshing sound effect to confirm it had been sent.

Macy flinched, looking around to see if Emilian had heard it—

He was already there.

The Dutchman had spotted her screen and silently risen up beneath her. His whip lashed out, the glow of earth energy running along it as it sliced through the catwalk.

The metal walkway's end section broke free. Macy screamed as she fell with it—

It smashed down on the lower catwalk, the impact flinging her hard against the wall. The phone flew from her hand and hit the floor below with a sharp snap of breaking glass.

Her leg hurt as she rose. But she knew she had to move. She broke into a limping run along the catwalk. 'Rain!' she cried. 'Rain, help!'

Where was Emilian? She glanced back in fear, expecting him to be flying after her. But he hadn't moved. He raised his left arm.

Something shone upon it, a curved piece of golden metal covering his forearm—

A missile shot from it, sprouting golden wings.

Macy shrieked and ducked – but the object changed direction to track her, passing close enough to brush against her hair. It looked like a bird, its shape clear in the darkness as earth energy roiled from its sharply pointed beak to its fanned tail. 'Stop there, Macy!' Emilian ordered as it swept out over the factory floor.

'Go fuck yourself!' Macy yelled back, running again. 'Rain!'

The metal bird came back around after her. This time, it didn't veer away.

Its beak slashed across Macy's shoulder, slicing through her clothing – and cutting a line into her flesh. She screamed, reeling against the railing. The ancient weapon made a tighter turn to return to Emilian, clanking back into its slot upon the vambrace.

Before Macy could recover, he rushed through the air towards her – and kicked her over the guardrail.

Macy screamed again as she fell the rest of the way to the factory floor. She landed hard on the dusty concrete. The staff clanged down beside her. She painfully dragged herself to it, using it like a crutch to push herself back upright—

Emilian landed in front of her.

She swung the staff at him. He jerked back, not expecting her attack. But he quickly overcame his surprise. The whip snapped towards her. She brought up the staff to block it—

Falling into his trap. The whip's glow vanished – and the metal snake coiled tightly around the staff. He yanked it sharply back, tearing her weapon from her grip and making her stagger. The whip uncoiled, casting the staff across the factory. Before she could recover, he kicked her in the stomach, knocking her breathlessly back to the floor.

He advanced on her. 'You only need one hand to use the staff,' he growled. 'The other one, your legs . . .' He let the whip wave menacingly from his hand, the earth-energy glow returning. 'They can go.'

He drew back his arm to strike. Macy cringed—

Lights swept through the room from outside.

Emilian turned in surprise. Macy looked past him – and saw an SUV pulling into the courtyard.

Who was inside, she had no idea. But it gave her the moment she needed to roll away from Emilian and hop back to her feet. She ran for the stairwell. The Dutchman spun back and followed, the whip whirling—

An angelic figure dropped down between them.

Emilian halted abruptly as Rain hovered above the floor. Her original sword had been lost in the Iron Palace – but she had found a replacement.

Excalibur.

She raised it in both hands. The gleaming blade shimmered with blue light. 'What are you doing?' she demanded, bringing the sword's tip towards Emilian's halo-shrouded face.

'He was working with Loost the whole time!' Macy said before he could reply. 'Those men in France, the attack on the villa – it was all planned. Emilian was part of it!'

'She's gone crazy,' Emilian countered. 'She can't handle losing her parents, so she's having a paranoid breakdown!'

'That's bullshit!' the redhead shouted back. 'Rain, what my mom and dad said about Loost in the Iron Palace, it's all true. He wants the staff so he can control whole countries – and gouge money from them. Emilian's trying to force me to use it for him!' To her dismay, her friend seemed unsure who to believe. 'He sent the mercenaries who killed your parents, and Fernando, and everyone else!' she cried in desperation. 'Emilian helped him. And he killed the other Knight so I'd replace him!'

Silence, Rain not moving . . . then she turned to look back at Macy. 'I believe you,' she said.

'That's unfortunate.' Any attempt at persuasion vanished from Emilian's voice, replaced by menace. 'I thought you'd believe your real friend.'

'Macy *is* my real friend,' Rain insisted. 'And – *did* you kill Gael?'

'I . . . did what I had to,' came the reply. 'And I'd do it again. But that's up to you, Rain. I only need Macy. So either you're with me, or against me. Which is it?'

The two Knights faced each other, unmoving, weapons poised in a tense stand-off. Rain broke it. 'Macy, *run!*' she shouted.

Macy raced for the exit.

Emilian jinked sideways – and snapped his whip after her. It extended, the tip of the glowing metal lash carving towards her legs—

Rain swept down the sword to intercept it. When charged with earth energy, the whip could cut through almost anything – but so could Excalibur, and its edge was far sharper. Sparks flew as the two weapons collided, a three-foot length of the whip clinking to the floor in Macy's wake as she ran on.

Emilian recalled the remaining length of his weapon in fury, immediately sending it back at a new target. Rain shot vertically, pulling up her legs. It cracked just below her feet. She swung around and readied her sword.

Macy reached the door to the accommodation wing. She hesitated, looking back to see Rain preparing to battle Emilian – then hurried through and rushed up the stairs, heading for the concealed vault.

'Someone's here,' said MacDuff as he, Nina and Eddie got out of the SUV. Another vehicle was parked in the courtyard.

Nina regarded the building. Lights were on in the upper floors of the wings at each end. 'Where will they be?'

'Probably up there.' He pointed at the wing to their left as Eddie opened the rear hatch. 'We turned that part into living quarters. The door's just over—'

Nina's eyes snapped to the large windows along the building's length. The interior lights were not on – but she saw other sources of illumination behind the glass. 'Oh my God, look!' she cried. 'Is that Macy?' Two of the angelic figures she had seen in the Iron Palace swooped around each other in an aerial dance.

But it was no aerobatic display. They were fighting. Weapons charged with earth energy slashed back and forth.

'That's Emilian – and Rain,' said MacDuff, shocked. 'What the hell's going on?'

'And where's Macy?' Nina demanded.

Eddie opened the case and took out the weapon that Zane had provided for him: a TS12 shotgun, a futuristic-looking piece of hardware with three magazine tubes that rotated like the cylinder of a giant revolver. 'Let's go and ask 'em.'

54

Rain and Emilian orbited each other, neither taking their eyes off their opponent. With her sword facing a whip, Rain was at a disadvantage; the Dutchman could attack from farther away. Her only hope was to try to damage his weapon again, but she knew that despite all her training, he was the better fighter—

The whip lashed at her.

She jinked sideways in mid-air, swinging the sword to intercept it. Emilian rose sharply, the metallic snake extending to sweep at her head. Rain dropped, rolling backwards to pull her weapon up faster. Excalibur was larger and heavier than the blade she had lost, harder to control. It met the whip barely ten centimetres from her head, catching it with the flat rather than its edge. Sparks of energy made her flinch.

The whip's damaged end coiled around the sword as if to snatch it from her grasp – but she was already moving, powering towards Emilian on the attack. He yanked the whip back. Rain was on him before he could make a second strike. All he could do was retreat and try to dodge. One of his wings clipped the catwalk, forcing him to change direction.

The movement slowed him. Rain braced herself, sword extended to impale him—

His left arm came up – and he fired the bird-like missile.

Its wings extended like miniature versions of his own as it left its mount. Rain barely had time to twist away from the unexpected attack. Its wingtip clinked against her armour. She recovered and brought Excalibur back up as she pursued Emilian. In moments she would have him cornered, and he still hadn't readied his whip for another attack—

The bird looped around, needle-sharp beak crackling with earth energy – and punched straight through her armour into her back.

Rain convulsed, a breathless cry caught in her mouth . . . then Excalibur dropped from her hands and clanged to the concrete floor. She followed it, slamming down hard near the roller door. Her wings retracted unevenly, their glow fading along with her halo. The bird slipped from her wound.

Emilian landed beside her and retrieved his bloodied missile. 'You could have been with me, Rain,' he said, drawing back the whip to slash at his defenceless target—

A window blew apart.

Glass and metal scattered explosively into the factory as Eddie emptied one of the TS12's five-round ammo tubes into the rust-scabbed framework. He rushed through as the cascade hit the floor, pulling the paddle to rotate the next tube into position. 'Ding-dong!' he yelled, locking the gun onto Emilian. 'Who ordered an arse-kicking?'

Nina hurried in behind him, followed by MacDuff. She saw the fallen figure. 'Oh my God! Rain!'

Emilian's wings surged with power, and he shot upwards. Eddie was momentarily startled, his shotgun's next blast passing harmlessly beneath the Dutchman. He hurriedly tracked his airborne target. 'Nina, get Rain out of here!' She ran to the wounded young woman.

MacDuff looked on in horror. 'Let me talk to him!' he said to Eddie, darting to block his line of fire. 'Emilian! What are you *doing*?'

Nina reached Rain. Blood ran from a thumb-sized wound in her back. Her strange armour shrank as the American watched, the metal scales moving seemingly of their own volition to

472

coalesce into orichalcum bands on her wrists, ankles and neck. Nina was taken aback, but she had seen enough seemingly impossible things in her lifetime to overcome her surprise and haul Macy's friend towards a nearby door. 'Rain, I've got you.'

Rain looked up at her, wide-eyed. 'I – I thought you were dead . . .'

'Not yet. And you're not either.' She reached the doorway, finding a stairwell beyond. 'Where's Macy?'

'Getting – her armour.' Merely speaking made Rain's face screw up in agony. Nina pulled her through the entrance.

'Get out of the way,' Eddie growled as MacDuff kept blocking his aim.

'I can stop this,' the Scot insisted. 'Emilian, please! Listen to me! I don't know what Rafael Loost told you, but you have to stop. You can trust me, you know you can! I found you, I rescued you!'

'You did.' Emilian slowly descended, touching down twenty feet from him.

Eddie sidestepped to get a new line of fire, but a call from Nina made him look towards the doorway. 'Eddie! Rain's hurt, bad – I need help!' He hesitated, but then, keeping his shotgun readied, backed into the stairwell to assist his wife.

Emilian approached MacDuff, the whip coiled in his hand. 'You rescued me,' he continued. 'But you didn't help my mother. I've seen your database. She had the same potential as me. But you didn't think she was worth saving, did you? All you saw was a junkie and a whore. And by the time I convinced you to go back to find her . . . it was *too late*!'

His last words became a roar of pure rage – and he launched himself at MacDuff, flying across the remaining gap to slam the Scot backwards against the wall. MacDuff collapsed, stunned and winded. Emilian kicked him hard in the chest and stomach, then snapped out the whip. 'You could have saved her!' he screamed. MacDuff looked up through pain-narrowed eyes, seeing his own impending death—

Something slammed into Emilian's chest from above.

The force of Macy's trikan, even with its blades retracted, knocked him back despite his armour. She jumped from the topmost catwalk where she had entered, deploying her wings as she fell. Both feet swung up to kick Emilian solidly in the chest. He reeled back, the glowing whip's tip slicing a chunk of concrete from the floor. 'Rain!' she cried, seeing only MacDuff slumped against the wall. 'Where are you?'

Someone rushed out of the stairwell – but it wasn't Rain. 'Macy!' shouted her father.

She froze, stunned. '*Dad?*'

Emilian recovered, bringing up his left arm—

Eddie didn't know what he was doing, but his movement – aiming a weapon – was clear enough. 'Look out!'

Macy whirled to face Emilian, ready to throw the trikan—

The bird shot from Emilian's forearm as Eddie pulled the trigger. The shotgun's blast made the Dutchman's shield flare like a fireworks display, sending him staggering.

But his missile had already been launched. The bird hurtled at Macy—

She threw herself sidelong. Not quite fast enough. Its beak caught her left arm, the earth energy charge piercing her armour. Macy shrieked as it tore into her biceps.

Eddie's face filled with fury. He locked the shotgun onto Emilian again. 'You fucking—'

Emilian straightened, regaining control – and the bird turned to hurtle at the Yorkshireman's head.

Eddie instantly switched targets to the greater threat and fired. The bird's wings were shredded by the storm of red-hot shotgun pellets. It spun out of control, hitting the wall.

The TS12 snapped back to Emilian. Eddie fired again, the armour's shield catching it with another sparking display – less intense than the first. The Dutchman lurched back, arms flailing as he was hit harder. 'MacDuff!' Eddie shouted. He used two more shots to blow out the window closest to the Scot. 'Get out!' MacDuff painfully stumbled towards the new opening as the Yorkshireman cycled his last tube of ammo. 'Macy, are you all right?'

'Yeah, I'm okay,' she gasped. 'Dad, his shield's just like the one on the Nephilim ship—'

Her father immediately understood – and fired relentlessly on the staggering angel. Two shots hit Emilian, a third, the flare weaking with each impact—

Emilian realised the danger. A fourth shotgun blast exploded against his chest, the auroral shimmer almost gone – but even as he reeled he lashed the whip desperately at his attacker. It extended, rushing at his head.

Eddie ducked, but it changed course, homing in—

He instinctively shielded himself with the shotgun. The whip sliced through the metal, cleaving it in half. He jerked his left hand from the forward grip a split-second before it would have also taken off his fingers. The barrel and magazine tubes clunked down at his feet, leaving him holding only the gun's rear end. 'Shit!' he yelped. The TS12's ejection port was built into the shoulder stock, meaning the chambered shell might still fire – but equally the damaged weapon could explode in his face.

He tossed down the bisected shotgun. 'Eddie, what's happening?' Nina called from the stairwell.

'Slight weapons malfunction,' he said, quickly backing up to the doorway. 'You stay in there!' He grabbed the door and slammed it shut, pulling the locking bar closed.

'Eddie, no!' came her muffled shout from beyond. *'Eddie!'*

He moved away, watching Emilian intently as the Dutchman

recovered his whip. The shotgun blasts had clearly hurt him . . . but the shield had held, the armour undamaged. 'Dad, get out of here!' said Macy.

'I'm not leaving you to fight him on your own!'

'You *have* to! Dad, I can do this.' She briefly dispelled her halo so she could look him in the eyes. 'You taught me how.' Then the light reappeared, and she raised her right hand, setting the trikan whirling in his holder.

Eddie reluctantly took the hint. He ran for the window he had blown open for MacDuff.

Emilian saw him go. Fury overcame pain. A whipcrack echoed through the room as he lashed out his weapon to decapitate the running man—

The trikan intercepted the whip, knocking the metal scourge away from Eddie. He jumped through the window into the darkened courtyard.

Emilian faced Macy, whirling the whip like a lasso. She drew back her hand, ready to throw the trikan. They warily circled, waiting to see who would make the first move—

Macy broke the stand-off.

She flung the trikan, sending it not directly at him but off to one side – before swerving it towards him. If she could entangle the whip, she could yank it from his hand—

He took off, still whirling the whip. She sent the trikan after him. Sudden excitement – he had left one side exposed as he climbed. If she could get the trikan past his defences, she could slice off one of his wings.

She guided it towards him, extending its blades—

Emilian spun sharply – and used his corkscrew motion to give the whip extra momentum as he cracked it at the incoming trikan. A clang as the two Atlantean weapons collided – and a chunk of the trikan's golden casing spun through the air.

Macy extended her own wings and left the ground, recalling

the trikan as Emilian triumphantly brought back his whip. The disc smacked back into place in its holder, but she could already *feel* that it was wounded. A thumb-sized piece had been gouged from the metal shell.

'You still need more practice,' said Emilian. An echo of their first fight. No casual mockery this time, but pure contempt.

'I'm just getting warmed up,' she replied in kind. Her weapon might be damaged, but it would still do its job. How well was entirely up to her. She set it spinning again. 'Like yo' momma after *twenty* guys!'

She did not merely hit a nerve, but dug a scalpel into it. *'Jij teef!'* snarled the Dutchman. He shot towards her, the whip scything at her head—

She hurriedly pulled back, throwing the trikan. It collided with the whip, both weapons deflecting away from each other. But the respite was only brief as Emilian attacked again, the two Knights spinning and swooping around the factory as they battled.

Eddie ran across the courtyard to the SUV. MacDuff was already at it, breathing heavily. 'Where's your gun?' he asked.

'In bits,' the Yorkshireman told him, going to the open rear hatch.

'I don't suppose your benefactors gave you a spare?'

Eddie already suspected not, the TS12's case containing only the shotgun and its ammunition, but opened a floor panel to see if Zane's associates had left him anything extra. All he found was the SEAT's standard emergency kit. 'Bollocks!' he said, looking back at the factory – where beyond the broken windows, the two glowing figures traded strikes in mid-air.

He needed a weapon to help his daughter. But there were none.

* * *

Macy drew in a sharp, fearful breath as the whip nicked her halo. She dropped and twisted out of the way as Emilian tried to hit her again.

How long could she keep fighting? She was already tiring, the pain from accumulated injuries burning through her body's energy reserves. And she had only days of experience with the trikan and armour. Emilian had years. Unless she did something drastic, he would wear her down . . .

Her only clear advantage was range, the trikan's wire far longer than the whip even before Rain sliced off its end. She changed direction to fly back along the factory's length. If she could open up enough of a gap, she could throw the trikan without his being able to counter-attack.

Emilian followed. But he had not expected her move, the distance between them widening. If she was fast enough, she had a chance.

She spun and hurled the trikan, using her motion to give it a slingshot boost of speed—

It went wide.

Emilian reacted immediately, angling away from it as he closed the gap. The whip surged with power, streaking towards her—

Just as Macy had hoped.

Now she banked the trikan, bringing it around behind him in an ever-tightening curve. She simultaneously made a hard turn to dodge the incoming whip, her body's momentum pulling the armour painfully tight around her.

Emilian's weapon pursued like a striking cobra. It clipped her leg, the earth energy-charged lash slicing her calf. She held in a cry. *Keep focus, stay in control, just another second—*

The trikan came back past Emilian – and she swung it around him, yanking back the wire to draw it tight.

It pulled his arms against his body. He tried to spin the other way to loosen it, but Macy was already making another loop,

ANDY MCDERMOTT

reeling in the wire. The whip snapped up at her, but with his right arm partially pinned it was too slow. She swung behind him. When he was fully entangled, he would be helpless and she could disarm him—

Emilian shot upwards.

'No, wait!' Macy cried. If he yanked the wire fully taut, he could chop himself in half. Despite everything, she didn't want to kill him, only stop him. She flew after him, halting the reel—

Emilian reached the wire's limit. He braced himself, forcing his armoured arms out as far as he could. The metal line pulled tight – and the trikan's holder was yanked from Macy's hand. She gasped as it skinned her knuckles. The metal grip fell to the floor, the wire spilling from it.

He spun in place, shrugging off the entangling line. Macy dropped down to retrieve the handgrip. But the whip cracked at her again, forcing her to retreat from it.

Emilian brought his weapon back to his hand and glided towards her, passing over the fallen trikan. 'Give up, Macy,' he said. 'This is your last chance. Either you do what I tell you . . .' The whip unfurled, flicking menacingly. 'Or I'll *make* you do it.'

55

Nina used her shirt as a makeshift bandage to staunch the bleeding wound in Rain's back. With the young woman stabilised, however crudely, she now had to help her family. She tried to open the door to the factory, but it was locked from the other side. 'God *damn* it!' she said, pounding a fist against the barrier in frustration.

Wait – the roller door . . .

She darted to its control panel – but before she could raise the shutter, Rain spoke. 'No . . . If you go out there, he'll – he'll kill you.'

'I've got to help Macy and Eddie!' Nina told her. To her alarm, Rain tried to sit up. She hurried back to her. 'What are you doing? Lie down!'

'Use my . . . armour,' Rain strained to say. She pulled at one of her thick bracelets – and to Nina's shock, what had seemed like a solid band of metal somehow *unfolded* around her wrist, separating and coming free before clinking back together into a single unbroken piece. 'Put them on. Macy has the . . . power to use it. So do you.'

She tugged at the torc around her neck. Again, it split and rejoined without any apparent seam. Hands shaking, she passed it to Nina, who felt a tingle of energy from it: a power she had encountered before. 'What do I do?' the redhead asked.

'Just wear them. They will . . . fit around you. To make the armour cover you, you have to . . . *want* it to. To fly, you—' She broke off, panting in pain. 'You—' was all she managed to

480

say, before convulsing – and then falling limp.

'Rain!' Nina cried. Was she dead? She quickly checked for a pulse. It took a moment to find it, but it was there, if only weak.

An echoing bang of metal hitting concrete came from the factory. She looked around in alarm – then began to remove the unconscious woman's other metal bands.

Macy hovered, watching Emilian approach. A glance towards the windows. Could she fly outside and escape? She dismissed the thought. Fleeing would leave those still here at Emilian's mercy. Rain, MacDuff . . . her father. She still hadn't overcome her shock at seeing him still alive—

She wouldn't get the chance now. Emilian suddenly rushed at her. The whip flicked backwards, about to strike. She flew upwards, twisting to avoid it. A supersonic *snap* as it lanced past. She dropped and turned again, trying to speed away, but he followed, a harrier chasing a sparrow.

She couldn't outrun him. She had no weapons. And she was out of places to go—

An idea: panicked, desperate. But it was all she had.

She made another hard turn, corkscrewing back upwards as the whip came at her again. A flash – and she felt a burning line of pain as the whip's end cut through her armour and sliced her hip.

She gritted her teeth and concentrated on her climb. Emilian followed, rapidly gaining height. The ceiling rushed at her. He was directly below, whip hand drawn back to lash at her again—

Macy willed herself to halt – then power straight back down.

The sudden reversal made the armour cut painfully into her body. But she kept control, plunging like a piledriver with both legs braced beneath her—

Emilian tried to dodge.

Too late.

Their shields cancelled each other out, her feet passing straight through his halo – and slamming into his face. The shock of the impact pounded up through Macy's legs. But the Dutchman came off worse, their combined closing speed making the collision as fierce as if he had run head-on into a wall. His nose broke with a crunching burst of blood, front teeth snapping.

They both fell. Macy managed to catch herself before hitting the floor. Emilian did not, landing hard on his side. His wings shrank away, the halo vanishing to reveal his bloodied face.

Breathing heavily, Macy came down beside him. Where was the whip?

He had landed on top of it. If she took it, he would no longer be a threat. She crouched, pulling his right arm out from beneath him. He was still clutching the weapon's metal handle. She grabbed it—

A sharp chitter as metallic scales formed a new shape – and Emilian stabbed the narrow blade jutting from his armour's left wrist into her torso.

Macy gasped, feeling not so much pain as a strange coldness. Then Emilian yanked back his hand. The blade came out, glistening with blood. She stared at it, realisation dawning that it was hers . . . then she toppled backwards to the floor. She clutched at the wound, feeling a tiny tear in her armour – and hot liquid running out of it.

Emilian forced himself upright and stood over her, the stiletto retracting. Energy rippled along the whip's length as he prepared one final strike. Macy tried to speak, but no sound came from her mouth—

A mechanical rattle echoed through the factory.

Emilian looked up in surprise. The roller door was rising – and a figure stood behind it, silhouetted by the light flooding into the room.

A new angel.

Nina, wearing Rain's armour, strode through the doorway.

Even distorted by the glowing halo, her voice had never been more dangerous. 'Get away from my daughter.'

Silence for a moment, then Emilian responded – with a disbelieving laugh. He stepped over Macy, swirling his whip in a slow and menacing spiral. 'You think you can fight me?' he said, mocking.

Nina advanced – seeing Excalibur where Rain had fallen. She broke into a run towards it. Emilian realised her intent. He launched himself into the air, wings springing back out from his armour – and rushed at her.

She was much closer to the sword, but the gap rapidly shrank—

Nina reached it first, snatching it up as the whip lashed out. The blade surged with earth energy as she gripped the hilt with both hands. Emilian hurriedly willed the whip away from the shining edge. But she swung the sword, catching it – and sliced a foot-long piece from its end.

Emilian landed and drew back his whip, shocked. Before he could ready another strike, Nina ran at him with a roar of pure maternal fury. He hurriedly sent the whip at her head. She batted it aside with the sword. The lash snapped back under his mental command, trying to loop around her weapon. But he misjudged its now-truncated length. It caught Excalibur, but not firmly enough, immediately coming loose when he pulled.

And now he had left himself open—

Nina swept the sword at him. He jumped back as the glowing blade sliced at his chest. His whip hand came back up, the Atlantean weapon cracking at her.

She released her left hand from the hilt to speed up her return swing, intercepting it. A clang of contact, but only the blade's flat met the whip. He jerked it away. The sword came back at the Dutchman. Another lash, this time aimed at her legs—

Nina yelled as she attacked again – targeting not her opponent, but his weapon.

The blade caught it just above its handle. Charged with earth energy, Excalibur was beyond razor-sharp. It sliced straight through the whip, severing it – and cutting off its own channel of power a split-second before it caught Nina's thigh. The shimmering shield surrounding her armour sparked with the contact, but the broken whip was now merely inert metal. It bounced off and fell to the floor.

Emilian hurriedly retreated. But Nina wasn't going to let the man who had hurt her daughter go. Excalibur slashed at him, again, a third time, the last swing making contact. The sword's tip cut a gash through his armour just above his waist. He snarled in pain as blood oozed from the new opening.

Nina again gripped the sword with both hands, about to swing it with all her strength—

Emilian saw his opening and lunged – cracking her on the head with the base of the whip's handle.

The blow was hard enough to dizzy her. Before she could recover, the Dutchman took off – and made a flying backflip to kick her in the face.

Nina staggered back, dropping Excalibur as she almost fell. Its glow vanished the instant she lost contact. Emilian completed his flip – and rocketed at her, tackling her forcefully into a tarp-covered stack of boxes. She crumpled to the floor as he touched down, wings retracting.

He tossed away the handle and turned to locate Excalibur. The sword was near the factory's blank outer wall, beside one of the cross-braced struts supporting the catwalk above. He went to pick it up. The blade's glow returned as his hand closed around it. 'I only need Macy,' he said, wiping blood from his mouth. 'So before I cut off her legs, she can watch you die!'

He raised the sword, turning back to the winded Nina—

Bright lights suddenly pinned him.

He whirled – as the SUV smashed through one of the windows,

Eddie at the wheel. 'Beep-beep, fuckface!' yelled the Yorkshireman as his vehicle hurtled across the factory.

The wings sprang from Emilian's armour. He took off—

Not quickly enough. The SEAT's nose caught his legs – and ploughed him backwards into the wall.

The SUV was doing almost seventy kilometres per hour, the crash caving in its front end and flipping its back wheels off the ground. The mangled vehicle rebounded a few feet and jolted to a halt as broken safety glass cascaded from its front windscreen. The catwalk above creaked and swayed, its support buckled.

The airbags had fired, saving Eddie from a brutal meeting with the steering wheel, but he was still left stunned and dizzied. He blearily opened his eyes . . .

To see Emilian splayed across the crumpled bonnet in front of him.

His armour had only partially protected him from being crushed. One leg was broken. His halo faded, exposing his face. He tried to move – and screamed, raw agony searing from his snapped femur. Writhing, gasping, he looked up . . .

His gaze met Eddie's just a few feet away.

Excalibur was still clutched in the Dutchman's hand. Pain turned to vindictive rage. The halo reappeared. Eddie tried to move, clumsily fumbling at the seat-belt release. Emilian drew back his sword arm to strike—

'*No!*'

Macy's shout reached them – followed by her trikan, which sliced through the damaged support pillar.

Emilian twisted to look up, starting to scream—

The sound was cut off as the catwalk crashed down on top of him.

The SUV bucked again. Eddie was flung against the steering wheel, the limp airbag this time providing no protection. But Emilian fared far worse. Only his outstretched hand and the top of his halo protruded from the catwalk's wreckage, the shield flashing and flaring as it tried to hold against the weight of steel. But the pressure was unyielding, relentless . . .

The light vanished – and the beams and struts abruptly dropped several more inches before crunching to a stop.

The trikan clanked back to Macy's hand. She dispelled her armour, then pressed her other palm to her torso wound as she staggered towards her parents. 'Mom!' she wheezed. 'Dad!'

Nina pulled herself upright. 'Macy! Are you okay?'

'No,' came the reply. 'I'm not.'

Overcoming her own pain, Nina limped as quickly as she could to her daughter. She held Macy, supporting her as she slumped. 'I've got you, honey. I've got you. I thought I'd lost you. Eddie!'

The SUV's door creaked opened. Mouth bloodied from a split lip, Eddie clambered out. 'I'm here, I'm coming.' He hurried to them.

Macy hugged them as best she could. 'Oh, my God. You're alive, you're both okay! I thought you were dead! I thought you were dead . . .' Tears streamed down her cheeks, finally released.

'We made it,' said Eddie, relief and joy in his voice. 'We all made it.' He squeezed her, then drew back, seeing her injury. 'We've got to get you to a hospital.'

MacDuff peered owlishly through the demolished window, taking in the scene of destruction. 'There's a phone in the offices. I'll call an ambulance.' He hurried away.

'For Rain, too,' Macy implored. 'Is she okay?' she asked her mother.

'She's unconscious,' Nina told her. 'If we can get her to an ER, I think she'll make it.'

'And . . . Emilian?' She looked almost fearfully towards the mangled car.

'He's got proper angel wings now,' said Eddie. 'Not that he's going in that direction, the little bastard.'

To his and Nina's surprise, Macy managed a faint laugh. 'I need to develop better taste in guys. The last one I liked turned out to be a member of a human sacrifice cult, and this one tried to kill me *and* my family! And as for Loost . . .' She shook her head. 'Please don't give me an "I told you so".'

'I wasn't going to, honey,' said Nina. 'I don't know how we'll make him pay for what he's done, but . . . we will. But first, we need to get you to a hospital. And tell the IHA about these artefacts so they can secure them.' She glanced at Excalibur, which had dropped from Emilian's dead hand to the floor.

'No.' Despite her wound, Macy's voice was suddenly firm, older than her eighteen years. 'The Knights will protect them.'

'The Knights have been destroyed.'

'Not all of us.'

Nina regarded her uncertainly. '"Us"? Macy, you aren't—'

Macy gripped her hand. 'Mom, you know how I wasn't sure what I wanted to do with my life? Well, now I am. The Knights have protected this stuff for thousands of years.'

'Until now.'

'Because they were betrayed. That doesn't mean what they do is wrong. Mom, even you don't agree with what the IHA is doing now! They're trying to reverse-engineer Atlantean artefacts for the US government. They want soldiers with shields, like this.' She released herself from Nina's hold and stepped back, summoning her armour. Both her parents flinched, startled by their first close-up view of the transformation. 'They want flying tanks and guns that shoot earth energy instead of bullets,' she continued, voice hollow behind the halo, 'and Earthbreaker, and the Staff of Afrasiab – superweapons there's no defence against.'

'The IHA wouldn't hand things that dangerous to the military,' Nina insisted.

But Macy detected the doubt behind her words. 'Maybe not right now,' she said, detransforming. 'But what if the next president is a fascist asshole who decides our soldiers need this stuff so we can invade Iran or Venezuela for their oil? Or that America shouldn't have democracy any more? I need to rebuild the Knights of Atlantis to stop that from happening.'

'You can't do that alone,' said Eddie.

'I won't be,' Macy replied, seeing MacDuff returning from his phone call. 'I've got Rain, Euripides, the other people who survived. And,' she took a deep breath, standing straighter to face them both, 'as long as you support me . . . I *won't* be alone. Will I?'

'You know we'll always support you, love,' said Eddie. 'But are you sure you want to do this?'

She nodded. 'I am.'

MacDuff reached them. 'The ambulance is on the way. I'd suggest we meet them outside. This might be a wee bit hard to explain.' He regarded Emilian's crushed body with dismay. 'Where's the staff?'

Macy gestured towards one of the rusting old machines. 'Emilian threw it over there. You need to hide it somewhere safe – that nobody else knows about. Once I'm out of hospital, we'll collect it and decide what to do with it.'

There was a clear tone of command in her voice. MacDuff eyed her. 'Do I take it you're staying with the Knights?'

She nodded. 'I am.'

The moment was one Nina had expected – feared – for some time, but the circumstances made it hit all the harder. 'So, you're really leaving?' she asked, voice catching.

More tears flowed from Macy's eyes as she faced her mother. 'Yes.'

'Oh . . .' Nina's own eyes brimmed as the reality sank in. 'But . . . I'm not ready. I don't want you to go!'

'It's not like I'll never see you again. It's just that . . . I won't always be there with you any more.'

'A baby bird's got to leave the nest,' said Eddie. He tried to sound stoic, but his own voice was close to breaking. 'But, I suppose . . . its mum and dad can't tell it where to fly.'

Macy gave them a tearful smile, returning to them. The family held each other for a long moment. It only ended when Macy drew in a pained breath. 'Come on, love,' said Eddie, wiping an eye. 'Let's get you to the hospital.'

'And Rain too,' she said.

While they talked, MacDuff had retrieved the Staff of Afrasiab. 'Got it,' he said. 'Mr Chase, if you'd help me with Rain?'

Eddie nodded, then, after kissing her head, let go of Macy. She took the staff from MacDuff as the two men headed for the stairwell. 'I'll help you outside,' said Nina, supporting her daughter's weight.

'Thanks, Mom,' Macy replied. They started for the nearest broken window.

'Are you absolutely *sure* this is what you want to do?' said Nina. 'It would mean changing your entire life, giving up everything you have at home . . .'

'I won't be giving up *everything* at home. That's where you and Dad are.' They shared a look of warmth. 'But I need to do this. It's important – and not just to me.' She held up the staff. 'Imagine if Loost had got what he wanted. If he had this, and someone he could force to use it.'

'He almost did,' Nina pointed out. They reached the window, and she helped Macy clamber over the broken frame. 'What if he tries again?'

'We have to make sure he doesn't. Like you said, he needs to pay for what he's done.'

They emerged into the courtyard. Nina drew in a weary breath as the soupy air surrounded her. 'Oh, God. It's so damn hot . . .'

Macy stopped, Nina halting beside her. 'Let me see what I can do about that.'

She gripped the staff more tightly, closing her eyes. The crystal at its end began to glow. 'Macy, what are you doing?' Nina asked in alarm.

'Don't worry, Mom,' Macy reassured her. 'I've got this.' A half-smile. 'It's funny. I told Loost I wanted to save the planet from climate change. Now . . . I can.'

She opened her eyes again and looked up. Nina did the same. The clear night sky lightened, clouds forming and reflecting the glow from the city below.

As mother and daughter watched together, a gentle rain began to fall.

Epilogue

New York City

Two Weeks Later

Nina checked the time on her phone – her old phone. Since returning from Portugal she had bought a new one, which was pointedly devoid of Uzz or any apps linked to Raphael Loost. But she had brought out her former device for one last hurrah. 'It's time,' she told Eddie.

Her husband picked up his own phone. 'I'll text Macy.'

He moved clear of her phone's cameras as she – with reluctance – brought up Uzz. Knowing that the app was constantly spying on its billions of users was deeply disturbing. More so was her discovery that any suggestion of such was dismissed as a paranoid conspiracy theory. Anyone publicly expressing concerns would be dogpiled by Loost's fans, a fanatical army rendered starry-eyed by the tech trillionaire's products and promises. Meanwhile, those she would have expected to be most concerned at the prospect, the politicians and lawmakers, were equally hypnotised by his sheer wealth. The fantasy that the world's richest man must also be its smartest, and therefore always right, was deeply ingrained.

Loost's actions had dispelled any illusions she previously held about him. Now it was time, as promised, to make him pay.

She found his name in her contacts and made a call. There was a good chance he would not reply. For a start, something was currently happening that would command his attention. It was also in his interests to deny all interactions with her.

But . . . he might be intrigued enough to answer. Nina had no idea if Loost even knew she and Eddie were still alive. If he didn't, the unexpected call would reveal he lacked information about a potential threat. Would he answer? It wouldn't change what was coming, but she wanted to look him in the eye before it happened . . .

Loost appeared on the screen.

'Professor Wilde,' he said. His face appeared impassive, but his voice gave away his shock at speaking to her. 'Before you say anything, I'll remind you that my lawyers will be reviewing all aspects of this conversation.'

'That's fine,' she said airily.

'What do you want?'

'To give you one last chance to confess to your involvement in everything that happened in Portugal and Turkmenistan, and to give yourself up to the authorities.'

A harsh, humourless laugh. 'I have nothing to confess to, and I have no idea what you're talking about. And any accusations you make will be leapt upon by my lawyers. It would be a shame if I had to take everything you've ever worked for in a slander suit. You'd have to live off Macy's charity. By the way, how *is* Macy?' He leaned closer to his camera, eyes narrowing. 'She's no longer using Uzz. A shame. I was hoping to talk to her.'

'She's somewhere safe. Off the grid.'

He shrugged. 'I'm sure she'll turn up soon enough. Now that I know you're alive . . . I can discuss that with her.'

Nina frowned at him. 'Was that a threat?'

A mocking smile. 'Not at all.'

'Because it sounds like you're intending to use my life as leverage to force Macy to give up the Staff of Afrasiab.'

The smile vanished. 'I wasn't bluffing when I said I'd take everything you have for slander.'

'You can't slander the dead.'

Surprise – then his lips curled in sneering disbelief. 'Was *that* a threat?'

Now it was her turn to smile. 'Not at all.'

Loost shook his head. 'You'll be hearing from my lawyers, Professor Wilde. See you in court – not in person, of course. Now, if you'll excuse me, I'm busy.' He reached towards the camera as if to disconnect.

'Oh, with your rocket launch?' was Nina's overly bright remark. He hesitated. 'Yes, I'm watching it too.' She turned the phone towards her nearby laptop. It showed a live feed from Loost's spaceflight company. One of his rockets stood on its sunlit launchpad, an overlaid timer ticking down to T minus one minute. A swathe of jungle spread in the distance beyond the area that had been clear-cut to create his spaceport in the South American country of Suriname.

When she brought the phone back to herself, Loost's expression had become one of deep suspicion – and concern. 'Why are you watching that?'

'Oh, no particular reason. But rocket launches are very exciting. Anything might happen. Say, isn't this a supply mission with your next blood transfusion?'

Now his face filled with full-blown alarm. 'How did you know about that?'

'Macy told me.'

'And where *is* Macy?'

'She decided to take a vacation. In South America.' Before he could absorb the full implications of that, she raised her eyebrows in response to something happening on her laptop. 'Wow, that's unusual. Look at those clouds! They're forming very quickly. Must be a tropical storm.'

The previously blue sky above the launchpad was rapidly turning coal-dark as a swirling vortex of heavy clouds coalesced above it. Loost's gaze snapped to what Nina presumed was his own live feed. He stared at it in disbelief – then hurriedly jabbed at a keyboard. 'Mission control, this is Loost! Abort launch, abort, *abort*!'

'Something wrong?' Nina asked innocently.

He ignored her, barking more commands to his ground station. The sky on the laptop's screen was now a churning mass of black, lightning flaring within. The countdown reached twenty seconds – then stopped.

But the storm did not.

A writhing column of raw power lanced down from the seething clouds. It didn't strike the lightning conductors on top of the rocket or its launch tower, but instead carved down the spacecraft's side like a knife through a hanging carcass. Great bursts of sparks flew as metal vaporised, the huge fuel tanks inside the aluminium skin exposed, rupturing—

A flash even brighter than the lightning lit up the distant jungle as the rocket exploded.

Loost cried out in horror. A colossal fireball erupted from the pad, swallowing the launch tower before rising as a burning mushroom cloud. What little remained of the rocket itself crashed to the ground as flaming, extremely expensive scrap metal.

'Ohhhh, that's a shame,' said Nina, in the tone of a mother who had just seen their child's sandcastle collapse. 'I suppose you'll have to come back down to earth for that transfusion now.'

'I can't! One of my nurses used the reserve capsule—' His eyes went wide in angry realisation. 'But you already knew that, didn't you? Macy told you. You set all of this up to trap me in orbit!' He turned back to his keyboard, typing rapidly. 'It won't work. Galibi has a secondary launchpad. And a manned launch was already scheduled for next week – I can bring it forward. You thought you

494

could kill me? You thought you could *outthink* me? I'm Rafael Loost, you bitch! I'm the richest man in the world – I'm the *smartest* man in the world! There's nothing I can't do!'

'Except produce your own haemoglobin,' she reminded him tartly.

'Oh, you think you're so fucking clever,' he snarled. 'But I won't be dying any time soon, because I can have a backup flight here in a few days. What are you going to do, blow that up too? You'd murder innocent people to try to kill me?'

'There's a lot of accusations flying here,' said Nina. 'You're saying I plotted to murder you by wrecking your rocket? How, by controlling the weather to blow it up with a bolt of lightning? Any jury would know that's impossible.' She glanced back at the laptop. 'And speaking of lightning . . .'

More electrical spears stabbed down from the dark sky. This time, they did not strike the launchpad's blazing remains, but something halfway between it and the giant building where Loost's rockets were assembled: the massive crawler that carried them to their take-off position. The crackling arcs burned into the vehicle, cutting through metal like lasers – before it too blew apart in a roiling conflagration.

Nina watched the spectacular display of destruction impassively. 'Gee, I hope that wasn't anything important.' The lightning stopped, the clouds within moments turning from impenetrable black to increasingly lighter greys. 'Do you have a spare?'

Loost took a long moment to compose himself before answering. His whole body was clenched with rage. 'You know god-damn well that I don't,' he growled. 'You planned this whole thing to kill me. You destroyed my rocket, and its crawler. So now you think I'm stuck up here with no way to get what I need.' He gave her a slow clap with trembling hands. 'Good try, good try. But I can *buy* a launch from somebody else, even my rivals. They'll bump whatever their next flight is carrying if I give them enough money. And do you know what else I can do with money?' He sneered into the camera. 'I can have you killed. And your husband – yeah, and Macy too. How does a billion-dollar bounty on your heads sound? Granit wasn't the only killer on my speed-dial. You'll all be dead long before me. You're *dead*, Wilde!'

'Now, that definitely sounds like a threat,' said Nina. It chilled her, but she controlled her fear – because she hadn't finished with him yet. 'I'm sure a video of the world's richest man threatening to murder three people would be big news, though. It'd mean the end of all your US government contracts, for a start.'

'There won't *be* a video,' Loost said with contempt. 'You forgot about Uzz's privacy controls. Even if you're running a screen recording app, all it'll show will be a blank window with no sound. You can't record me on your phone.'

'Not on *my* phone. Eddie?'

'Ay up,' said Eddie, leaning into the frame of Nina's camera. He had been standing just out of Loost's sight the whole time, recording the entire exchange on his own phone. 'Smile, bell-end. You're on Candid Camera.'

Loost was briefly speechless. When he spoke again, he was stuttery, flustered. 'This – this isn't over. You've fucked with the wrong person. Both of you! I can buy my way out of anything. You just made the biggest mistake of your lives. I'll, I – fuck you!' he finally shouted. '*Fuck you!*'

'Bye,' said Nina, waving at him. 'You'll be hearing from *my* lawyers. Good luck with the blood thing.' She ended the call. 'Did you get it?'

Eddie stopped the recording, then scrolled back through it before tapping play. '. . . with money? I can have you killed,' said Loost on his screen.

The Yorkshireman nodded. 'I got it. Think he'll still try to do it?'

'Now that I've finished my anniversary piece about discovering

Atlantis, I think we should take an off-the-grid vacation for a couple of weeks. Which, oh hey, we were already going to do. After we send the video to any people and organisations who might find it interesting.'

'Funny, that,' Eddie said, grinning. 'I just happen to have a long list of 'em ready right here.'

Nina returned the smile. 'What a coincidence!' She picked up her replacement phone. 'I'll call Macy.'

The village of Plage des Hattes was at the very north-western corner of French Guiana, the neighbouring Maroni river marking the border between that country and Suriname. Once a sleepy fishing settlement, it had become a tourist destination in recent years due to its proximity to Galibi spaceport in the coastal wetlands of the neighbouring nation. Visitors who stayed there a week were almost certain to witness at least one launch, sometimes even two.

Anyone who had booked to visit after today would be disappointed, Macy mused. The clouds she had summoned using the Staff of Afrasiab had already dissipated, but the plumes of smoke from the destroyed rocket and crawler were still rising into the sky. 'Wow,' said Rain, peering over her sunglasses from the deckchair beside her. Under false names, the pair had rented a small beachfront villa with a view across the Maroni. 'Remind me never to piss you off.'

'I think you're safe,' Macy told her with a smile. Her phone rang; she answered. 'Hi, Mom.'

'Hi, Macy,' Nina replied. 'How's the vacation?'

'The weather looked kinda bad a few minutes ago, but it's okay now.'

'Yeah, I saw something about that.' Even without Uzz on their phones, they had previously agreed not to mention Loost or anything connected to him; there was always a chance that someone was listening. 'Did you do everything you needed to?'

'Yeah. What about you?'

'We recorded an . . . interesting video. I'm sure you'll see something about it on the news soon. But we're going to get out of the apartment, take a break from any potentially stressful situations.'

'I got you,' said Macy, understanding. 'Is Dad there?'

'Hi, love,' Eddie chipped in; Nina was on speaker. 'You and Rain both okay?'

'We're good,' she said. 'Getting better.' She had been lucky with her wound, if it could be considered that way. Emilian's blade had pierced her large intestine and liver, but his weapon had been so thin the damage was relatively straightforward to repair. She still felt a dull pain if she was not careful with her movements, but the prognosis for recovery was good. The same was true of Rain, who had a dressing covering the now-sutured hole in her back.

'Glad to hear it. Nice work, by the way. With that . . . thing you did.' Macy could almost see Nina nudging him not to give anything away on an unencrypted line. 'Thought I was the one who was good at blowing stuff up.'

'I learned from the best,' she said, smiling. 'Listen, Mom, Dad: this break you're going to take? If you want to come see me . . . ?'

'We'd love to,' said Nina, 'but . . . I get the feeling you're going to be busy for a while.'

'You could say that, yeah.' Even with the help of MacDuff and the other surviving members of the Order of Behdet, relocating the headquarters of the Knights of Atlantis and all the artefacts they were protecting to a new, secret location was proving a complicated business.

'We'll come and see you once you've sorted everything out,' said Eddie.

'And also once we're sure there won't be any problems from . . . certain people,' Nina added.

'That'd be great,' Macy told them. 'And obviously, you can stay with me for longer than a day. Wherever *I* end up staying!' She meant it as a joke, an echo of what she had said to them in France, but found her voice unexpectedly catching. Then, she had known she would be returning to her lifelong home in New York; now, she wasn't even sure where her home would be.

'I know,' said Nina, with the same deep feelings. 'But wherever you go, and whatever you do . . . we'll always be there for you when you need us.'

'We love you,' Eddie said. Even he struggled to contain his emotions. 'Take care of yourself, okay?'

'I will,' Macy promised. 'I love you both.'

'We'll see you soon, once all this is over,' said Nina. 'Love you, honey.'

'Love you, Mom, Dad. Bye.'

Her parents echoed the goodbye. Then the call ended. Macy found herself blinking away tears.

Rain stood, concerned. 'Are you okay?'

'I'm . . . I'm good,' the redhead assured her. She smiled; Rain returned it. She glanced down at the Staff of Afrasiab, on the ground beside their deckchairs. 'Looks like I have a new job.' She looked off into the distance, not at the smoking spaceport, but the horizon of the deep blue ocean. It stretched away before her, like the future: unknowable, but filled with infinite possibilities. 'Time to get to work.'

Have you discovered Andy McDermott's bestselling Wilde and Chase series?

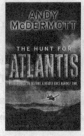
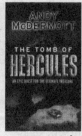

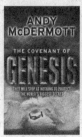
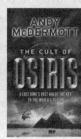
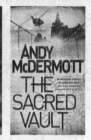

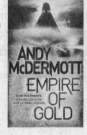

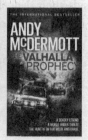

Available from Headline

Have you discovered Andy McDermott's bestselling Wilde and Chase series?

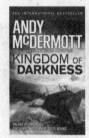

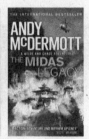

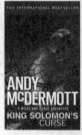
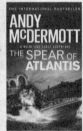
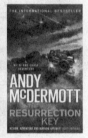

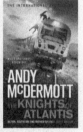

Available from Headline

If you can't get enough of Andy McDermott, explore the action-packed Alex Reeve series…

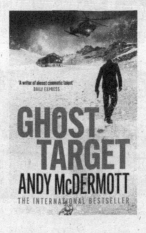

THRILLINGLY GOOD BOOKS
FROM CRIMINALLY
GOOD WRITERS

CRIME FILES BRINGS YOU THE LATEST RELEASES FROM
TOP CRIME AND THRILLER AUTHORS.

SIGN UP ONLINE FOR OUR MONTHLY NEWSLETTER AND BE THE FIRST
TO KNOW ABOUT OUR COMPETITIONS, NEW BOOKS AND MORE.